Saint

Saint and Sinners

Ruby Vincent

Published by Ruby Vincent, 2021.

Chapter One

Bodies crushed in on me. Pushing, shoving, and chancing a crafty grind to entice me to dance.

The speakers thrummed, vibrating to the beat of an unfamiliar song. I felt it as I slipped away.

Felt sound.

Battering my eardrums. Thumping in my chest. Silencing everyone and reducing us to flirty glances and gyrating hips.

This is what I loved about clubs. We humans were as we were supposed to be when the lights went down and the music turned up.

No awkward conversations about our plans for the future. Or dancing around an attraction for nigh on months waiting for one of us to make a damn move.

Inhibitions were shed at the door, and we finally gave in to acting on impulse. Eyes meeting across the bar. Hands roaming free on the dance floor, and then stifled giggles and racing hearts as we escaped to the bathrooms.

I headed for the vaulted velvet rope, passing by more grasping hands, and snagging some sap's cocktail off a server's tray. The guy whipped around, searching for the thief in the crush of bodies.

Roddy, the bouncer, eyed me as I approached. I said nothing, simply padded my jacket pocket, and he lifted the VIP rope for me to pass—as he did the night before. The night before that. Three nights before that. And as he would the following nights to come.

Opium was the best club in Cinco City. I logged more hours here than I did at work.

Darkness swallowed me as I stepped through the curtains. In the gloom, a shadow moved and someone brushed against me. My eyes adjusted to the sight of brown hair and a Cartier watch slipping through the door at the end.

I loved the pounding music. The crush of people on the dance floor. The tipsy hands groping me as I danced.

Loved it all, but the real party wasn't inside Opium. It was beneath it.

The footfalls of me and my silent friend reverberated through the staircase, leading down, down, and down.

Music leaked under the double doors at the foot of the stairs. Not as loud as what we left behind, but dancing wasn't the particular activity of choice for those of us on the bottom floor.

The man pulled open the door and swept to the side, pausing to hold it open for me. He looked up, locking eyes, and the breath was snatched from my lungs.

Sooty black pools sought me under thick lashes and sprung the trap. Fixed on them, I tripped off the final step, earning a grin that revealed a dimple on that scruffy cheek.

"You okay?" The voice was thick, rich, and smooth like a river of dark chocolate.

Yum.

"Fine." I righted myself, clearing my throat.

"First time here?" he guessed.

You'd have to think so from the tripping-over-my-feet and flashing moon eyes like I'd never seen a handsome man before.

I raked him up and down. *Though I haven't seen this brand of ropey muscles, thick, autumn-brown hair, and cupid lips before, to be fair.*

"No," I said aloud. "I'm a regular."

"After you."

Murmuring thank you, I passed through the final set of curtains and stepped into the heady embrace of cigarette smoke, mingled laughs, and clinking poker chips.

I turned to my new friend and caught his back as he strode off, making for a side hallway leading out of the main room.

I let him go and took in the true club.

The place had high ceilings for an underground casino. Chandeliers threw soft light on the black tuxedos and sparkly gowned revelers playing their odds at blackjack, roulette, poker, and craps.

Women strode around the felt tables wearing dresses cut down to their areolas and hems flashing thongs as they bent over patrons, serving drinks, or multitasking flirting with keeping an eye out for cheaters. Written on their name tags were undoubtedly fake monikers and three gold words.

The Pleasure Center.

To be honest, I thought they could have gotten more creative with the name, but it did the trick.

The bar took up the entire opposite wall of the room. I crossed the reddish-gold carpet, practically tasting the whiskey sour on my lips.

"The fuck!"

A crash sounded to my right.

"You're cheating!"

I didn't have a chance to turn as a body slammed into me, knocking me into a passing worker and their loaded tray.

We went down in a shower of alcohol and shattered glass. I gasped, air punched out of me, and flailed on top of the poor woman who cushioned my fall.

"Dozy prick! How do you cheat at roulette?!"

Eyes flashing, the hulking mass of greasy hair and bulging muscle who attacked, seized the man on top of me and slammed his head on my collarbone.

"Get off!" I screamed.

Hands grabbed under my arms, tugging me and the server free. I fell onto a warm, hard chest, secured by a hand wearing a familiar watch. I tilted my head to my new friend.

"Are you okay?" he asked.

I snagged his arm. "Neither one of us will be if we don't move."

"What—"

Shoving him back, we scurried behind the players and servers clearing the space, giving the fighters a wide berth.

"I didn't cheat!"

The shorter, blond man punched his accuser across the jaw. They rolled over the carpet, knocking into a table and tipping it and another shower of drinks onto the floor.

"Someone should stop them," he cried.

"Someone"—the back door flew open—"will," I finished.

Three men in suits even nicer than the one against my cheek, streamed out of the door. Two laid hands on the men scrapping and pulled them apart. I winced as the first gut-punch doubled the blond man in half. Security swept his leg, dropping him in a groaning heap on his ass, and joined his partner in beating the guy who started it.

The final man stood apart from them. Still, silent, and blank-faced as Greasy Hair went from blustering to pleading.

"Stop," he shrieked. "It w-was him! He called it every time. He's a fucking cheat."

Angelo flicked to the supposed cheater currently trying to crawl away.

Angelo Castillo wasn't as pretty as the man whose arm I held. His voice scraped hard and guttural out of his throat. His hair was shaved close to the scalp. And a web of tattoos running down the left side of his weathered face covered the jagged scar that marred his cheek. All the same, Angelo didn't need looks to strike the room speechless.

He didn't react as another punch dealt by his enforcer splattered blood on his white coat. "Is this true, Mr. Jensen?"

Jensen snapped his neck shaking his head. "I got lucky. I swear, I wasn't cheating. I wasn't!" His voice went up in pitch as the guys stopped their beating to drag his fleeing ass back.

"Gentlemen," Angelo began. "The first rule of TPC is do not cause trouble. The second rule is do not break the first rule." He shook his head like a disappointed parent. "You fight in my club. Disturb my guests. Spill my alcohol. Knock down one of my girls. I'd say that's causing trouble, wouldn't you?"

"It was his fault," Jensen pleaded. "Please, Angelo—"

"Get them out," he ordered. "Break something, but don't kill them."

The men were hauled shouting out of the door and carried up the same staircase we came through.

Angelo swept a smile over the watching crowd. "I'm sorry you had to witness that unpleasant business. Please, friends. Sit, drink, play, and enjoy yourselves. It's what we're here for."

Only when he disappeared into the back room did anyone actually move.

"I see it's actually your first time here," I murmured.

He laughed mirthlessly. "Does this happen a lot?"

"Rarely ever for the reason you just saw. Angelo doesn't stand for people making trouble down here." It suddenly occurred to me that I was holding on to him longer than I needed to. I quickly stepped back, smoothing down my clothes and hair. "I should get going. The auction is about to start."

"Watch out for yourself."

"I will," I said. "Wait, what's your...?" I trailed off. He was already walking toward the hallway he went down earlier.

It figured he was here for the fights. Strong, quick-thinking guy like him was probably one of the underground fighters—though that perfect face didn't look like it met with too many punches.

Enough with him, a voice reminded. *He's not who you came here for.*

I rubbed my jacket pocket again, riding a triumphant thrill to the bar. After receiving my drink, I made for the opposite hallway leading off the main floor.

I wasn't interested in the cage matches. Two half-naked people stepping into the hold to beat the shit out of each other until one went down and didn't get up. All the while howling hyenas urging them on and placing bets faster than their bank accounts could keep up. Fun, but not my vice.

In this world, our base desires were catered to excess. The lust for brutality, riches, and wine. But all I was after—

Fevered moans blanketed the casino music. This hall was a museum of glass doors, showcasing the activities inside.

—was lust itself.

Pert, round breasts flattened on the glass, slicked by sweat and the condensation of her hot breath. Her screams bordered on overenthusiastic as a portly man who was thinning on top pounded her from behind.

Nearly every room was filled with adults engaging in good, clean fun. Place a single full bed in the midst of three walls and a pane of glass, and the Pleasure clubbers took over from there.

I paid them minimal attention, even to the few flashes of interest that came my way.

A black velvet-covered door waited for me at the end of the hall. A man emerged from the shadows as I reached for the handle.

"Name?"

"Winter Phoenix." An obvious alias.

He consulted his phone, and nodded at my name on the list. "Do you know the rules of the auction?"

"I do."

"Do you know the consequences for breaking the rules?"

I shuffled from foot to foot, hand tightening on the handle. "I do."

"Minimum bids are three thousand dollars US. Payment is to be transferred immediately upon conclusion of the auction. If you cannot cover your bid, you will be asked to leave The Pleasure Club."

By way of a broken jaw and carried feet-first out of the door.

"I understand," I replied.

He opened the door for me. "Take any seat. Your bidder card is eighty-six."

The room that greeted me was the high-class scene Angelo worked to maintain.

Antique, upholstered chairs formed neat rows in front of the stage. Gold damask wallpaper stretched up to a ceiling that was painted to envy the night sky, and a young man stood behind a large ornate podium, watching the hands as they ticked the final seconds to eleven o'clock.

I was one of the last to arrive. Men and women in their jewels, silk, and finery spread through the space. *And now I'm one of them.*

I claimed a seat toward the front, heart thumping loudly in my ear. I'd been waiting two months to be let into this room. I wasn't leaving without my prize.

"Welcome, everyone," the auctioneer began. "I'm Mr. Black. We'll begin in just a few moments. If you'd like to order a drink or take care of other business, do so now. Once the auction begins, the door will remain sealed."

No one moved.

"Excellent. Let's begin." Mr. Black swept out his hand and the curtains behind him parted like his long, tapered fingers conducted magic. A raven-haired, jewel-eyed vision revealed before us, clad only in a lace bustier and matching black thong. "Ladies and gentlemen, welcome the lovely Champagne."

Polite applause broke out, and Champagne did a little shimmy and twirl, showing off all her assets.

"Champagne is new to TPC, and joins us for the first time tonight. She enjoys double penetration, being tied up, and spanked." Mr. Black rattled this off with no inflection. He could've been talking about what she liked on her pizza. "We'll start the bidding at five thousand. Do I have five thousand for a night with Champagne?"

Bidding cards shot in the air.

My tongue darted out, tasting pure carnal lust in the air, and I held back a grin. Beneath the layer of wealth and civility, we were not better than the rutting, grinding clubbers above our heads—eager for a night of no-holds-barred, wild sex with a complete stranger. We just left nothing to chance.

While what we were doing wasn't strictly legal, it was a less risky and exceedingly lucrative arrangement compared to the potential hook-ups that pawed me on the dance floor.

Angelo only brought in escorts from the best services. All clean—drug- and STD-wise—and all wanting to be here even more than we did. These auction spots were highly sought after by those in the know. One night with a TPCer could clear you six months' worth of rent payments.

"Ten thousand," Mr. Black announced. "Ten thousand going once. Twice." He banged his gavel. "That's ten thousand to bidder fifty-two. Thank you, Champagne."

The curtains whisked shut with another wave of his hands. Behind them, I heard movement as someone else took Champagne's place.

I leaned forward in my chair, visions of the man I came for dancing in my mind. I recalled every second of the first time I saw him. The spotlight illuminating the stage of the male strip club. The scent of sweat and lavender rolling off him as he thrust his scantily covered crotch in my face. I remembered searching for him after his dance, and the weight of my frustration when he cuffed my chin, chuckling as he said I couldn't afford him.

I rubbed my pocket and the new bank card within. *He won't be saying that to me tonight. Thanks to my new friends, there's nothing I can't afford.*

"Next up." Mr. Black cut into my runaway fantasy. "We have Candy."

Another whoosh of the curtains and the blonde, ruby-lipped incarnation of Aphrodite winked at us in a see-through bra and panties that left nothing to the imagination.

"Candy is another new addition to the club." I listened with half an ear as he listed her skills and preferences. Why didn't they list the order of escorts coming out? How long would it be until we finally got to him?

"Let's begin the bidding at three thousand. Do I have three thousand for a night with Candy?"

A paddle went up.

Then two. Then three.

"That's five thousand," said Mr. Black. "Do I have six?"

Candy shimmied on the platform. She gave her best *come hither* grin as she swept her bra strap off her shoulder.

No bid cards went up in the air.

"Five thousand going once. Twice—"

Twisting, Candy gave the audience her back and bent at the waist. Bold as ever, she pulled her underwear aside and plunged two fingers in her pussy. Half a dozen cards flew in the air as she licked her fingers clean, grinning with thinly disguised triumph.

"Eleven thousand. Twelve. Thir— That's fourteen thousand." Mr. Black was keeping up without a hitch. "Seventeen."

An older man with silver hair and a suit to match raised his card. "Twenty thousand."

Black banged the gavel. "Twenty thousand to bidder seventeen."

The curtains closed once more. I gathered my jacket tighter around me. My pocket's contents dug into my side, reassuring me. If twenty thousand was the going price around here, I was secure. My bank account was freshly topped up with three times that amount, and more was only a text away.

"Now, ladies and gentlemen, we have a club favorite." I moved with the curtains, rising out of my seat as inch by agonizing inch obsidian locks... jasper-green eyes... russet-brown skin... and that grin was unmasked.

"Montecito.

"Of course, you know the minimum bid for a club favorite is fifteen thousand," Mr. Black continued. "As he needs no introduction, let's start the bidding."

My paddle shot in the air.

Montecito flicked to me, and I swore recognition lit in his eyes. He tossed me a wink that burned a fire from my roots to my toes.

"I have fifteen," Black announced, gesturing to me. "Do I have sixteen?"

On and on we went.

I trounced every bidder until it was me and a regal brunette woman left in the bidding war—though the glares she was throwing me had me thinking the wealthy noble act was just that.

"Thirty thousand," she cried.

"Thirty-five."

She flushed an alarming shade of purple. "Forty," she forced through gritted teeth.

Montecito stood on the platform. Arms folded and lips teased with amusement.

I jumped to my feet. "Fifty thousand dollars."

Black banged the gavel. "Sold! Bidder eighty-six."

My knees gave out, dropping me hard on my seat as black velvet concealed that devilish beauty.

I won. My mind hardly made sense of the sentence. *Montecito is mine. After all this time, tonight he goes home with me.*

The rest of the auction was a blur. My heart fluttered out of control. I wiped my damp palms a dozen times and finally sat on them. The parade of skin and sex had no effect on me. I got what I came here for, and knowing he was on the other side of the door waiting for me was unraveling the threads holding me together one by one.

"Thank you for coming," said Black. "This concludes the auction."

I bolted out of my seat, brushing past the woman who tried to outbid me and collecting a glare for my trouble.

The door was opened by the man who checked me in earlier. And waiting in that darkened hallway to a soundtrack of gasps and slapping skin was him.

Montecito glanced down as I approached. "I guess I don't have to ask if you want to skip dinner and get straight to dessert."

A flush went up my neck.

My cock strained against my lining—on display for all to see. I usually had more control over myself than this. But then again, no man had ever captivated me to the point I was driven to tap all my resources to have him.

"Is it a problem that I'm...?"

"A guy?" Montecito brushed my hair from my eyes. Lingering, he skated over my temple and traced my lips with his thumb.

His mouth was on mine in a breath. Scraping my bottom lip between his teeth, he drew a groan and captured it in his kiss. A slow, gentle temptation that blew apart the last of my self-control.

I almost came on the spot.

"Why would it be?" he whispered.

"What's your real name?"

"It's whatever you want it to be." He dropped his hand. "My place is close by. Nothing against the club, but their rooms lack privacy, space, and toys. I gotta make sure you get your fifty thousand dollars' worth." He cuffed my chin reminiscent of the first night we met. "Meet me outside? In the alley?"

"Okay."

He disappeared into the auction room. After handing over my card to the ever-watchful guard, I hurried upstairs—mind split between Montecito below and him in his apartment spread on his sheets among the *toys*. Rushing upstairs would get me to the latter faster.

A whipping wind smacked me as I stepped into the alley, playing with my collar. I turned it up to the cold and crossed to the opposite wall.

Overhead, a lightbulb flickered its last breath. The alley wasn't dirty per se. The only trash littering the concrete were cigarette butts, and the graffiti covering the walls bordered on artful. A dumpster backed onto the fence at one end. At the top of the street, cars streaked by, carrying the mindless inhabitants of Cinco City to their dull, pathetic lives. A life I once had until I embraced the true rule of survival.

If you want something, take it.

Montecito was only the beginning, and this would be far from our last night. I'd get him out of the life. Set him up in the best apartment in the city and make him mine in every way. After that, I'd buy my partner out of the business. That stupid fool has held me back for long enough. Then—

The door opened, spilling music into the alleyway. A smile broke out as I recognized my new friend who saved me from the fight.

"Hey," I called.

"Hey." He placed a cigarette between a cut, weeping lip. His left eye was already beginning to swell. "What are you doing out here?" He closed the distance as he dug in his pockets for a lighter.

"Waiting for someone." I jerked my chin at his bruises. "So, I was right about you being a fighter."

"Retired until tonight," he said. "A friend of mine suggested I put my skills to use. Make myself some money."

"Did you?"

His grin sought me through the dark. "Cleaned up."

"I didn't catch it earlier," I said. "What's your name?"

"Doesn't matter."

"Why not?"

"Because this." He drew out his searching hand and the flickering light glinted off the metal.

I had enough time to register it wasn't a lighter before he grasped my shoulder, shoving me against the brick as he plunged the knife in my gut.

I gasped, eyes widening as emotion leaked from his. "N-no. Plea—"

He stabbed once, twice, and three times. Shredding my insides as pain ripped apart my soul. I tried to speak and choked. Warm, gushing blood that should have been my pleas splattered on his cheek.

I sank onto his shoulder. Strength leeching out and loosening the hold on my life. My friend's grip was almost gentle as he brought me to the ground. His jacket he removed, placing it under my head.

"You know why." Light spilled over him, mimicking a halo. My vision was going quickly. I couldn't feel my legs to put them under me and run. It was no wonder I sought an angel. "Take comfort that your death will serve a purpose."

My lips parted and one final word rose to the surface.

"Kieran."

"Yes," he replied.

The warm hand left my forehead. The last thing I heard as my lids fluttered shut on eyes that stopped seeing, was his soft footfalls fading down the alley.

Chapter Two

Four Years Later

"You're not seriously going to wear that, are you?"

I looked down at my purple one-shoulder top and jeans. "What's wrong with it? You ordered me to show skin and I am."

Gianna threw herself on my bed. "You gave me *one* shoulder. You're going to have to do better than that. I want both shoulders. Cleavage. Thighs. And a little bit of ass if you're feeling generous."

"I'm not," I deadpanned.

She laughed. "Then just the shoulder, boobs, and thighs, please."

Rolling my eyes, I stuck my head back in my closet, searching for my rare and well-hidden sexy clothes.

It was amazing the dresses could hide. My closet was so small, I could barely shove myself inside. The same could be said for my room in general.

Five strides brought you from one end of the room to the other. I squeezed in a twin bed. A dresser with a television on top, and all the paintings and photographs I could fit on the walls. Somehow all of it just made the space smaller.

"What kind of job is this?"

"I told you, Addy. We're servers." Gianna turned the television on low. "We carry a tray of canapés around in a tight dress and walk away with five hundreds at the end of the night. I couldn't think of an easier way to make money than if I got paid to flick my bean."

I heaved a sigh. "Why do you say these things to me? You know I'm an innocent, delicate flower."

Her guffaw was followed by a soft missile striking my back. "You're innocent like I'm a virgin."

"Seriously," I said, abandoning my clothes. I picked my pillow off the floor and threw it, and myself, down next to her. "If we're just passing out the cheese and crackers, why are boobs, thighs, and skin required?"

"Kayla said we have to dress up. That's all I know." She nudged my shoulder. "I know you need the money. Salvatore's been cutting shifts on you, or we wouldn't be lying here chatting."

I groaned. "Ryan had me covering for him so often, I was racking up too much overtime pay. Salvatore put a quick stop to that. Striking off two of my regular shifts. I'm barely part-time now."

"Cheap ass," she spat. "Why haven't you quit that job? With your skills, you could work for any restaurant in the city."

"Yes, but those restaurants won't be two blocks from the home or have Ryan Sinclair in the kitchen. The man's earned three Michelin stars," I said. "Learning to cook from him is like being taught to swim by Michael Phelps. Did I tell you he invented a new way of making aspic? What you do is—"

Gianna's head fell back. A loud snore ripped from her body.

"Jerk." It was my turn to smash her with a pillow. "Get out."

"Nope," she said, sienna eyes dancing. "Not until you slut up, my friend."

Gianna was already dressed in a sleeveless sequin bodycon dress that looked amazing on her. Her mane of wavy locks was piled on top of her head in an effortless bun, and just a swipe of glittery lip gloss adorned her full lips. Gianna Cross was the kind of girl that turned every outfit into a fashion statement. Even ripped sweats and holey T-shirts with Cheeto stains.

I, on the other hand, managed to look like a little kid playing dress-up every time I attempted an outfit fancier than jeans and a plain blouse. Twenty-three years old and I hadn't yet shed that fresh bloom of youth for the mature lines and full figure age promised me.

"I do need the money," I admitted. "Dad cut open his mattress to hide his poker winnings inside. The director says I have to pay for a new one."

"Daddy Red is incorrigible." You know you've been friends for a long time when your bestie calls your father Dad too. "How did he get something sharp?"

I pinched the bridge of my nose. "He made a shiv out of a toothbrush."

"I've got nothing for that."

I heaved myself off the bed, making another attempt to find an outfit Gianna approved of. My dad and his incorrigibleness aside, I hadn't let on just how much I needed this money. But seeing how Gianna and I had been best friends since we were thirteen. We went to middle school, high school, and Cinco University together. She lived with me for a year when we were fifteen, and I've been telling her everything since then, she likely knew how close I was dancing to disaster.

Overtime was barely covering my share of the rent, utilities, and bills from the nursing home. Part-time had me straight-up looking at eviction. And I had three other roommates who would be happy to help pack my bags with how often I asked them to turn their music down, or take the fun to their friends' places, so I could get some sleep before work. They were twenty-three and looking to party. I was twenty-three and looking for a nap.

I pulled a cute sweater dress off the hanger. It was snow white and lovingly fuzzy. The V-neck offered a little collarbone action and the hem didn't make it past mid-thigh. This would have to do.

"G, toss me the black boots under the bed."

"Addy, look at this." Something in her voice stopped me with my shirt half over my head. "They struck again."

"The Merchants?" Yanking my clothes down, I tripped rushing to see.

"They hit a jewelry store a few days ago."

Sure enough, "Jewelry Store Robbery" scrolled along the bottom of the news report in big, bold letters. A grainy video accompanied it. Huddled figures dotted the floor, cowering in the face of masked men brandishing shotguns. That in and of itself did not separate them from run-of-the-mill robbers. I gave that honor to the "M" stamped on the side of each mask.

"How much did they get away with?" I asked.

"Half a mill worth of gems."

I whistled. "I swear these guys didn't exist a year ago and now they're everywhere."

"Like Cinco City doesn't have enough problems," she mumbled.

Cinco City.

I loved this place. I wouldn't want to live anywhere else, but remove the "-co" from the name, and you knew what our little slice of earth truly was. Forget Las Vegas.

Cinco was so named for a quirk we mirrored from New York City. Five distinct boroughs that were like their own mini-cities. Hundreds of cultures. Thousands of people. A multitude of foods, museums, theaters, and clubs.

A beautiful façade concealing the highest number of fatal overdoses in the nation. Rampant illegal gambling. Underground fight rings. Corruption that made *House of Cards* look like child's play.

We had enough gangs and crime families running through the neighborhoods. Who asked for another one?

"The masked part I get," I said. "But why do they call themselves the Merchants?"

"I heard they trade or sell everything they steal. Not exactly Robin Hoods, but a few of the paintings they knocked off from the Aurora Gallery ended up in a private home. They found out when they arrested the guy for tax evasion. They get their hands on the merchandise and peddle it to whoever is buying. Merchants."

I nodded. "You get into that kind of business, the masks are necessary."

"No one knows who runs their crew. Or even how many there are." She gestured at the screen. "This store was in Harlow. Whoever these guys are, they have a death wish. Harlow is the Kings' territory."

"If the Kings want to kill them, they'll have to find them first. The Merchants aren't making that easy." I turned off the television. "Enough about them. Where is this party?"

"Leighbridge. East side."

I whistled. "Are we talking penthouse?"

"You know we are."

"Are we talking rich, hairy creep who's used money to get what he wants for so long, he can just demand a bunch of scantily clad women traipse through his living room for a couple of hundreds?"

"The rich, hairy creep in question is Raiden Spencer."

"I'll be ready in ten minutes."

I ignored her knowing look on the way to the bathroom.

Raiden Spencer was rich, and naturally he was used to using his millions to get what he wanted. But the young, full-bearded former model was no hairier than the average guy. In every other respect—including his extensive catalog of tight, white briefs shots—he was far from average. The best part, the only woman he was creeping on these days was the famously infamous Hazel O'Hare. Daughter of Leonidas O'Hare. The man who owned half the city.

Her wild child days of table-dancing, boob slips, coke nose rings, and the boot from every prestigious boarding school in North America was well-documented in the media. The story they were running these days was of Hazel and Raiden's impending wedding, and their attempts to woo Ryan Sinclair into catering their event.

If Ryan took the job, I could weasel my way onto his staff telling stories of the night I wowed the future Mr. and Mrs. Spencer with my ability to smile and carry a tray at the same time.

"You should've led with that," I called to Gianna.

"You should've known I had your back."

Fair point.

I rinsed off in my minuscule box shower, pasted on a little eye shadow and amber lipstick, and then I blew the female-version of my father a kiss in the mirror. Despite the man's many jokes that he should've gotten a paternity test, I resembled him down to the plump lips, cleft chin, and desert-sand eyes. My mother's only contribution was to burnish strands of red in my brown locks, round my nose, and leech enough melanin from my skin that people have been asking "What are you?" my whole life.

Dear old Mom.

But let's not ruin a perfectly good mood by thinking of her.

I left the bathroom, wiggled into my fluffy white sweater dress, and tugged on my boots. Gianna fussed with my hair while I dug into my jewelry box for earrings.

"Are we just handing out drinks and mini quiches?" I asked. "Any chance I can get in the kitchen and put my stamp on those trays?"

She chuckled. "That's another reason why your roommates want rid of you. You're on this one-track mission to feed everyone around you until they burst out of their clothes."

"A healthy goal for a chef."

"I'm sure they've got the menu and caterer sewn up by now, Addy."

"Might try anyway."

Gianna finished wrangling my hair into two messy buns. I reached for my purse on the nightstand and slipped my pepper spray from the top drawer inside.

My roommates were spread out on the mismatched threadbare couches passing a bowl of popcorn back and forth. They forgot about their movie when we stepped out.

"Are you going out, Addy?"

Corinne's surprise was deserved. I rarely walked past them out the door in anything but my work clothes.

"Yes. We're going to a party in Leighbridge."

Corinne snapped her fingers over her shoulder, signaling for Alisha to get on her phone. "Are you staying out all night?"

I quirked a brow. "Do you want me to?"

She shrugged delicately. "We just want you to have fun. You're always working. You've got like one friend."

I noted she didn't include herself, or Alisha and Sage in my circle of friends.

"Stay out all night. Meet someone. Let them fuck the stress out of you. You deserve it."

"Thanks, roomie," I said with an eye roll. "Is Alisha calling up everyone so that you three can do the same?"

"Hmm." She was barely listening. Her phone was out and fingers tapping away too. "See you tomorrow."

"Sure," I said. "Don't let anyone in my room, and you can eat the last of my fried apple pies."

"Oooh. Thanks, babe. You're the best."

I'm pretty sure she only heard the last half of that sentence, but Gianna was already dragging me out.

"You need to move out of this dump," Gianna said. "They're the main reason you've got stress."

"This dump charges me next to nothing in rent, and it's right on my bus line to work and the home."

I had no issues calling my home a dump. Between the worn, stained hallway carpets, cracks in the ceiling, peeling brown wallpaper, and the clinging odor permeating the entire building—calling it a dump was being kind.

"I keep telling you to move in with me."

"Can't." Our heels stomped down the wooden staircase. "You've got a Raul problem."

She heaved a sigh. "Isn't there some kind of rule that the best friend has to pretend to like the boyfriend? Being supportive and all that."

"Def not a rule."

She elbowed me. "Would living with him really be worse than living with the Terrible Trio? Last month, Alisha stumbled home drunk, burst into your room, and threw up on your bed. While you were in it. You'd rather deal with that than Raul?"

I crossed the cracked tile ahead of her and held open the door. Wind whipped in my face, teasing my earrings to chime. "He can't keep a job. Spends all your money on weed. And he's cheated on you half a dozen times. I'd rather kill Raul and stash his body in a trash can."

She laughed. "I've cheated on him more than that, but he only knows about a few of them. Dysfunction works for us, babe. If I kicked him down the stairs, he'd probably propose to me." Gianna popped a kiss on my cheek. "But I love you looking out for me."

"Now it's your turn. Kick him down those stairs, so we can move in together."

Gianna howled, striding off. I did believe she enjoyed the color and drama Raul Perez added to her life. She was a theater major currently working a hotel front desk in between auditions. She couldn't have the least interesting part she played be her own.

I linked arms with her as we rounded the building, heading for the stop at the corner of Brixton and Canal Street.

"Mhhmm. Ay, ay, ay, ladies." A group of guys broke their huddle to eye-fuck us from across the street. "Damn, you looking good."

"Where you going so fast?"

"How much for a date?"

I stifled a groan. "Oh no."

A stooped, wrinkled missile shot across the road, cutting off a driver who had to swerve to avoid him. Captain skidded to a stop, pulling us up short.

"How much for the both of you?" He flashed broken, rotting teeth. "Ain't got much, but you can give an old man a discount."

"Old man is right," Gianna said. "You're old enough to be our grandfather."

"But I'm not." He thrust his hips at us, ratcheting up the howls from the group of guys watching. "No reason we can't have a little fun."

I grimaced at the piss-stained crotch coming at me.

Captain was a permanent fixture on my street. He'd taken a liking to the couch someone threw out behind my building, and violently defended it from removal. I found this out when he popped out from behind the dumpster on my move-in day and said the only way I was going near his couch was if I rode him on it.

"Move on, you leathery, senile perv," said Gianna. "I swear we do this every fucking day."

"That's because we do." I took out my pepper spray and shook it. "You know I keep this just for you, Captain. Six feet at all times."

He scowled—put out like he didn't know this rejection was incoming. I looked him up and down.

"How are you doing, C?" I asked. "Did you go to that shelter I told you about? Get you some food and clean clothes?"

But looking at him it was clear he didn't. The bottom half of his pants were in tatters, and the waist was held up by a rolled-up strip of cling wrap. Under two jackets was a brown shirt that used to be white. Still, his clothes were in a better state than him. There were unknown bits of something tangled in his scraggly gray beard. Above his eye was a cut I noticed days ago that dripped blood onto his eyebrow that he had yet to clean off. Didn't look to be healing properly.

He flapped a hand. "Nah. If I leave, someone will take my couch."

"No one is going to take your couch. Go to the shelter," I said. "Jeanine is super sweet. She'll hook you up, and take a look at that cut. Do you remember the address?"

"Lost the card."

I dug in my purse and fished out the shelter's business card.

"If you're really worried about me—" Captain seized my outstretched hand and smeared his face on my palm. "—there's plenty you can do to make me feel better."

Gianna snatched my pepper spray can. Captain received a hard whap to the head. "Told you to move your ass on!"

"Frigid, teasing bitches!" he howled, taking off across the street. "Cocksucking sluts!"

"We're not sucking your shriveled-up dick!"

Captain's tirade continued as Gianna tugged me away.

"You're too nice, A. Next time, I'm spraying him before he opens his mouth."

"Captain is all talk. Besides, if he gets on his feet and off the couch, I'll finally be able to throw out my trash without his weekly description of the things he wants me to do to his dick."

"Do you feel sorry for him because he's a vet?" she asked as we reached the bus stop.

"A vet?" I repeated. "Oh, no. That's not why he's called Captain. He stole a naval captain's hat off a corpse he tripped over in the park, and took a liking to it. Wore it every day and the name stuck."

"Again. I have nothing for that."

The number twelve bus rode up on time. We climbed on and settled in for an hour and forty minutes of bumps, stops, jostling, and two transfers. Leighbridge had plenty of distance between it and my borough, Rockchapel, and that's how they liked it.

I gazed out the window as overturned trash cans, graffitied storefronts, and lecherous old men were replaced by soaring skyscrapers, passing Lamborghinis, and women walking dogs with diamond-encrusted collars.

The bus spat us out in front of Prestige Apartments. My neck bent in half following the shiny silver windows to the very top.

"Kayla," Gianna said into the phone. "We're here. Can we come right up? Uh-huh. Okay. Cool." She hung up. "We give our names and IDs to the dude at the front desk. Then take the service elevator to the top floor." She nudged me. "Network the living hell out of those people, A. Get on the O'Hare-Spencer wedding. Become the go-to celebrity chef. Then I'll be moving into your swanky downtown penthouse."

I hummed. "You don't think I'd have traded up to a better best friend by then?"

A sharp pain zinged through my backside. My yelp was followed by my laugh.

"Doesn't get better than me," she said, "and I'll pinch you the next time you forget."

I kissed her cheek by way of an apology. I had Gianna when I had nothing. There was no clawing my way to the top if she wasn't coming up with me.

The doorman sized us up as he bowed, but didn't say a word. We walked over to the front desk as ordered, and handed over our identification.

"These will be returned when you leave." The guard, Daniel, spoke to his clipboard rather than our faces. "You will be searched upon exiting the Spencer residence and again before you leave the building. Mr. Spencer's private security will have further instructions when you arrive. Do not disturb the other residents. Do not..."

I scanned the space as he droned on. Swanky in the extreme but I expected nothing less.

A glass waterfall installation stretched from floor to ceiling in the middle of the room. Surrounding it were synthetic flowers and palm fronds that swayed under the air-conditioning. Through walls of glass, I peeked a dining room and state-of-the-art gym.

The bottom floor was empty this time of night. I pictured my empty-bank-account, working-from-open-to-close, sleeping-in-a-shoebox life trying to fit into all of this.

"—Mr. Spencer's private security will have further instructions when you arrive," Daniel continued. "The service elevator is at the back of that hallway."

Gianna and I headed in the direction he pointed to.

"I plan on breaking nearly all of those rules without shame." She tugged her dress down, popping the girls out to play. "Yes to sneaking the food and wine. Yes to snagging a rich, handsome guest. Yes to both of us slipping away from the party. And yes to pocketing a memento of the night."

I pressed the button for the elevator. "Take a sock or something like that. People expect to lose them, so they don't question if they go missing."

Gianna tapped the side of her nose. "That's why you're the mastermind in this operation. Got any tips for the cute, wealthy stranger?"

"Strut around in that outfit and they'll come to you."

The elevator whisked us high in the sky, opening up to a darkened hall-way with a single door. Darkened, but not silent. The bass thumped through the walls, letting us know we were in the right place. Kayla poked her head out like she sensed us.

"GiGi. Madeline." She threw her arms around Gianna, squeezing the stuffing out of her.

"Adeline," I corrected, waving to her. The flying-hug greeting wasn't for me.

Kayla was more Gianna's friend than mine. The three of us went to the same college, but they were the drama majors, while I was hospitality man-agement and working two jobs. Didn't leave much time for hanging out.

"Come on in, guys. It's totally chill." She took both our hands. "It's a pre-engagement party Raiden threw to surprise Hazel."

"Pre-engagement?" I said as the doorway swallowed us. "Aren't they al-ready engaged?"

"Yes. The real engagement party will be in two weeks when Raiden's par-ents return from Europe. This is the pre-party for all of their close friends."

A low whistle escaped my lips. *All two hundred of them.*

Everywhere I looked, people were grinding, dancing, and sweating on something or someone. Raised platforms were in and around the living room—complete with pole. Ladies and gentlemen professional and amateur were giving them a go. Purple glow lights replaced the function of the chan-deliers, casting an otherworldly vibe on the party.

Overhead, a banner congratulated the happy couple, but I'd hazard a guess this soiree was less about Hazel and Raiden and more about getting shit-faced.

"Are we late?" I shouted over the music.

Kayla shook her head. "They started early. Going before any of us showed up." She held out her hands. "I'll skip sending you to security and take your phones now. Sorry but they've gotta be locked up till the end of the night. Stay out of the rooms. Don't have sex with the guests." I swore she looked at Gianna when she said that. "Don't dance. Don't drink. Otherwise, it's a par-ty. Have fun."

I squinted at one of the women on the platform. More like I squinted at her neck.

"Hold on. Isn't that Hazel?"

Kayla followed my line of sight. "You don't have to ask. No other woman on the planet is walking around wearing that."

Drifting closer, my lips parted, releasing a soft, "Wow."

The diamond dangle choker shimmered in the colored glow, trapping the light and tossing it back in pure, mesmerizing beauty. It swayed as she danced, and my eyes with it. Tick-tocking side to side like a pendulum clock.

"The Symphony of Stars." Gianna stepped to my side, surrendering to the same hold. "Why can't I snag a man who gifts me like that?"

"Because there's only one Raiden Spencer," I whispered.

Gianna couldn't have heard me, but she nodded all the same.

Raiden Spencer wooed the sultry, enchanting heiress with the promise of gifting her a diamond for every week they were together. Set in brilliant white gold, the symbol of their love and commitment adorned her neck, growing in time to their march to the altar. One single chain held thirteen diamonds and valued at almost three hundred thousand dollars. Hazel was now up to eight chains splayed on her chest and bound to the band of white gold around her throat.

"Can you imagine walking around with over two million dollars around your neck?" Gianna asked.

"No point," Kayla spoke up. "It's never going to happen." She drew us away from the dancing Hazel, recapturing our attention. "The kitchen is through there. Grab a tray, circle the party, and collect your money at the end of the night."

I spotted a few women who had been given similar instructions. One ducked a flailing arm and toppled the champagne glass on her tray. The contents spilled down her dress, earning a round of catcalls.

"This'll be fun," I muttered.

Kayla collected our phones and sent us off.

Heading for the kitchen, we passed portraits of Hazel, Hazel, a half-naked Hazel, and half-naked Hazel and Raiden on the walls. The future Mrs. Spencer was quick about putting her stamp on this place.

"We're in the home of Cinco royalty," Gianna said. "We're witnessing how the other half lives, and no surprise, it's pretty fucking sweet."

My jaw fell open. I stopped dead on the marble, eyes rolling in my head trying to take everything in at once.

The room was one long galley. A massive fridge claimed the middle of the action. Three grown men could fit in that cooler and you'd still have room for the kombucha. A wooden wine rack stretched to the ceiling—splashing old-world charm in the modern white-and-silver kitchen.

A stainless-steel canopy range hood floated above a professional dual fuel cooktop. Two ovens. Handcrafted burners. Eleven—count 'em—eleven knobs.

If appliance catalogs were porn mags, this oven would be the centerfold.

"Wow, G. Want to steal this whole damn kitchen for me?"

"Best I can do is a baggie full of stuffed mushrooms and a fork."

Laid out on the island were the trays of food and glasses. The caterer had come and gone. I suspected they'd return in the morning to clean up. Until then, the rest was up to us.

It was like Christmas.

I popped said mushroom in my mouth and moaned. "Good. Very good. The only thing that would make... this better... is..." I brazenly opened the cabinets and pawed through. "There has to be some in here."

"I'm going to find a playmate before you get us kicked out," Gianna said. "Good luck."

I waved over my shoulder. "Ah ha." The cabinet above the toaster held my prize. I grabbed the bag of pine nuts and got to work crushing and sprinkling it over the mushrooms. Then I set my sights on the rest.

The salmon toast was sprinkled with fresh dill. The mini quiches received a helping of minced chives. For the shortbread cookies, I went whole ham. Hunting down a saucepan, I filled it with water and set it to boil on the pornographic stove.

Whether Raiden fed himself or had a chef doing it for him, they kept this place well-stocked with everything I didn't know I needed. I got weak-kneed holding a melon-baller, and had to fight myself to not claim a Gianna-style souvenir.

With the chocolate melted down, I set to work dipping the cookies and placing them on the rack to cool. Why did I waffle on coming? This is the best party I've been to in years.

A server wandered in. "Hey, I need more—"

"Take the salmon," I ordered. "Those should be eaten before the quiches. Don't bother carrying around drinks. People are bound to knock into you, and we don't need broken glass on the floor. Put them on the dining table."

"I— Uh. Yes, ma'am." She scurried out with her tray.

Now that I'm talking alcohol. I need to change the pairing to match the new flavor profile.

I went to the wine rack, pulling out bottles in search of a cabernet sauvignon. A complex wine with a smoky, black pepper taste was exactly what I needed.

"Perfect."

A deep, husky baritone filled the room. "I believe that's mine."

Jerking, the bottle nearly slipped from my hand.

"I'm so sorry, Mr. Spencer," I said, spinning around. "I didn't— You're not Raiden."

Thick, manicured eyebrows crept to the hairline. I followed them up, breath catching as he moved around the island.

This stranger was tall. Topping out at six feet at least. I imagined that sudden growth spurt made him clumsy as a preteen, but he'd found his stride in the years since. He moved with a fluidity that dancers envied, and stretched his suit over a different part of his toned body.

I took all of this in during the brief second I was able to look away from his face. Then he cocked his head, elongating the creeping vines inked on his neck, and I was back.

Heaven have mercy on us. We mortals weren't meant to look upon such beauty.

"Aren't I?" he said.

"No."

I can't say why that made him smile. His entire being transformed and the impact bowled me over.

Eyes a slightly spooky, gunmetal gray captured me as he straightened, passing so close his exhale brushed the tip of my nose. I locked on to them, counting the river blue specks swimming around his dilated pupils. A lock of hair fell between us, cutting off my view and ripping me out of the trance.

"How do you know?" he asked.

My back bumped against the wine rack. He had pushed me back without laying a hand on me. Unthinkingly, I returned the favor—reaching to push on his chest and getting the same result when he moved to avoid my touch.

"I know because Raiden Spencer doesn't have blue hair." I flicked to the waves of electric blue sprouting from his roots. "If you wanted to impersonate the guy, you should have looked at a photo or something."

He laughed—a deeply pleasing sound that curled my toes. "Fair point. But that's mine all the same. You're going to hand that over without a fuss, aren't you, Bunny?"

"Bunny?" I blurted—though the white, fuzzy dress and two balls of hair piled on top of my head made my new nickname easy to guess. "I, uh, yeah." I passed over the bottle. "Are you a friend of Hazel and Raiden?"

"Friend of a friend's friend."

"Oh." I was usually more articulate than this. But then again it wasn't every day I ran into men that looked like him.

I flicked over his shoulder. "Do you like shortbread cookies? The chocolate should be cool by now." I went over to the rack, picking up one for him and for myself. He smiled at the offering.

Damn, he really is handsome.

His bottom lip was fuller than the top. Both were stained a light pink that clashed with the raven shadow lining his jaw and continuing up and over his mouth. "Did you make these?" he asked as he took it.

"Can't take the credit. My only addition is the chocolate." The melty, floury treat crumbled on my tongue, drawing a moan out of me. "My name's Adeline. What's yours?"

"Sinjin."

"Sinjin." I rolled it around on my tongue. Decided I liked it. "I thought my name was unique."

"It's a nickname."

"What's it short for?"

"An old and ill-matched name."

I waited for more, lifting my brows as a hint, and was gifted with his mirroring my "And?" expression.

I laughed. "All right. Fine. Don't tell me."

"The chocolate was a good touch, Bunny." He tucked the bottle under his arm and scooped up some more.

"The name is Adeline," I corrected. "They are yummy. A pot of steaming chamomile tea would be perfect with this."

"I'm picking up your hint, but I don't have time to take you for tea right now. We'll have to hook up later."

Heat blossomed in my cheeks. "I wasn't dropping a hint," I cried.

"Sure you weren't." He swooped in quicker than I could blink and kissed my cheek. "I've got business, so meet me back here in… about two hours? You can drizzle all the chocolate you want on me then."

My jaw fell open, preventing a response as he boldly claimed another cookie and walked out of the kitchen.

"Rich people," I muttered.

I caught my fingers tracing the ghost of his kiss and ripped away. I was not meeting this blue-haired devil in two hours or at all. I was doing my job, collecting my money, making sure Raiden and Hazel knew who upgraded their appetizers, and then taking my ass home. Despite what Corinne said, I did not need a stranger to screw away my stress.

I should toss him Gianna's way. I grabbed another bottle to replace the wine. *Though if all of Raiden's friends are like him, she's having no trouble finding someone to commemorate the night.*

Carrying my trays, I abandoned the safety of the kitchen. There was even more people packed into the space than when I arrived.

A group of women danced near an expensive-looking statue by the front door. One look at me and they descended, clearing my tray of every drop of alcohol. I offered the salmon, got wrinkled noses in response, and continued on.

The penthouse boasted a sunken living room that did little to contain the guests. I weaved around the bodies, darting through a hole when one appeared, and watched my treats disappear as I sought the middle of the action.

Bodies parted and the arm of the couch peeked through. I edged around a particularly amorous couple. The two were making out like starving hyenas. The guy had her skirt pushed up so far, no one had to guess what his hand was doing between her legs.

She lifted one up for better access and kicked me square on the hip. I gritted my teeth.

I need this job. I need this job. I need this job.

Pushing through, I escaped the crush and fell on the chair. I anticipated a coffee table and the slight space around it. This was my spot until my food was gone.

I turned my back to the furniture and landed on the group sitting on the couch. Three guys huddled over a slim pair of legs ending in green spiky heels. One of the guys twisted his neck to laugh with his friend, revealing the young woman underneath them.

Her eyelids fluttered as her head fell on his shoulder. The man on her left tilted her chin forward, holding her steady as he put the tumbler to her lips and made her drink.

My tray crashed to the floor. "What the fuck are you three doing?!"

They jumped like the guilty pieces of trash they were. "What? Nothing," one cried. "Who are you?"

Shoving him aside, I bent down in front of the barely conscious woman. "Hey, are you okay?" I patted her cheek and she dropped her head forward. Out.

"Get me water," I ordered.

"Fuck off and pick up that tray, bitch. I don't—"

I whacked him upside the head. "I'll show you bitch, boy!" I shouted into his wide eyes. "Get me some water now!"

He tipped over, landing on his friend who hauled him up. The three of them ran off—maybe to fetch the water or maybe not. All that mattered was those shits were away from her.

"Lady? Are you—"

Her eyes snapped open. I shot out of the way as she doubled over, spewing her stomach's contents on the rug.

"Okay. Time to go." Draping her arm around my shoulder, I dove into the throng of people. The tips of her heels skimmed over the carpet. She put all her weight on me, forehead tucked under my chin, but lucid enough to hold tight to my neck.

I picked up the pace, veering down the opposite hallway from the kitchen. Double doors peeked between the wall and another statue. I tried the handle.

Locked. I had to get her into a bathroom before she was sick again. *Where the hell is it?*

This hall had one more set of doors for me. I crossed to the end and twisted the knob. The door swung open, revealing a bedroom.

Her stranglehold constricted.

Moving fast, I carried her past the bed and raced to the bathroom. I positioned her head over the toilet just as she heaved.

"You'll be okay," I said over her retching. "Get it all out."

The bathroom we forced ourselves into was Hazel and Raiden's. Double sinks loaded down with matching colognes, gels, razors, and on the other side, perfume, makeup, and contact solution. My entire apartment could have fit in this bathroom. The whole of my room would've sat square into the jetted bathtub with space left over.

I wandered over to the sinks and began opening the cabinets. *Gotta be something I can use... There.*

Nestled under Hazel's sink next to the spare toilet paper, was a stack of rinse cups. I filled up one with water and brought it to my new friend.

"Here. Drink this."

She knocked my hand aside, spilling the water on my shoes.

"Nice," I muttered. Going back, I filled it up again and got it into her hand. "Drink, please. When you're feeling better, I'll get security to help you home."

It took some more gentle prodding but finally she swallowed the mouthful. I made her drink more until I was satisfied.

"Good. Now, let's go."

The muted sounds of the party turned up to maximum, pouring in as someone came into the room. *Must be Raiden or Hazel. I'll tell them I was helping out their friend. They can't fire me for that.*

"—a conversation."

Wait.

"You know what this is about."

Sinjin? What's he doing here?

I poked around the wood, and immediately grabbed the door, swinging it shut as I ducked down. Through the crack in the frame, the electric-blue Adonis strode into the bedroom carrying the pilfered bottle. Behind him, three men dragged in a guy I recognized on sight.

Raiden Spencer.

"I have no idea what this is about!" Raiden thrashed in their grip. "Get the fuck off me!"

"Stop all that bleating, Spencer," said one of his captors. He looked down at him with such distaste, I felt his revulsion like it was my own. "No one can hear you."

It was a terrible look on such a sculpted face. Jaw hard enough to split a rock set in stone. Golden eyes burned through Raiden's bravado, and the man ripped him out of the other guys' hold and threw him at the foot of the settee.

I crouched low on the frame, narrowing the crack to a sliver. My spot gave me a clear view of the door, the settee, the entry to their walk-in closet, and part of the bed. The backs of the four men faced me as they bore on Raiden. Sinjin's hair couldn't hide him from me, and one of the other men carried a black backpack. Otherwise, it was only Raiden I could see clearly.

What was going on? What did Sinjin want with Raiden?

Why am I hiding in here? I need to get out.

I twisted. My unnamed companion had closed the toilet lid and rested her head on it. She was out cold.

"Stupid bastards. It was a mistake to come here." Seeking through the crack once more, I saw Raiden scour their towering figures, lips peeled back from those gleaming, white teeth. "You're not making it out alive."

"Who's going to stop us?" A voice smooth and savory like melting butter tickled up my spine. One of the guys jumped on Raiden's bed, crossing one leg over the other, getting comfortable. I saw only a wisp of crow-black hair as he passed. "Your security is busy making sure none of your friends rip the symphony from your pretty girl's neck. No one will look for you until it's much too late, my friend."

Goose bumps rippled down my skin. *I need to get out of here now.*

My knees locked—feet rooted to the spot. My instincts screamed that I had stumbled into something bad. They screamed it almost as loudly as the knowledge that it would cost those four men no effort at all to catch me as I fled to the door and throw me down next to Raiden.

"Funny you should mention the symphony," Sinjin said, "because that's exactly what we came to chat about."

"Wh— What about it?" Raiden edged away, his retreat blocked by the couch. "That's what you want, isn't it? Fine. It's yours." He threw out his hands. "Take it! Will that settle this? Are we good?"

The men fell silent. I don't know why that had been the wrong thing to say, but I sensed it was all the same.

"Are we good?" Sinjin crouched before him. "You think we're here for that gaudy trinket?" He laughed. "Like I couldn't have taken it myself any time I wanted? Like the lovely Hazel wouldn't have happily slid it off her neck and put it in my hand while her mouth thanked my dick for the pleasure? I'm fucking Sinjin Bellisario! Since when do I need your permission to take what I want?!"

He smashed his fist in his jaw. I clapped my hand over my mouth to pen my cry.

"How could you do this, Spencer?" he asked over Raiden's groaning. "Insult me to my face? I thought we had a mutual respect. Businessman to businessman."

The hard-jawed, golden-haired man actually patted Sinjin on the back like he needed comforting.

"I almost wish the symphony could settle our business, but you know we've gone beyond that now."

"I didn't do anything," Raiden cried. "I swear, Sinjin. Whatever this is, we can work it out."

"Whatever this is?" Sinjin looked up at the blond guy. "Cash, will you lay it out for our friend here?"

"What this is," Cash began, "is you tracking us down through Memphis for a jewelry store job. Buying your lady love's affections with diamonds seemed like a good idea when she refused to let you lock her down, but you're over it now. Your money is better spent on pussy you can't get for free."

Cash knelt next to Sinjin. It was hard to make out Raiden between them.

"Everyone knows Old Jimmy's shop is a front for his real business," Cash continued. "The guy keeps a stash of jewels waiting to fence when the heat dies down. Everyone also knows, he works for the Kings.

"We told you we wouldn't take that job. Going after Jimmy would kick off a war that we might win, but we'd lose a shitload of our guys trying. The Kings aren't a gang you take on without a strategy, stockpile, and a contingency for your contingencies. They're for fuck sure not guys you piss off because some spoiled, rich prick wants to cheat his old lady."

"But you didn't like hearing no, did you?" That deep timbre spoke up—cool and relaxed as he reclined on the man's bed. "Decided you'd hire a bunch of guys, put them in our masks, and get the same result."

"Our masks?" I whispered. "Jewelry store?"

These guys... Sinjin... They're the Merchants?

"No. No!" I saw him toss his head through the crack in their bodies. "You have it all wrong. Someone else framed you. Someone who knew about the job. Memphis!" he burst out. "I bet that shit saw his chance and took it."

"Really?" asked Cash. "Because I'm betting you saw your chance and assumed your overpaid guards would protect you from us for the short time we have left on this earth. The Kings will come after us now. They lost millions in that hit, and they're not about to take that lying down. They'll hunt, torture, and kill every member of our crew. Cinco City will bathe in our blood, and for the next decade, no one will dare wear a face mask, even if it's for a cold.

"You get what you want, and the Kings handle the rest. The plan should have been foolproof," he said. "But your staff takes bribes."

"And we didn't have to pay them that much," Sinjin stage-whispered. "Your ass really is cheap."

"It's not true! I had nothing to do with the robbery. I'm telling you someone is setting us both up."

Sinjin got to his feet, bottle dangling from his fingers. "Someone is playing a game, Spencer. That much is true. We keep our circle tight. Only do jobs for those we've vetted, and our contacts know not to pass our names up for something like this. Knocking over a Kings' front doesn't factor into our immediate plans.

"We're working behind the scenes. Laying the foundation for big moves that will one day see the Kings whimpering pups at our feet, and the Merchants running Cinco City." Sinjin inclined his head. "But that day is not today. Someone put you in contact with us who shouldn't have. Did they also tell you to frame the Merchants if we refused?"

"It wasn't me," Raiden roared.

"We're making someone nervous," said the man on the bed, ignoring Raiden. "Someone who knows more than they should, or doesn't want to risk that we do."

It was then I realized the guy with the backpack had yet to utter a word. He stood silent and immobile as though observing a scene he wasn't a part of.

"That someone wants the Kings to take us out," Cash added. "You're going to tell us who that someone is, Spencer."

"I don't know what the fuck you're talking about." Raiden pushed himself up. Blood cut macabre lines down his face, aiding the flames in his eyes.

Raiden Spencer was handsome, wealthy, charitable, and my stepping stone to an enviable culinary career. And if what Sinjin said was true, he was a liar, cheat, thief, and the catalyst of a gang war that would claim more lives than just the Merchants.

I can't just sit here and let this happen. My heart thumped audibly in my ears. All too soon they would hear it.

They would find me.

They haven't done anything to Raiden, another voice said. *One punch in exchange for framing and painting a target over their heads isn't as bad as he could get. Besides, in all the news reports of the Merchants, there's never been a murder. They're not killers and they likely won't become them here with a party full of people on the other side of the door. If I sit tight—if we both keep our heads, we'll make it out of this room.*

My pulse slowed. Breaths evened out.

Everything would be okay.

"—played for fools," Raiden was saying. "I don't have the diamonds."

"Who put you up to this, Spencer?" Cash asked calmly.

"It wasn't me."

"Who gave you my name?"

"Memphis. I said I needed a job done and he told me he knew just the guys."

"Liar," Sinjin sang.

"I'm not lying!"

"You approached Memphis with my name in your mouth," Cash said. "That you're lying about it proves we were right about you."

"Fuck you," Raiden spat. "It's Memphis you want. Turns out you can't trust your precious contacts."

"I can trust Memphis."

He chuckled. "You think so?"

"Yes. He's my cousin."

"He— He's what?" From across the room, I watched the color bleach from Raiden's face.

"I ask for the final time," Sinjin said. "Who put you up to this?"

Raiden didn't speak. His cleft jaw was starkly pronounced under clenched teeth.

"I see." Sinjin bowed, flourishing his hands. "Brutal, I defer to you."

"Brutal?" Raiden snorted. "Oh, very scary, but I'm done with this shit. And you know what, yeah, I hired those guys to do the job you pussies were too scared to do." He waved his hands. "The infamous Merchants. No one knows who they are or where they'll strike. So terrifying until you find out they're just a bunch of clowns in masks, shitting their pants in face of the Kings."

As he spoke, the man revealed as Brutal slid his backpack off his shoulder.

The frame dug lines in my skin. Flattened my nose. I had stopped breathing long ago.

"Get out," Raiden bellowed. "You're jokes! I give you a week before the Kings cut you off at the punchline."

Shut up, Raiden, you fucking fool! Why don't you see how far you'll have to go to get to that door?

A cold sweat slicked my back. Brutal had pulled something from his bag. As he unfolded it, the crinkle of plastic undercut Raiden's carrying-on. He smoothed it out on the carpet, still not having uttered a word.

"Is that for you? Lie down on it, cunts," Spencer ordered.

Brutal reached into his bag again. He turned and I missed what he took out.

"I'll have my guys take out the trash when the party's over." He shoved past Sinjin. "The next job I make those boys do in your masks, I'll have them paint 'fuck you, Kings' on the—"

Sinjin struck, smashing the bottle across his back in a shower of wine and glass. Raiden staggered into Brutal's waiting grip.

He threw him down on the plastic with such force, the floor rumbled beneath me. Raiden had no chance to recover. Brutal raised a now gloved fist and sunk it in his gut.

I shot out of sight. My nails dug furrows in the shell of my ears as the pleading started.

Everyone knows the theatrical movie sound effect of a fist striking flesh. Heightened so the audience knows, feels, and hears each strike. The reality of witnessing a beating was nothing like that.

There was no "pow," "boom," "crunch." You couldn't hear anything like that over the poor soul screaming and begging for it to stop.

"Okay, okay! No more!" Raiden cried.

"What was that? More?" Sinjin asked. "Alright, Brutal. Give him more."

"No! No, please—"

Pow.

Boom.

Crunch.

"Stop! I'll... t-tell you. Please, stop."

"You're giving in to a couple of jokes like us?" That Sinjin was enjoying this was obvious to everyone he did and didn't know was in the room. "So easily? I don't believe it."

Easily? Shaking hands clutched my writhing stomach. Brutal had beat him for what felt like eons.

"Break his thumb and middle finger."

"No, no, no!" His voice reached a new pitch. "I don't know who it was, I s-swear. I needed someone to do the job and a friend said they could hook me up. He asked around and came back saying some guy in a bar told them the Merchants would take any smash-and-grab job that pays," Raiden got out in a rush.

"Which bar?" I heard Cash say.

Slowly, I crept to the crack. The curled-up, broken man that was once named Cinco's most eligible bachelor forced the reply through red-painted lips.

"Shalimar's." Raiden clutched his fists to his chest. "They told him Memphis could get me in contact with a man named Killian Hunt. James & Co. Jewelers had to be the target because his security is a joke. Cheap cameras in the front room, but none in the side alley where he does his business with the Kings.

"The Merchants are new. Clueless. Reckless," he said. "You'd take the job, and if the Kings sought retribution, they'd come down on you and I'd be in the clear."

"And if we didn't take the job?" Cash probed. "He said to make it look like we did."

"No. He told my friend you'd take it for sure. He didn't say what to do or who to go to if you didn't. Hazel's expecting another chain in time for our engagement party." He gazed at them through swelling lids. "Don't you see? I didn't have a choice."

"What was his name?"

He tried to sit up and Sinjin kicked him back down. He slid across the drenched plastic. I couldn't tell what was wine or what was blood.

"Name!"

"I don't remember! Started with a K. K-Kevin? Kyle?"

"Kieran."

"No."

"No?" Sinjin repeated.

"It wasn't Kieran. I'm not an idiot. Even I know that name." A strange sound rattled from Raiden's chest.

Is he... laughing?

"A guy named Kieran appearing in the right place at the right time to lend a hand? I would've dropped the job right there and then. Bought Hazel a thousand diamonds. Kieran's name was never mentioned, but if he did orchestrate this..." A terrible smile spread across his face. "He's played us all. Nothing that has happened—you turning me down, me pulling it off anyway, the five of us here tonight—is by chance. It's all going according to his plan."

He laughed again. "Whatever big moves you were setting up in the shadows, Kieran has brought you into the light. He'll destroy you. Stamp out your little girls' after-school club like roaches beneath his boot." Raiden rose up, kneeling at Sinjin's feet. "My only regret, Sinjin, is that I won't be there to see you die."

Sinjin bobbed his head, lips stuck out almost comically. "Well... you're right about one thing."

He jabbed, plunging the jagged shards of the wine bottle's remains in Raiden's neck. The man fell over choking and gurgling, showering Sinjin in arterial spray.

My scream leaked through my fingers. *What did I do? What did I do?! I should have helped him. Stopped this! Raiden Spencer is dead and it's all my fault.*

"Ugh."

I snapped up, eyes widening.

"Uhhhh."

My forgotten companion reasserted her presence. Moaning, she tried to push up, lost her balance, and landed between the toilet and the tub with a smack that shotgunned my heart in my throat.

I bolted, racing for the linen closet with a half-formed thought to hide myself inside.

Bang!

"Oh ho. What's this?"

It's too late. Think. Think of something now! I narrowed on the small glass cabinet of perfumes and shaving creams. I latched on to the handle as hands grabbed and spun me around.

"Get off!"

"Bunny?"

Sinjin didn't spare a glance to the woman sleeping on the floor. He blocked her from view, standing before me as Brutal and the still unnamed man flanked him.

I blinked rapidly, wondering for a desperate moment if panic was making me hallucinate.

Brutal wore the simplest of suits to match the plainest black gloves. But his attempt to downgrade his appearance could go no further than his clothes. Long, fine lashes framed eyes the color of whiskey.

Soft, sweeping hair. Gently sloping cheekbones. Plump, bee-stung lips. Everything about this man made you think of a deity sculpted by worshiping artistic hands, and nothing about him evoked savage beatings. Was impending death making me see angels?

Shaking his head, Sinjin tsked. "Just couldn't wait, could you?"

"You killed him. You're a Merchant. You're a monster!"

He shrugged and my gaze fell on the dark, wet patches on his suit. "Depends on your perspective. If you were listening, Bunny, you heard him admit he sparked an impending war to save himself a few bucks." Sinjin smiled. "I ask you, who is the real monster?"

"You!"

He sighed. "What's the point of a moral debate if you dig in without considering all sides? A bit close-minded, Adeline."

I tensed. Hearing the name I ordered him to use was worse—so much worse than Bunny.

"You know this girl, Sinjin?" Cash's grip was a shackle around my wrists. "Where the hell did she come from?"

"Wrong place, wrong time."

"What do we do with her?" The man had left the bed but calm cloaked him like he'd drift off to sleep any moment now. The face I peeked through the crack was dusted with a trimmed beard, adding a ruggedness that belied moss-green pools. "We can't let her go."

"Hmm. A sweet little bunny hopped into the path of wolves. Do they go against their nature? Set the bunny loose to snitch to the *fuzz*?" He made big eyes, leaning back and waving his hands. "Or do they do what wolves do?" Sinjin put his face in mine. "Rip the pure white fur from her flesh.

"How does the story end, Adeline?"

My gaze was steady even as I shook in Cash's hold. "If you think this is the part where I beg and plead and say I'll forget what I saw tonight, I'll have to disappoint you. You wouldn't believe me anyway." I lifted my chin. "Do what you're going to do, Sinjin, but don't touch her. She didn't see anything.

When she wakes up tomorrow, she won't even remember the ride up the elevator."

Sinjin cocked his head. "Final words and you use them for someone else's life? That's a first."

"What's it going to be?" Cash snapped. "Spencer's bleeding out on the fucking carpet. We need to leave."

"Intriguing little bunny," he whispered, running his bloody fingers down my cheek.

I wrenched away, a snarl leaking through my teeth. "Don't touch me."

Sinjin was gone in a blink. He strode to the door, grabbing a towel on his way out, and tossed over his shoulder, "Let's go. We're taking the girl."

"Taking me?"

Brutal got my other side. The two hauled me out of the bathroom, screeching the whole way.

"Let me go!"

Raiden Spencer lay on his plastic resting place—an unrecognizable collection of glass, bruises, and blood that had been freed from pain.

I didn't know what to think of the mess he had made for himself, or his taunting of danger to come right up to his end. All I knew was his death would not be mine. I had to get free.

The music rushed into the room. Pounding on my eardrums. Covering my cries.

I was carried out the door and into the hallway without a hitch in their step. "Kidnapping women something you do every day?!"

Sinjin slid a smirk over his shoulder.

The party was going strong. More people had arrived in the time I was trapped in the bathroom, and I could barely see the door.

The blue-haired demon parted the crowd effortlessly. The remains of their host lay a few feet away and none were the wiser. They danced and partied unaware of the tragedy about to careen their carefree lives off track.

"Help!"

A mound of muscle shifted to the side. Pressed against the wall, feverishly making out with a red-haired back-of-the-head, was a sequin dress and a pair of heels she borrowed from me.

Sinjin closed on the knob and I thought fast. Heaving up in their grip, I kicked the statue. It toppled with a splitting crash that ripped Gianna and her date apart. Screaming, shouting, and dozens of eyes flying to me.

Cash and Brutal dropped me. They slipped out of the door behind Sinjin, ducking the witnesses that now had my face burned into their memory.

"Addy?" Gianna threw her arms around me. "What happened? Are you okay?"

I buried my face in her neck. My knees shook struggling to hold me upright.

"No. I'm not okay."

SINJIN

The bunny scurried to the idling vehicle, holding tight to a buxom young thing in lethal heels. The cab peeled away from the curb and melded into traffic.

"Do we follow her?" asked Cash.

I shook my head. "Not tonight."

"She could be speeding to the police station."

"I don't think so."

"Fuck it, Sinjin. Why wouldn't she?"

"Because making an enemy of a gang full of masked men isn't a smart thing to do."

"She's seen our faces. She's heard our names. She saw you kill one of the richest men in Cinco City. We're not masked anymore."

I nodded, fixed on the glowing red lights that was her cab. "I didn't say we weren't going to grab her. We know about her too. She was melting chocolate and pouring drinks. A friend of Spencer's wouldn't be able to find the kitchen if it fell out of their ass. Adeline was working the party. Track her down."

"And when we do?" Mercer drawled. His reflection leaned on the car door with his eyes closed. "Will you kill her then?"

"I haven't decided yet." My reflection flashed all of his teeth, grinning. "The fun's in not knowing."

Chapter Three

" ——Found murdered in his downtown penthouse. Witnesses say they spotted him at various times during the night, but can't recall the moment he left the party or who may have been with him. Mr. Spencer's fiancée, Hazel O'Hare, is devastated," said the reporter. "She asks that anyone who has information regarding that night, please come forward."

Gianna took the remote from me, shutting off the television. "Addy, what are you going to do?"

It had been a week since that ill-fated night, and she had asked me that question every day for the last seven days.

I went to my closet and pulled out my work clothes.

"They're going to come after you," she pressed. "This wasn't gangbanger-on-gangbanger beef. You witnessed the Merchants kill Raiden Spencer. They can't have you walking around free."

"It's been a week and I haven't gone to the cops. They'll know that by now."

A hand gripped my shoulder, gently turning me around. "Why did they try to take you? This... Sinjin... could have killed you right there and then. Why didn't he?"

That was the question that had been plaguing my waking and sleeping mind. Despite the risk to him, the violent, brutish thug that came on to me within thirty seconds of learning my name, tried to whisk me away. Why? What did they plan on doing to me when they got me alone?

"He said I intrigued him," I rasped.

Hard lines appeared around pursed lips. Concern shone in her eyes, shining a spotlight on my fears.

"They won't come after me." I spun back, yanking out my polo and khakis. "I haven't gone to the police and I'm not going to. Sinjin, Cash, Brutal, Mystery Man, and their band of masked Merry Men have nothing to fear from me. I'm going to cook my food, live in my shitty apartment, and go about my life. I will," I repeated.

"You shouldn't go to work today. Tell Salvatore you're taking a long overdue vacation."

"I can't. Understandably, we never got paid for working the party. My dad's sleeping on a torn-up mattress and rent's due in a week and a half. I'm picking up extra shifts until I pass out on the stove."

She hugged me from behind, resting her cheek on my shoulder. "Fuck the rent and fuck Raul. I mean it, Addy. I'll kick him to one of his friends' couches and you can stay with me. I'll feel better if you're with me. If the Merchants break in the front door, we both know Corinne and Alisha aren't throwing themselves in their paths."

"But you will?"

"Without a thought."

I hugged her tight, loving her so much at that moment I was tempted to say yes.

"Thanks, G, but that's the reason I can't move in with you. If—" I swallowed and tried again. "If they come after me, I'm putting you in danger."

"I'm going to work with you at least," she said. "Picking you up after too."

"You don't have to, G. Seriously, I'll be okay."

I was hauled around to face her again. "I'm not asking. There's a body in a downtown morgue that's been beat to shit and stabbed in the neck with a broken bottle. Until we're sure the Merchants haven't marked you for next, I'm sticking close."

I found myself nodding. "Alright. But you have to let me get ready, or I won't have a job to go to."

Gianna let me go. She sat on my bed, turning the television on to the report running on every news station.

Raiden Spencer.

SALVATORE'S WAS A HALF an hour bus ride from my humble digs, located in the Waterford borough. In my borough.

Waterford was where I grew up. My former elementary school was a few streets over from the restaurant. My all-time favorite gelato shop sat across from my bus stop. Waterford rent prices drove me out after college, but this was no less my neighborhood. When I was running Salvatore's, it'd be official.

"Bye, G," I said as we hit the pavement. Gianna's hotel was only a twenty-minute walk from Salvatore's, so I hadn't put her too far out of her way. "I'll text you if I'm running late."

We kissed cheeks and then I headed inside, looping around the alley to enter through the back door. Colorful stained glass set in red brick served as my backdrop. Salvatore's offered a high-class menu and the boss underwent massive renovations—at Ryan's orders—to provide the atmosphere. The restaurant I started working in during college looked like an old-school pizzeria. Checkered tiles and all.

This new-and-improved Salvatore's spread white linens on the tables and placed a single lit candle on top. The wooden chairs were replaced with upholstered pieces, and the entire kitchen had been gutted and replaced with the newest and best. Second best to only Raiden Spencer's kitchen.

Don't go there, Addy.

I stepped into the chorus of clanging pans, sizzling onions, shouted orders, and disinfectant. Tension leaked out of my body like it was never there. This was my domain. My home. Nothing can touch me in the kitchen.

"Adeline!" Ryan latched on to me from the other side of two stoves, five cooks, and the warmers. "Where have you been?"

I checked my watch. A move he caught.

"On time is an hour late in this business," he barked. "I needed your help to scale the fish and prep the marinade."

A task he hadn't bothered to inform me of beforehand, and yet I said, "Yes, Chef. Sorry, Chef."

"The fish. Now."

Snagging my coat off the rack, I entered the fray, getting the halibut from the walk-in, and beginning the cold, slimy task of stripping their scales and filleting them from the bones. Normally a job for a kitchen grunt, but not in Ryan's kitchen. As his sous chef, I and I alone did the prep for his specials.

I woke up at the butt-crack of dawn to wrangle with the fishmongers. I drove out of the city to a farm that sells fresh, organic herbs. I stayed until three in the morning to taste-test as he worked to perfect a recipe.

Man, I loved this job.

"Adeline."

Hands covered in fish, I just opened my mouth. Stevie popped the serving spoon in my mouth.

"Delicious, Stevie. Couple sprigs of thyme and the soup's done."

"Yes, Chef."

"Lorenzo," I called. "Where are my potatoes?"

"Coming now, Chef."

The nonstop on-your-feet hustle of work sucked me in. I cooked at my station while simultaneously barking orders and fulfilling my destiny as Ryan's bitch.

"Adeline, mince the shallots and toast the sesame seeds." He blew into my space and dipped a pinky in my marinade. "Too much lemon juice." The bowl was snatched from me and dumped in the trash. "Start again."

I fished the bowl out of the garbage, washed it, and did as commanded. Ryan Sinclair's tyranny over my life didn't bother me in the least—though Gianna had plenty to say about it. She thought I put up with him because I low-key had a crush on him. Broad shoulders tucked inside that chef's jacket. Ebony curls sprouted under his hat, and classic good looks couldn't be hidden by his perpetual frown. On top of all that, he could cook. On paper, he should be my type, but that wasn't why I endured him.

A kitchen was built on hierarchy and everyone knew their place within it. Those under me did what I said without question and I obeyed my chef with the same respect.

This was the order in the chaos. The rule of law beneath unfettered creativity. If the entire world was like a professional kitchen, fewer men would die with a bottle in their necks.

Ryan was on me before I set my spoon down. He took it from me and tasted.

"Perfect, Adeline."

I feel no shame to admit I beamed like a six-year-old who nailed her first ballet recital. To win any measure of approval from him was reason to feel ten feet tall. Sinclair was a genius wooed into working here with the promise he'd have full reign over the kitchen and front of house. I thought he'd give me the boot when he first arrived. I worked hard, proved myself, and Ryan came to love that I was "fresh and unspoiled" by the culinary world. He dubbed me a blank canvas on which to pour his talent.

Natalya poked her head into the kitchen. "Chef, we have a special order. Lobster tails with chive butter and sage rolls. Short ribs with mushrooms and lentil pilaf. They ordered our best vintage."

Ryan didn't look up from his fish. "Adeline."

"On it, Chef."

Our best wine and lobster tails? These were the kind of customers we wanted becoming regulars.

I marched through the kitchen, collecting ingredients for the portions I'd make myself, and doling out the sauce and rolls to Stevie and our pastry chef, Milos.

Soon, I had the lobsters grilling and the scent of the lemon butter was wafting in my nose. Maybe I'd pop to the grocery store after work and then visit Daddy. The meal I made us would be nowhere near as fancy as this, but Dad never complained about my steak and potatoes.

Stevie brought out the sauce, setting it beside me as I presented the plate and then added the final touches. It went out the door with my final thoughts about it. On to the next dish and customer.

"Order of macaroni crab and squash salad," said Ryan. "Adeline, get on it."

"Yes, Chef."

Another trip into the walk-in fridge, I returned loaded down with ingredients and found Natalya at my station.

"Something wrong?" I asked.

"Just the opposite. The guests took one bite and asked to compliment the chef. Do you have a minute to talk with them?"

I glanced at the clock and then at Ryan who was already frowning at my standing there and chatting.

"Tell them their compliment is received and appreciated."

Natalya saw where I was looking. "I know you're busy, but they were most insistent on speaking to you in person. Please, Addy. They're the kind of patrons we want coming back."

"Okay. Just one minute."

I followed Natalya out, smoothing down my jacket, and quickly taking off my hat to fuss with my hair. Waterford was middle- to upper-middle class. The cute mom-and-pop eateries were found in this borough while Leighbridge laid claim to the fine dining and Michelin-starred restaurants. Salvatore slashed staff pay to the bone in aid of bringing that fine dining to our side. Helping him achieve that dream meant good things for my financial future.

Natalya led me around the bar. The dinner rush hadn't quite started. A few couples and small families murmured to each other over candlelight, basking in the soft classical music.

"Sirs," Natalya said. I made out an elbow and jacket hung over the chair from around her back. "This is your chef, Adeline Redgrave. Adeline is a promising young talent which I'm sure needs no announcing."

"Absolutely not."

I froze.

Sweeping aside, Natalya left me bare and exposed to their eyes. Sinjin and Cash sat eating my food as though it was the most natural thing in the world.

"I only wish I could've tasted what she does with rabbit," Sinjin said.

His smile stuck two pins through my feet, leadening my bones. They found me. In a week, they discovered my name and restaurant.

Natalya laughed. "I'm sure we can make that happen, sir. If you book a catered evening with us, we'd tailor the menu to your liking."

My internal voice screamed for Natalya to shut up. These were not patrons we ever wanted back.

Cash set down his glass and waved a hand at her. "You can go."

Bowing, Natalya left us alone.

The silence stretched between us, and my jaw clenched feeling that smile corrode my insides one molecule at a time.

Sinjin took another bite of his lobster and moaned. "Damn, girl. You don't mess around in that kitchen."

"How did you find me?" I rasped.

"Prestige scanned your license at the front desk," Cash replied easily.

"To the man's credit," said Sinjin, "he wouldn't be lowballed. Demanded a high price to serve you up to us on a platter, Adeline Redgrave of 145 Broad St, Rockchapel, apartment 4... B." His lips made a little pop around the final letter.

I glanced to the left and the charming couple sucking down plates of tomato pesto and salmon.

"You won't do anything to me here. Not in front of all these witnesses."

"We know how to handle witnesses, Bunny."

"You're not going to handle me."

"Oh ho," Sinjin crowed. "Didn't I tell you I liked this girl, C? Normally, I'd love to play this out and see how long the tough act lasts, but I'm afraid we have to eat and run."

"We're leaving," Cash told me. "Now."

"I'm not going anywhere with you two, *Killian*. Wake the fuck up from that dream."

"Sweetie, I suggest you wake up and come to understand the situation you're in." The muzzle poked out from under the tablecloth. "I'm not asking."

My eyes bugged. "He—!"

Sinjin was out of his seat in a flash. Grasping the back of my neck, he pressed my face into his chest and leaned over my ear. "None of that, Bunny." His whisper was warm breath sending shivers up my spine. "We're going to have a chat. That's it."

"You don't have to do this. I didn't go to the police, and I'm not going to. You have no reason to see me as a threat."

"Who says that we do?" Sinjin skated down my chin, tracing a line with his mouth that curved my jaw. He tipped me back, raising me to lose myself in swirling pools of blue and gray.

The breath trapped in my chest as he curled around my neck. Heart hammering, heat suffused my body.

He's feeling my pulse.

The racing traitor was letting him draw all the wrong conclusions. Then I noticed something pressing into my abdomen.

"Don't speak. Don't scream." He was so close, I felt his lips form the words on my cheek. "Wave to the nice people and walk calmly to the door. Understand?"

With a knife in my stomach and a gun trained on me, I understood.

"You're putting in quite a lot of effort into trapping the bunny that got away." Slowly I turned, taking one step. Then another. "Should I be flattered?"

"Deeply."

The three of us passed an empty table when Sinjin spoke up.

"Wait. Almost forgot." He doubled back and scooped up his plate. He grinned at me. "Shall we?"

I stared at him in disbelief. *This fucker is certifiable.*

And I'm letting him lead me into a dark alley at night.

We walked out, receiving a curious glance from Natalya on the way. Cash smoothly stepped into my path as I made eye contact with her. These men weren't stupid.

The darkening sky brought frigid blasts of wind with it. It sent a plastic bag whipping wildly through the alley, skimming close to the men posted up on the nail salon's back wall.

Cash prodded me to the center of the narrow space, enclosing me on all sides in their web.

"This better be the spot where you kill me," I voiced. "Because wherever it was you tried to take me the other night, you've seen I won't go quietly."

"What are you afraid of, darling?" Mystery Man said. "That we'll pass that pussy around until we get tired of you and then put a bullet in your head?"

I held his gaze. "Yes. I'll skip to the bullet, thank you very much."

To my surprise, he chuckled. "I've racked up quite an impressive rap sheet, if I say so myself, but rape isn't on it."

"Then who are you people?!" I burst out. "What do you want from me?"

Sinjin circled me, still picking off his plate. "It's like this, Bunny. You've seen our faces. Know that we're the Merchants. You saw Spencer meet with his unfortunate end. You say you won't go to the police—"

"I won't. I *haven't.* I had that option for an entire week and I didn't take it."

"Why is that?"

I jumped. I hadn't noticed how close Cash had gotten to me. His exhale tickled the hairs on my neck.

"Because..." I dropped my gaze. "Raiden knew what he was doing when he framed you for that job. He knew it'd paint a target on your heads and set off a war that no one wants. Not you and not this city. I'd gotten used to walking around with just the pepper spray for a lewd old man, instead of the spray, pocket knife, spiked key ring, and quick step from my bus stop to my apartment.

"People like Raiden Spencer live high in their towers, far from the fear and spilled blood, and they don't care about the people dying for their greed. I'm sorry he's dead." I glared at Sinjin. "And you are a sick, twisted son of a bitch, but I won't have the Merchants declare war on me to avenge the death of a man who is little better than you."

"What'd I tell you guys?" Sinjin threw at them. "This one's got some common sense in her head, and damn"—he ripped off a bit of his sage roll—"she can cook." He nodded. "Alright, decision made.

"We did bring you into this alley to kill you, Bunny. Put your body in that dumpster over there and let the pretty Natalya find you." He shrugged. "You understand that men in our position can't let a witness run around free, even if she *promises* not to say anything."

"But I—"

"Shhh." He passed his plate to Cash to put a finger over my lips. "It's not you, it's me. I have trust issues."

I stepped back and bumped into a hard body. I looked up into Brutal's eyes, recalling visions of plastic and gloves. "Where does that leave us?"

"It leaves us with this. We're offering you a job."

"A— Excuse me?" It wasn't possible I heard that right.

Sinjin jerked his chin. "Mercer."

The man I now knew to be Mercer slipped a card out of his pocket.

"Be at this address tomorrow. Three o'clock," Sinjin said.

The men strode off like the matter was settled.

"Wait— Hold on!" I cried, reading the address scribbled down. "I already have a job, and even if I didn't and was sleeping on that couch cuddled with Captain, I wouldn't work for you."

"Oh, did I forget to mention?" Sinjin faced me, walking backward out of the alley. "If you don't show up, we'll pay your friend, Gianna Cross, a visit. Maybe pick her up when she's out back behind the Harmony hooking up with her boss. After that, we'll swing by Papa Redgrave at Waterford Retirement Home."

My lips parted, but nothing came out.

"Goes without saying that if you rethink your no-snitching stance between now and then, they'll both be dead before the cops track me down. Matter of fact, Brutal and Cash are off to babysit them now." He waved. "Until tomorrow, Bunny."

The card crumpled in my fist.

I stood there long after they'd gone, tears transforming to stinging ice in the bitter wind.

"Adeline!" Ryan burst outside. "What are you doing out here?"

My mentor towed me inside.

"I need you cleaning and steaming the bok choy. There is nothing more important."

SINJIN

Glowing specs passed by below. Hundreds of people moving too fast. Seeing too little. Feeling nothing at all. They were foolish not to stop and breathe in this city.

Cinco was a marvel that deserved to be admired. Malice and corruption seethed under the surface like writhing worms under a kicked-over rock.

It was a criminal's wet dream.

In Cinco, the stakes were higher. The women fucked harder. The alcohol burned sweeter.

The fear was palpable.

I tasted it on my tongue every time we did a job—surging on the power that we could take what we wanted, when we wanted, and no one would ever stop us. No one would get in the way of what we were truly after.

"Sinjin."

"What?"

Mercer joined me at the window. He placed a drink in my hand. "Do I have to ask, Sin, or will you just give it up?"

"Unlike what you're used to, I make you work for it."

"Why her?" The question flowed smooth and calm. "Why did you give that girl our address? Why are you bringing her on?"

"She'll be useful to us."

"How's that?"

"Bunny will reveal that to us as time passes. I have no doubt about that."

He fixed out the window. "I don't understand why you didn't kill her the first or second time you had the chance."

"You're asking me that? Usually you're whining and whimpering in the corner when things get bloody."

"I don't do the whimpering," he said, amused. "I'm a lover, not a fighter—though I recognize lethal measures are sometimes necessary. We wouldn't be on the same side if I didn't. I'm not saying I wanted to kill her. It brings me no satisfaction to kill an innocent woman, but I know a little something about breaking a person, Sinjin. She's got that look in her eyes that says we'll die trying."

"I know." My cock twitched in my pants. "Doesn't that sound like fun?"

I thumped his shoulder. "That's what we need. Fun. The knights drank till they pissed themselves and visited every brothel in the village before they went off to war. Why shouldn't we?"

"We should... until she inevitably becomes a problem. What will you do then?"

I sighed. "The bunny intrigues me. The second that's not the case, I'll get rid of her. Does that put your mind at ease, Santos?"

He swept out his arm, bowing deeply. Mercer took off and surrendered to the hold of the party while I returned to admiring my city.

The music turned up, bass thumping and rattling the ice cubes in my glass. The perfume touched me first, then the hands snaking around my waist.

"Sinjin," she whined. "Why are you standing over here being boring? Come play with me."

I gritted my teeth. For the fucking life of me, I'd never understand why women put on that little girl voice. What could be less fucking sexy to a grown man than for his date to pout like a seven-year-old?

Adeline wouldn't pout or whine. She'd give it back as good as she got—even while a man put her on her knees.

My tongue darted out, seeking the ghost of her on my lips. Twice she faced me and twice she didn't cower. Didn't plead. Didn't show the respect I'd come to demand from those who did and did not know my true self.

"A little bunny hops in the path of wolves," I whispered, "and she wasn't afraid."

"What?"

I lifted my arm, hooking around her neck and bringing my drink to her lips. She drained it without complaint.

Cash and Brutal were taking care of our new pet. Mercer and I had our own shit to do.

The party he got us into was in another rich boy's penthouse and filled with another stable of drunk cokeheads that couldn't tell the girl they were trying to hump from the crack in the couch cushions.

Except for Mercer, of course. Sober as a judge and knowing exactly what to do with the two naked women on his lap.

"Candy," I said. "If you want to play with me, you have to deal first."

"What do you mean?"

"You're Corbin's favorite ride."

She swatted my chest, giggling.

"The guy spends every last cent he has to slither into bed with you. Someone that taken has deluded himself into thinking you're his girlfriend. Don't tell me the guy doesn't share more than he should with you."

Candy shrugged delicately, smiling away. "Client confidentiality is binding between escorts too. Sorry, Sinjin. There's nothing I can say."

"No?" I molded her to me, slipping my hand under her shirt and stroking the small of her back. Candy immediately rubbed my crotch, enticing my uninterested fella to sit up and take notice.

Corbin of the Harlow Kings couldn't stay away from Candy, but I personally had no trouble turning her down. The little girl voice killed my erections stone-dead.

But tonight, my cock would get over his hang-ups.

"I'm not asking for his deep dark secrets here. I want to know if the Kings plan on striking back for the jeweler."

She winced—which said more than enough.

"Oh yeah, Sinjin. Angelo's raging. No one strikes the Kings in their own territory and gets away with it. What were those guys thinking?"

"I heard it was a frame job," I said. "Anyone can put on a mask and knock over a shop."

Candy shook her head. "No, these guys had a yellow M stitched on their masks. Only the Merchants do that. It was definitely them."

If Candy doesn't buy it, the Kings won't either.

"They've got the word out for anyone who knows who these guys are to give them up. They'll be paid more money than they can count if they do. Makes me wish one of those guys was deluding himself into thinking I was his girlfriend too."

I chuckled along with her.

"How much money we talking?" I asked.

"Hundred grand for a bitch taking orders. Quarter of a mill for the guy giving them."

I whistled. "They got any takers?"

"Not yet. No one's talking. Why?" She squeezed my dick through the fabric, stroking more insistently. "Do you know something?"

"Nah. Just whispers. Couldn't go to Angelo with that."

"Then why are you interested?"

Grinning into her eyes, I shifted them to burning, fiery cognac brown. Her ivory skin turned tawny. Blonde hair darkened at the roots and spread to the tips. I wound it around my finger, catching flecks of red in the light.

"Because," I began, "when I finally know what I need to know, Angelo and I are going to have a chat."

"As long as you split that finder's fee with me, daddy."

I refused to let the voice destroy the image of Adeline.

"You'll have to give up a lot more if you want your cut."

"Oh, I can give it up."

ADELINE

I looked from my phone to the building and back to my phone. Stubbornly it insisted I had arrived at my destination.

What the hell am I doing here?

I meant that in so many more ways than one.

I had allowed myself to believe, as the days went past, that the Merchants would give up on me. Then two plates of lobster and beef later, and everything changed.

Someone bumped into me, scooting me closer to the red metal fence. On its other side, looming over the surrounding buildings was a fire station.

I swept the street.

This part of Cinco was boringly named North Quay. It backed onto the main port bringing in cargo ships and cruise lines. This particular slice of the neighborhood was active. Kitschy bars and little craft shops lined up on both sides surrounding the fire station. Young, attractive people joked and traded conversation as they popped into the cafes.

Why did Sinjin tell me to come here? I turned my head to the lone, quiet structure. *What awaited me inside?*

Go in and find out. My nails cut tracks in my palms. *There was never another choice with Gianna and Dad at risk. The only two people I have left in this world. The Merchants found what was priceless to me and traded to devastating effect.*

I pushed on the gate and it swung open easily.

Those bastards are well-named.

A fire station in the middle of a city is a simple, no-nonsense space. An enclosed parking lot held four cars each more nondescript than the last. I walked up to large red doors and raised my hand to knock. I thought better of it and tried the knob.

They're very trusting, I thought as I stepped into the dim entry.

"Hello?"

"Come up."

I recognized the voice as Cash's—he could not be confused—but I didn't see the man that went with it.

I stepped further in, passing a lone door, and met with a staircase. Peering up, I spotted a pair of legs go past.

"What am I doing here?" I called.

Nothing.

"Hello? Hunt?"

"The name's Cash," came the dry reply.

"What do you want with me, Cash?"

"Answered that question already."

I took a step back. "I won't work for you."

"You haven't heard the offer yet." Sinjin's voice floated down the staircase. "At least listen to the pitch."

"I—"

A faint click sounded behind me. Realizing what it was, I flew at the door, banging and screaming as the lock denied me.

"Let me out!"

"Not until you hear what we have to say. Don't make this harder than it has to be, Bunny. They're serving cheeseburger casserole in celebration of bingo night. It'd be a shame if Daddy Red didn't make it to the first course."

I slapped the frosted windowpane. "You're not going to touch my dad!"

"Absolutely not... as long as you walk up the fucking stairs."

Breathing hard, the visions of what I'd do to Sinjin Bellisario assaulted my mind. Rip those blue strands from his skull. Light that trimmed beard on fire. Whale on him until I pounded this threat out of my life.

Straightening, I released the doorknob and climbed the stairs. Echoing footfalls secured the nails in my coffin. One by one by one.

My head crested the top, and the whole of the converted station unveiled before me. Brows snapping together, I stopped on the third to last step, working to reconcile what I pictured with the reality.

It was spotless.

Gleaming hardwood floors held the reflection of the four men sitting on the stools lining a steel table. On the far side of the room, three big windows cast light on brown leather couches and the big screen they sat in front of.

There were no plants. There were no pictures or paintings on the brick walls. The home—for now I realized it was their home—boasted little décor. A typical bachelor pad if not for the mentioned fact that I had never been anywhere so clean.

A faint scent of bleach filled the room like potpourri. I didn't even see flecks of dust floating in the air.

Sinjin pointed to the stool in the middle of the room. "Sit."

I hesitated, but only for a moment. There was no plastic on the floor. The men looked to be relaxed and weapon-free. Considering they had two opportunities to kill or assault me and didn't take it, I was relatively assured that wasn't what I was here for.

Taking the last few steps up, I got a clear look at the kitchen on my left. In that glance, the personality of these men began to unfold. You can tell just about everything you need to know about a person from their kitchen.

Loving, proud parents posted their kid's scribbled drawings and reports to see every morning as they reached for the milk. Parents with a bare fridge either weren't too loving and proud, or their kid was no Einstein. Busy people who cared about taste had a toaster oven. Busy people who shoved the nearest thing in their mouth on their way out of the door, did not.

I scanned the toaster oven, espresso machine, fridge without so much as a magnet, and an empty sink that had been wiped clean.

Obsessive workaholics that care about nothing and no one, and never deny themselves an indulgence.

This was the kitchen of a home you needed to leave.

Immediately.

I did not. Crossing the distance, I sat on the stool, facing the four silent men.

"Well?" I prompted when the quiet began to itch. "You've lured me here with threats and violence. You wanted me that badly. Tell me what for. What's the job?"

Sinjin swept out a hand. "This is the job."

"Excuse me?"

"We've been looking to fill this position for a while." He gestured at Brutal. "My friend here hates mess like it killed his mother. Everything has to be clean and in its place even if it holds us up when we have matters to attend to."

I looked between the two of them. "And?"

"It's becoming inconvenient." Sinjin lifted his tightly fitted gray shirt and pointed to a scar on his torso. "I got this when I exploded the pasta sauce in the microwave and refused to clean it up."

"Well, that's pretty rude," I said mildly. "Deserved it if you ask me."

Brutal tilted his head and I thought I glimpsed a grin. Studying his impassive face, I decided I imagined it.

Sinjin didn't have to tell me he was responsible for this sterile living room. I'd never seen a man as neat and tidy as him. Not a speck of lint graced his black slacks. Leather shoes were polished until they shone, and the shirt buttoned all the way to his neck was a blinding white. You could say his features were organized too.

Almond-shaped eyes not too close or far apart, Greek nose, and a pair of shapely lips beneath them. It was said those who achieved perfect facial symmetry were the most attractive among us. In Brutal's case, that was one-hundred-percent true.

The gorgeous man gazed at me without flinching as Sinjin spoke, and I found myself unable to look away.

"Deserved it or not, I need a few problems off my plate. I've already got to deal with the plastic on the floor and gloves on before he beats a bitch, I don't need to be that bitch every time I leave a plate in the sink."

"That's where you make yourself useful," said Cash. "From now on, you're doing the cleaning around here."

The trance broke. I ripped away, goggling at Cash. "I'm doing what now?"

"You're cleaning."

"And cooking," Sinjin added. He rubbed his hands. "I've got the lobster tails thawing for you, Bunny. We'll have that tonight."

"The job you're offering me... is cook and housemaid?"

Saying it out loud didn't help either. The myriad of sick and depraved things they'd try to force me to do, kept me up all night. I didn't get a wink of sleep preparing for the consequences of refusing to be pimped out, smuggle drugs up my crack, or terrorize the streets in a mask. Hidden in my bag were the pepper spray, spiked key, and pocket knife my dad gave me on my fourteenth birthday. All of that to be told I had to clean a fire station.

"Is this a trick?" I snapped. "You threatened my father and best friend because you want me to clean the floors? What the hell is wrong with you?"

Sinjin lifted his shoulders. "No one knows. The doctors have given up."

I bristled. "You think this is a joke?"

"We think you're assuming this job will be easier than it is," Cash cut in. "Like he said, we've wanted someone to take over for a while, but of course, we can't have just anyone in our place. You know who we are, you have a refreshing resistance to snitching, and it was either we find a use for you, or we kill you."

Cash dropped that like he was deciding between movie selections. Neither outcome stirred his peaceful dreams.

He propped one elbow on the table, leaning back to spread his V-neck wider and allow his soft-looking chest hair to peek out. "You'll have to clean this place to Brutal's standards on a near daily basis—"

"—and deal with his fucking tantrums when the next jar of pasta explodes," Sinjin finished. "You have no idea how this is going to free up his life, Bunny. He's wicked excited to have you."

Wicked excited looked eerily like disinterest on Brutal.

"What are your standards?"

"No point asking him," Sinjin said, motioning to Mercer. "Brutal only speaks when there's something worth saying."

"Really?" Curiosity piqued higher than disgust and irritation. "Is that by choice?"

"Don't know." Mercer picked something off the table and handed it to me. "He never said."

My eyes rounded as I read.

"Dust the lightbulbs? Clean bathroom daily? Soak dishes in a bleach solution every night? Handwash your clothes?!" I cried. "There are five sheets here. This is ridiculous."

"Don't forget three meals a day," Sinjin added. "We're not going to mess around and act like Brutal won't make your life a misery until he's satisfied, so you can name your price."

"No."

"No?"

"No," I repeated. "I'm not naming my price because I'm not taking the job. No."

Sinjin looked at the guys, pulling a face as he mouthed, "No?"

"No," I drew out. "I can't get through a list like this before my shift. On top of the bus ride from North Quay to Waterford to Rockchapel. I'd never sleep."

"Bunny, you're saying things that are not problems. You don't work at that restaurant anymore." Sinjin delivered that with such a wide smile, the instinct that I received good news almost tugged a smile in response. "Did I also forget to mention this is a live-in position? Your room is ready for you to move in tonight. I hope you like blue."

Silence spread through the space.

Cash's smirk. Sinjin's bordering on insane grin. Brutal's slow blinks, and Mercer's preoccupation with something he spotted under his nails. All of it clashed with the information my mind worked to comprehend.

Four homicidal criminals expect me to quit my job, leave my life, move in upstairs, and serve them hand and foot?

"Is killing me and dumping my body in a dumpster still an option?"

Sinjin tossed his head back laughing. "Damn, Bunny, the more I'm around you, the more taken I am. It's getting to the point you'd have to commit a serious offense for me to get rid of you."

"Name it."

"What reason do you have to turn us down? I've seen where you live, and where you're keeping Papa Redgrave. I'm betting the money that could be going toward getting you out of that crack den, is spent keeping your old man comfortable."

His words struck me through the heart. Sinjin knew so much more than he should.

"I respect that," he said. "People who don't look after their blood are a useless waste of skin and bones. But you don't have to choose, Adeline. Seriously, name your price."

"You're not hearing me, Sinjin. Okay, I am struggling to make ends meet," I admitted. "Even so, I love my job. It's where my future is. I won't walk away from it to clean your toilets."

Grinning, he climbed off the stool. "It's a shame you're refusing our kind and generous offer." Sinjin caressed the neck of the wine bottle that had been behind his back. "I had hoped we toast the conclusion of this Raiden Spencer business and move forward."

I slowly stood up, putting the stool between us. "Go on. Threaten me some more. That bit is getting old. I was willing to keep quiet if it meant living in peace, but you're making it clear I don't get that option either way. So here's what's going to happen"—I mirrored that grin—"you're going to unlock the front door, I'll walk out of it, and the five of us will never see each other again."

He hummed. "And if that doesn't happen?"

"My dad hits send on a lengthy email I wrote CCPD, detailing the night I saw four men beat and kill Raiden Spencer. It's complete with your names, descriptions, and the address you gave me which—oops—turned out to be where you live." I tsked. "If I'm not sitting down to enjoy that cheeseburger casserole with him in two hours, you'll have the cops here in three. Visiting hours for non-family members ended forty-five minutes ago. You can try to go after him, but you wouldn't get through the gates until it was far too late."

Mercer wasn't picking at his nails anymore. He looked to Cash, who half rose out of his seat as if preparing to test the theory he couldn't get to my father in time.

"Sinjin," Cash barked.

His smile was nowhere to be found. Sinjin studied me through hooded eyes, knuckles whitening around the bottle. "Calm down, C. Adeline is going to rethink this current course of action and make a better decision."

"What I'm going to do is walk out the door and you'll never have to worry about me again. I won't be your overpaid prisoner and you're not hurting to be an actual prisoner. This way, everyone gets what they want."

"I'm not a man concerned with *everyone* getting what they want." Sinjin closed the distance between us. My grip was firm on the stool, though his hands were empty. He got in my face, flattening his nose on mine. "Only me."

Stand your ground, I told my jackhammering heart. *If he wanted to hurt me, he would have done it already.*

My tongue darted out to lick chapped lips, and skimmed over his in the process. I jerked back. "What a coincidence." I was proud of my voice for remaining steady. "I don't give a fuck if you get what you want either. That said, you still can. All you have to do is open the door."

A swirling torrent raged in his eyes, battering my surety that he wouldn't kill me. Sinjin looked like he wanted nothing more than to hurt me. To loom over me as blood and wine spread over the plastic.

"Open the door."

"Fine."

"What?" Now Cash was on his feet. "I didn't want her here in the first place, but now it's a different situation. She can't make threats like that and then go walking free."

"Maybe next time you'll check the bathroom before you murder someone."

Cash bared his teeth. "There's no one in ours."

"Whoa." Sinjin put his hands up between us. "Easy. I said the lady can go and she can. Brutal, show her to the door."

"I don't need an escort."

Brutal acted like he didn't hear me. Dusting imaginary lint off his coat, he bore down on me and the resounding screams of a beaten Raiden Spencer forced me to move to keep the distance between us.

At least he doesn't have his backpack.

I clambered down the steps, sensing him behind me. The red exit made shape and sang that my freedom from the Merchants was on the other side. The cute couples, cafes, fashionable young moms, and artisan beer that existed side by side with their orderly house of pain. At least on that side, I was broke, desperate, and... safe.

"You didn't really want me here, did you?" I heard him behind me, descending the stairs. "It's not just the things you have to do. It's the knowledge they're being done correctly. And the only person you can trust to get it right is you."

"What would you know about it?"

I jumped, whirling around on him. There was no reason I should have formed ideas about his voice, and still the silvery sotto voce surprised me. Reminded me of the smooth jazz radio host my dad would play on the long drives to get me to sleep.

"I know your friends up there think they're helping when what they're really doing is introducing another mess for you to sweep up behind. You're happy to see the back of me, so remember that in case any of them get the idea to come after me. I saved you a headache. You owe me."

The twist of his lips that time, I did not mistake. "Do I?" he asked, smiling.

I dropped my voice automatically. I got the impression that to hear him speak was a rarity. One I didn't want to share with those upstairs.

"Yes. This is what's best. The four of you don't want someone you can't fully trust in your home, and I want nothing to do with you period. So cool that rage burning in Sinjin's and Cash's eyes"—I swept aside—"and open the door."

Brutal closed the final step, and grabbed me. I screamed as he threw me over his shoulder, securing my waist.

"What are you doing?!" I pounded his back. "Put me down."

Brutal threw open a door, but not the one that led outside. I was swallowed by darkness, carried down into a sub-basement. The last thing I saw before the door slammed shut was the polished tips of Sinjin's shoes.

"Brutal, or whatever the fuck your name is, let me go now!" Clasping my fists together, I struck the small of his back, ripping a grunt out of him. "My father will send that email. You'll be cleaning up after your new cellmate/boyfriend, Lo Ryder, in the next twenty-four hours, if you don't put me down!"

Brutal laughed without reservation, shaking his whole body and the woman riding on top. Light flicked on, and my cries died in my throat.

The bright, clean space I left behind was night and day to the room I was brought into, and I meant that in every way.

It was the knives I saw first.

Shaped metal of various shapes and sizes hung on the wall with white outlines to mark their spots. From cleavers to butcher knives to a collection of swords.

The basement was a concrete cave. Circular spotlight recess lighting cut odd, triangular beams of light on the walls, showing off the whips and clubs decorating wall number two.

My pounding resumed in earnest. I pummeled his back, shouting for him to let me go, and promising to rain hell on the Merchants until the jury voted guilty.

A soft clang and then I was tossed away, flying past metal, I landed on a surprisingly soft surface. He slammed the cage shut and the sound of the padlock snapping reverberated through my body.

"Brutal, no, don't do this. Let me go." I scrambled off the cushion and fisted his pant leg through the bars. "It doesn't have to end the way it will if you don't release me. Think about this! Let me go!"

Bending over, he untangled my death grip and left. The lights went out, plunging me in darkness.

It seemed telling me I was not getting out of here wasn't something worth saying.

Chapter Four

S *injin*

"Now what, Sinjin? Are you still intrigued?"

I felt the muscle above my eyebrow twitching. Mercer and his contributions couldn't be denied. All the same, I ached to punch in that self-satisfied smirk every time it came my way.

"I assumed she wouldn't make it easy."

"Right. So, we hold her in the basement for a few days, do what it is we do, and then we let her out and put her to cooking our food?" He scoffed. "We'll die of poisoning within a week."

"Men more ruthless than her have enjoyed our accommodations and came out licking our boots. You think I can't handle one bunny?"

Mercer pushed away from the table, striding off toward his room. "I think you chose her precisely because you can't."

"Why do we keep that fucker around?" I snapped at Cash.

"For his people skills." Cash grabbed a beer out of the fridge and was next to take off. "Do something about that email, Sinjin. Or I will."

"Will everyone relax? Do I look worried?"

Brutal topped the stairs, holding out the item I was waiting for. I plopped on the couch while I poked around in her phone. *Daddy* came up as the second most called number. Right after *Gianna* and on top of *Salvatore*.

"Damn, this girl needs excitement in her life," I said, dialing her father. "I'm doing her a favor."

"Hello. Thank you for calling Waterford Retirement Home. How may I direct—?"

I hung up.

Unfortunate. The home's business line wouldn't be the second-dialed if Daddy had his own cellphone. I couldn't send a text pretending to be her, and my gravelly voice wouldn't fool the man. Adeline would have to get on the phone herself and tell him to delete that fucking email.

I flicked to the clock.

Our basement was impressive, but even the weakest weaselly bitch wouldn't break after being down there for three minutes. Adeline doesn't have to obey my request. She just has to wait one hundred and ten minutes.

Brutal watched me out of the corner of my eye. The man didn't say a word, and still I heard loud and clear, "You look worried now."

"Fuck you," I said, "and let's go. We have to speed up the timeline on this one."

He peered over his shoulder.

"Midday traffic," I replied. "No time to get across the city, bribe our way into the home, and grab the old man's laptop before five. You coming or not?"

Brutal stared at me.

"Don't give me that shit. I brought her here, so that we're not three hours late to the next job because you've got to dig the dirt out of the tires with a toothpick. Don't hurt yourself forcing the words 'thank you' out your mouth."

He didn't break eye contact.

"Alright, fine. That's not the only reason." A lopsided grin curled up to my cheekbone. "But you know what they say, a man can never go wrong if he follows his dick."

Pushing off the chair, I headed down to the basement, Brutal on my heels. Adeline's shouts burst out of the soundproof room. I flicked the light on.

"Hello? Brutal? Let me out of here, asshole!"

"Bunny, stop all that racket. It's just us. No one else can hear you."

She smacked the bars. "Now!"

The air around her charged with hatred, bending the atmosphere like heat on a sweltering day. She hadn't worn a provocative outfit for her meeting with a couple of crime bosses. Just a simple pair of worn jeans, scuffed suede boots, and a T-shirt that read "Food Is My Life."

It was quite possibly the sexiest thing I'd ever seen a woman wear.

The jeans molded to her hips like she was dipped into them, reminiscent of the chocolate cookies we ate the first night we met. The outline of her black lace bra peeked through the shirt's thin fabric, and the bars uniformly breaking up the sight made my pants tent.

"Adeline, sweetie, I'm gonna need you to call Pops off."

I knelt before her. The cage was big enough for her to stand but if she held out her arms, they'd reach through the bars. Barely any room to move. No chance of sleeping comfortably. Though this cage only had one tenant before her, and they begged for the privilege.

Adeline took a swipe at me. "Let me out of here, you over-primped psychopath. I'm gonna take the plunger you tried to put in my hands and shove it down your throat! Then I'll use my Sinjin pinata stick and beat your friends into a coma!"

The question could be asked if one was truly brave in the face of someone they didn't know to fear. Adeline may have seen what I do to my enemies. She had no idea what I did to pretty little enigmas who plagued my dreams.

On the next swipe, I caught her hand and kissed it. "You can't believe empty threats will get you out of here."

Adeline snapped back and slapped me across the face. "A real one will," she hissed. "How long until five o'clock?"

I took the hit in stride. I did have the woman in a cage after all. Tensions were bound to get heated. "Touché. There are a pair of handcuffs under the cushion. Put them on."

"Like hell."

Reaching behind, Brutal smacked the hilt onto my palm. I leveled the gun on her. "Let's try this again. Put on the handcuffs. Please."

The artery pulsed in her neck, jumping for what I suspected were different reasons than mine. Slowly, attention on the gun, she reached beneath the cushions and got the cuffs. "At least you said please."

I laughed. "Defiant to the last." Getting up, I gestured to Brutal. "Get her out. I'll do the hook."

Like I said, our basement was a masterpiece. After death ended our reign of Cinco, they'd bring gawkers through our house like Yeoman Warders led tourists through the Tower of London.

"Right down here, folks, is the Merchants' torture chamber. Did you know Sinjin bought that handcrafted medieval rack at a yard sale? The execution chair he traded a guy who needed a job done."

I bypassed the chair and rack. They were just for show anyway. I mean, come on, what did we look like?

Monsters?

I grasped the pulley at the back of the room, lowering the hook until it was just about Bunny's height.

She gave Brutal plenty of trouble as he hefted her out. She kicked at his ankles, landing solid blows that winced his impassive mask to shreds. He made to hang her and Adeline moved fast, looping her cuffed hands around his neck and clamping down.

"Argh!" Struggling with her, another kick knocked him off-balance and they both went down.

I rolled my eyes. "I've watched men twice her size come after you and they couldn't put you on your ass. This is real embarrassing for you, B."

His middle finger shot above their flailing bodies.

Laughing, I hauled Adeline off and helped him suspend her on the hook. Brutal slammed out the door with his hair a mess and a rip in his collar.

"He'll make you pay for that," I mused. "But that comes later."

I circled her, drawing close to scent that sweet smell of sweat, perfume, and fear.

"You and I are going to chat first."

ADELINE

"I won't do it. I'm not calling off that email."

My toes skimmed the concrete floor. I was hung like a stuck pig, revolving gently to the full view of the knives, whips, chains, guns, cage, and other instruments of torture that decorated this room.

Sinjin moved to the chair. He set his gun on the seat and then placed his jacket on top of it. I stiffened as the tie came off too.

"Why are you taking off your clothes?"

"Not for the reason you think," he said mildly. "What Mercer said applies to my entire crew. Rape isn't on our rap sheet."

"Is that supposed to reassure me?"

"Doesn't it?"

I pressed my lips together. I wouldn't say that it did, but my relief was felt despite not being voiced. No one would ever touch me like that.

Not again.

"I didn't think murder was on your rap sheet either," I said. "All the banks, stores, and stalls that I heard the Merchants knocked over, you didn't kill or hurt a single person. Forgive me if all I accept about you now is you're unpredictable."

Sinjin unbuttoned a few off the top and rolled up his sleeves, revealing veiny, muscled arms covered in a spiderweb of tattoos. The word "powerful" was sometimes ascribed to men's bodies. I didn't understand why.

What made a man powerful instead of strong, tough, or rugged? Was it just people getting free with their adjectives? Or was there something about that guy in particular that made you believe he had total mastery of himself and those around him?

Looking at Sinjin Bellisario, my question was answered.

"Bunny," he began. "Do you know why I'm the leader of the Merchants?"

"I'm sure a few wine bottles have something to do with it."

He chuckled. "Fair guess, but no. I sleep like the rest of the mortals. Cash, Brutal, and Mercer have had endless opportunities to snuff my lights out and take over. I'm sure they've thought about it too."

Sinjin put his arm around my waist, pulling me close. His arms were like two tree trunks. Thick, hard, and impenetrable. I was handcuffed and hanging off the ceiling, but it was him around me, warmth pressing in on all sides, that I felt I would never get free of.

"Mercer is the kind of fellow that can start out with a paperclip and trade his way to a million dollars. Cash is cold, quick, and ruthless." Sinjin swayed side to side, moving in a circle. "He plans our jobs down to the millisecond. In and out. We've never run into a problem he didn't account for. Brutal can— Well, you've already witnessed his talents."

Is he... dancing with me?

Sinjin rocked me to a tune only he could hear. As tall as I was, I reached as far as his shoulder—nose buried in his open collar and tickled by chest hair. Cinnamon, bergamot, and sweet notes of vanilla fogged my mind with each inhale.

"They all have the ability, and the lust, to run the Merchants, but they take my lead for one simple reason.

"I'm unpredictable."

Sinjin whipped me around like he was spinning me out, and then snapped me to his chest. "I think linearly. Horizontally. Diagonally. Even in zigzags. I turn a problem into a solution. A threat into an asset. And a witness into a pet," he said. "I do what needs to be done, Adeline. No hesitation. No second-guessing.

"We've never killed anyone on a job because we take them for people who need the product, but not the heat. We're traders. Middlemen. Merchants. The products themselves have no value to us, so why have the major crimes cops hunting us down as murderers, when the property crimes unit is doing a bang-up job chasing their own tails?"

"Raiden Spencer answered that question," I said.

I felt his nod against my cheek. "He did. We planned our strike against the Kings to happen in at least eleven months. We needed the time to build the capital, turn enough men, and fortify our defenses. They're the first piece that has to be taken off the chessboard if we're to reach the endgame, and they weren't supposed to see us coming. Spencer blew that to shit, and I made the decision to kill him for it over a bowl of cereal while doing a crossword.

"That's why I'm the boss, Bunny. My crown isn't heavy. I fucking love the way it fits."

I swallowed hard. The gentle embrace. Heady cologne. Soft cheek on mine. It was at odds with the horrid speech dripping from his lips.

"Why are you telling me this?"

"So you understand that as quickly as I decided to spare your life, that's how fast I'll change my mind." Stepping back, Sinjin took my phone out of his pocket. "Tell your father to delete that email."

"No."

Sinjin heaved a sigh. "My mistake. I'm not communicating the gravity of the situation. Let me make this clear, if that email goes through at five o'clock, you die at five oh one." He shrugged. "Sure you can go to your death knowing you got your revenge on us, but it will take a while before the police get here, and we'll be long gone by then.

"How long can we stay ahead of the police? As long as it takes to buy off the investigating detectives. Three— Maybe four weeks."

"You can't—"

"Can't I? You'll die, Adeline. Right here, in this dark, concrete room, and it'll all be for nothing."

"Not nothing," I rasped. "Living under someone else's terms, I might as well be a walking corpse that hasn't found my grave. Does your live-in maid get time off? Will I see my friends and Dad whenever I want? Can I nip out into that yuppie paradise outside and grab a beer on a whim? Or will that door always be locked, Sinjin?"

He said nothing.

"That's what I thought. You'll let me out of this dark, concrete room, but the handcuffs won't come off. I might as well die here, knowing I gave you four weeks of hell as the price."

Sinjin stared at me for so long, the chill in his empty gaze crept into my bones. I trembled and each shake filled me with anger. Sinjin was shifting before my eyes, and in that glance, I understood the true reason Brutal, Cash, and Mercer didn't take their chance on a sleeping Sinjin. Under the wild hair, recklessness, and can't-give-a-shit jokes, there hid a swirling, boiling pot of pure madness.

Staring directly at this had consequences akin to staring at the sun. My response couldn't be controlled, and still it killed me that he should think I was afraid.

"Is that so?" Sinjin brushed my cheek like he did that night with blood-stained fingers. "I admit, I'll feel something close to remorse after you're gone. You're the first woman I've met who is... like me."

Holding my chin between two fingers, Sinjin leaned in. He didn't move fast or hold me tight. The gulf between his approach and my chance to turn away stretched eons. But it was a chance I never could have taken. I had seen something no one was ever meant to see, and it stripped me of all my defenses.

The heart of Sinjin Bellisario.

Soft lips touched mine in an impossibly tender kiss. Sinjin didn't force or press. He didn't take more than I could give. The barest meeting of our mouths, and then he was gone.

I blinked up at him. "What's your name?"

Why that was my first question, I couldn't say. I just had to know. Needed it at that moment even more than my release.

"Tell me."

"I will." His smile returned. "Tomorrow. Of course, you'd have to make a call for that to happen."

The spell shattered. "Fuck you." With dawning reality came the rest he said. "I'm nothing like you!"

"You are," he replied, moving away. Sinjin went to the wall of knives and ran his hand over the hilts. "Everyone around us has been drawn, coded, and programed like non-player characters. They behave the way they're expected to no matter what is thrown at them. Not you and me."

"I'm not a killer."

He flapped a hand over his shoulder. "This has nothing to do with social constructs of morality, Bunny. It's all about unpredictability." Sinjin's hand came to rest. "See, when I bring guests down here, I can count down to the second when they'll crack, but you..."

A long, thin blade similar to a boning knife was taken from its place.

"I honestly don't know how long the three of us will play down here before you break. Or if you will at all." He faced me, and that heart-stopping grin made me yank at my binds. That, and the bulge in his pants. "And damn if that doesn't get me excited."

"Sinjin? Sinjin, don't! What are you doing with that?!"

"I'd let you in on a secret, but it's already been given away." He gestured at his erection. "There is something about you. It's not only that I want to fuck you," he said, blunt as a rolling pin. "It's everything.

"It's that look in your eye that the man who could tame you, hasn't been born yet. It's that sense that you know you're the most beautiful woman to walk into a room, but you don't flaunt it because why put effort in for those beneath you.

"Even the way you smell." He bobbed his head all over the place, inhaling me like a line of coke. "Coffee, jasmine, and lemons. Overpowering scents that fill the room and let everyone know you're there. You're a queen, Adeline Redgrave, and you've finally met your king."

I followed the knife through his speech. "That was a hot load of projected bullshit," I said, tensing as he moved closer still.

Sinjin laughed. "Don't ruin the moment, Bunny. I'm here baring my soul to you."

Dropping to his knees, Sinjin grabbed the cuff of my jeans and slashed. My scream covered the sound of ripping fabric.

"Sinjin, no!" Panic crept into my voice. "Stop!"

"Don't squirm. That's how accidents happen."

I bit my lip, containing my cry as he sheared the second pant leg to my knee. "Such clean, smooth cuts," he mused. "There's something to be said for the katana, but call me old-fashioned, I prefer a short, handy blade that gets me up close and personal."

Sinjin cut around my knees, turning my pants into shorts. His next stop was my button.

I tried to fling myself away from him—swinging on the chain-link hook. "You said you wouldn't!"

Grasping my hips, he held me steady and got to his feet. "Bunny, I will have you many, many times. And all of those times, you will want it. I dare say, you'll beg for it. Understand?"

"I'm supposed to believe someone as *unpredictable* as you?"

"About this? Yes."

His sincerity reached deep inside of me, flicking off a deep-rooted fear. "Then put away that knife," I said, "and get your hands off my zipper."

"Ah. That I cannot do unless— Are you ready to make that call?"

"Are you ready to live in a cell like this one? Minus the décor."

This man found everything I said amusing. "I'll take that as a no." Sinjin punctuated his sentence with a hard tug that ripped my jeans off my thighs. "A word I don't hear from my Merchants, and I'm definitely not about to hear it from my bunny. It's time you learned respect," he said, moving to the executioner's chair. "If the lesson sinks in on time, it won't have to be your last."

Sinjin pressed the back of the chair to my stomach and then lowered the chains suspending me. I draped over the back, face smooshed in his sweet-smelling jacket and ass in the air.

His leg brushed my cuffed hands moving around the chair and behind me. I was a girl who preferred boy shorts, so Sinjin wasn't getting much of a look.

"Do you know why you don't have a boyfriend?"

The question was so out of left field, my jaw worked for a full ten seconds before I pushed out a reply. "Who says I don't?"

"He'd be in the top three dialed calls."

My cheeks warmed though it was nothing to be embarrassed about. "So what? I'm focused on my career—"

Thwap!

A sharp stinging blossomed from my left butt cheek.

Did he just spank me?!

"That's not why," Sinjin said. "You don't have a boyfriend because you've never met a man who wasn't intimidated by you."

Thwap!

My right cheek was given a slap to match, pulling a cry out of me.

"Everything you've got, you've fought for. From proving yourself to an overinflated chef to looking out for your old man. When a woman like you learns how capable you are of taking care of business, you start to wonder why everyone said you needed an other half."

Thwap.

"And every guy that tried to get close to you could sense it," he went on. "That they could never do for you what you couldn't do for yourself. Isn't that right?"

Yes.

"No!"

"They couldn't support your career."

Yes.

"No."

A harder smack tightened my thighs—crossing my legs at the ankles.

"They couldn't help you claw your way out of a dead-end life."

Yes.

"No," I gritted out.

"If all that wasn't enough, none of those useless shits satisfied in bed. Their hands shook undoing your bra." *Thwap.* "They grunted like western lowland gorillas, rutting on top of you for a few minutes, and then passing out before you got close." *Thwap.* "Have you ever had a toe-curling orgasm that you didn't give yourself?"

Thwap. Thwap.

"Ahh," I cried.

No.

"No— I mean, yes."

Sinjin draped himself over me. Kisses dotted my hair till he found my ear. "You don't have to lie to me, Bunny. The frustration is what makes you smell so lemony."

My whole body was burning from my stinging backside to the pants heating the air between us.

"Deep down, you've ached for a guy to bend you over just like this." A finger ran up my thigh and ended with a playful swat. "And spank you just like that. But you knew if you shared your true needs, they'd slink out the door and never come back. Which, of course, they did anyway."

My chest heaved, bobbing my hardened nipples on the expensive fabric. "You don't know anything about me."

"I've got you spot-on, Bunny, and we both know it. So, here's what you need to know about me." His weight disappeared. "I am that guy."

I scoffed. "You're the guy who'll support my career and build a white-picket-fence future with me? Is that before or after your reign of terror over Cinco City?"

"No, Adeline. I'm the guy who isn't afraid of you."

Thwap!

I didn't know much about torture, but I assumed it wasn't tailor-made to the individual. The tried-and-true methods worked on everyone, so no need to mix it up. On my honor, I wished Sinjin prescribed to the same belief. I would have taken the knives, guns, or even the rack compared to what he did to me.

"—guess your fantasy," he said. "Tied to my bed and covered with a bottle of hardening chocolate sauce. I'd have to bite, lick, and tear to get to that sweet center." Another slap arched my hips off the seat.

I'd lost track of time somewhere around the declaration that Sinjin was the man I'd been waiting for. Since, it'd been a never-ending loop of spankings and detailed descriptions of the various things he planned to do to my body once I became his girl, and a deep-rooted hatred sprouted in my soul.

I prided myself on my control. On being the very same woman he named me. Strong, independent, and unshakable.

Sinjin unraveled that woman with a gentle tug of a loose thread. I wondered if she was ever truly there. He had me hot, sweaty, and shaking. Thighs quivering. Breaths ragged. Panties damp.

"If you think you're wet for me now, Bunny, just wait till we move past my hand."

My legs squeezed under the unsummoned vision flashing in my mind.

I hated him. I hated him so fucking much… because I was about to come.

Sinjin spanked me again, zinging electricity up my middle like a finger stuck in a socket. Then his presence retreated.

"So, how did you cook that lobster?" he asked. Through my fogged vision, he propped himself on the rack—the picture of coolness if not for the raging hard-on. "Butter, of course, but did I taste some paprika as well? Also, is it true that you have to boil lobster alive? I'm a cold bastard, but even I think that's harsh."

The pressure faded, swirling down the depths to start the ride again.

"Sinjin!"

"What's that, Bunny?" He cupped his ear. "If you want something, ask for it."

I bore a hole in him, poured magma into that twisted mind and saw with perfect clarity his exploding head. Over and over again, he brought me to the brink of orgasm and then retreated to a corner to prattle on about nonsense. He said I'd beg for it and, heaven help me, any more of this and I would.

"Are you ready to make that call?"

"No," I cried.

"Then I'm not ready to give you that orgasm." Sinjin rubbed himself through the fabric. "You held out much longer than expected. This is becoming torture for both of us. Isn't it time we skip to the chocolatey part of the evening?"

Calm down, Addy. I took a deep breath and held it, willing my heart to slow. *Sinjin was right about one thing. The man to own me has not been born yet.*

"Love to," I croaked. "Let me out of these handcuffs and I'll show you where I'll shove that bottle."

He hummed. "Tempting."

A creak cut off my response.

"It's five minutes to five," Cash called down. "Is it done?"

Sinjin cursed. "I lost track of time. It's not done, but one way or another, it will be in four minutes. Prepare to move out in case." Advancing on me, Sinjin claimed the gun his jacket concealed. He held my phone in one hand, and dug the muzzle into my scalp with the other.

"Wait, Sinjin!"

"Playtime is over, Redgrave. Tell him to delete the email, or Daddy gets a front row seat to me blowing your brains out."

"You're not going to do it. You just spent the last two hours detailing your obsession with me!"

"Three minutes." Sinjin put the phone to his ear. "Yes, I'd like to speak to Oscar Redgrave. It's urgent."

Mrs. Rowe's faint voice replied.

My mind screamed at me, silencing the rational thought that fought to get me out of this mess.

"Hello?" I heard my dad say.

"Alright, stop. Hang up," I half-screamed. "I lied. There is no email. I said that to get out of here."

Sinjin covered the phone. "If that's true, there's no harm telling him you're home safe, you won't make it to dinner, and should he feel the need to get on his computer—don't." He held it up to me.

Taking a steadying breath, I said, "Hi, Daddy."

"Adeline? What's wrong? Rowe said it was urgent."

"I wanted you to know I won't make it to dinner tonight, so don't wait up for me." I raised my head and was pushed down, muzzle pressing deeper.

"I'm home doing a movie night with the girls, so... there's no need to send any emails."

"Send emails? What are you talking about?"

Of course he didn't know. My bluff was just that.

And it didn't work.

"Nothing, Daddy. I'll see you tomorrow. Love you."

"Alright, baby girl."

Sinjin ended the call. "Interesting," he said. "It was putting your father on the phone that did it, wasn't it? None of my threats moved you until the promise of Daddy hearing them carried out. You didn't want him to know you were in trouble, so it was all a bluff."

For no good reason, the bastard laughed. "You let me go through all of this for nothing, enjoying the ride while me and the guys were sweating. I'm almost tempted to reward you with that orgasm."

"You want to reward me? Let me go."

He lifted me up, setting me on my feet. "We're back where we started, Redgrave. You didn't have the option of walking out of here when you came in, why would you have it now?"

"I won't work for you."

"I also didn't expect you to take us up on our offer from the start," he said. "Why do you think that cage was open and ready for you? Now that we've settled this email situation, we can resume negotiations. Here is my offer: take the job now, or stay down here until you do."

"You wouldn't."

Sinjin told me what he thought of that by uncuffing me, throwing me over his shoulder, and tossing me inside my new accommodations. He left me in the dark without a backward glance.

Chapter Five

S *injin*

"They're searching hard for us," said Cash. "One of the Kings questioned the Donatello brothers, asking if they hired us to do the Cinco Savings and Loan job."

"We knew they'd get to the Donatellos," I replied. "They told the whole family they got us to do the job and suggested the entire outfit look into outsourcing. It was only a matter of time."

"I had this planned down to eleven months minimum." Cash's fist came down on his stack of now worthless plans. "With their full attention on us, we're looking at a couple of months before they finally get the right person to talk."

The four of us were bent over the dining table, having the same argument we've been fighting for four days.

"Then that's how long we have," I said. "Figure out how to take them out in two months."

"Impossible," Cash forced through gritted teeth. "They're the oldest gang in the city. They've survived for over forty years. What the fuck are we going to do in two months?"

"The Roman Empire lasted a thousand years, and they crumbled like the rest."

"Yeah," Mercer drawled, "but they didn't do it in two months."

I propped my knuckles on the table, letting them bear my weight. "What do you two suggest? We give up? Throw open the fucking door and invite them to slit our throats before dinnertime, so it's not too inconvenient? Do I need to remind you that they're the first and only lead we have to Kieran?"

Three pairs of eyes hardened as they always did when I said that name.

"They're coming for us either way, so I say we strike hard and we strike first. If you're not with me, walk away now."

Cash scoffed. "Keep your hair on, we're not going anywhere. You're going to get us all killed, but we're in this to the end."

The kitchen timer went off.

Mercer peered over my shoulder. "What are you making?" he asked.

"Food for my pet. A bunny's got to eat." I took the pot off the stove and poured the contents into a bowl. "Overthrowing a gang is the same as an empire," I said. "Drain their funds, shake their followers' loyalty, and cut off the head. I expect your new plan in two days, Cash."

He stood from the table. "You'll get it when the fuck it's ready."

I let him walk away unharmed. Cash could get away with more than most.

He was my brother after all.

Whistling, I jogged down the stairs and entered the basement. Adeline shrank against the bars, wincing under the harsh lights.

"Good morning, Bunny. Ready for breakfast?"

I knelt before the cage. The woman inside looked nothing like the one we locked up four days prior. Plump lips were shrunken and chapped. The wild mane of bronze hung in limp, greasy hanks. I reduced the outfit I loved so much to tatters by day two, leaving its remains on the floor. On day three, she jumped me with the rope she made out of the scraps, trying to strangle me. The result of that scuffle gave her a lump on her forehead.

"Break... fast?" Adeline saw the bowl, and threw herself at the bars. I dodged her swipe. "Give it to me."

Her eagerness was understandable. Four days without food would do that to a person.

"It's yours," I said. "First things first. Handcuffs. Can't have you attempt to kill me again."

Adeline was too weak to argue. It took her three tries to get the cuffs on her wrists. Attention on her, I drew my shirt over my head and tossed it to the side.

"You... said food?" Her voice was barely a rasp.

"And that's what I have." Unlocking her cage, I beckoned her out. "Here."

I held the bowl just above her head, making it impossible for her to see inside. She inched forward, distrust etched into the haggard lines of her face, but hunger pushing her on. "What is it?"

"What else would it be?" I tipped the bowl over, splashing the melted, warm confection down my chest. "Chocolate."

The white of her irises shone stark in the spotlights. Her breaths came faster, rattling in her half-exposed chest.

"I promised you'd get to lick this off me, and I'm a man of my word."

Adeline didn't move. She watched with rapt attention as a dark line traveled down my abdomen and soaked into my waistband.

"What's wrong? Not hungry?" I made to get up. "In that case—"

Adeline tackled me to the floor. I struck the concrete hard, skull bouncing off. Twice I was surprised by the burst of strength she could summon in her weakened state.

She attacked me like a savage beast—licking, slurping, and scraping her teeth over every inch of me. I was hard in seconds.

I sat up, holding Adeline between my legs. She ducked down, seeking where the chocolate soaked my waistband, and stuck her tongue through the lining.

I clamped hard on my jaw. Just like that, I regretted my little joke.

For four days she resisted me, fought me, refused to cower when men in her situation had given up by day two. Cinco City was a dangerous place that twisted men and women alike. It's not that I never met another woman with my dark needs. I never met one who looked into the soul of me and didn't blink.

A sharp pain shot up my abdomen. Scorching desert sand trapped my gaze, daring a reaction to the teeth ripping through my skin.

She got one.

I raised the bowl over our heads and poured the rest over my collarbone, trickling down my chest. Adeline was a thing of beauty tearing at me—biting my chest, stomach, and nipples. She came for every speck of chocolate, and punished me for the insult. That she saw no reason the former should hold her back from the latter, tightened the chains binding me.

I was sick of her being down here. I had long stopped enjoying our game, and every day she refused to give in stirred equal parts resentment and respect. I couldn't end this until she let me.

Placing a finger under her chin, I raised her to meet me. Glistening smears of red and brown covered her mouth and chin, so like the strands running through my fingers. No wonder it suited her. Blood and chocolate.

"Take the job, Adeline," I whispered.

She was coming toward me. Or maybe I was closing the distance. It didn't matter because her mouth was on mine.

The kiss was gentle at first—as if both of us were remembering how to do this. Then my tongue darted out, tasting her sweet, metallic lipstick, and Adeline clamped down, drawing me in.

Warring tongues battled for dominance, clashing in a shower of sparks like those cast off when I sharpened our blades. It was hungry—almost frantic. We fell over, her leg between mine, and the other wrapped around me. Sweet and sharp. Soft but fierce. An addiction that would be the end of me. I knew it as though I woke with a vision of my future. The worst mistake I ever made was letting her out of that bathroom alive. Now my heart would lie on her palm until she inevitably squeezed.

I flipped us over and Adeline made a distressed noise. I didn't think twice in removing the key from my jacket and freeing her trapped hands. They were around my neck in a flash, shoving me back.

My nose hovered centimeters above hers. We gazed at each other, both of us likely wondering what she'd do and if I'd stop her.

"What's your name?" The question left her unbidden—if I named the look of surprise that followed correctly.

That she wanted to know so badly made the devil in me refuse to tell her. "St. John."

But it seemed he had been tamed by her too.

"Saint," she whispered.

"As I said, the name doesn't suit me."

Her hands fell from my neck. "Two thousand," she stated. "In cash. That's my price."

It took me a minute to realize what she was talking about. "Two thousand a month?"

"A week." She shoved against my chest with no real strength. I climbed off without a fight. "A thousand for the cooking and cleaning, and another for dealing with you four."

"Done," I said with a slight chuckle.

"We're not done. I've got a list longer than Brutal's." She put her arms around my neck. "Get me out of here first."

I obeyed—gathering her in my arms and carrying her up the stairs, past the guys' watchful eyes, and to the second floor. Adeline's new bed was ready and made for her. I tucked her under the brilliant blue sheets, riding a high of triumph that made it obvious even to me what a bastard I was.

"What happened to you?"

Cash didn't have to lower his voice. Adeline was already asleep.

I paid a disinterested glance to the half a dozen marks weeping on my body. "Our bunny bites."

"Mercer is right, then." He leaned on the doorjamb. "We'll have to watch her cook everything she serves us, and assume when we enter a room that she'll be waiting behind the door to bash our heads in with a frying pan."

I chuckled at the thought. *She has tried to strangle me once already.*

"You going to tell me again that I should've killed her?"

"No," he said, "because I agree with you. She'll be useful to us."

I narrowed on him. "What does that mean?"

"It means I've got a plan. Or I should say the start of one." He gazed at my little bunny asleep in her bed. "And she's the key."

ADELINE

Exhaustion carried me away, and gnawing hunger brought me back.

I woke in a bright space devoid of bars and weapons, and panicked not knowing where I was.

Then it came back to me.

Sinjin. The chocolate. The kiss. My new job.

A plate of chicken, cucumbers, and tomato salad sat on the nightstand. Next to it was a bowl of chopped avocado and a glass of water. Plate on my lap, I rested against the headboard while I ate, taking in the room he claimed was mine.

It was more spacious than I was expecting. The queen-size bed and nightstand took up one corner of the room. In the other corner was a dresser, a stand and television, and sliding doors that led to a closet. That was it for furniture.

The real personality of this room reflected on the walls.

Posters of bands I grew up listening to. Smiling, silly photos. And the larger print over my head of Cinco City at night. I loved it all, of course, because it was mine.

It should've shocked me that Sinjin and his crew charmed—or broke—into my apartment, took my stuff, and set it up in the room they knew would eventually be mine. It should've. But that was the least horrible thing done to me in the last few days. Honestly, they'd done me a favor packing and hauling it up themselves.

I finished my light meal much too quickly. I shifted the dishes to the nightstand and banged on the wood.

"Sinjin? Sinjin!" I kept this up for a full five minutes—according to my alarm clock.

The door swung open. In its place was my blue-haired, raven-bearded captor. "You summoned me?" Sinjin had changed into a pair of black pants and a button-up shirt that hung open. It provided a nice peek to the bandages covering his torso.

"I'm still hungry. Get me a bowl of chicken or vegetable soup. And another glass of water."

"I don't fetch for anyone, Bunny." He gestured at the empty plates. "Mercer's the one who fed you. If you're lucky, he'll do it again. Mercer!"

"I'm on it." A figure strode past him. "The least we can do for our new valued employee."

"I'm glad he brought that up," I said. "It's time you heard the rest of my conditions."

"Oh? This should be good."

I glared at the grin coming toward me. "You're the freaking cat who caught the canary, aren't you?"

"Cat who caught the rabbit to be accurate." Sinjin stretched on my bed, propped up on his elbow. "Why did you give in?"

Take the job, Adeline.

"Because you finally said please."

His brows snapped together. He didn't have to understand because I did.

"Here's how it's going to work," I began. "I'll be mindful of allergies and diet restrictions, but otherwise, you eat what I put in front of you. Making four different meals, three times a day is too much."

"I'd say it's not for two thousand a week."

"On top of the *misery* Brutal will wreak upon my life?"

"Fair point," he said. "Fine. We'll eat what you deign to serve us. None of us have allergies or restrictions, but Cash and Mercer are the only ones who eat tomatoes. Obviously, Brutal prefers a neat plate and doesn't like his food to touch."

I nodded. "I can handle that. Next, I want new locks on my door. Ones that are opened with a key, and two deadbolts."

The grin was in full force now. "Don't trust us?"

"A rhetorical question, so we'll skip over it."

He flopped on my bed laughing, arms folded behind his head. The sound gripped my heart and squeezed. Sinjin Bellisario truly was the most beautiful thing you'd ever seen when he smiled. So free and relaxed, you could almost see through to the person who was once called St. John.

"I get one day off every week to visit my dad."

"A condition we can accommodate when you earn the privilege."

"I doubt I have a job at Salvatore's after falling off the grid for days. Plus, I've been evicted from my apartment," I said, waving my hand. "I have nowhere to go. Nowhere that you don't know about anyway. You don't need to keep me locked up."

"All the same."

I let it go. For now.

"Where's my phone?" I asked.

"In my room." He pointed. "Right next door. I've got an open-door policy. Feel free to drop in whenever you want me to finish what those spankings started."

"This should also go without saying, but just to be clear, you and I are never going to happen. We won't fuck. We won't get handsy in the stairwell. We won't even stare longingly into each other's eyes. All hope you had of fulfilling your numerous deep and disturbing fantasies blew into smoke the night I saw you kill a man."

"I know you have to say that to maintain your pride," he said, "but let's be honest, the permanently damp patch on your underwear blew that into smoke." Sinjin sniffed the air. "I can smell how wet you are for me right now."

I clenched my teeth. "Is this the real way you came to lead the Merchants? You irritated the other three so fucking much, they gave in to you to shut you up."

Sinjin's smile remained. "No, love. It's definitely the deep, abiding pleasure I relish from pain and mutilation. I deal with disrespect swiftly and efficiently. Do you need a reminder?"

I drifted over his shoulder. The time to antagonize Sinjin was not before I outfitted my door, or when he was on the wrong side of it.

"No, thanks," I said simply. "There's one final thing. My phone—get it. I want to speak to my dad and Gianna. Now."

"Not possible."

"Then it's not possible for me to lift a spatula or sweep a broom," I replied, folding my arms. "They haven't heard from me in days and must be worried sick. I just want to tell them that I'm okay and that I've found a new job and a new place. Also, that I'll see them as soon as I've settled in. If you don't let me talk to them, we start the last four days over again."

"That would be worse for you than me."

"Exactly. That should give you an idea of how important this is to me, and what a stubborn nightmare I'll be until I speak to them."

Sinjin stared at me for a long time, eyes unreadable. I held his gaze till it became unnerving and I had to look away.

"I'll be listening to every word you say," he said. "Don't veer off script."

I nodded.

Sinjin walked out and returned steps behind Mercer. A bowl of vegetable soup and water rested on the tray he placed on my nightstand. Mercer bent over me, tucking the blankets in around me. I pressed my lips together, keeping in a surprised noise as he adjusted my pillows.

Mercer smiled into my eyes and it hit me we'd never been this close be-fore... and I was better for it.

Sweet, citrus tones overwhelmed my senses, fogging my brain to lesser ef-fect to soften me to the full impact of that one-sided grin, pointed canine, and roguish stubble that tempted me to reach out and touch.

I stopped my hand halfway to his face and pulled the blankets tighter around me instead. His grin grew knowing like my fake hadn't fooled him.

"Need anything else?" Mercer asked, placing the tray on my lap.

I found my voice. "What? So you're the nice one?"

He winked. "I like to let people think so."

Mercer swept out leaving me with that enigmatic statement to chew over while Sinjin made himself comfortable. He stretched out on my legs, prop-ping his chin between the crook, and handed me the phone. I had plenty to say about him getting homey on my lap, but it stayed in my head. Like I said, the time to piss Sinjin off wasn't when he was on top of me.

I called the home first. Dad's gruff voice poured out of the speaker, loos-ening the tight ball of tension in my chest.

"Addy. Where you been?"

"Sorry I fell off the map, Dad. It's"—I cut a look to Sinjin—"been a hec-tic few days."

"Something wrong?"

"No, I'm okay," I said. "I moved out of my apartment. Found a new job too."

"New apartment? Where?"

Sinjin rested his cheek on my thigh. The other received a slow, kneading massage through the comforter.

With two fingers, I picked up his hand and dropped it off the bed. It found its way back in an instant.

"North Quay."

"That's a nice area," said Dad. "Expensive though. What's this new job?"

"Personal chef."

"Those are good gigs. Better hours, more money. Didn't your old man say it? You were meant for more than running around a sweaty kitchen."

Sinjin had moved his massage to the inner thigh. It felt better than I wanted to admit after being in a cage for days. My cramped muscles purred under ministrations creeping close but not close enough to my middle. Heat was sprouting from the source, carrying a burning undercurrent of embarrassment. There was a damp patch forming, and I hated myself for it.

I grabbed his hand to fling it away a second time and Sinjin struck, sinking his teeth in my palm.

"Ow!" The cry was more out of shock. "You bit me!"

"Adeline, are you okay?" Dad asked.

"I'm fine." I glowered as Sinjin resumed his activities, smirking at me like the psychopath he was. "The owners have a dog. Vicious, evil little creature. Probably have to be put down."

"Stay away from that thing."

Would that I could, Dad.

"Anyway, I just called to give you the update. *This Sunday*, I'll swing by with dinner and we'll talk then."

"Good. We need you at the game, baby girl. Kenny's kid is a national poker champ and he's cleaning up. The Redgraves have to retake their pride."

"You take great pleasure in robbing these fixed pensioners blind, Daddy."

"An old man has to get his kicks some way."

I laughed. "Just don't cut up any more mattresses."

"Don't have a choice. Rowe confiscates our winnings if she gets her hands on them. The fucking nerve saying it's not appropriate for us to gamble. I was counting cards while she was still swimming around in her daddy's testicles."

"Once your dad says the t-word, it's time to go. Love you. See you Sunday."

"Bye, brown eyes."

Sinjin switched to the next thigh. I dialed Gianna, leaving him to it rather than risking another bite. I was beginning to see the effectiveness of his unpredictability.

The call picked up.

"Hey, G—"

"Addy! Where the hell have you been?"

Wincing, I switched to the other ear. "Sorry. I wanted to call you sooner."

"Why didn't you? What was I supposed to think when I showed up at your place and the Sanderson sisters tell me a couple of guys cleared your stuff out? I've been losing my mind." Gianna dropped her voice. "Is it them?"

The steady look Sinjin was giving me said he was waiting for me to make a wrong move.

"Yes," I said. "It's a long story. I'll get into it later. The short version is I got a new job. New place too."

"You're living with them." It wasn't a question. "Are you safe? Are they listening to you right now?"

"I'm fine. It's a decent job, G. Pays well."

"I'll take that as a yes. They're listening."

"On Sunday I'm swinging by the home to see Dad. Meet me there. We'll talk then."

"Alright, Sunday or I burn the city down looking for you. And if those guys forget their manners, kill them while they're sleeping."

I cracked a smile. "Got it."

"I guess there's one good thing to come out of this."

"What's that?"

"I never have to see Captain again."

"Love you, babe," I said, laughing. "Bye."

"Bye."

I set the phone down and reached for my spoon. Sinjin tucked the cell away in his pocket.

"You're cute," he said, "but you're not going anywhere."

"I am going somewhere. I'm seeing my family on Sunday, and tomorrow I'm going back to my apartment to get the rest of my things. Feel free to tag along. I could do with a ride."

"We got your things."

"Out of my room," I replied. "The armchair in the living room I bought with my own money. Plus, most of the appliances in the kitchen and all of the cooking stuff."

"We have all of that here." Sinjin pushed himself up, climbing off the bed. "Forget it."

"You say you understand me." I stopped him halfway to the door. "If you know how hard I worked to get the little I have, you understand what it means to me to hang on to it. I saved for three months to buy that chair, Saint."

"It's Sinjin."

"It's important to me," I pressed.

"Fine. We'll go tomorrow. There's something I gotta do anyway."

"Yes, you do. Buy and install my locks."

"And copy the keys," he returned. "Good night, Bunny. Sweet dreams."

He closed the door and I was up like a shot. Setting my tray aside, I raced to the dresser, and shoved it into place in front of the entrance.

I sank to the floor—back pressed to the wood. Heart hammering.

A beast stalked into my territory. Scented the air. Smelled the blood running through my veins. Tasted the fear. Then he slinked out with the mercy of sparing my life.

I closed my eyes, preparing to sleep against that dresser for the rest of the night.

This was my life now. One wrong move, and the beasts would strike.

SINJIN

Stepping out of my room, I passed Adeline's and tried the handle. It swung open easily. I stuck my head in and saw she wasn't there.

The night before my check ended with the door banging into her dresser. She could barricade herself inside all she wanted, as long as she was where she was supposed to be.

Speaking of. Where did she get to?

I moved silently, recalling her first attempt to kill me, and peered around the frame into the bathroom.

Nothing.

"... or small?"

My ears perked up, leading me to the banister.

Mercer and Brutal sat at the table, tracking Adeline fluttering around the kitchen with the same attentiveness I now afforded her.

Her hair was held back by a headband, allowing those impossibly thick locks to sweep down her back. It fell around her as she bent to look in the under-sink cabinet, peeking a strip of likely another pair of boy shorts over the waistband of her jeans. Sin was my name and hers for daring to turn these simple outfits deadly.

The denim clung to her curves fit to drive me to tear the presumptuous bastards off. The cheap cotton T-shirt didn't dare to hug her. It also did nothing to conceal the red bra underneath.

"What time do you all get up?" she asked. "I can have breakfast ready by seven. Does that work?"

"Eight is better," said Mercer. "You can't pin us down for lunch, so stick whatever you make in the fridge and we'll grab it on our way in or out."

I ducked into my room, snagged a gift bag off the nightstand, and jogged down to join the party. Adeline frowned at my arrival. One day soon that would change.

"You've emerged from your lair," she said. "We were talking breakfast preferences. I assume you feast on the flesh of virgins and only drink the blood of newborn lambs. We're out of both, so you'll need to take me to the store today too."

"Nope. You eat virgin and you're hungry again two hours later." I snaked around her waist, pulling that warm, shapely body to me. "I prefer my meals with a little more... experience," I whispered in her ear.

"Do you also prefer your limbs attached to your body?" She broke away from me, putting six feet of distance between us. "Was it you who tried to get into my room last night?"

"Just checking on you, Bunny. Wanted to make sure you were comfortable."

Her eyes narrowed to slits. I didn't blame her for seeing me as a danger. I was, in every sense of the word.

I placed the gift bag on the countertop. "For you," I said. "It's your uniform."

Adeline crept up, eyeing me like she thought it would explode. Finally, she tipped the bag over, and the two-piece, naughty maid costume landed in a pile of sheer lace and an apron skirt.

Brutal laughed. Mercer's sniggering wasn't much softer.

Adeline snatched up the lingerie and flung it in the trash.

"Just so you know," I said. "Every day you're out of uniform, I'll have to dock your pay."

"Just so *you* know, every day you piss me off, I'll spit in your food."

Brutal's laughter came to an abrupt stop.

"Oops," I crowed. "Shouldn't have made that joke." I backed toward the stairs. "We leave in an hour. Don't care what you serve these pricks, but I expect fried eggs and bacon on my plate in thirty minutes."

An eye roll was her reply.

An hour later, my breakfast was consumed and the two of us were standing before the front door. I unlocked it through our phone app, and swung it open for Adeline to step outside for the first time in almost a week.

"Black truck," I said.

Three cars sat in the lot. One down from Cash's convertible. I expected him to be MIA as he worked out the details of our suicide mission against the Kings.

I slid a look to Adeline climbing onto the passenger seat. *A mission where she'll be instrumental.*

I didn't talk on the drive to her old apartment. This didn't slow her down.

"Mercer says you're in and out all day, and up to who-knows-what at night, so I'm thinking I'll prep a bunch of make-ahead lunches on Saturdays and put that in the fridge. I'll make a hot meal for dinner, and if you don't want to eat it out of Tupperware, you'll be home by eight to eat it fresh. Consider this my part to play in keeping the Merchants off the streets."

I swerved at the sight of brake lights. "You talk a lot," I remarked.

"You drive too fast," she said. "Slow down, Saint. We're in a school zone."

"Are you refusing to call me Sinjin because you think it will get a rise out of me?" My tone was curious.

She made a noise in her throat. "I'm not that petty. I will only call you Saint or St. John, and my reasons are both psychological and self-serving."

"I gotta hear this."

"There was once a sweet, innocent boy whose parents named him after a saint. Somewhere along the way, he became what you are now. Sinjin. Every time you're with me, I'll remind you of who you used to be."

"Interesting. Does your theory take into account that most sweet, innocent boys become men like me because their childhoods aren't worth remembering? Every time you call me Saint, may just flay another strip off a twisted mind."

"Am I?"

Smiling, I winked at her. "Another excellent attempt to manipulate me, but you haven't been playing at my level for long enough, sweetheart. I won't tell you anything about my past."

"You've already told me your name, agreed to an outrageous salary, and gave me early release from my cell. I suspect I'll get a lot more out of you than you think."

I grinned ear to ear. "Touché, Bunny. Here's a tip to play fair, walk around in that maid costume and I'll spill my blood, give you all my account numbers, and recount every single day in the life of St. John."

"I put that *uniform* down the garbage disposal and that's the last we're talking about it." Adeline continued over my chuckling. "After we pick up my stuff, we'll swing by Waterford Organic Produce. It's next to the mall."

"That matters because..."

"I need a few cooking essentials. A mandolin, fish spatula, potato ricer, melon-baller, immersion blender—"

"Aren't I driving you to your fucking place to get all of that?"

"I don't have that stuff. I couldn't afford it, and your kitchen is lacking quite a few things. We'll outfit me to do my job in one afternoon."

"It all comes out of your pay, Bunny, so go wild."

I caught her look out of the corner of my eye. "Do *you* call me bunny to get a rise out of me?"

"I call you bunny because you like it. Makes you feel like you're all mine."

"I— You— Where the fuck do you get this shit?" she snapped.

"Am I wrong? Because I'm picturing a pert, red bottom and quivering thighs that says I'm not." I was picturing it, and my cock hardened at the vision.

She flapped her hands. "You've fooled yourself into thinking adrenaline, stress, and placating equals attraction."

"None of that applies now. Let's pull over and see who is fooling themselves."

"This is sexual harassment."

"Take it up with your boss."

Adeline turned her head, and I couldn't confirm if that quick quirk of the lips was a smile.

"We're almost there," she said. "Turn on Canal Street. It's faster."

I slid too fast into the right lane and earned another squawk. "There was an old homeless man lurking around when Cash and I went to get your stuff," I mused. "He explained in graphic detail how he wanted his dick sucked and the positions in which he'd fuck me. My payment was to be a go on his couch."

"I would've paid good money to see you go up against Captain."

"I'm sure you can picture it," I replied. "He tried to climb in the car with us, so I killed him."

"You did what?" she cried.

"Shot him in the head and hid his body behind that blessed couch."

"He was a sick, old man! Harmless! How could you?"

Adeline continued in the same vein for the rest of the drive—ranting and yelling at me. I parked on the side street next to her building and climbed out. She was out and running up on me before I shut the door.

"Is this what you do?" she demanded. "Hurt people because you can?"

"Sounds about right."

"I swear, Saint, if you don't—"

"Addy!" Someone rushed out of the alley. "Knew you'd be back, gorgeous, and you brought someone. I've got more than enough for the both of you."

Adeline took one look at her apparent best shelter-deprived friend, and gave me a withering glare.

"I'm confused by your anger, Bunny. Are you mad I lied, or mad he's not dead?"

She turned her back on me and walked off.

ADELINE

Sinjin fell in step with me. Captain was a few steps behind, telling our backs the sexual favors he'd like for free.

"Was that your idea of a joke?" I asked. "Do you get your kicks from shocking people?"

"It was amus—"

Sinjin jerked, eyes bugging. He whipped around on a smirking Captain whose outstretched pinchers revealed what he'd done. Sinjin shot to his waistband and the knife holster concealed beneath his jacket.

"Whoa." I jumped on his arm, wrestling it down. "Calm down, cowboy. Captain is going to be on his way, or find himself with a face full of pepper spray."

Captain winked. "Meet me 'round back in twenty minutes."

He went one way and I dragged Sinjin the other.

"Decrepit little shit!"

"Bet that's the first time in years someone's p-pinched your ass." I bit hard on my lip, fighting to keep it in.

"You think that's funny?"

A snort burst out, and then I couldn't stop. Howling, I clung to Sinjin's arm, unable to hold myself up. "Seeing karma hit you with your sexual-harassing payback so soon after my prayers? It was priceless." Tears ran down my cheeks. "The look on your face!"

Sinjin grunted something. His irritation came off him in waves. The arm keeping me up slipped out of my hold, and went around my waist. I pressed into his silk shirt, laughing myself breathless. Every struggle for air parting the hole between buttons, and peeking the hard, rippled body I licked clean only days ago.

Awareness hit with a cold bucket to the face, waking me up to a wayward finger tracing slow circles on the small of my back.

I looked up at him. That wasn't irritation he was radiating.

It was satisfaction.

I shot away like he burned.

"Let's go," I snapped—suddenly pissed. "We've got other things to do today."

Sinjin strode by my side into my building and up the stairs, lips curled into his cheeks.

"Stop it," I said.

"Stop what?"

"You know what. Stop reading into things."

"I'm not reading into anything. I have the exact measure of this situation."

The smooth, easy answer only served to heat my blood. I stomped across the landing, banging on my old door. "You have just as much chance with me as Captain does with you."

His grin widened.

"Ugh."

"Alright, I'm coming," Corinne said through the door. "Calm down."

My former roommate opened up in an old shirt and panties, looking like she just rolled out of bed despite the fact it was pushing noon and she worked on Wednesdays.

"Addy? What are you doing here?"

"Came for the rest of my things."

She made no move to let me in. "We gave your things to your boyfriend. Where did you pick him up, by the way?" She licked her lips. "Blue hair and all, he is hot as hell. I'd ride that dick till it fell off..." Corinne trailed off as a presence pressed in behind me.

"Please, stop. You're making me blush."

Corinne was the one blushing. She lit up like a traffic light, hands flying to her messy bun. She glanced down at her half-dressed state and took off running.

Shaking my head, I went inside and made the two steps into the kitchen. I wasted no time opening the cabinets and taking down the cooking tools Corinne *forgot* to pass off in their sweep. To be fair, without my contributions, the three of them were down to one frying pan and the egg timer we found when we moved in.

"The brown armchair," I said. "The two of us should be able to get it downstairs."

"I've got it."

He disappeared into the living room. I heard Corinne's return.

"Can't believe she's got you doing the heavy lifting by yourself."

"What kind of man would I be if I let beautiful ladies lift a finger?"

Giggle. Giggle.

"I'm happy to help. You get that side."

They carried the chair past me. Corinne had ditched the stained shirt for a flowy white dress and her hair was combed and falling in waves down her back. Sinjin flirted with her all the way down the hall.

Unplugging my rice cooker, I slammed it on the tabletop.

Why should I be annoyed? I hope Corinne does ride him till his dick falls off. Saves me the trouble of cutting off the damn thing and shoving it down his slick-talking throat.

The two returned laughing about something.

"I know," I spoke up. "It was hilarious when Captain felt him up. His eyes popped out of his head and rolled down the sidewalk."

Corinne scoffed. "That guy is a menace, Addy. It's not cool how he drools and chases people down the street. Someone should do something about him." She squeezed his bicep. "I hope he doesn't keep you away. See you soon, Sinjin."

She went off, wiggling her fingers goodbye.

"Is she?" I asked. "Are you meeting her in two hours to drizzle some chocolate?"

Sinjin leaned against the door, letting his knowing smile speak for him.

"What? It's not like I care," I said. "Let her be your new obsession. Maybe then I can get back to my life— Stop fucking smirking!"

Peeling himself off the door, Sinjin moved behind me. I stiffened at his body pressing on my back. He gripped my thighs, rocking me on his middle, and my breath stopped.

"You're a possessive little bunny, aren't you?" He licked the shell of my ear, and electricity singed my nerve endings from head to toe. "You realize you let a perfect chance slip away? You could've run out of here while I was hauling that thing down the stairs, and never been seen again."

My lips parted, shock stealing away my reply.

He was right. I could've run, and it didn't even cross my mind.

"But you didn't," he whispered. "Because that would've meant leaving me alone with the lovely Corinne, and you won't stand for me to have another woman."

Hands slipped under my shirt, drawing the hem over my breasts. Sinjin traced the lace of my C-cups, brushed over the sensitive flesh. I bit hard on my lip.

"If anyone is going to ride my dick, it'll be you. Right, Bunny?" His teeth clamped on my earlobe, making me cry out. "Now I am going to blush."

My shaky knees gave out on me and I bore down on his erection.

"Say it." He ground into me, squeezing harder on mounds that fit treacherously right in his hands.

"No," I forced out.

"Say it."

"No." I clamped down on his wrists, but didn't put in the strength needed to pull him away. "I don't care who you fuck. Corinne is probably bucknaked and waiting for you to knock on her door. Go ahead. I'll melt the chocolate myself."

He traveled up my straps and inched them off my shoulder. This was the part where I shoved him off. Reminded him of his promise. Cursed him till his ears lit on fire. Kneed the cock rubbing against me.

I tightened on his wrists. *This is your chance.*

"Doesn't bother you at all, huh?" His lips burned a trail to my throat and pressed a light kiss. All too late, I realized he was once again feeling my pulse. "You're lying."

The accusation quickened my heart—which further gave me away.

"You lie to me. Stopped me teaching that old pervert a lesson. And got your kicks laughing and spreading his disrespect around." Sinjin licked my throat. "What should your punishment be for this list of offenses?"

"Nothing," I rasped.

"Wrong answer."

The world blurred.

I looked up at the faded buttons of my rice cooker. My face was shoved onto the tabletop. A firm grip around my throat.

Sinjin ripped my jeans down around my shins. "Say it," he growled.

"No."

The first slap arched my back. The second I rose to meet.

"Do it, Adeline." In his voice, I heard the tenuous threads of his self-control snapping. "Admit it. Beg for it."

"You beg."

Thwap!

A moan mixed with my cry. Reaching behind me, I wiggled my boy shorts down, catching his sharp intake of breath. The hold on my neck tightened.

"Don't take that as an invitation," I gasped. "We'll make this a rule, Saint. I won't admit, give, or beg for a thing unless you ask nicely. Put a please on top. Get on your knees if you're feeling generous. Want those fantasies to come true? Then you'll fucking earn it."

"Here's what you need to know. The only way to win a game against me... is to be holding all the cards."

Thwap! Thwap!

"Ahh." My eyes rolled up in my head, blinking the rolling pin out of sight.

All I had to do was grab it. Smash him over the head, yank my panties up, and take the opportunity I missed earlier.

There was no locked door. Three beautiful, dangerous men weren't waiting to intercept me. I could run from this deranged man who demanded my submission like a dog is ordered to sit and shake.

"Say it."

"You first."

I was playing a dangerous game. Knew it as surely as the wetness slicking my folds that I had taken a wrong turn. I was hurtling headfirst into my destruction, and there was no way back.

Sweat beaded my feverish skin. I'd stuck my finger in that light socket and my entire body was alive and aflame like it had never been. In the deepest, darkest recesses of my mind, I imagined the man who'd take without asking. Dominate without apology. Find my clit without aid of a porno.

But that man is not him, my sense screamed. *It can't be.*

Sinjin spanked me again, and I shoved the pin away, sending it crashing to the floor. I grabbed the table edge, digging deep grooves into my palm. Anchoring on my toes, I raised my ass to give him better access.

Whoever the fuck he is, I was getting that orgasm.

Thwap. Thwap. Thwap.

My cries were reaching a crescendo, likely that's why I didn't notice she was there until I opened my eyes.

Corinne gaped at us, eyes huge. The crash no doubt bringing her running out of her room.

I opened to say something.

Tell Sinjin to stop. Shout at her to leave.

I hadn't decided which when the sound of his zipper drawing down penetrated.

"Beg, sweet bunny."

"No."

His spankings began anew. Harder. Faster. Zinging equal mixes of pain and pleasure up my core and throughout my body.

Corinne drew her dress up, slipping her hand down her underwear.

"Last chance," Sinjin whispered.

"If you stop—" My words came out as ragged pants. "—I will kill you."

He chuckled deep in his chest and I had to ask myself who in this situation was holding the cards.

The smack landed square on my raw right cheek. My legs crossed in an X, straining to hold in what I just demanded.

Thwap. Thwap.

Choking on a scream, my body seized. I came hard—jerking and flopping on the table in a way that couldn't possibly have been sexy. Seconds later, Sinjin grunted and warm, sticky wetness covered my backside.

He bent over me, kissed my cheek, and just like that, released my throat.

Stunned, I slid to the floor. Eye level with Sinjin's cock, my jaw worked as he tucked his impressive length in his pants over the sound of Corinne's moans.

What. Just. Happened?

How had I ended up half-naked on the floor, butt stinging and covered with his cum?

Sinjin held out his hand. "Shall we go again, or do you need me to get on my knees and say please first?"

I scrambled to my feet, yanking up my pants. I grabbed the first thing within reach and bolted for the door.

"Wait," Corinne called. "You don't have to go yet. Alisha and Sage won't be back for hours."

I broke into an all-out sprint. I heard Sinjin say something to her and then his trailing footsteps.

My ankle twisted on the third step, and I pitched forward. I grabbed the rail, stopped, and took a breath.

I felt him before I heard him.

"We didn't come all this way for a chair and a mixing bowl, did we?"

I didn't have to ask if he was proud of himself. Satisfaction rolled off him in waves.

I looked down at my stainless-steel prize. That's exactly what we did. I was never setting foot in that apartment again.

"It won't happen, Saint," I said so softly I barely heard myself. "You won't have me."

A light kiss landed on my shoulder. "The game's not over yet."

Sinjin continued downstairs, leaving me to follow. After a minute, I did.

I had my chance to get away and I didn't take it. There was nowhere else for me to go now... but with him.

Sinjin held the door open for me to go out. I avoided eye contact, cheeks warming at the fact his surprise ending was still all over me. I fought hard for this reprieve and all I wanted then was to return to my fire station prison, shower, and make a new home in my powder-blue comforter where I'd remain until I died.

Sinjin drew ahead of me, rounding the building.

"Something I can do for you, gentlemen?"

I stepped into view, landing on the group of guys circling Sinjin's truck. The five of them zeroed in on us. I recognized their faces as the men who often stood on the corner, catcalling me and Gianna as we went by. I recognized the red bandanas wrapped around their heads, arms, and hanging out of their pockets, denoting something else.

I took Sinjin's hand—a move so natural it barely registered. "Saint, be careful," I said softly. "Those bandanas mean they're—"

"—Blood Brothers," he finished. "I'm well-versed in my gang knowledge, Bunny."

"This is a sweet ride, man." Ronin—the one who always shouted the filthiest things at us—broke out of the pack. Ronin ran his hand over the hood like a doting mother caressed a baby's cheek. Laughing, one of his boys jumped in truck bed and reclined in my armchair.

"Nice to have you back, mama," Ronin said to me. Lips peeled back over stained brown and gold teeth. His least attractive feature by far, but Ronin had a thick head of brown hair and a strong jaw to make up for it.

"Move on, boys," I said.

"Oooh," Ronin crowed. "You're telling us to move on? What happened? Got yourself a rich daddy and now you're too good for us?"

"That's exactly what happened," Sinjin said. "For your sake, listen to the lady, and move on."

"Hmm." Ronin screwed up his face, tapping his chin while his jackals cackled louder. "I don't think I will. Not unless I'm riding off in my new truck." Ronin raised his shirt, flashing the gun tucked in his waistband. "Hand over the keys, john, or we'll fuck you up worse than that hair."

John, he called him, not because he knew his name, but because he assumed Sinjin bought my pussy like he did that truck.

Sinjin made a strange noise. I stared at him in disbelief strong enough to draw my attention from the gun.

He was... laughing. A loud, full-bellied laugh that shook his blue strands. "Well done. You're going to steal *from me*?" He clapped. "This is just too good."

Ronin's pack shared amusedly confused looks behind him. "Glad you think so, guy," one of them said, "so, toss 'em over."

"I would, fellas, but if you lay another finger on my truck, I'll have to slit your throats and throw you in"—he pointed—"that dumpster."

My eyes bugged, holding the fear of which Sinjin was fatally devoid. Five guys with guns against our knife and mixing bowl.

"I would hate to do this," Sinjin continued over my mental screaming. "Because I respect what you do. Thief to thief. But you chose the wrong one today.

"All of you, run along. Except you." Sinjin leveled his gaze on Ronin, amusement drying up like it was never there. "You stay. I'm afraid your death was sealed when you disrespected my girl."

"Me?" I squeaked. *Leave me the hell out of it!*

It was the Blood Brothers laughing now.

"Did you hear that, guys? I disrespected his girl and now I have to die!" Ronin crouched down, pretending to bite his nails in terror. "What do I do?"

"I know." Ronin whipped out his gun and erased the distance with two strides. "Put a bullet in his head while his ho watches."

Sinjin blinked lazily down the barrel. "Thank you for drawing first. Now all the witnesses will back up it was self-defense."

"You don't get it, do you? You're not walking out of—"

Sinjin shoved me. I went flying around the corner, falling out of sight.

A shot pierced the busy intersection, and the screams followed like the expectant chime of Rockchapel Cathedral's noonday bells.

I scrambled to my feet, darting around my battered, brick obstruction, and stopped dead.

Ronin gawped into Sinjin's pearly-white grin. Bravado gone—wide, desperate pleas screamed in his gaze. Pleas unable to pour from his ruined throat.

Blood spurted from the gash, showering Sinjin ruby red, and the dripping knife held above their heads told the story of what I missed in that blink of an eye.

Sinjin gripped Ronin's wrist, pointing his gun over his shoulder. The man slid to his knees and the gun into Sinjin's hands.

"Whoo!" Sinjin laughed. "Who's next?"

They rushed him. Drawing their own weapons, they roared their rage for the dead banger bleeding out at Sinjin's feet. The guy who defiled my chair drew another gun. Sinjin fired as he leaped from the truck bed. One shot and he struck the pavement.

He didn't get up.

Three on one. Two of them broke off, ducking behind a parked car for cover to approach him from the back. The final man bore on him—gun and all.

"Son of a bitch!" he roared. He slashed his switchblade. "You killed my brother!"

"Which one? This shit?" Sinjin kicked Ronin's body. "Or the one over there licking cement?"

"Argh!" He ran at him.

Sinjin flung the gun away, twisting as the knife drove through the spot he was standing in. Clamping his forearm, he spun him to his chest and secured him in a hold almost similar to the one he had me in upstairs. Sinjin encircled his neck and, without a whisper of hesitation, plunged the blade in his chest.

The dying man coughed and sputtered, calling on the remains of his strength to buck free. A primal noise tore from Sinjin and he buried it deeper.

"Sinjin, look out!"

The final two broke from cover and ran at his back. My body moved without command. The man with the bandana tied around his neck charged, knife out, and honed on Sinjin.

I smashed my mixing bowl across his temple.

He stumbled into his partner, recovered quick, and turned on me. "Big mistake, bitch."

Straightening, I held my bowl like some kind of shield. "I don't appreciate being called a bitch by a Harlow King wannabe who attacks a guy while his back is turned. Last chance: run along."

He ran... at me.

I swung and metal clanged on metal. The knife went flying.

He launched at me, wrestling the bowl from my grip. I tripped and hit the ground hard—one hundred and sixty pounds of violent brute landing on top of me.

My bowl was wrenched from my grip and brought down. Pain exploded in my face.

"Adeline!"

Dazed, I struck blind, burying my fist in soft flesh.

A grunt. Then I reared. Jerking my knee up between his legs.

"Stupid slut!"

My vision cleared on his balled fist drawing back. I caught it and twisted, wrenching his arm the wrong way to screams that bordered on high-pitched.

Forcing him off me, I kicked him in the gut and dropped him on the pavement. I left his moaning heap and searched for Sinjin.

Gone.

There was no one on the street. Not so much as a fleeing bystander.

"Sinjin? Saint."

A faint grunt drew my attention. I ran into the alley where Saint and the final attacker faced off. The guy jabbed and slashed in a frenzy. His wild swipes were less effective in killing him, but worked to keep Sinjin back.

And that was all he could hope for.

Blood soaked from the tip of the blade to his dimpled cheeks. Sinjin darted smoothly in and out of reach, batting around like a cat playing with its food, and as he turned my way, our eyes connected. At that moment, I understood.

St. John Bellisario was not of this world.

Mortals may have birthed him. Human hands may have molded him. But surely as my name was Adeline Redgrave, this man was a demon.

Forged in flames. Warped in agony. Nursed in dark delight.

He was a being sent to rule us all, and to defy him, was to sign our death and seal it with a kiss.

Yes. I finally understood what it meant...

... that he chose me.

My demon looked at me, and his expression changed. "Adeline!"

A shadow fell over me.

I whipped around, and my risen opponent charged, his knife plunging toward my stomach.

I seized his wrist with both hands, forcing the tip back. He bellowed and drove harder. I scurried backward until I hit stone, screaming as he threw his weight into the thrust. Face purpling. Muscles straining.

The knife inched closer.

And closer.

The tip pierced my skin.

"Addy!"

Something streaked past me. The knife flew away and went down with him. Captain straddled him, raised his weapon high, and struck him once. Twice. Three. Four. Five times in the face.

By three, his legs stopped flailing.

Captain climbed off of him and threw the metal bike lock in the alley. "Are you okay, Addy?"

"I'm fine, thank you. I— Saint?"

I sought him in time to witness the last ill-fated thief shoved against the wall. The knife sank into his gut. There was no stopping it.

Sinjin dismissed him in the removal of the blade. He walked off before he slid to the ground, thunder storming in his eyes, advancing on me.

"Saint?" I almost took a step back. "Are you okay? What's wrong?"

Grasping the back of my neck, he tilted me up and grabbed my chin.

I gasped. Heart hammering in my chest, and slowing as quickly at the look in his eyes.

His hands moved down my face, feeling me all over.

"I'm okay," I whispered. "I'm not hurt."

Sinjin touched my temple and I hissed. The rude purpose my mixing bowl was put to came back to me.

His fingers came away with blood. Sinjin slowly turned, looking down at the still man with the ruined face.

"Saint, I'm—"

He pounced on him. The hilt was buried in his chest before the plea left my lips. Sinjin wrenched, twisting the blade in his heart.

It was over in seconds.

His life.

Saint's rage.

The brief chance there ever was to leave him.

Sinjin stood and drew me to his side. I curled into him willingly.

"That'll teach those Blood bastards to mess with us again," Captain said.

"You did well." Sinjin held me tighter. "Here."

I saw him pull something out of his pocket.

"Call this number and say Sinjin sent you. Candy will hook you up with a lady, or guy, or both, who will fulfill all those dirty fantasies, friend. Bill's on me."

"Really?" Eyes huge, Captain cradled the card with more care than he did the numerous ones I gave him for food, shelter, and medical care. "You're welcome on my couch anytime."

Sinjin chuckled, holding me closer.

"Saint?" His grip was tight. Too tight. "Saint—"

He dropped.

"Saint!" My devilish tormentor slipped from my hold, collapsing on the ground. My stained hands betrayed the blood soaking him was partly his own.

"Fuck," he hissed.

I cradled his head on my lap.

"He got in a shot while I was distracted. A better one than I thought."

"Where?" I lifted his shirt and choked. Ichor seeped around the piece of the blade still in his body. "We have to get help."

I scrambled for his phone.

He took my hand. Warm. Strong. Steady.

"No ambulances," he said. "No hospitals."

"Then what do I do?"

His eyes fluttered shut.

"Saint? Saint, can you hear me?"

Sinjin's hand slipped from mine, falling on the pavement.

Chapter Six

I turned off the stove and crossed to the cabinet by the fridge. My silent shadow trailed me.

"Brutal, we've been over this. I was kidding about spitting in your food. You don't have to watch my every move."

His response was to follow me to the stove—a step closer.

"You've got a vindictive streak, you know that?"

Brutal laughed.

Swallowing a retort, I finished putting together the meal and piled it on-to a tray.

Three days.

It had been three days since that trip to my apartment. Three days since Sinjin was attacked. Three days since Captain and I lifted him unconscious into the truck, and I of sound body and mind, sped past three police stations and two hospitals to rush back to the Merchants and my gilded cage. And in those three days...

... Brutal made my life hell as promised.

"No good deed goes unpunished, right?" I tossed over my shoulder.

Silence was my answer.

Of all my newfound roommates, Brutal was the hardest to place.

That he had a need for neatness and cleanliness, I understood. That he spoke only when he chose to, I understood as well.

That was where my understanding stopped.

He may not have been verbal, but Brutal was physical. If I missed a mi-cro-speck of dust, he had no qualms picking me up and dropping me where he wanted me to do the job again.

Which he did. Four times. Ignoring my shouts that the mantle was spot-less and the next place I'd put the Swiffer was up his ass.

That only made him laugh which further compounded my confusion.

How could someone who laughed so freely be so reserved in every other manner in his life?

I did not understand it, but then, I did not understand him.

I didn't so much as know his real name.

"Hitch a ride," I said. "We're changing locations."

The two of us trekked upstairs. Brutal followed me as far as the door and stopped at the threshold.

Sinjin raised his head at my arrival. He was propped against the head-board. His shirt was discarded in favor of letting the multitude of bandages covering his torso conceal his body.

I swept the space as I did the last dozen times I'd been in this room. As always, there was nothing to see.

Less than nothing.

The walls were free of posters or photos. He had a king-size bed with a single pillow and sheet. A nightstand with a clock. A closet with suits. And, hanging above his bed, a cross. That was all.

"There you are." Sinjin flung the sheet off his lap, gifting me the full view. Pants apparently were no more needed than the shirt. He patted his bare thigh. "Hop on. You'll have to do most of the work, but I'll make it up to you next time."

I heaved a sigh. *Yep. He's feeling better.*

"I'm not hopping on anything," I said. "You seem to have mistaken de-claring your ownership to a band of bangers in the midst of a street brawl as a change in our relationship status."

"Actually, I amended our relationship status when I came on that tight ass." He winked. "Nice job, by the way. That level of perfection takes work beyond genetics."

"We're done talking about my ass."

"I'm done talking period," he said. "I'm past ready to consummate our new arrangement, and Cash says I'm good to go."

I skated past the innuendoes. "Cash says, does he?" I set the tray down and bent over him, carefully peeling back his bandage. The wound was clean and neatly stitched. I wasn't an expert on this, but I guessed Sinjin would make it out with only a faint scar. "Still, I should've brought you to a real doctor."

"The one you brought me to was real enough," he replied. "Cash went to medical school."

"Excuse me? Cash? As in Killian Hunt? He got into med school?"

"My boy's got a storied past that would blow your mind, Bunny. Yeah, he got in. Did a couple years. Then dropped out."

"Why?" I waved a hand. "For all of this?"

"Can't be that bad a life if you willingly returned to it."

I flicked away.

I couldn't skate past this. It demanded to be acknowledged by him... and me.

"I wouldn't say I willingly returned so much as I accepted my fate," I said. "Where else am I going to go, Saint? You got me into a pseudo-threesome with my ex-roommate, and painted a target on my back that the Blood Brothers will be more than happy to riddle with knives.

"I can't set foot in Rockchapel for at least the next five years. Running somewhere else doesn't turn up better odds either since I'm broke." I gave him a look. "Congratulations. You've got me right where you want me."

"I had that already," he replied. "Still, it pleases me that you're right where you want to be as well."

"Eat your soup," I snapped.

I plopped the tray on his lap, ignoring his chuckles, and claimed a spot on the edge of his bed. We fell into silence. Me watching him eat and Sinjin enduring being watched without discomfort.

Likewise, the way a person ate said as much about them as their kitchen. Slurpers, spitters, open-mouthed chewers, dainty nibblers, and talk-while-you-eaters.

Sinjin was none of the above.

He cleared his bowl without sound or pause. Up, down, up, down his spoon went in perfect time. Sometimes he met my gaze. A few times he looked down at his food. What he did not do was give anything away.

And I'm looking close for a sign.

I traveled the length of his body and carried on around the room. Though I would never say it out loud, Sinjin was right. That day at my apartment did change our relationship. In what way or to what consequences, I didn't know, but I was determined to know the man I'd be living with for the foreseeable future.

At this rate, I thought to his impersonal space, *I'm better off with the direct approach.*

"Why St. John?" I asked. "Why not John or even Saint? Is it a family name?"

"No."

"Are your parents from overseas?"

Sinjin set down his spoon and reached for the water. "Why would they be?"

"St. John isn't a common name in the States. I assume your folks are from a place with a strong Catholic population."

"Europe," he said.

"Is that where they're from?" I asked, sitting up straighter.

"No."

I huffed. "Want to help me out here?"

Sinjin chuckled. "That's not how it works in an interrogation, Bunny."

"This isn't an interrogation. I'm trying to get to know you better." My eyes drifted up. "A cross hangs over your bed. I think your parents were religious. What happened?" I asked. "Were they struck down in some way that made you lose faith in God and humanity? Is that how you became Sinjin, leader of the Merchants?"

He thrust out his bowl. "Get me some more of this."

I plucked it from him and placed it firmly on the nightstand. Planting my hands on either side of his hips, I bore into that amused expression. "Why St. John? It's a simple question. One that can't be used against you in any way. Just tell me."

Sinjin leaned back, openly raking my body and sparing no shame for it. "I laid out my terms for opening up."

A frilly maid costume floated through my mind.

"And I laid out my terms for *opening up*," I hissed. "You want something from me, Saint, get on your knees and beg for it."

"I don't beg any more than I fetch, and you'll never see me on my knees." His fingers skated up my arm, sparking a shiver that curled my toes. "So, it seems we're at an impasse."

"It seems so."

"Good." Sinjin clapped, startling me. "That means the interrogation is over. I'll have more of that soup." He kissed his fingers. "Truly delicious. You outdid yourself."

My lips parted, but nothing came out. *How did he do that?*

The crafty fucker steered me right into the trap, and I didn't see it coming. He may have been correct about me not being on his level.

I snatched up the bowl. "This isn't over," I warned.

His laugh followed me out the door.

I have to try another tack.

I descended the metal stairs, casting an eye over Cash writing in a binder, Mercer reading in his armchair, and Brutal rising from his seat to mold to my side.

I knew nothing about these men except that they were dangerous, unrepentant killers. Ignorance in a situation like this didn't look good for my odds of making it out alive.

I returned to Sinjin with his second helping. "If you won't tell me about yourself," I said, handing it over. "Tell me about the guys. What's Brutal's real name?"

"Ask him yourself."

"Cute," I deadpanned.

"He likes you," Sinjin replied, grinning away. "I bet you could get him to give it up."

"He likes me? When did you pick up that vibe? When he was helping you hang me from the ceiling, or when he made me scrub my armchair half a dozen times before it could come in the house?"

"Somewhere in the middle there."

I stretched out at his feet. "I'll also take the tale of Cash's storied past."

A low whistle cut through the room. "Truly wish I could tell you that. It's good."

"You both seem closer to each other than you do the others. How long have you known him?"

Sinjin smiled at me.

"Fine. What about Mercer?" I asked. "Why doesn't he have a cool nickname like the rest of you?"

"I don't need a nickname."

I jerked, twisting on the leaning figure in the doorway.

"The one you choose inevitably gives something away about yourself. The cold and efficient Cash. The hard and merciless Brutal." Mercer drifted off my face. "Sinjin."

Mercer didn't need to add descriptors. Sinjin summed it up just fine.

"But Mercer Santos—the name a well-intentioned couple gave a squalling infant—tells you nothing about the man he became."

"Fair point," I said. "Why don't you tell me about the man he became?"

"I will one day. When I have time to savor your reaction." He picked himself off the frame. "Cash finally took his head out of the binder. I've been given my marching orders. We'll know something by the morning."

"Is Brutal going with you?"

"No."

"Fine. Tomorrow."

My skin tightened. Once again, I was witness to a conversation where nothing was revealed.

Maybe that was a good thing. Knowing too much about their criminal enterprise didn't work out too well for Raiden Spencer.

Still, I had the feeling being kept in the dark would keep me safe... until it didn't.

I flipped back to Sinjin after Mercer left and pushed down the urge to ask what they all knew. Why was it important that Cash had closed the binder?

"Where are your keys?" I asked.

The up, down, up, down stopped. "Why?"

"I need them. I'm leaving early in the morning to see my dad. Spend the whole day with him."

"Ah," he said, resuming his meal. "No."

"Your breakfast, lunch, and dinner are made and sitting in the fridge. Tomorrow is my day off. Give me the keys. And whatever code you guys use to get in and out of this place," I added.

"No."

The calmest of replies and my temper flared all the same.

"I told you I was going to see my dad days ago."

"I remember. It was right before I said you weren't going anywhere."

I jumped up. "And twenty-four hours before I proved beyond a shadow of a doubt that I wouldn't run away if given the chance. What's up, Saint? I just want to see my family."

"You haven't yet earned unsupervised leave."

"Yes, I have," I said through gritted teeth.

"Tell you what. We'll settle this right now." Sinjin transferred his bowl and glass to the nightstand. I tensed as he reached into his drawer—recalling chains, knives, and rolling pins.

Sinjin set his find on the tray.

"Playing cards?"

"Playing cards," he said. "I'll play you for it. If you win, you get the car, the code, and twenty bucks for gas."

My eyes narrowed. "And if you win?"

"You stay right here and continue catering and pampering me with that lovely smile on your face."

It was guaranteed my lovely smile was nowhere to be found.

"Also." His eyes met mine. "You stop asking to leave. Agreed?"

I lifted my chin, biting the chill and throwing it back.

"Agreed." I climbed up and straddled his knees. "What's the game?"

"Blackjack. Know how to play?"

I gave him a look to which he grinned.

"You're more and more my girl every day."

"Shuffle it up, Romeo. We'll see if you've got any sweet talk left in you after I win."

His grin widened. "Definitely all mine."

If a flush crept up my neck, he couldn't tell, so it couldn't be proven. I settled in as Sinjin shook out the cards. He cut the deck and the show began.

Watching him shuffle was mesmerizing. He moved so quickly, reds, blacks, golds, diamonds, and spades blurred in my vision. Sinjin bent the deck, sending the cards cascading through the air and landing effortlessly on his palm. He fanned them on the tray.

"Check 'em."

I did—searching to see if they'd been marked or messed with in any way. I nodded to him.

Sinjin gathered the cards and placed one facedown in front of him, and then two faceup for both of us. Ten of clubs for him. Two of diamonds for me.

"Hit," I said.

Me. Seven.

Sinjin. Ace.

"Hit," I said.

Sinjin dropped a five of spades on my pile. He flipped his cards and his facedown revealed with a smirk on her face.

Queen of hearts.

An ace. A ten and a queen.

"That's blackjack, Bunny."

I gaped. He said it. I saw it. And I still didn't believe it.

He folded his arms behind his head, leaning against the headboard. "Now that that's out of the way. I repeat, hop on."

"Again." I picked up the cards and reshuffled them. "That was a lucky draw. We play for real this time."

"We can play as many times as you like."

We did.

Three.

Five.

Nine times.

Over and over again, I dealt, hit, and stayed, but in every combination of cards, Sinjin either won or we ended in a stand-off.

I threw a two down on his nineteen, eyes rounding to capture his smugness in my periphery.

"You cheated," I breathed.

"How'd I do that?" The man was breezy like he wasn't risking another stab wound.

"You did mark the cards." I held them up to my face, squinting at the red curlicues. "Where is it?"

"You keep looking," he said, sliding under the sheets. "I'm taking a nap. Feel free to join me."

"When I figure out how you did it, you're handing over those keys for good." I snatched up the tray—cards and all—and stormed out.

SINJIN

"... uh..."

My eyes opened in the dark.

"... ah..."

I turned my neck, falling on the white paint, plaster, and wood that separated us.

Pushing back the sheets, I stood up, ignoring the shot of pain that went through my side. Soundlessly, I crossed the room and stepped into the hall.

The cries were louder out here. They slipped easily under the door crack.

I tried the handle.

Locked.

I did not slip as easily under the door crack.

My head tilted up to the ceiling.

But this was not the barrier Adeline would have liked it to be.

I slipped away in the dark, traveling to the single room Adeline didn't know about. After some time and more than a little difficulty, I stepped into her bedroom, passing by the barriers she placed in front of the door.

"Uh."

Adeline thrashed beneath her sheets—kicking and flailing at the unknown demons in her mind, and from the whimpers leaking through her lips, I feared she was losing.

I crossed to the bed, gazing down at her.

Sweat plastered autumn locks to her forehead. A streak of moonlight sought her through the window, laying a stripe over puffy eyes and darkened circles. In the morning, she would cover it with makeup, and have a plausible explanation for the split lip. This was not the first time she'd drawn her own blood during a nightmare.

I reached out and stopped myself, hovering within inches of her.

This was also not the first time I stole into her room.

I noticed the nightmares while she was in the cage and put her distress to her accommodations. But they continued after she moved into the space next to mine, waking me from the light sleep that was my curse. Another in the way we were alike.

Night did not bring peace. Day brought us no restfulness.

Closing the scant distance, I brushed away the ruby stain on her lip.

"Mm." Adeline shifted—mouth parting as if she sensed the touch.

I cradled her cheek, feeling a peculiar emotion as she lay on it, pressing me between her and the pillow. Her thrashing eased. Whimpers lodged in her throat where they stayed.

As I traced small, gentle circles on her cheekbone, Adeline settled into sleep. Her hand flopped on my arm, and immediately her fingers curled around me. She couldn't have known I was there, but still she kept me close, and another strange sensation went through me.

"Curious," I whispered.

What was it about this woman?

She saved my life though I threatened hers. She pulled down those boy shorts in the middle of saying I'd have her when I begged for the privilege. She attacked me with savage ferocity, and cradled my head in her lap as I bled out.

Adeline sought to know me, but she was the mystery. As were the feelings she stirred in places other than my cock.

I stroked her cheek, arm tensing under the handprint burning into my skin.

Is this love?

My mind had no answer for me, and there was nowhere in the winding recesses I was likely to find one.

Love was something I assume I was capable of a long time ago. In the years since, the only emotions I indulged were anger and pleasure.

I traced the sloping outline of her nose.

Adeline Redgrave made me feel both in equal measure. Along with a deep, consuming need to own her in every possible way there was to have a person.

Maybe that's love. Can't say, I thought. *I'll ask someone.*

"She named me St. John in honor of my father," I told her. "My parents were born here in Cinco City, where you're correct, that name was not common. This didn't faze her. My mother did exactly what she wanted to do without hesitation. A trait that's served me better than the name she gave me."

Adeline stirred, face scrunching up.

"The name you give a squalling infant has no impact on the man he becomes."

ADELINE

"... man he becomes."

I blinked awake. Sitting up, I scanned the empty room.

I thought I heard someone, but of course, I was alone.

I pressed a hand to my cheek.

The strangest sensation lingered on my skin. My fingers traced what felt like the mark of a handprint and then fell upon my lips.

I winced.

The nightmares had increased since I became the Merchants' newest roommate. Not surprising. The anxiety I hid during the day, plagued my sleeping mind.

Still. Why should Saint's voice whisper in my dreams? Or was it Mercer?

Turning over, I spotted the playing cards on my nightstand. I went over every inch of them, but how Saint cheated hadn't revealed itself to me.

I'd be here for a while. I had to find a way to survive.

A way to sleep.

Chapter Seven

S*aint*

"Stop. Let go!"

I peered over the railing.

"Brutal, I fucking swear! This isn't for you," she cried. "It's for Cash."

Adeline held tight to the plate, straining to free it from Brutal's grip. What he found wrong with her breakfast, I didn't know, but he was as determined to get it away from her as she was to get it back.

"If you throw another plate away, I'll feed you cabbage soup for a week."

Unheeding of her threats, he moved back, skidding her across the floor after him. He opened the cabinet that housed the garbage can.

"Let go— Ah!"

Brutal snagged her around the waist, lifting a shouting Adeline one-handed. The other tipped the French toast and sausage directly in the trash.

He set her back on her feet and strode off.

Adeline chased after him, leaped on his back, and—

My brows shot up my forehead.

—ran her hands through his hair, thoroughly messing it up.

"Argh!"

Dropping down, Adeline took off running. Brutal closed the distance in two bounds, setting upon her. The two collided and tipped over the back of the couch, grappling.

"This is not going to work," a dry voice spoke up.

Cash stepped to my side, taking in the scene.

"You don't trust your own plan?"

"I don't trust her," he corrected. "Look at her. She's too defiant. Unpredictable."

"I've always admired unpredictability."

"Not when our fucking lives and everything we've built is on the line, Sinjin. She's the key variable in all of this, and the only one we can't control. If she doesn't do what we need her to do when the time comes, we're all dead."

"She'll do it."

"Why?" he challenged. "Because you imagine this dance you two are doing means something to her? Far as I'm concern, she's dangling that pussy above your head to keep herself above ground."

"I wouldn't say that," I replied mildly. "Bunny has made it clear her pussy will be for the taking if I do something I'll never do."

"Which is?"

"Surrender."

"Doesn't look to be something she does either."

Adeline escaped Brutal's grip and went for the hair again. I laughed.

"No, it doesn't," I said. I made up my mind. "She's coming with me today."

"What? What the fuck are you talking about?"

"She's coming with me to get the shipment."

"I'm going with you," Cash said. "Mercer put all his considerable skills toward getting us the time and location. The boys are locked and ready to go. If we mess this up, we won't get another chance for three months, and as I mentioned, we'll be dead by then."

"All this I know."

"She can't go, Sinjin."

"She's going." I turned on him, leaving Brutal and Adeline to their fight. "She's gotta be a part of this. Implicable in this."

"That's not a word."

"All the same, I'm right. Adeline won't sacrifice for the Merchants unless our fate is tied to hers."

Cash slid a look down below, frown losing its edge. "You mean we turn the snappy, whisk-wielding princess into one of us?"

"A Merchant."

ADELINE

Brutal snatched me free of his locks—ever-silent though his whiskey eyes raged his unfiltered thoughts.

We tossed against the couch cushions. Brutal was trying to get a hold of me and who knew what the hell I was doing. A month ago, I was sous chef in Waterford's famed up-and-coming gourmet restaurant.

Yes, a month.

A month of cooking, cleaning, tense meals, conversations I couldn't follow, Brutal's tempered amusement, Cash's cold dislike, Mercer's enigmatic smile, and Sinjin's open lust.

In that time, I tested my boundaries and fought to have them expanded. Winning our fiftieth game of blackjack, got my phone returned. Threatening his life to find out how he'd been cheating got me tied to his bed and spanked until I almost broke and demanded more. It's been a very confusing time but my fall from grace was not lost on me.

Now I was forced into petty antics to keep my food out of the trash.

This is what the Merchants reduced me to.

I straddled him, pinning his arms to his side with my knees. "I banned you from my kitchen three weeks ago, Brutal. You brought this on yourself." I smirked down at my captive. "Aren't you supposed to be the big, bad fighter? And you let a little lady like me sneak up and pin you?"

I tsked. "This is real embarrassing for you, Brutal. Might want to consider a name change."

Brutal bucked, and the floor rushed to meet me. I let out a cry. It wasn't fully out of my mouth before he was there.

My head landed softly on his arm. Brutal lay on top of me, leg between mine, weight trapping me to the floor more effectively than mine did him.

The corner of his mouth rose.

For the last few weeks, I'd watch the guys have entire one-sided conversations with Brutal where he'd never do more than raise a brow or twitch a facial muscle. I assumed it was a running gag to piss him off.

As I looked into those impossibly light eyes and traced the curve of his lips, I heard with complete clarity, "What was it you were saying?"

I knew him no better than I did a month ago, but then I understood, Brutal Last-Name-Unknown said more with every part of him than people spoke in their whole lives.

Brutal brushed a strand of hair from my cheek and my breath caught.

But what he's saying right now is not coming through.

I wasn't able to shift his weight as easily as he did. I wasn't going anywhere. This was his chance to take revenge.

Brutal continued the path down, skating across my jaw and continuing to my shoulder. His hand was on my arm gliding over the bumpy flesh.

My heart beat so loud, I was certain the entire house could hear it. I peeked over his shoulder toward where Cash and Sinjin had been standing. Both were gone, but what if Sinjin peeked his head over the banister again and saw the two of us?

What's there to see, Addy?

Brutal closed over my hand.

Nothing is happening. This is nothing.

He pressed me against his thigh. His grin widened in time with my eyes.

Brutal guided my hand into his pocket. My knuckles bumped into something. He pressed it to my palm, pulled me out, and I glanced at my prize.

A comb.

Brutal popped my hand on his head and again his intent needed no translation.

"Fix the mess you made."

I placed the teeth on his temple and, brown locked on brown, glided the flyaways into their proper place.

My breaths were picking up. Brutal rose and fell on my heaving chest, and his hand found my cheek again.

Another look to the landing.

We weren't doing anything wrong, so why did it feel like we were?

Brutal bent, giving me better access, and his forehead bumped my lips. He made no move to pull back.

The comb formed neat grooves in his hair. Hair that I now knew was as soft as it looked.

Softer even.

Wider grooves were made as I replaced the comb with my fingers, running them through his locks.

There was no roaring. No shoving me back. No flinging threats with his gaze.

He turned, moving against my mouth, and as though it was the most natural response, I kissed him.

"Saddle up, Bunny."

I jerked.

Sinjin thundered down the stairs. "We're going out."

"Out?" I repeated.

"That's right." He stood over us. If he had something he wanted to say about the scene, he held on to it. "We've got business to take care of. Get dressed and let's go."

"But I—" Brutal was still on top of me. "I haven't finished breakfast."

"The guys can feed themselves."

"Makes me wonder what the hell I'm doing here, then."

He cracked a smile. "In the grand scheme of life? No one can answer that but you. Or if you meant right now? What you're doing is wasting time," he said. "Let her up, Brutal. We're expected across town in half an hour."

Brutal twisted his neck, looking up at Sinjin.

His smile disappeared. "She's coming," Sinjin said. "I know what I'm doing."

A clock ticked the passing seconds. I couldn't put my finger on why, but I sensed tension permeating the room. Brutal wasn't letting me up, and clouds were darkening Sinjin's face.

"One month, Brutal."

Slowly, Brutal pushed himself up—gaze on Sinjin the entire time. A silent communication seemed to be passing between them.

"What's going on?" I asked. "Saint, where are we going?"

"We're playing delivery men," he replied. "No big deal. Just picking up a shipment for a friend who doesn't drive."

"Why am I coming with you?"

"I need help unloading. The others are busy."

"Excuse me?" I mimicked cleaning my ears. "Did the great St. John just say he needs help? Isn't that the first sign of the apocalypse?"

"No, I believe it's a man on a white horse." He held out a hand. "You can rest assured the only thing bobbing between my legs in the near future will be you."

Accepting the hand, I stood up. "You're a good gambler, Saint, but here's a tip: Don't put money on that."

His chuckles followed me upstairs.

I changed into a simple pair of jeans, an old band shirt, and beat-up sneaks I wore on days I wandered the city aimlessly—soaking in my home.

I didn't do much of that these days, but once I was out of the house, I'd convince Sinjin to extend the reprieve.

I'll talk him into going to Citronella's. They serve the best coffee in all five boroughs. Who knows, he might be more open to interrogation over a cup and a plate of chocolate scones.

Sinjin waited for me at the front door. He held it open for me and pointed to the parking lot's newest addition. A large white van.

"Who is this friend of yours?" I asked. "I didn't know you had friends other than the people in this house."

"I've known her a long time," he replied. "Years create ties like proximity forces relationships."

I chewed over that for a while, not speaking up until we were out of the gates and idling at the first traffic light.

"I guess, in a way, proximity does force relationships. Which makes me wonder why you guys live together." I eyed him. "You four are in your late twenties and flush with blood money. Why not get your own places?"

"For the same reason married couples live together," he said. "We don't trust each other."

I pulled a face. "That's not why married people live together."

"Of course it is. Mary doesn't trust Jim not to sling his dick at everyone that moves unless she's always got an eye on him. Now that they are married, she has to know where he is and what he's doing at all times. And vice versa." Sinjin dove into the right lane. "It's the same with the four of us. It's harder to plan a coup against the guy looking over your shoulder."

"Couples live together because they love each other," I said. "And you live with Cash, Brutal, and Mercer because you're friends. You don't spare attention for people you don't like, Saint. You may not want me to, but I know you."

"Do you?" Amusement laced his voice. "I'm quite interested to hear what you know about me, but I'm expecting an important call in thirty seconds. Afterward, you and I will be busy. We'll put this chat on hold."

Thirty seconds on the dot, Sinjin's phone rang.

"Hello. Yes, I'm on the way. How many?" He paused for the person on the other end. "More than we expected. Nothing changes," he said sharply. "Do what you have to do and it'll be fine. It has to be done, and it has to be today." Another pause. "Good. I'll be there in twenty minutes."

Their conversation faded in the background. I leaned against the partially opened window, breathing in the curious scent that was Cinco City. It was hard to describe. The closest I could come to was iron, smoke, and cayenne pepper. The last didn't make much sense, but there it was.

Sinjin got on the express leading to Leighbridge.

"Leighbridge," I said. "They have the best themed cafes near the animal sanctuary. We should stop by and get something. Neither one of us has had breakfast yet."

"Not now. We'll grab something after."

Turning, I squinted at him. The Sinjin I knew would've jumped on the insinuation that I was asking him on a date.

"What's going on, Saint? Why were you and Brutal acting strange?" I sat up, scanning the endless row of luxury skyscrapers and penthouse apartments. "Where are we really going?"

"We're going to pick up a shipment as I said. Where do you think we're going?"

"To the alleyway where you'll dump my body."

"Oh?" He was definitely amused. "What would you have done that requires your death?"

"Who knows? Today I messed with Brutal's hair. Yesterday, I blended smoothies while Cash was watching the news and got bitched out for it. Tuesday, I called you out for cheating at poker," I said. "You've already locked me up and forced me into servitude for *not* turning you over to the cops. You're unpredictable, Saint. I've accepted it."

"I—" His phone rang. "Be quiet."

Sinjin answered. "What's the problem?"

He delved into another conversation I couldn't follow. I put my head to the window. Whatever was going on, I'd find out soon enough. What I needed to do right then was soak up my city before I returned to the fire station and forgot what it looked like.

The turn for Leighbridge's borough came up and Sinjin drove past it. Two exits down, Sinjin veered off the highway and merged onto Foxwood Street. This part of Leighbridge was less skyscrapers and more funky art museums, public gardens, and warehouses. Less noise. Less traffic. Fewer people.

"What are we doing here, Sinjin?"

He didn't answer.

Sinjin turned right onto a one-way street sandwiched between an artisan bread bakery and an organic food store. I held on to a shred of hope that this was our stop. Sinjin was taking me food shopping and then we'd pop next door for fresh croissants.

He kept driving and left the smell of fresh bread behind.

The street narrowed on us, closing in on the van. Sinjin hit the brakes with barely room for us to open the doors and climb out. Reaching over me, he pulled something out of the glove box and tossed it on my lap.

"Put this on."

I took one look, and flung it at the windshield. "No. No, no, no." My fingers scrabbled at the door handle. "I don't know where we are or what the fuck you think I'm going to do here, but it's not happening. Let me out of this car right now."

"I can let you out, but I'll just pick you up and bring you right back." Sinjin fit the black, knit cap over his hair. "It's a one-way street with limited escape options. Where do you think you're going to go?"

"Why did you bring me here? Tell me right now, or I'm giving escape my best damn shot."

Sinjin blew out a breath like I was being difficult. "I told you. Multiple times. We're picking up a few boxes, putting them in the back, and bringing them to a friend." He secured the mask over his pretty lying mouth, and the blue-stitched "M" shone like neon.

"That's all," he said. "Trust me."

I yanked at the door. "I would trust a con artist in the process of stealing my wallet before I'd trust you!"

Sinjin laughed out loud. "Bunny, the mask is to protect your identity." I threw a glare to the mask I tossed away. "Ten feet up is the first security camera. This is all aboveboard, but I mentioned my trust issues. Just in case my friend is attempting to serve me up to the Kings, do you want your face to be one they know?"

"What kind of friendships do you have?" I hissed. "If this could be a set-up, what are we doing here alone?"

"Relax." Sinjin took my hand, placed the mask on my palm, and closed it. "Those calls were my men confirming it's not an ambush. They've been staking the place out all morning because one can never be too careful. Even so, I'm not taking chances with you." He kissed my knuckles. "You're welcome."

"Don't even try it. If you're that concerned about a simple pickup and delivery, why didn't you tell your *friend* to figure it out themselves?"

"Are you kidding? I couldn't do that. I love Edie. I'd open my veins for her if she asked."

"Oh, you love her, do you?"

"Don't be jealous." I didn't need to see his smirk to know it was there. "I'm not her type." Sinjin kicked on the engine and continued on. "Last chance. Put on the mask."

I looked from him to the piece of cloth, and scanned the buildings for the security cameras. Nothing but anonymous red brick walls.

This is ridiculous. I looked to Sinjin. *But the threat from the Kings is not.*

A piece of white plastic poked out from the corner wall and I reacted quickly, clapping the mask over my nose and mouth as we passed by the camera.

It's a precaution like he said, I told myself. *I know what it's like to have a band of rogue psychopaths chase you down. No measure is too extreme in covering your tracks.*

Something I should have remembered.

Sinjin passed the opening for a side alley that cut back to the main road. He parked behind what was clearly a loading dock. There were no signs to say what was on the other side of the metal door.

"What is this place?" I asked.

"Lombard Integrative Health Clinic."

"Lombard Health." My grip loosened on the seat belt. "I know that company. They've got free clinics all over Rockchapel."

"See? Nothing to worry about." Sinjin climbed out. "Hurry up. They open in two minutes."

I got out, falling in step next to him. "Aren't they going to have something to say about the masks?"

"A couple of doctors? Pretty sure this is a sight they're used to."

"Fair point."

We stepped out of the alley. The sign for Lombard Clinic hung proudly over a yellow door with a flower basket. Inside, I spotted someone puttering behind reception. Cars were already filling up the parking lot. For once, the situation was exactly what Sinjin said it was.

He held open the door for me to go inside. The chime made the man pause in straightening the desk. He was a stout guy with wide-framed glasses and a buzz cut. The badge on his chest read, "Henry."

"Good morning." Wrinkles formed at the corner of his eyes. "What can we do for you?"

Sinjin coughed. "The missus and I caught a bug. Fatal. Or at least, we wished it was last night while we were spewing from every hole."

My cheeks heated up. If it was from being called his wife, or the incredibly embarrassing picture he painted, I couldn't tell.

"I'm sorry to hear that," Henry said. "There is a virus going around. We had a few people in the last few weeks with the same symptoms, but none had the foresight to wear a mask when going out. Thank you for that."

Unbelievable. The man walks in wearing the calling card of a dangerous street gang and is thanked. I shook my head. *Leighbridge is a bubble of privilege unto itself. Anywhere else, and the residents would have known exactly what that M meant.*

"Are you both new to the clinic?" he asked.

"First time," said Sinjin. He stepped up to the desk, drawing me to his side. "But we're not here for us. We're here to pick up."

"Pick up?" He glanced at the papers on his desk. "I wasn't informed of this. What exactly are you here for?"

"We're here for you and the seven guys in the back room."

Henry's smile dimmed. "I don't know who you're referring to."

"Then you're wasting my time, aren't you?" Sinjin flashed out, clamping the back of the man's neck. He wrenched, knocking Henry into the monitor and tipping it crashing to the floor. The man's shout was ended in a headlock.

I ran.

Spinning around, I bolted out the door and onto the sidewalk. They were on me in a blink.

A dozen mask-clad men rushed me from all sides. I screamed, hands flying up to protect myself, and someone lifted me off my feet.

"Now where do you think you're going?" Sinjin's voice poured in my ear. "He's out. Diego, did you take care of the security cameras?"

"Yes, boss. If they're watching, all they are seeing is an empty lobby and parking lot."

Eyes huge, my heart hammered on Sinjin's arm. I knew of course the Merchants were more than four men, but to find myself surrounded by them and trapped like the rabbit Sinjin named me, struck me numb. I didn't move. Didn't think of running even if it was possible.

"I want three in the alley. The rest take out the men in the back. No blood on this one," he ordered. "Lombard CEOs will cover up a robbery. Can't say the same for seven murders. Understood?"

"Yes, boss."

"Get the fuck in there. One of them may have heard me take out the front man."

They streamed inside orderly and silent like soldiers marching to their captain's command.

"What the hell, Sinjin?!" Free from the crush of his men, I bucked in his hold. "You said this was aboveboard. A favor for a friend!"

"This is a favor for a friend," he replied. "But yeah, I lied about the rest."

"How could you bring me here? What is wrong with you?"

"It's past time you got a sense of what we do. Afterward, you'll agree we did what needed to be done. I'm certain of it."

I bucked harder.

"So certain, I'll put something new on the table. Everything you want to know about me, my past, and the Merchants. I'll tell you everything."

I stilled. "Excuse me?"

"You heard me. No tricks. No lies," he said. "The unedited story of St. John Bellisario. If my actions today don't meet your approval, I will offer all of me up for judgment."

I couldn't believe what he was saying. For weeks I tried and failed to scratch the surface of this man who enraged and seduced me in equal measure. If he'd told me any lies that day, that would surely be it.

"I don't believe you," I whispered. "You lie as easily as you breathe, Saint."

"This is true. But what I don't do is back out of a bet."

"If you have a justifiable explanation for knocking over a free clinic that helps the vulnerable people in this community, give it to me now."

"No time," he said, releasing me. "Cash clocked twenty-one minutes to get in and out before the first nurse shows up for her shift. Keep an eye on our friend." He guided me back inside. The friend in question, Henry, was slumped on the floor—out cold. The breaths fluttering his name tag let me know he was alive.

Fighting floated through the wooden shield concealing the back room. Shouts and crashing assaulted my ears. I couldn't imagine blood was not being shed.

I bent down next to Henry, checking him over. Out of the corner of my eye, Sinjin rounded the desk. I heard the door open and the shouts flooded in.

He had left me alone with Henry. The thought to run came and went.

It'd take me hours to get back to Leighbridge's city center, beg a phone off someone, and get Gianna to come pick me up. There was also the tiny, but important detail of almost eight thousand dollars in cash hidden away in my room. That was getting-far-away-and-starting-over money. The kind of money I'd need to make a clean break from the Merchants.

"They're loading up." Sinjin emerged from the back. "Keep a lookout."

"I'm not aiding and abetting until I hear that explanation."

Sinjin snaked a hand around my waist and kissed my cheek through the masks. "I appreciate that you trust a good one is coming. Loyalty is handsomely rewarded. Tonight we'll go down to the basement."

I wanted to say being chained up in his torture room and spanked raw wasn't a reward. I might've if the desire pooling in my core wasn't so strong, I feared he smelled it on me like an animal knows when its mate is in heat.

Sinjin lifted Henry under the arms and put him in the lobby bathroom. He swept outside, expecting me to follow, and I did.

The white van was open. Masked men loaded boxes into the back, working quickly and efficiently.

"Five minutes," Sinjin said. "Pick it up."

They did without argument. As the men loaded the last few boxes in the back, I noticed the sideways glances cast over me. Our mask concealed our faces, but nothing was hiding that I was the lone woman in the bunch.

"Alright, head out," Sinjin said when they were finished. "Take different routes. Do not meet up, discuss the job in public, or at all."

"Let's go," said one man with a deep voice and blue eyes. "Racer, you're driving."

The guy he pointed at—Racer—made no move in the direction of the car. "Boss."

"What?" Sinjin looped a finger through my belt loop, pulling me behind as he pried open a box to check the contents. I peered around him, confirming it was vials of antibiotics and packs of butterfly needles.

"What's the cut for this job?" Racer asked.

"Cash handles the payments. It's in the name."

"He said we'd get five grand each."

Sinjin opened another box. "Then why the fuck are you asking me?"

A click sounded behind me, and a wave of musky sweat hit my nose. An armpit was in my face, attached to the hand holding a gun to the back of Sinjin's head.

"I'm asking because why should we settle for five grand, when turning you over to the Kings would get us four times as much?"

"Hey!"

"What the fuck are you doing?!"

The situation changed in an instant. Half a dozen guns were out. Some trained on Racer. Others on the men threatening him.

"Put the gun down, Racer."

"Sack up, Diego," Racer growled. "What's playing their bitch got you? A war with the Kings."

Sinjin hadn't moved or spoken. I inched around, positioning to strike.

Racer snatched my throat and shoved me against the van door. "Don't try it, bitch. You can't move faster than I pull this trigger."

"Let her go." I didn't recognize the dark, grasp gruff as coming from Sinjin until he turned, leveling the gun between his eyes. "Now."

"Happy to." Racer sounded almost friendly.

He bore tighter on my throat.

Almost.

"This girl—whoever the hell she is—can go right on her way as long as you put those cuffs on and get in the van without trouble, *Boss*."

Gun aimed, one of the guys moved closer, holding a pair of cuffs.

"Hawk, Gunner, Viper, and I have a quarter of a mill coming our way. If these fools don't want in on the payday, that's just more for us."

"The four of you thought this up, did you?" Sinjin tsked. "This is why we warn you not to talk to each other. You come up with stupid ideas and they spread through the men like cancer. Let her go. Every second your hands are on her, I tack another hour on the long, agonizing death that awaits you."

Racer slammed my head against the door. I cried out, black spots taking over my vision.

"Put the cuffs on!"

Saint cast a cool eye on me. "Dear Lord. It seems I'll reach a new level of savagery with you."

"Stop this, Racer." A pair of blues and a black suit inched closer. "You know you won't make it out of here."

Racer's men weren't backing down. "I'll drop you if your finger fucking twitches, Diego."

"All of you, relax," Sinjin said.

"You're not in charge here." The cuffs smacked Sinjin's chest and fell to the ground. "Put them on or"—Racer choked a gasp out of me—"watch me kill her."

"I'm always in charge, Donald Seward, aka Racer. Current address: 486 Ridgeway Drive, Waterford. Baby mama's current address: 323 Crystalview Apartments, 2B, Rockchapel. Parents' current address: 1010 Maynard Street, North Quay."

Racer stumbled back and his hand fell off my throat.

"We set up the Merchants so that you wouldn't know each other, but did you honestly believe we don't know you?" Sinjin shook his head like a disappointed parent. "Did you, Viper, aka Liam James? Gunner, aka Adrian Westwood? Hawk, aka Noel Harvey?

"We know where you live. Where your wives, husbands, mistresses, and your cousin twice removed on your mother's side lives." The shaking muzzle pressed into Sinjin's chest as he closed the distance. "We know where sweet little Debbie Seward goes to preschool. You can hand me over to the Kings, Donny, but I ask you, what good is all of that money if you don't have anyone to share it with?"

"You wouldn't," he hissed.

Sinjin shrugged. "I couldn't. I'd be under Angelo's tender care by then. No, it'd be my associates' job to hunt down and kill your families before making examples of you that will sicken every person who hears the name 'Merchant' for the next fifty years.

"Debbie won't like being an orphan, Donny," Sinjin sang. "Cinco's foster care system is shit."

Sweat dripped down pale cheeks, soaking the lining of Racer's mask.

"Put the guns down, gentlemen. And all can be forgiven."

Slowly, Racer's men lowered their weapons.

Shots pierced the morning.

Viper, Gunner, and Hawk dropped where they stood. Dead.

Racer whirled around, and Sinjin was on him. He grabbed his arm and twisted the gun from his grip.

"No," he cried. "You said we'd be forgiven!"

"I lied. I do that." Sinjin's expression was terrible to behold. Yanking Racer's hand up his back, Sinjin kicked the back of his legs, dropping him to his knees. "Hold him."

Diego and the others held him down. The wind whipped at Sinjin's coat, spreading its tails to honor the blackened wings of a fallen angel. I backed away and tripped inside the van, bumping into the boxes.

I knew this man. I knew the coldness in his words and delight in his eyes. I knew as surely as I knew it was time to look away. And if I could have, I would. Sinjin held me captive in all ways proclaimed by the word.

"But in one thing I intend to keep my word," Saint said. "I promised you a slow death."

"No, please—"

Sinjin fired, ending Racer's plea in a shout.

He doubled over. A red stain growing above his belt.

"That bullet will immobilize you, but it won't kill you. Not for hours, maybe days. You'll bleed out in some abandoned warehouse knowing you could've been saved if only someone found you in time. Which, of course, they won't because no one will hear your cries for help."

Sinjin tipped his head to Diego. "Hold his mouth open."

I crawled further in, feeling every hair on my body stand on end. *A new level of savagery.*

Racer bellowed. He thrashed and tossed his head, fighting on pure adrenaline to stop Diego and two other men prying his jaw open.

The wings drew back on the web of leather that held his blade. Sinjin held it aloft, reaching in to pull his tongue out of his head. The hold broke.

I looked away.

Something dropped at my feet—small and wet.

"We've been here too long," Sinjin said. "Once the nurse finds our boy Henry, she'll call the police if she hasn't already. Take Racer out a few miles where he can die in peace and seclusion." Choked, muffled sobs struggled to be heard over him. "My gift to you for making the right choice in the end."

Shuffling. Gruff conversation. Then Racer's noise faded.

"Bunny."

I snapped my head up. I hadn't heard Sinjin's approach.

"Let's go. We're running late."

My gaze fell on the outstretched hand and flicked over his shoulder. The bodies were cleared away though their blood remained. Sinjin was right, this was not a place we wanted to be when the police arrived.

I rested my palm on his. Sinjin snapped me to his chest. I hissed when he touched the back of my head.

"There's a first aid kit in the glove box. I'll take care of this when we're out of Leighbridge."

"Okay."

We shut the back doors, climbed in, and drove out of the alleyway. Miles were between us and the clinic when I spoke.

"Are we going to the house?"

"No. The van's due back in three hours. Can't have the person we stole it from return and report the theft."

I shook my head—whether at his casual disregard for felonies or my lack of surprise, I didn't guess.

"I didn't say this before because I assumed there wasn't a need, but you don't have to make examples of people who hurt me, Saint."

"Because you shudder to see what needs to be done?"

"Because I can take care of myself." I bore into the side of his head till he met my eyes. "You got that?"

Sinjin gave me a long look. One that prompted cars to honk us at the changing light. A grin broke out over the racket. "Understood. Next time, you choose the punishment."

"There won't be a next time." I probed my skull and came away with spots of blood on my fingertips.

"Here." Sinjin pulled off two lanes over from the turning lane. A car slammed on the brakes to avoid hitting us, sending up another wave of blaring horns.

We turned into a bowling alley parking lot. Sinjin leaned over me, propping himself on my thighs, and I lost focus gazing at the knit cap covering the telltale blue hair. Waves of sandalwood, leather, and a fresh woodsy scent hit my nose.

Sinjin always smelled like he'd just gotten out of the shower. A feat that should have been impossible after this morning. He subdued an employee, pulled off a twenty-minute job, was betrayed by his own guys, and cut out a man's tongue. Any other man would be buckets of sweat and damp stains. But those men were not Sinjin Bellisario.

Still, I suspected he wasn't as cool as his stature conveyed.

Sinjin risked himself, me, and the Merchants on this job.

Just who is this friend that he loves so much the risk is worth it?

"I'm ready for that explanation whenever you are."

"It'll become clear when we get there," he said. "Turn around."

I obeyed. Holding still, he checked and cleaned the small cut.

His touch was gentle. Fingers weaved through my strands. Soothing me under the soft exhalations he blew to dry the antiseptic.

"Wasn't that bad." Sinjin moved down the nape of my neck, cupping my throat. "But you'll have a bruise."

My swallow bobbed against his fingers. My pulse was fluttering beneath him, and the slow, light circles he rubbed opposite of their wild dance was not helping. "Won't be my first," I said. "Weaponless muggers go straight for the neck too."

"You've had an eventful life."

"I suspect not as eventful as yours. A hunch I'll have confirmed tonight." I curled my hand around his, dropping it on my lap.

Sinjin pressed on my stomach and drew me closer. I made a small noise in my throat as he licked a stripe over the bumpy ridges of my spine. Then he was gone.

"Here." Sinjin tossed his cap at me. "Cover up. A bleeding head wound will scare the kids."

My mind was a beat behind struggling to reconcile his sudden switch from intimacy. "Kids? What kids?"

His reply was to start the car and pull out onto the road.

Sinjin didn't get on the highway this time. Instead we weaved through our gloriously grimy city, stopping once to pick up breakfast from a drive-through bakery. I fed him mini butter croissants while he drove. Mostly to save my life. Sinjin driving while eating was ten times as dangerous as him using both hands.

"What did you mean about your men not being allowed to talk to each other?" I tapped on his mouth to get him to open up. "How does that work? Don't they have to?"

Sinjin closed over my fingers, wrapping his lips around them. I couldn't find my voice to say stop.

"It's the way we've set it up. The only person you know in the gang is the guy who got you in. Everyone else goes by a nickname, and when we meet up, we're in masks and gear. They know the guys in charge are me, Cash, Brutal, and Mercer. They have a number to call us if something goes down. But my own men could pass me in the street and not have a clue who I was."

I hummed. "A fact that's coming in handy now that the Kings are after you."

Sinjin inclined his head. "I thought Cash was overdoing it like he does fucking everything. But his plans haven't led us wrong yet."

"So, Cash is the brain. Brutal is the muscle. You're the unflappable leader. What does that leave for Mercer?"

"Mercer has a very specific skill set." I heard the humor in his tone. "Believe me, he's invaluable."

"Okay, then what does that leave for me?"

Sinjin took his eyes off the road, forcing me to grip his chin and face him forward. "Leave for you?"

"What's my place in all of this, Sinjin? You didn't need me to go with you today. You also don't need me to cosign your motives. Was the clinic some kind of test? To see if I'd run if I saw you in action?"

"What if it was?" he challenged.

"Then I ask what's the point? Some days I feel like you're fashioning me into your mafia bride. Polishing the arm of your throne where I'll perch until the kingdom falls down around us."

"Loving the image."

"But then there are other days," I continued, "when you refuse to bend the slightest inch to take what you say you want. The days you shut down on me, and look at me like I'm another card to put in your deck. That guy doesn't want a bride, queen, or partner. He wants to defeat a challenge, and what he'll do after he does, I can't begin to guess."

"We're still talking about me, right?"

"Yes," I gritted out. "So, tell me, Saint. What do you want from me?"

"That's a loaded question, my bride. I eagerly await the results of our bet to find out if I'll answer." Sinjin jerked the wheel, careening me into him. "We're here."

I straightened, looking up the sloped driveway to the structure rising out of a green mound. It came together slowly in my vision. Steeple. Stained glass. History soaking the weathered stone and the inscription above the arched entrance.

Our Lady of the Sacred Heart Cathedral.

"I don't understand."

"We'll drive around back and unload," Sinjin said. "Edie will be waiting for us."

Sinjin rumbled up the hill to the small parking lot behind the church. I hopped out, running around the car to stop him opening the door.

"Wait," I cried.

"What is it?" He stuck his head out of the window, hand flying to his holster.

"This is hallowed ground. Won't you burst into flames if you set foot here?"

"You're very amusing, Redgrave," he said without a trace of a laugh.

I stepped aside, letting him out. The real question was how he could drive up this hill with a van full of stolen goods after what he did to Racer/Donald Seward.

Sinjin hooked through my belt loop again and tugged me along.

What does it take to faze you? What makes you sweat?

"Once a month, Sister Edith opens the church to the community," Sinjin began, throwing open the van. "Members donate food. Nurses and doctors donate their time. They set up cots for anyone in need of a warm night indoors.

"Word spread over the year. Last month, they had a hundred people come through the doors looking for food and medical treatment."

"Wow," I said. "It's wonderful what she's doing. Must be a lot with only donations to work with."

"It is." Sinjin placed a box in my waiting arms. "She receives plenty of food, but antibiotics and the like aren't as easy to get your hands on. That's when Lombard Integrative Health came in."

I glanced down at the swirly logo. "Lombard?"

"They announced to the press that they'd donate whatever Sacred Heart needed to keep the doors open. They put on a huge show. Camera crews came in to photograph the CEO shaking her hand. The church received one box of diabetic test strips and some insulin, and that was it."

My brows snapped together. I couldn't have heard that right. "That was it? What happened?"

"The entire thing was nothing more than a publicity stunt to distract from Joseph Lombard's latest leaked sex tape. After the cameras go away, no one checks to see if these faceless companies follow through with their promises. Edie called politely asking when they'd receive the next donation. Everyone she spoke to either said they didn't know anything about it, refused to let her speak to Joseph, or put her on hold until the line went dead."

"Oh my gosh," I breathed. "That's terrible. How do you feel good about yourself after ripping off a nun and a church full of needy people?"

"There are worse men in this world than me, Bunny." Tilting my chin up, Sinjin pecked the tip of my nose. "That's why men like me exist."

"To steal from them and give to those in need?" I cast an eye over our haul. "Did the sister ask you to pull this job as her last hope?"

Sinjin gave me a crazy look. "No, Bunny," he said slowly. "She did not ask me to knock over a health clinic. She's a nun."

My cheeks warmed. "Alright, then why did you do it?"

"Edie was going to give up. That heavenly piousness wouldn't allow her to continue chasing down freely given offerings like she had a right to them. Something Lombard was banking on. I told her to let me handle it. I'd go down to headquarters, meet with Lombard myself, and clear up this mix-up." Sinjin hefted a box under his arm. "This is me handling it."

I tossed my head, mouth hanging open. "Let me get this straight, in response to her decision to let it go and be content with what she has, you robbed Lombard and showed up on her doorstep with a van full of stolen medicine. What will her heavenly piousness say about that?"

Laughing, Sinjin strode off. "Beggars can't be choosers, Bunny. That's in the Bible."

"No, it isn't!"

His rich honeyed laugh filled the courtyard and echoed to the tip of the steeple. A laugh like that was a beacon to all who heard it.

"Sinjin?" asked a silvery voice. "There you are. Looks like the meeting went well."

"Cleared up the whole mess, Edie. It was a miscommunication like we thought."

Peeking around the van, I laid eyes on a diminutive woman in sensible shoes and a habit. I placed her in her late fifties. Sixties at a push. She turned a cheek up at Sinjin, granting the full look at her kind face and pleasant smile. He dutifully kissed her.

"Hello," she said, spotting me.

"This is Adeline Redgrave. She volunteered to do the heavy lifting."

"Hello, Sister." I set my load in the van and ran up to shake her hand. "It's nice to meet the woman Sinjin would open his veins for."

Sister Edith's laugh was warm and unrestrained. "It's nice to meet you too, Miss Adeline. How do you know our Sinjin?"

"We met at a party," Sinjin cut in. "Adeline put her stamp on the appetizers and I hired her to be my personal chef on the spot. I'll bring some of her creations to the next potluck."

"Wonderful. Bring yourself too," she said to me. "You're welcome any time."

"I'll put away the meds while you give her the tour."

"Thank you." Edie patted Sinjin's cheek, brimming with fondness. Whatever devotion he had for her was clearly reciprocated.

Tucking my hand under her arm, she led me inside the cathedral. The interior was as striking as the exterior. Light flooded through the stained glass, casting a myriad of purples, blues, and reds over the pulpit. Shining marble floors stretched to grand wooden doors, and brown pews were covered with deep red cushions. The thick cobwebs stretching from mirror to mirror, cracks in the floor, and worn, ripped threads did not make the church less magnificent, though it did speak to their troubles.

"How long have you known Sinjin?" I asked.

"Many, many years." She led me to a door that spilled out into a courtyard. "He was the first face that greeted me when I walked through those doors. A sweet boy that's grown into a kind young man."

With that, I know it's useless interrogating you. You don't know Sinjin at all.

A long row of bushes hugged the cathedral walls. Tucked between them were comfortable wooden benches. Sister Edith settled on one, drawing me down next to her. I could tell this was her favorite spot because it had instantly become mine.

A limestone pathway split the lawn down the middle, leading to a babbling fountain. Over the head of the serene stone woman, all of Cinco City lay before us. The bustling, smoky, loud, charming wonder I'd call home until they put me in the ground.

"Wow. I'd take holy orders for a view like this too."

She laughed. "It was fifty-five service to the Lord, and forty-five percent this view."

Right then, I decided I liked Sister Edith too.

"Sinjin mentioned kids," I said. "Are they inside having Bible study or something?"

"No, they're across the street at Our Lady of the Sacred Heart Catholic school. The school doesn't have a playground, so the teachers bring the kids over to run around the courtyard."

"That's nice of you. Everything you do—opening the church to the community, housing the homeless, helping the sick—it's needed, Sister, and it's appreciated."

"A wise man told me that this is what a church is meant to be. A shelter for the homeless. Refuge for the ill. Safe haven for children. Anything else would make us a bunch of pompous pricks flouncing around in black dresses while pretending to care for our fellow man."

I made a choked noise. "Sister!"

"What?" A smile played at her lips. "I told you, a wise man said it. Not me."

The noonday bells chimed, sounding through the courtyard.

"Ah. The children will arrive soon. Would you like to meet them?"

"Love to."

There was still a chance I could fall asleep tonight dreaming of laughing children and sweet missing-tooth smiles, instead of wretched cries and bloody tongues.

We stepped inside as they did. Neat lines of uniformed, knobby-kneed munchkins marched past the pews. Sinjin was nowhere to be seen though the back door hung open.

"Hello, children."

"Hello, Sister Edie," they chorused.

"This is my friend, Miss Redgrave. Say hi."

"Hi, Miss Redgrave." One kid broke out of the pack to hug me.

"Hi, guys. What are your feelings on tag?"

A dozen hands shot in the air. "I wanna play! I wanna—"

"Arrgh!"

My heart shot in my throat. Spinning around, I nearly tripped over my feet as Sinjin ran at me.

"Children!" he bellowed.

Shrieking, the kids took off in every direction.

"Saint, what are you do— No!"

He snatched up a little girl no more than seven years old and threw her over his shoulder. "Children! Children in the nave. Children in the pews." He bolted—girl and all—after a boy racing fast for the confessional. "They're everywhere!"

Sinjin caught the boy around the stomach and hitched him up like a saddlebag. My cries died on my lips. The children were screaming their heads off... laughing?

He strode into the courtyard, innocents in hand, and all I could do was trail the baffling sight out of the door.

Sinjin carried the screaming kids to the fountain, and dumped them in without preamble. The children popped out of the water laughing so hard they weren't breathing. He blew past me running inside for more victims.

"Be careful," Edith called. She returned to her bench, folded her hands on her lap, and closed her eyes. I sought the kids' teacher to make sense of the madness, but she was on another bench, marking papers.

"This is the worst infestation I've ever seen!"

I went inside and found a seat on the stairs' bottom step. The kids had endless places to hide. An obvious group were shuffling and giggling behind a tapestry that was probably priceless. Sinjin rousted them and snatched up the ones who weren't quick enough. They were taken to the fountain to receive the same fate.

I got the feeling this was a game they played often. And Sinjin was a man they knew well. If this was the side Sister Edith got to see, she was lucky. As lucky as I was to see it now.

"Adeline." The sister poked her head inside. "Would you like to help me prepare lunch for the children?"

"I'd love to."

Edith took me to their bare-bones kitchen. It was attached to a modest-size hall. We chatted about her plans to open the church to the community once a week. It was possible now that Sinjin handled the "Lombard mix-up."

Which means this won't be the last time the Merchants steal from Lombard to help her. Sinjin's good intentions—if they can be called that—could land her in hot water.

Didn't Lombard bring this on themselves? another voice spoke up. *They promised her this medicine and then dropped her when the cameras turned off. He's only taking what was owed her.*

I halted in the middle of buttering a cheese sandwich.

So this is how Sinjin does it. Worms in with his amoral logic and has me questioning right and wrong. He said I'd agree with his actions that morning, and dammit, that's exactly what I was trying to do.

The children filed in soaking wet and grinning from ear to ear. The sister and teachers passed out food and towels, and then sat down at a table near the window with their lunch.

I hung back rather than join. These were good people doing right without reward or expectation. Not many people like this survive Cinco because of the Joseph Lombards in every borough. On every street corner.

Maybe what good people need isn't an overworked pro bono lawyer doomed to fail against an army of suits on retainer. Or a drawn-out media battle where the other side lies their way into slapping you with defamation of character.

It's possible what good people with no options need is someone who comes in and solves the problem without restraint. Someone like a middle-man.

"That's why men like me exist."

Or a Merchant.

I left the hall in search of Sinjin. The van was locked and empty. Sinjin was finished unloading, but I didn't hear cardboard ripping or a hulking mass of wickedness and beauty moving around.

Climbing the stairs, I moved to the second floor that wasn't included in my tour.

The space was narrow. Cinderblock walls pressed in on me, imposing and cool to the touch. They bounced my echoing footsteps through the nave—alerting Sinjin that I was coming before I rounded the corner.

There he was. My avenging angel or merciless demon depending on the day. Depending on my traitorous pulse or sneaking smile recognizing the first man to ever challenge me.

Sinjin stood in a small office. It barely held him, the desk, bookshelf, and a small fireplace. He hadn't looked up at my arrival, though he faced me. His attention was fixed on the frames, crosses, and rosary beads adorning the mantle.

I leaned against the frame, giving him the same rapt focus. "How long have you been going here?" I asked.

"Do I seem like a man who attends church every Sunday?"

"My mistake. I meant, when did you *stop* going here? The cross that hangs over your bed is the same size, color, and style as the one hanging on that wall."

The corner of his mouth drew up. "I'd say you were impressively observant, but in this case, Edie likely helped you along."

"She said you were the first person she met when she arrived. Did you go to the Catholic school?"

He gave the barest shake of the head—gaze fixed. "The school opened ten years ago. What she meant is, she walked into the cathedral and found me sleeping on a pew where my mother abandoned me. Hell of a first day."

My jaw slackened. "Your mother..." I trailed off.

"Don't mistake me," he continued, voice soft. "She was a good woman, and took care of me for all the years she was able. When the cancer brought her to the point that she couldn't, she brought me here, so I wouldn't have to watch her die. I never saw her again."

"Oh." There were other things I could've said. Better things. None would come to my lips.

"Edie wanted to call child services and get me placed with a family. The priest at the time wouldn't let her. He decided I'd stay here. Live here."

"He did?" I whispered. "Wow. I didn't know priests could do that. I mean, you can't be the first child that was left in a church by a desperate parent."

"I'm not, and they can't. The diocese gave him hell for it. He argued with the bishop at least once a week about turning me over. He refused. For six years, this was my home."

I smiled. "He was the wise man Edie spoke about, wasn't he? The one who said this place should be a refuge. A safe haven for children."

"He used to say that, yes."

"Hmm. It's wonderful that he stood by his convictions, and by you, but why was he so resistant? You could've found great adoptive parents. Did he not trust the system?"

"He resisted." Sinjin broke his gaze and brushed past me. "Because he was my father."

The statement hung in the air long after Sinjin's footfalls faded. Slowly, I stepped into the room, taking Sinjin's place.

On the shelf sat a black-framed photo of a man in priest's robes holding the hand of a little boy who was undeniably Sinjin. His hair was black. His smile wide and beaming, but the glint of mischief in his eyes connected man and boy. As did the strong resemblance an older Sinjin had with the man looking back at me.

No, this little boy isn't Sinjin. He's St. John.

And as surely as I knew it would crush me to find out why Edith and Sinjin spoke about his father in the past tense, I knew it was the first chapter in how that boy became this man.

I placed my hand over my heart. Wild, racing, and fluttering.

Just like I know I'll spend the rest of my life waiting to hear that story.

Sinjin won.

I was his, and heaven help me, he would be mine.

Chapter Eight

Sinjin leaned against the van, throwing the keys up in the air. "Took you long enough. Let's go. You're making me another one of those malted chocolate drip cakes."

I slipped out of the door, smiling. "It takes three hours minimum to make that cake. I only bake for you when you're good."

"I gave to charity today." He gestured at the van. "I was very good."

"You stole for charity," I corrected. "You and I will have a discussion about your definition of good."

"Lesser men than you have tried to educate me."

"Then let me step in when they failed." I molded to him, laying my head on his chest. Sinjin stilled. "Your mind is a place no person can comprehend. In there, everything you did today was justified. Part of me even agrees that it was. Right and wrong isn't as rigid as we'd like it to be. It can change in any circumstance, on any given day.

"Which is why you won't get my approval."

"You crossed a few signals there, Bunny."

"It's not black and white. Part of me agrees and part of me doesn't. Going down the spiral to choose one would only leave me split. There is the answer to your test, Saint. We end in a draw."

He hummed. "I'll take it."

"You'll take this too." I rose up and captured his lips. Soft and chaste, I moved against him, indulging the tangy spice that was Sinjin.

Head spinning, I broke away. My skin was tingling like millions of bubbles were bursting beneath the surface. I knew all the reasons why I waited to do that, and still I waited too long.

"See what happens when you give me what I want," I teased.

I turned away, reaching for the door handle.

A hand clamped on my wrist and the world spun in a riot of white, blue, and gray. Then there was Sinjin.

His mouth crashed on mine, swallowing my yelp. I was slammed against the van, crushed between metal and his powerful body as if to rid me of the idea I was going anywhere.

He spread my legs, wrapping them around him, and ground between my middle until I moaned. The invitation was all he needed to plunge in.

Every second of every day with Sinjin Bellisario had been a battle. Why should kissing him be any different?

He curled around my tongue—tugging and demanding it surrender. I pushed back and dipped into him. Shockwaves thrummed through me. Tightening my body. Clicking on sensations for the very first time.

I'd never wanted anyone this badly in my whole life who wasn't an unattainable member of a boy band.

Sinjin was real. He was hard, rippling flesh under my fingers. He was fine hair tickling my forehead and punishing teeth scraping my bottom lip. He was a throbbing cock demanding entrance.

I was done with our game of "will we, won't we." I was going to attain the fucking crap out of him. To borrow a phrase, I'd attain him until it fell off.

I broke away gasping. "I give you an inch and you take a mile," I said, grin impossible to hold back. "Why am I not surprised?"

He growled. "This better not surprise you either. I'm taking whatever I want from here on out. Consent signed, dated, and sealed until the end of time."

"That's not exactly how it works."

"Got something you want to say about it, say it now."

"I—"

Sinjin grabbed my jaw, trapping my reply, and licked me from the tip of my chin to my crown. It was the weirdest, sexiest thing any guy had done to me, and my recovery time was zero. He kissed me again. Rough. Insistent. Hungry.

The fantasies he outlined that day in the torture room came flooding back. It was past time we'd gotten to those. Starting with the hardening chocolate.

"Ahem."

Reality crashed in, tearing me free of Sinjin.

Edie raised a brow from the back-door steps. "Thank you for handling the Lombard issue, Sinjin."

He wasn't listening—too busy sucking and nipping his way down my cleavage.

"I hope we'll see you next week to help set up the cots and put out food. Bye now."

"Bye, Edie." I pushed on his shoulders, moving him the barest inch I needed to wiggle free. "I'm so sorry about— We'll see you next— Sorry again, we're leaving now."

I climbed inside, slammed and locked the door. I didn't put it past Sinjin to haul me out and continue where we left off.

I OPENED THE DOOR TO climb out but Sinjin was already there. He threw me over his shoulder and strode into the fire station.

"As arousing as this caveman impression is, I can walk, Saint."

Naturally, he ignored me.

Sinjin carried me over the threshold and turned left. I bit my lip, heart thundering under the Sinjin-standard brand of whirling emotions he ignited in me.

He stepped into the dark space, venturing down, down, down.

"I'm confused," I said. "Am I being punished?"

"Pain can be a gift in itself."

"I was thinking we'd indulge in another activity today."

"So was I."

The torture room was just as I remembered it. Instruments of death covered every wall, singing tales of misery and last words.

Sinjin was on me before I was on my feet. His ferocity burned hotter than outside the church. Nothing would stop him this time.

Our mouths clashed in a furious battle of tongues, moans, and teeth.

I bit his lip. Hard. Earning a grunt on the back of tangy blood coating my tongue.

Leaning back, I smirked into those eyes. "Was that a gift?"

"Dear Lord. I'm going to reach a new level of savagery with you."

I licked him chin to nose. "You'll want my tongue attached."

Roaring, Sinjin seized my collar and tore my shirt a new opening, ripping it clean off. A mark of strength both terrifying and heady. Like the snarl on his lips and the lust in his eyes. He wanted to worship and torture me in equal measure, and honestly, I wasn't certain which he'd choose.

The rest of my clothes met the same fate. My bra straps snapped. Jeans shoved off my legs, and my underwear—

I grabbed his wrists, halting him in pulling them down. "Isn't this the part where you say please?"

"No." Sinjin lifted me in the air. "It's the part where you do."

My body slammed into metal. *The cage. My old friend.*

I grasped the bars out of instinct, and wrapped my legs around Sinjin when he let go. He slipped inside the lining, finding my clit, and rolled it over rough callouses and knife scars. His other hand probed my folds, tricking a gasp out of me that caught as he plunged in without warning. Weeks and the only one to touch the poor thing was me. My toes curled on his knife holster, eyes rolling up in my head.

Waves of thrilling agony ratcheted up my body. Sinjin set an inhuman pace, fingering me so hard and fast, the *slap, slap, slap, slap* of our skin on skin beat a tempo faster than my pounding heart.

I clung desperately to the cage. The cold metal bit back, reminding me of the days they separated us. I felt his anger then, burning me because my stubbornness kept us apart. And I felt his anger now for so long being denied what I knew was his.

"Ahh, Saint," I breathed.

A fourth finger joined the rest—the two inside and the one tormenting my clit. The double attack was unkind. I couldn't last for more than ten minutes under an assault like this.

The pressure converged on a single point, building to burst me apart at the seams. I threw my head back and my jaw cracked in a silent scream.

I came hard. Jerking and shaking, I lost my hold and Sinjin had to catch me.

"Fucking hell. That's what I've been missing all this time?"

"I tried to tell you." He pressed against my lips, pushing fingers dripping with my arousal inside me like feeding me croissants. "But don't worry. You won't go a day missing out from now on."

"Every single d-day?" My traitorous voice squeaked. "That's quite a promise."

"Fuck promises. It's a bet."

I don't know who went for his zipper first—him or me. But it was me who guided his length to my entrance, stroking him as I did so. I wouldn't say I had extensive experience with cocks, but if I had a type, his was it. Long and thick. Molded to my palm as if it belonged there.

Sinjin slid in to the hilt, gave me a nanosecond to adjust, and then fucked me like a wild animal.

I bounced up and down on the steel. Sinjin had me by the thighs and my feet flapping behind him. The cage rattled in protest—clanging and banging to rouse the entire street. We weren't much quieter.

"Yes, right there," I cried. "Fuck yeah, I'll take… one of these… every day."

My nipples were pointed missiles striking his face. He captured one, growling like it was a naughty tease in his way, and sucked it into submission. He struck that spot, and a violent orgasm of such magnitude wracked me, I broke two nails in his back and almost blacked out hitting my head on the cage.

Tensing, he flattened me on the bars and exploded inside me. I was sure pulling out didn't occur to him. Fortunately, being on the pill occurred to me.

Not that I was concerned about all of that at the moment.

I slumped into his arms. Sinjin was warm and wet and holding me as I slowly came down.

"Mmm," I hummed. "So that's what it takes to make you sweat."

"I got carried away. I had planned to put this room to its use. Extract each orgasm on the pain of begging me for release."

My lower belly tightened.

"Then you bit me and I lost my head."

"Best-laid plans, Saint." I kissed him slow and languid. "They always go awry."

His voice was a low, husky murmur. "I haven't given up yet." Sinjin carried me to the rack. "And we assumed we'd get no use out of this. Arms up."

Refusing didn't cross my mind. I raised my arms over my head and was strapped, locked, and secured. My legs received the same treatment.

He bent over me, I thought to kiss me, but his lips ghosted over mine and he drew back. Sinjin straightened to his full height. He stripped unhurriedly, eyes locked on mine to hold me captive. I broke free and drank him in.

"You asked me a question today."

"Did I?"

He nodded. "I told you I'd give you an answer if you won our bet."

"We ended in a draw," I murmured.

"We did," he said. "Changes the rules, but I always hold up my end. You'll get your reward, Bunny, if *you* answer the question."

I was having trouble remembering the damn question. Sinjin was walking away from me and my mind screamed to get him back and have him inside me again.

"This room isn't for sex." Sinjin circled the space, casting his eyes over the walls. "Everything here is made to kill, and each guest I've brought down here has been intimately acquainted with what they can do."

Sinjin selected a knife off the hook. A sharp point and narrow blade made that knife perfect for removing bones. That's how it got its name.

I was calm as he came toward me. A single knife in his hands was ten times as deadly as a fully equipped army, but I had nothing to fear. Not from him. Not ever again.

"Except you," he said. "I had my chance to kill you. End your threat. Your distraction." The blade tip pressed between my breasts. "But I couldn't."

"Is that so bad?" I asked softly.

"Yes." The blade traveled down, gliding harmlessly over my skin. "You have some kind of... hold on me. I lead the Merchants because I do what needs to be done without question. That has always been the case, but never with you."

He reached my middle, lifted the blade, and slid the hilt inside me.

"Ah." The softest sound escaped me as he moved in and out.

"I was going to kill you that night in the bathroom. Instead I took you. I would've followed you in that cab. What I did was let you go. I should've found another woman to give me what you denied. But I stopped fucking your imagined imitations and moved you into my house.

"Why, Adeline?" He raised the knife, gazing at it unseeingly. "Why can't I hurt you?"

And then it came to me. The question I had asked him.

"It's simple," I said. "It's because you love me."

"Is it?" Sinjin sounded genuinely curious.

"'Fraid so."

"Hmm." The knife clattered to the floor. Sinjin climbed on the rack, lying on top of me, and rested his forehead on mine. "Why? How do you know?"

My throaty laugh floated over us. "Because you told me you did. You couldn't kill me because you respected me. You can't sleep with other women because I'm the only one on your mind. And you keep me here because you can't live without me. You need to see me every day, and go to bed each night knowing I'm next to you.

"That's the answer to the question, Saint. All you want from me… is me."

Sinjin kissed me—neither sweetly nor loving. It was a fierce, rough, hungry kiss because to this man those emotions came out no other way.

"Aren't you going to ask me if I love you?"

"No." Sinjin got up and loosened my leg restraints. He angled me over his knees. "By the criteria you set, you do."

"Excuse me? My second point mentioned not sleeping with other people. Celibacy by lovesickness is very different than celibacy by imprisonment."

"You could've fucked Cash, Mercer, and Brutal at any time." He pushed in deep, cutting my protest off with a moan. "We even agreed we wouldn't get possessive about it if you decided to get your employee benefits from all of us. But you chose me, because you love me."

I laughed. "Well, I've told you how you feel and you've told me how I feel. Maybe one day we'll speak for ourselves. If we lose a card game or something."

"Bet."

He started pumping, and conversation was lost from that point.

Was it his intent that we make up for weeks of lost time in one day? I'd have to say yes from the marathon blow jobs, orgasms, and relentless pounding that took place in every position I knew of, and a few I didn't.

At one point, I stumbled upstairs for food and water, dizzy and giggling from the sex high. Or maybe just delirious from lack of sustenance.

Sinjin caught up to me, reclined on the table, and made me eat my treats off him. Of course that is when Brutal showed up. We ran upstairs under pain of death and went at it all night and into the early morning.

I passed out exhausted by his side.

For the first time since I moved in, I slept without dreams.

THE NEXT DAY, I WOKE to a growling stomach, clock that read eleven, and an empty bed. Sinjin would have business today like he did every day.

I went downstairs to find he wasn't the only thing missing. The dining table was gone. How Brutal removed it without me hearing a thing was one of the many mysteries he'd keep close to the vest.

I wasn't surprised. The table was destined for the incinerator the minute he caught us. I just hoped the next one they got was two inches lower and bamboo. Much better for prep. And sex.

I got started on lunch, making due with minimal counter space. On today's menu was roast chicken with loaded baked potato salad and green beans. Because that's what I was in the mood for. The guys were out around lunchtime. If I was eating alone, I was eating what I wanted. I called Gianna while I peeled the potatoes.

"Hey, G."

"Hey." Rumbling and conversation sounded on the other end. I suspected she was riding the bus to her lunch. "What's up? Still on house arrest?"

"There's a chance terms can be amended. What about you? Have you been in to see Dad?"

"I went the other day. He asked what's going on with this new job that you never have time to visit. Otherwise, he's good."

"About the bill—"

"Don't start, Addy. I've been begging you to let me help pay his nursing home bills. You know I don't mind."

"I will pay you back," I said. "The home refuses to take a mailed wad of cash. Once I earn my leave, I'll settle my debts and treat you to dinner at the most expensive restaurant in Leighbridge."

"I'll hold you to that."

"How's work? Did you hire a new maintenance man?"

"No. You wouldn't think it'd be this hard, but so far, none of the applicants have passed the background checks. The boss has me looking for a night manager too."

"What was wrong with the old one?"

"Fell asleep on the job. Guests walked in on her drooling on reception."

"Nice."

"I'll get it figured out. What I really care about is seeing you," she said. "It's been a month. We have so much to talk about. Face-to-face. Over my obscenely expensive dinner. Seriously, babe, do I need to storm the place and murder those guys?"

I laughed. "I'm thinking that won't be necessary. Sinjin and I have reached a new understanding."

"Code for you fucked him?"

"I wasn't going to put it that crudely."

"Meaning you rode him hard and went to bed wet. I don't know if I should mentally high-five you owing to him being one of your captors and this could be Stockholm syndrome, but it's like six months since you've gotten any, so I'm just glad it hasn't closed up by now."

Laughing, I got a knife and cutting board out of the drawer. "I'm pretty sure vaginas don't do that."

"I'm not about to find out, and neither should you."

"I'm confused. Are you now encouraging me to sleep with my captors?"

"I expect you to do whatever it takes to see me. You better love me that much."

"You know I do."

We talked about what I was missing out on while I made my lunch and sat down on the living room couch to eat. I tore a bite off my chicken and moaned.

"Damn, I'm a good cook."

"So good Ryan's still asking for you. I swung by the restaurant the other day, and the guy accosted me at the host stand demanding to know when you're coming back."

I groaned. "When I got my phone back, there were seventy missed calls from him. Not kidding. Seventy. I made up something about getting in a horrible accident and falling into a coma. He bought it, but as you saw, he wants my coming-back-to-work date."

A chime rang through the house, signaling the front door was opened.

"I've got to go," I said. "Talk to you soon."

"*See* you soon."

I hung up and called over my shoulder. "Good timing. Lunch is ready. You can eat it while it's hot."

"It'll have to wait," the deep baritone replied. "Let's— Where the hell is the table?"

"Brutal saw fit to throw it out after it made contact with bodily fluids."

Cash cursed under his breath. "You've finally stopped dangling and I've got to shell out for another table."

"Dangling?" I asked, twisting around.

"Your pussy."

My mouth fell open. "I wasn't dangling anything."

"The fuck you weren't. Next time, keep it in your room. We haven't done a real job since Spencer turned the Kings on us. Coffers are low, Redgrave. Can't waste money replacing everything you come on."

I gaped at him. "You are one frostbitten asshole."

"So I've been told." He crossed the room and took my plate. "Let's go."

"Go? What are you talking about?"

Cash stood over me—tall, imposing, handsome. "Things are moving quickly, and after yesterday, we're down four men. Their example should make the others think twice, but a quarter of a mill is a lot of money. It's time we take care of the problem."

"Again. What are you talking about?"

"Sinjin says you're ready," he went on. "You understand what needs to be done. We'll find out tonight."

"What's happening tonight?"

"I'll explain in the car." Cash ripped a bite off my chicken. "Mmm. For all your faults, I can't say anything about your cooking."

"I don't have faults."

He cracked a smirk, walking off. "Up. I have 'buy a new table' on my list of shit to do today now. You're slowing me down."

"Wait," I said, getting to my feet. "From what I got out of that nonsense, there is a problem that needs taking care of. But why are you the one taking me? Did Sinjin say—"

"Oh, Sinjin," he drew out. "My mistake. I should've realized you only sit, stayed, and begged at his order." He held up his phone. "Want to call and ask his permission to come with me?"

If I did have hackles, they'd be rippling down my back. "I don't need his permission."

"Good. Hurry up." Cash swept out, missing the middle finger I raised at his back.

Of all the guys, he never warmed up to me. Brutal found me amusing. Mercer dropped flirty, enigmatic comments whenever he got the chance. Sinjin was inside of me less than eight hours earlier.

But Cash—he looked at me like he'd have been just as happy, or happier, if I'd been left in that dumpster.

I grabbed a pair of shoes and met him downstairs. Cash's white convertible was the understated ride out of the bunch. Until you slid inside.

Leather molded to my backside like it was fitted for it. Everything in here was buttons and touch screens. Even the gearshift was done away for the sleek silver buttons in its place.

The dash screen lit up on the slam of Cash's door. A robot voice filled the car. "Good afternoon, sir."

"Start," he ordered. The engine purred to life.

"Even the car has to kowtow to you. And all the people who were shocked raised their hands." I made a show of looking around. "Look at that. No one's hands are up."

"Play Count Basie," Cash said.

"Playing Count Basie. Enjoy your music, sir."

"Count Basie? I'll raise my hand for that. I didn't peg you for a jazz fan."

"Why would you?" He reversed out of the drive. "You know nothing about me."

"We could do something about that. I'm told you've got a story worth hearing."

Cash turned the music up to deafening.

At this rate, I could chip at that iceberg for a decade and not make a dent.

I gave into Cash's obvious request for silence and turned my attention to my phone. Dad didn't text, but his nurse and home aides did. I checked in with them, seeing how he was doing. I was caught up in the fascinating story of how my father tried to help his neighbor escape over the wall when the music shut off.

"Listen up, Redgrave."

"Ah, you're bestowing your attention upon me now. This must be... important." I looked up and noticed my surroundings.

We weren't in Waterford anymore. Surrounding me were chic and stubby little buildings that hadn't reached their skyscraper potential. Orderly rows of trees stretched out of the concrete. Narrow streets lit by lampposts all bore the only mark of graffiti that dare grace this borough.

A crown.

"What are we doing in Harlow, Cash?"

Cash drove into a pizzeria parking lot. He killed the engine in a spot facing the street. "See that club over there? Paradise."

"Yeah. What about it?"

"How much do you know about the Kings?"

"I know they're not to be messed with. That was enough for me to go on."

"Sex, pain, and money," he stated. "That's their business in this borough and the rest. The high-priced escorts are managed by them. The underground fight network is promoted by the Kings. Plus, the big business, the illegal casinos. They run the games Cinco high-rollers play in, leaving Joe Broke stumbling in after his shift at the steel mill for the rest of us. They're unstoppable for the mere fact that at any given weekend, they're raking in hundreds of thousands."

I nodded slowly. "Makes sense."

"It also follows that if one is to bring a gang like this down, they have to cut off the tap. End the fight rings. Lure their escorts away. Drive off the coked-up trust fund babies."

"It follows."

"Four years ago, Angelo kept it all in one place. An underground club called The Pleasure Center. Then someone was murdered on their doorstep. The police swarmed the place and discovered the club beneath the club. Angelo barely got out of there in time, but half of the members weren't as lucky. It was a huge bust. So big you must have heard about it."

"I did," I admitted. "Our dean was one of the men arrested. Something about an underground sex room and a barely legal girl. But I didn't know the Kings were involved."

Cash leaned in his seat, fingers silently drumming the dash. "Since then, Angelo's gotten smart. He's split the operation into so many parts, you could shut down one ring and not make a crack in his business. The fights are held by sponsoring members in their penthouses. The 'sex rooms' are run out of hotels but we don't know which.

"Angelo still oversees the casino himself, but the location changes every week. You make a plan to move on one warehouse and it's already cleared out. That leaves the auction."

"What's the auction?" This was the longest conversation Cash and I had, and we saved it for a good topic. I was rapt.

"Exactly what you're thinking. Men and women with money to spare, bid for a night with the best Cinco's sex trade has to offer. And tonight, the auction will be held beneath Paradise. That's where you come in."

I hummed. "No, I don't think I do."

"Angelo handed charge of the auction to a guy named Corbin," Cash continued. "Corbin has no family. No friends. No pets. His only weakness is Candy."

"The hardened gangbanger likes candy?"

"I'm told she gives a wicked blow job, so who can blame him?"

"Ah."

"This is our way in, Redgrave. In the highly unlikely event we survive and take down the biggest gang in Cinco history, it starts here. Candy convinced Corbin you're a friend looking to make extra cash quick. Tonight, you have two jobs. One is clocking each entrance, exit, and where the guards are stationed. Two is going up for auction."

"No."

"Having to split the business was an inconvenience that Angelo does his best to minimize for the valued customers. According to Candy, they're sent the new locations directly, instead of tracking down a King and paying extra for the knowledge. I've narrowed down the people with enough money and influence to get on the valued list. Problem is we can't get close enough to lift their phones. Their security is too tight.

"Four of the people on our list will attend the auction tonight. As luck would have it, Bryan Acker is one of them. Young, racially ambiguous, sorta redheads are his top choice every day of the week."

"Too bad he's not getting any tonight."

"He'll outbid everyone for you no question, and once you're alone, you'll put this SD card in his phone." Cash pulled the tiny bit of plastic from his pocket. "It'll download the spyware that lets us intercept his texts, calls, and emails. You can't bring anything in but the clothes on your back, but this will be easy to hide in your bra."

"Not happening."

"So will this." A small baggie holding two white pills was held between us. "Suggest a glass of wine before the fun starts, slip this in his drink, and he'll be out in three minutes."

"Definitely not happening."

"I'll follow close behind. Once it's done, get out of there and I'll pick you up."

"And no," I announced. "This has been a fun field trip, but it's time to go. Let's not do this again soon."

Cash gave me a look that said they didn't make them any more irritating than me. "It has to be you, Redgrave. Putting aside the anatomical differences my boys and I can't overcome. It'd be fatally stupid to set foot in that club when we're public enemies numbers one through four. It has to be a woman. It has to be one we can trust. So, it has to be you."

"Get Candy to do it."

"I circle back to point two. A woman we can trust. Candy told Sinjin to his face she'd turn the Merchants over to the Kings at the first opportunity.

She thinks we're doing this because Bryan Acker paid the Merchants for a job and might have information. She believes she's splitting a finder's fee. She doesn't know we're coming after the Kings."

I clicked my tongue. "That's too bad. But you better get to work. You've got ten hours to find someone else."

Cash fished something out of the glove box and tossed it on my lap. "I found my someone, and this is your payment."

"Car keys?"

"To your car," he stated. "Consider your lockdown lifted. If you do this, you can come and go as you please. Visit your old man. Go to lunch with your friends. We'll give you the codes to the house and the car to speed out of the drive."

I didn't pay the shiny, Chevrolet-stamped metal another glance. "You'll end my unlawful incarceration if I auction myself to a random guy who'll take me back to his mansion and cut me to pieces while singing showtunes?"

"My research doesn't point to serial killer tendencies."

"I'm not doing it," I snapped at the dry reply. "Why would I? I should think a change in status was coming anyway."

Cash raised a brow. "Why? Because you're fucking Sinjin?"

"You know, 'sleeping with' is a perfectly acceptable term for sex."

"Call him." Cash tossed his phone on my lap next. "Ask him how loyalty is proven. You should also ask what he thinks of you being content to kick back on our couch, taking our money, while the Kings hunt and slaughter us in the street."

"This isn't my fight. I didn't ask for any of this."

"None of us did."

I scoffed. "Raiden Spencer was the symptom. You're the disease. We both know the Merchants would've gone after them eventually. Whoever you planned to use on that day, call them up now. I'm not your soldier."

Cash trapped my gaze, holding it steady. It was cruel how mesmerizing he was. I suspect even if he released his hold, I wouldn't be able to look away. Cash was hard lines and sharp angles. Beautiful and unyielding like the bars of gold desperate to match his glittering pools in brilliance.

"When they find us, and they will find us, it won't be quick. First, they'll drain us of money, weapons, and men. After dismantling what we've built to the last pickpocket scamming tourists in the park, they'll track us down in the fire station. It's fortified, but not impenetrable, and when it comes to Angelo—where there's a will, there's a way.

"He and his guys will get in. And any of us left standing"—he dropped his chin, piercing me through—"including you, will be subjected to torture the likes of which you can't imagine. Rape is not on our rap sheet, but it is on his."

A lump hardened in my throat.

"We'll try to stop him, of course, but we'd be outmanned and outgunned. Angelo will violate you while we're forced to watch, and then you'll be passed off to his guys—who will either kill you after having their fun, or one of them will keep you. That's your most hopeful option since you'll get the chance to make it out alive. Sinjin, Brutal, Mercer, and I won't receive such mercy. We'll be mutilated bodies on a fire station floor."

He raised his head. "You think I'm saying this to scare you. I'm not. My job is details. Numbers. Research. I've studied ten years' worth of King kills—those that made the news and those that didn't. There's a reason they flaunt their ownership of this borough for cops, soccer moms, and Petey's Little League team to see. They have nothing and no one to fear."

Cash was so hard and cold. I feared I would touch him and find he truly was formed in ice. So I did.

I rested my palm on his wrist, starting at the warm, smooth flesh beneath me. A steady pulse thrummed in his veins. As slow and unrattled as the rest of him.

"You are being honest," I whispered. "Never thought I'd come to hate that trait."

He glanced at our hands, his mask of impassivity intact. It was hard to read, but I'd guess my act made him curious, not annoyed. "Our only chance is if we bring the fight to them, Redgrave. We strike when they're least expecting it. A blow to their empire they can't come back from."

"Trojan horse style. The horse being me." I released a long breath. "This is really the only way?"

"If I had any other option, I assure you I would take it. You're a wild card. Just as likely to seduce Bryan Acker as kick him in the balls and make a run for it. For all I know, you're planning to do just that."

I shook my head. *For all you know...*

"It's a simple job, Redgrave, and I'll be out here the entire time. Are you in or out?"

A million thoughts, rejections, and arguments went through my head staring at Paradise's bland sign, waiting for nightfall to light the street neon pink. This was not my fight, but it was my life. I would live it on my terms and with the infuriating, blue-haired psycho that got me into this mess until I decided otherwise.

"I'm in."

Chapter Nine

"Did you know about this?"

"I know everything, Bunny."

"Is there a reason you didn't tell me?" I huddled low in the seat, hugging Cash's coat tighter. The two of us were back in his car, idling in front of the pizzeria.

Harlow's club street transformed with the setting sun. Sharp-suited men and women in slinky dresses scurried across the road in their heels, hitting the packed pizza place before running back for more booze, dancing, and bathroom sex.

Fourth Street rattled with the bass of a hundred speakers. Coupled with the screaming, shouting, and shrieks of my twentysomething peers, I practically had to yell into the phone for Sinjin to hear me.

"I'm surprised you're okay with me going home with another man."

"Why wouldn't I be? You pull this off and he'll be drooling into his pillow while you win me my prize. If the plan doesn't go off that smoothly and he touches you, you'll kill him and I'll still get it. That's a win-win."

"I don't resort to murder as quickly as you do, Saint."

"Remember that, Bunny, because if he lays one finger on you and walks out of that room alive, I'll have to take over from there."

"My night isn't complete without listening to one of your death threats." I shifted again—skin pimpling at the silk brushing my bare flesh. "Seriously, why did I have to wear this outfit? A little black dress would've been fine."

"You don't display half of the item up for auction," Cash said. "Bidders want to see it all."

My middle finger wasn't raised at his back that time.

"Whatever you're wearing, don't take it off when you get home," Sinjin threw in. "We're holding a little show of our own."

"Fuck you." *And fuck me for being turned on.* "Where are you anyway? Why aren't you here?"

"We've all got our duties. I was ambushed by my own men and now we're down four. I have to refill the ranks while reminding the boys why having me as an enemy is more dangerous than every King in Cinco City."

My nipples pebbled in the sequined bra thinking of the harsh lessons those calloused hands imparted. Yes, it was definitely me with the problem.

"You'll be fine," Sinjin said. "Pour that bottle of wine, and if he doesn't drink it fast enough, make him wear it around his neck."

"What's with you and wine bottles?" I mumbled. I was stalling. I knew it and felt no shame.

"Ever notice how you're never too far from one? I'd be concerned about this country's alcohol consumption if it didn't provide a handy weapon whenever it's risky to sneak one in. Use it. Kill him. Clone the phone."

"What happened to killing him being the last resort out of self-defense?"

"I changed my mind. The sad, flabby dick shit should not for a second hold the thought in his head that he can have you. Kill him."

The line went dead. In Sinjin-land, death orders passed as goodbyes.

I slid the phone in his coat and the coat off my shoulders. The outfit shone on full display.

Large blue and gold sequins decorated the cups and spilled down my stomach on dangly strings. My penchant for boy shorts was ignored. Covering, or I should say not covering, my backside was a matching sequin thong. The look was completed with gold glitter heels that would surely kill me before I could Bryan Acker. Or Cash.

"I look like a clown in the glitter circus cabaret, Cash!"

He openly and aggravatingly smirked. "I wouldn't say that."

I blinked. "Is that a compliment?"

"Is it?"

"Ugh. Why did I agree to this? I'm still not convinced you couldn't have come up with a good lie for Candy."

"I could've but it wouldn't have done any good. Corbin doesn't let her in the auctions anymore."

"Excuse me?" My voice was a low hiss. "If she's not allowed in there, how do you know her information is any good? This Bryan guy might not even show up."

"Candy might be out, but her friends are not. They say he's a regular and you're his type."

"But—"

"Get out of the car." Cash leaned over and shoved open my door. "Exits, entrances, guards, Bryan, and phone. Go."

I got out but not quietly. My steaming tirade didn't end with the slammed door or my march across the street, collecting appreciative looks and whistles.

"—rigid, unfeeling prick." Skirting the line, I went around back and spotted the lone man standing before the alley entrance. "Cat-eyed, walking, talking block of ice in a skin suit."

"Excuse me?"

"Nothing. My name's..." My lips fought to form the word. "Serenity. I'm here for the auction."

The guy sized me up with the same scrutiny I gave him. A sturdy mass of muscle topped with a bulbous head held up by a neck the size of a baked ham. He didn't need backup. No one was getting through him.

"Referral."

"Candy," I repeated as Cash told me.

"Code."

"Whippoorwill." An odd password but not one easy to guess.

"Rules."

"Rules?" *Cash didn't mention anything about rules.*

"Rules," he insisted.

I scowled. "The rules are I shiver my ass off in this ridiculous costume for the enjoyment of hooting hyenas. After literally being bought and paid for like an object, I leave with 'name redacted' to 'location redacted' and we engage in 'activities redacted.' I keep my mouth shut and tell no one about anything. That about cover it?"

A smile stretched across his face more unsettling than the dead-eyed stare. "Have a nice night, Miss Serenity."

He opened his door and bowed me through. I stepped into a pitch-black hallway. Dark, but not silent.

Club music banged on my ears, drawing me forward as my vision adjusted.

Cash says it's another club within a club. There has to be a—

There.

At the end of the hall, there were two doors. Pulsating, multicolored lights seeped out of one, causing me to try the other.

The knob gave way easily. I peered down a staircase. The soft glow of fluorescent lights peered back.

"Waitin' for an invitation, honey?"

I jerked. Two women in high heels and frilly pink and blue sheer lingerie stood behind me. The music so loud I hadn't noticed their arrival.

The dim light played with my mind, making their big hairstyles into living beings consuming their scalp. Heavy makeup caked their faces and caused a waxiness that warped them in the darkness.

"Wide-eyed little doe," one said. "You must be new."

"Uh. Yeah."

"Figures," the other scoffed. "Move."

She shoved me none-too-gently out of the way, clomping down the stairs. I stumbled in my shoes, ankle giving way. The other woman caught me.

"Careful. Don't bruise the fruit before it goes on the stand." She righted me and continued on. "Better get moving," she called. "Corbin doesn't like it when we're late."

Her warning didn't instill the urgency she intended. I paused, steeling myself.

It's simple. I stand on a platform, whisk off with Bryan Acker, fashion him a special drink, and do what I need to do.

What Cash said chilled me, but he was right. If the Kings took the fire station, they wouldn't let me skip out the door while they handled their beef with the boys. While I'm attached to the Merchants, their threat is my threat.

The guard let another pair inside, giving the final push to pick up my feet. The low emanating light grew closer, falling on my blue toes, my shaved legs, my exposed stomach, and my jangly bodice. It revealed me as it did the room.

I halted on the bottom step, lips twitching.

This is not what I expected.

Cash said the Kings were pulling in north of a quarter mill every week. If they were, you wouldn't know it from this place.

Losing the battle, my twitchy lips curled into a grimace.

The dim glow wasn't mood-setting. It was the result of half the lightbulbs burning out. It looked like an attempt had been made to replace a pair, but the janitor lost interest halfway through and let the plastic case hanging off the fixture. A man swilled his beer, lazily ducked the obstruction, and took his seat at the table.

Despite Cash's info that the games had been moved elsewhere, poker tables were full, and as old and grimy as the room they sat in.

Stains turned the green felt brown. The leather lining the tables was ripped—a few cuts deliberate—and spilling white cotton. A dank, heavy cloud of smoke hung in the air. Pungent from unwashed bodies and—

A sweaty, topless man leaned over and spit on the floor.

—the general aura of not giving a shit.

Where the fuck am I?

Swallowing hard, I stepped to the side, clinging to the wall. Until a proper look at the concrete showed red stains eerily similar to blood. I shot off, skin crawling.

Relax, Adeline. Just do what you came here to do.

I swept a closer look around and noticed I was receiving a few in return. I was standing there in a glittery bra and thong. It wasn't surprising.

One door leading into this room that has a single door opposite, and on my left, it spills into a hallway.

I glanced down the long tunnel of stained concrete. The light flickered overhead, plunging it in and out of darkness, but allowing me just enough to see it branched around a corner.

My next stop was that hallway. First, the door.

Cash needs to know what's an exit and what's a broom closet. Only one way to find out.

I hugged close to the wall without touching it. My heels carried me as quickly as they were able and my gaze pointed straight ahead. This did me no good.

Wolf whistles went up in the fetid air.

"I'd buy a night of that."

"Yeah, girl. Don't be shy. Take it off."

"Damn. How much are you?"

A hand swung out and smacked my ass.

"More than you can afford," I hissed. "Keep your hands to yourself or I'll take a hammer to you filthy pigs and see if there's money inside."

They laughed raucously, crowing about feisty treats and teaching mouthy sluts a lesson.

The banged-up brown metal door loomed straight ahead. I closed on the knob and drew it open. A figure moved in the corner of my eye and slammed on the metal, ripping the handle out of my grasp.

"Can I help you?" One of the men who'd been playing poker got between and shoved me back with his girth alone. "Did Corbin ask for you?"

"No." *Guard number two. Steps away from his post but keeps an eye on it just fine.* "I was looking for the auction."

"It's down that hallway, sweetheart," he said, pointing over my head. "This is Corbin's office."

"Got it. Sorry."

I returned the way I came, collecting disgusting, graphic catcalls. Captain prepared me for a lifetime of this, and if I had my pepper spray, I'd be making them do the screaming.

It was a mistake to come down here alone and unarmed. Something's not right.

This seedy crack den was not the picture Cash painted of high-priced escorts and wealthy clients. Why would a slicked-back congressman or diamond-dusted heiress sully themselves in a place like this when a phone call could bring the party to the penthouse doorstep?

Rounding the end of the hallway got me two more doors. One with an askew bathroom sign and the other blocked by my two new friends. They passed a cigarette back and forth like the dark little hole we were stuck in didn't reek enough.

"There she is," the friendly woman called. "Thought you made a run for it."

"Give me a minute." I poked my head in the bathroom, confirming it didn't hold another way out. "I've gotta ditch the heels first."

She cackled. "I'm Tandy. This is Pearl. What's your name?"

In the proper light, their hair was bigger, makeup cakier, and the reasons obvious. Concealer worked hard to cover the dark shadows under their eyes. Bright lipstick reddened peeling and cracked mouths. There was a subtle two tones in their hair that said most of it wasn't theirs.

"I'm Serenity." I stuck out my hand. Tandy shook. Pearl looked at it like she just saw me wipe my ass without toilet paper. "Nice to meet you guys."

"Nice to meet you," Pearl mocked. "Where do you think you are, bitch? Book club?"

She flicked the cigarette at my feet and stormed through the door. Tandy rolled her eyes at her back.

"Ignore her. She's pissed because her old man made her sign up. They need the money."

"I can't blame her," I muttered. "I didn't think it would be... like this. No offense."

She rolled her head. "You're not offending me. I've been in cozier crack dens. This place is a dump." Tandy pulled another cigarette and lighter from her bra. "Want?"

"No, thanks. I don't understand. I thought The Pleasure Center Part Two catered to rich bidders. Can't the Kings afford to operate out of nicer digs?"

Tandy gave me a long look, stretching the silence past comfort. "You really don't know what you've gotten yourself into. Part two is under new management, sweetie. It caters to a very different clientele."

"What does that mean?"

"You'll find out." Tandy stepped aside. "Go on."

Hesitating for only another second, I went inside.

My heels sank in the carpet. Another wall met me but it didn't reach the ceiling. What did come through the ceiling was pounding house music from Paradise. Soundproofing was skipped in this part of the basement.

I wandered left and stepped out from the partition. Two dozen faces swung to me. One of them a guard standing at the foot of the stage. He moved in my direction.

A hand yanked me back.

"Wrong way," Tandy said. "We wait over here."

I let myself be dragged. The opposite direction of that silent, watchful group seemed like the right way to go.

The other end of the partition opened up to the back of the stage. Men and women loitered around picking through a clothes rack or huddling in front of two vanity mirrors. Heavy drapes dropped down from the ceiling and fell over the steps to the stage.

That is Serenity's way up the auction block.

I noticed something behind a group of men.

And this is another way out.

Behind the stage, another short hallway hid a door. This one didn't need to be checked. A burned-out exit sign hung from the ceiling.

Two exits. Three guards. Secrecy and the Kings' reputation must be their best main walls of protection.

I backed out and headed for the door out.

"Don't bother." Pearl's snarl slid in my ear. "Once your name is on the list, Corbin will get his money either from these dickless cunts, or from you."

"Don't know what you're talking about. I'm just going to the bathroom."

"Play someone else, bitch." She got in my face, blowing stale alcohol breath up my nose. "You're running off with your fucking tail between your legs. I don't know your manager, but he's one cold bastard for throwing you to the sharks on what must be your first night. I can smell virgin on you."

"Wow." I laughed. "I have no idea how, but I really pissed you off."

"Yeah, you have."

"That's enough, Pearl," Tandy said.

I sidestepped them both and left. Footsteps followed me out.

"Wait, girl." Tandy pulled me up short outside the door. "Whoever fooled you into coming here won't like that we scared you off. Neither will Corbin. Pearl wasn't lying about that. Get him his money, and then never piss him off again so that he sends you back here."

My stomach flipped. Tandy assumed I got on the bad side of my pimp. I had come out here for the bathroom, but they had me questioning how big a mistake it would be to go back in that room. What went on on the other side of that door that two steely, hardened escorts classed it a punishment?

I'm not finding out. I turned my back and walked off.

"Seren— No. You know what? Go on, girl." She clapped. "Good for you. You don't have to take his shit."

I rounded the corner and slammed into someone. She stumbled, bumping into the girl behind, and crumpled in heels too high for her.

I gazed down at her—frozen to the spot. Her makeup was garish. Hoop earrings gold and expensive. Curls piled on her head. White halter dress tight and short.

None of that disguised the fact this girl couldn't be older than twelve.

A mass shove through the group and snatched her up. "What did I say?!" He backhanded her across the face, ripping out a scream.

From me.

The young girl made no sound. Her trembling lips were pressed together tight.

"Walk, sit, keep your fucking mouths shut!" He threw the girl away from him. "Who else can't get it right?"

Silently, the girls reformed their line. They continued shuffling with the girl in white limping behind the rest.

Children. Every single one of them. From thirteen to eight years old.

I watched them go, body wracked with tremors so fierce only the wall held me up. I clutched my stomach. My nails slid through the sweat from my slick palms, burrowing piercing grooves in my skin.

One by one, the girls walked past Tandy whose downcast gaze avoided them and their brutish escort. The auction room enclosed them—door shutting with a bang that reverberated in my soul.

I pitched forward and vomited. Spewing on the floor and down the wall.

Sinking to my knees, I hugged myself as I retched and retched until there was nothing left.

"Serenity." Tandy's soft whisper broke through. "If you can leave this place, go.

"Please, just go."

SMALL, SQUARE EYES too close together. A piggish nose that sniffed or twitched every five seconds. He was big on top. Beefy arms and rippling abs burst out of his wife-beater. Compared to the twig-like legs contained in ripped jeans.

I couldn't stop looking at him. Not at the bruised knuckles he flexed at the silent girls. The yellow crown riding his shoulder. Or the gun tucked in his waistband.

Tandy told me to leave. She flashed me surprise when I returned from the bathroom—makeup gone, face dripping, and heading in the wrong direction. She told me not to get any ideas. I wouldn't walk out of there at all if I did something stupid.

I heard what she said. It didn't matter.

There was no hope of leaving after seeing those girls.

"Welcome, everyone." Speaker feedback ripped through the room. "We will begin momentarily."

The man and the girls stood across an invisible divide. The escorts stood on one side, the King on the other, and six girls huddled behind him in the corner. Everyone looked or angled away from them, pretending they weren't there.

Except me.

Corbin's man snatched a girl from the huddle, and an iron grip clamped my wrist. The small bones ground in agony. Tears filled my eyes in time with hers. My head lolled, snapping back and forth in his jerking, shaking hold.

"Shut up," he barked.

"*Shut up!*" The slap twisted my neck. Pain blossomed in my cheek—as real and stinging as the first time, and the times after that.

"Stop," Pearl hissed in my ear. "Don't do it."

The King raised his hand to hit her. I surged forward.

Pearl nearly dislocated my shoulder yanking me back and throwing me against the vanity. The banger whirled around, but Pearl and the others were already moving in front of me, shielding me from view.

I breached the haze, gasping. My chest heaved like I'd been held underwater and ripped up for my last blessed breath of air. The phantom hands slapping, punching, grabbing, and tearing at me dissipated. Blurred vision cleared on the people surrounding me.

"You can't," said a guy in tight jeans and a tank top. "We know. Trust us, we know. But you can't."

"That gun ain't for show," Tandy said under her breath. "I've seen him use it. Those kids bring in a lot of money for Corbin. More than the rest of us ever will. He'll have you killed, girl, and who is that going to help?"

I swallowed around needles.

I wasn't thinking, but there was no time to think. I had to do something.

I felt for a phone that wasn't there. Why did they send me in here alone? I had nothing. Two pills and an SD card for a man who liked racially ambiguous, brownish-redheads. All around us was a den of monsters. What did I have to stop them?

The auctioneer sliced through the chatter. "All right, let's begin. Bidders, you know the rules. Special lots are up first. We have six special items up for auction tonight."

Bile rose in my throat, burning and screaming to come out.

"Payment is to be remitted immediately at the end of the auction," he said. "Let's begin with Special Item Number One."

Through the bodies, the King grabbed a nonresistant girl around the neck and marched her up the stairs.

"The only thing you can do," Tandy whispered, "is never piss that man off again. Do not give him reason to send you back here."

I didn't piss off any man. This was a simple job. A den of luxury. Adults that knew the score and what they wanted. A night that ended with glasses of wine. It was not supposed to be this.

Or was it? Cash appeared out of nowhere and told me to get in the car. He never wanted me around and made no secret of—

I cut the thought off at the knees. As it went through my head, I knew it couldn't be true. Cash wasn't that kind of man.

A killer? Yes.

Ruthless? Yes.

A sneaking, lowlife piece of trash that would sell me to a demented pervert in an orderly line behind children?

No.

I couldn't say why I knew he wasn't the last. I just did.

This wasn't on Cash. Corbin refused to let Candy near these auctions for reasons now blindingly obvious. She didn't know about this, so she couldn't warn Cash—who couldn't warn me.

We walked into a situation we did not understand, beneath the nose of a man we underestimated.

No. We *overestimated* Corbin. We didn't think he could be this heart-shreddingly vile. This soulless.

"We'll start the bidding at ten thousand. Do I have—? Ten thousand to bidder twenty-four. Do I have fifteen? Fifteen to bidder ninety-one."

Our gazes locked through the crush of people. Her eyes bled a thousand pleas—that girl in the white dress.

We didn't know, but now I do. I won't leave without you. I promise.

"Sold."

Another girl was taken up to the block.

Breathing slow, I willed my mind to clear. Running headfirst at him was never going to work. Especially if Pearl and the others get in my way.

Our eyes were locked, holding through the music, pounding, and shuffling. It was because of that I saw the moment they hardened.

She bolted and I shot up. Shoving Pearl aside, I caught her by the shoulders, stopping her as Corbin's man lifted his head from his phone.

"Of course, sweetie," I said loudly. "I've got something to put on that."

"What the fuck are you doing?!"

I smiled at him. "I've got the perfect shade of blush to cover the mark on her cheek. You know Corbin doesn't like the goods going out bruised."

His snarl twitched. "Corbin?"

"Yeah. I'm Candy's friend." The words were dropping from my lips too fast for me to stop them. The tiny little wisp of a girl shook in my hands. Her skin freezing to the touch. "Didn't they tell you I'd be here?"

"Candy?" He looked me up and down, brows furrowing. "Corbin's girl?"

I nodded. "Let me fix up her cheek."

He moved as I did, reaching for her. "No, she's fine. Leave it."

"Dude, for real?" I pushed past Pearl and Tandy, picked up the blush, and shook it at him. "It's just a bit of pink powder. Relax."

My confidence must have thrown him because he didn't stop me kneeling in front of her and sweeping the brush over her cheek.

I spoke so softly, my lips didn't move. "Don't run. I will get you out of here. I promise. Trust me?"

"Yes."

"That's enough." He hauled off and tossed her at the corner.

Calmly, I straightened, set the makeup down, and left the room. The hallway was empty like I left it. No one had even cleaned the vomit off the floor.

I paced the length of the space, heart thrashing in my rib cage. I didn't have a plan. I had the beginnings of one and the rest was tumbling in my head in real time.

Go. Now.

I messed up my hair and pushed a strap off my shoulder. Ripping open the door, I burst in the back while the piece of garbage stepped down from delivering *Special Item Number Three.*

"Help," I cried, falling on him. "Help."

He drew his gun with one hand and pushed me back with the other. "What the fuck's your problem?"

"In the bathroom," I gasped. "A man. There's blood everywhere."

"What?" Alarm bled into fury.

"I tried to wake him but he's not moving. I think he's one of the bidders. What do I do? Get Corbin?"

"No," he said quickly. "It's probably some drunk fuck who mouthed off at the tables and caught it while on the can. Corbin won't be happy if we bother him for that. Don't move," he barked at the girls.

He followed me to the bathroom.

The still unnamed brute shoved me aside. He ran in first—gun ready—and met with an empty room. "Where is he?"

I kicked the door, sending it careening into his back. He hurled forward, and I raced inside, using the momentum to shove him headfirst into the wall.

Roaring, he spun on me. A seeping wound painted his raging fury in blood.

His gun came up and I jumped on his arm like I'd seen Sinjin do. I jerked his wrist trying to loosen his grip.

The King swung his whole body, lifting me off my feet and throwing me across the room.

"Ahh!"

I crashed onto the toilet. Pain ricocheted up my back. I slid off and fell on the trash can, knocking over the contents. My vision cleared, and I threw myself to the side.

The bullet whizzed through the space my head had been.

A deep, guttural scream built in my chest. I launched at him, tackling him into the counter, and seized his arm again. I twisted so violently his shout penetrated my scream.

Grabbing his neck, I smashed his face down on my thigh. If his nose wasn't broken before, it was then.

"Disgusting, evil, child-raping monster!"

I ran him at the toilet, holding tight on the hem of his shirt. His head hit the metal flusher. He glanced off, groaning dazedly. I held his neck the way he did the little girl, and struck his face against the toilet seat again. And again. And again.

I staggered away from his still body. Only his rising chest let me know he was alive. "What did I tell you?" My sore rasp tinged sinister. "Some piece of trash is bleeding on the bathroom floor."

Hurry.

Three girls had been called up. I had to get them out before they called the fourth.

Tandy blocked my path coming in backstage. "Serenity, what did you do? Where's Felix?"

"Is that his name? Oh, he had to take care of something." My veins were on fire. Humming on pure adrenaline. "He told me to look after the girls."

Ducking her grasp, I raced to the final three children. "Let's go. I'm getting you out of here."

"Go?" Eight years old, she shook in the purple bathing suit they'd forced her into.

"Yes, go." I picked her up, causing the final girl to come to life. Crying out, she ripped her from me, clutching her with a protectiveness that spoke volumes.

"—thirty thousand to bidder twelve. Thirty thousand going once."

"It's okay," I said. "You have to go now. Quickly."

I tripped over my heels running to the exit. A little hand slipped into mine. The girl in the white dress.

"What's your name?"

"Kaylee."

"There's a pizza place across the street, Kaylee." I twisted the handle. It didn't budge. "Marco's Pizza. Go in there and hide. I'll come for you."

I threw myself against the door. "No matter what happens. I will come for you." I rammed it again, a cry leaking through my teeth. "Come on! Please!"

"On three." Suddenly, Pearl and Tandy were there.

They squeezed in next to me. "One, two, three!"

We hit the metal hard enough to rattle my skeleton.

"Again," Pearl ordered. "One, two, three!"

My muscles strained to their limit, then stretched past it.

Screech.

The exit gave an inch. Fresh air poured through the slit, giving me new strength.

We shoved against the obstruction, forcing it out of the door's path until there was just enough room for a child to get through.

"Hurry," said one of the guys. He steered the two remaining girls to us. "Run, little darlings, and don't look back."

"Marco's," I told them. Kaylee slipped out, still holding my hand. "I'll find you."

"Sold."

She let go, and was gone.

Chapter Ten

"This doesn't make any sense. Why would Felix leave?"

The auctioneer left his podium. He stood before our passive group, bloodshot eyes narrowed to slits. His gray suit and polished shoes cut an impressive figure compared to Felix, but all I saw was a monster masquerading as one of us.

"Do you think he shares his plans with us?" Pearl rolled her eyes. "All we know is Felix said he had to take care of something. He took the girls and left."

"We promised them six," he hissed.

"Well, now they'll have to go home with someone their own age." She spread her hands. "I'm ready to pony up."

"Yeah," someone said. "You're acting like the auction is over when we're all standing here."

"Let's go." Tandy strode over to the staircase. "The bidders are waiting."

Snarling, he scanned us, looking for a trace of deceit.

I faced my bruised back to the wall. The marks on my skin. Swelling lump hiding in my hair. Soreness in my shoulder. Unconscious man in the bathroom. What I'd done was written on my body, and on his.

Balling my fists, I hid them behind me when the auctioneer passed over me. Pearl said she'd say we got into it if anyone noticed I was banged up.

He stopped, zeroing in on me.

"You." He grabbed my chin and twisted my face side to side. I was so stiff it was a feat my muscles responded to the act. "Who are you?"

"Serenity."

"Bryan Acker."

My eyes widened imperceptibly. "What?"

"Candy told us to put your name down. Said you'd be a good fit for Acker. She was spot-on."

The flood of panic cleared. His sneer was gone, and in its place, a smirk.

"We'll get a shitload of money for you. Almost enough to make up for those last three until I can track that stupid fuck down." At this point, he was mostly speaking to himself.

"Fix yourself up." He roughly towed me to the vanity. "Put some makeup on for fuck's sake. You're next."

The others edged between us, shielding my back, and saying they'd do me up. Their caution wasn't needed because he'd already moved on.

"Hello? It's Donovan," he said into the phone. "We've got a problem. Felix took off with three of the special items. How would I fucking know? Yeah. No."

I hardly felt Pearl and Tandy tugging at my hair.

"Don't tell Corbin. Not yet. If we can get them back here before the end, this doesn't have to be a problem. Just track him down."

"Are you done?" he shouted.

"Almost," Tandy said. "Two minutes."

"One." He swept onto the stage. "Sorry for the delay, ladies and gentlemen. We've changed the bidding order. The final three special items will be auctioned at the end of the night. But don't be disappointed, our next item up for auction is a rare beauty."

"All right." Tandy patted some color in my cheeks. "That should do it. You get yourself out of here, girl, and don't stop running until you hit the coast." She guided me to the stairs. "Don't worry about us. We'll stick to the script."

"Welcome, Serenity."

I took a step. Then two.

I stopped. "Thank you."

"We didn't do it for you," Pearl said. "Just go and... get those girls to safety."

"I will."

Pushing the curtains aside, I stepped onto the platform.

A row of stage lights shone on me, showcasing my body and burning my retinas. I strained to see into the crowd.

Were the people who bought the first three girls still here? Maybe. But the ones waiting to buy the final three were.

"Let's start the bidding at ten thousand. Do I have ten— Ten thousand to bidder fifty-seven. Do I have fifteen? Serenity?"

I started.

"Give us a twirl, would you, love?"

"Oh, uh, right." Propping one hand on my waist, I did my best impression of sexy. Lips pouty. Eyes lowered. Hips swaying. Slowly, I turned, and before my back faced the audience, I bent over and flashed my thong-covered ass.

"That's fifteen. Twenty— Twenty-five thousand to fifty-seven."

The auctioneer's distraction gave me the chance to complete my twirl—bruises unseen.

The bids were soaring up, but not because everyone wanted me. Fifty-seven. Twenty-one. Sixteen. Those three bounced back and forth, lobbing their money at the Kings until two inevitably failed to claim the prize.

Me.

I assumed Bryan Acker was among those three. I couldn't see him or anyone else, which I quickly accepted was by design. The stage lights shone stark on the sweat running down my chest. The twitching corner of my smiling lips. My nails cutting half-moons on my hips. They could see it all.

I saw nothing. No other way forward but one. And as I stood there—besieged once more by the phantom fingers and dozens of crawling, leering eyes—I bent my neck to the fist ripping the hair from my scalp, gazed up at the ceiling, and made my choice.

"Sold! Forty-five thousand to bidder fifty-seven. Congratulations, sir."

The auctioneer gestured to me, pointing to my left. I understood. The girls hadn't returned backstage and neither would I.

I climbed off the stage into the waiting hands of security. He grasped my arm with more gentleness than I'd been receiving that night, and led me to the door where a lone man awaited.

"Mr. Acker."

The picture of this man I formed in my head, shattered on sight. A waxy-faced, middle-aged man who was balding on top and strutted around in three-thousand-dollar suits was my bet.

Middle-aged he was, but his waxy, Botox-ed skin was actually smooth and unblemished barring a few lines around his eyes and mouth. Sprinkles of salt laced a full-head of pepper hair, and the three-thousand-dollar suit was left in the closet in favor of a coat, half-zipped red fleece shirt, and brown pants.

Between the big-framed glasses perched on his nose and nervous smile, he passed for the everyday, casual geek.

But it's definitely not every day a casual geek drops almost fifty thousand dollars for a night with an escort.

I think.

The guard retrieved a tablet from his coat. "You may leave after payment is transferred."

He didn't spare a glance for him. "Hello."

"Hi," I rasped.

"Wow." He traced me inch by inch, popping goose bumps on my skin. "You look just like her."

"Um. That's cool."

"Except for this." Acker shrugged off his coat and draped it over my shoulder. "There. You must be freezing."

Gaze fixed on me, he accepted the tablet and made the transfer.

"Worth every penny," he said, offering his elbow. "Shall we?"

"Yes." *And quickly.*

We passed into the hallway, strolling past the small crowd gathered around the bathroom.

"Did you see anything? Who did this?"

"I didn't see nothing. Is he dead?"

"Felix? Felix!"

"Huh," Acker voiced as we left the chaos behind. "Wonder what happened?"

"Me too."

"THIS WAY, SIR. YOUR room is 204."

Cash wasn't exaggerating about the security preventing him from getting to Acker himself. We left the club and walked into the waiting hands of four personal bodyguards. They escorted us from the door of the alley, hands on their clips like they were waiting for one of the drunk clubbers to make a move. We slid into a limo with three more guards inside.

"A lot of security," I commented.

"Yes."

Bryan and I didn't exchange more conversation on the drive. I watched the pizzeria grow small in the distance, then we turned and it—they—were gone. Each mile that took me away from them was a band around my throat. I couldn't play the teasing, charming companion when the seconds I wasted with this man brought those girls closer to danger. Luckily, he wasn't in a chatty mood either.

Out of Harlow we drove, veering on the express for Leighbridge. Two months ago, I couldn't afford the bus fare to Leighbridge. Fast-forward to me cruising through the borough, wearing belly dancer lingerie in the back of a limo.

How your life can change in one month. One night. With one turn around a corner.

The vehicle pulled up to the Imperial Majesty Hotel. A valet sprang forward to meet us, but a guard was already there.

Walking into the lobby was passing among elegance, class, and wealth made tangible. Palm fronds brushed their tips over my hair and shoulders. They reached down from the plant beds on either side of us, forming a living, green walkway. They led a path to reception, and at their back, a waterfall installation stretched to the ceiling. Crystal chandeliers spread shimmering light over the perfect picture.

This was the nicest place I'd ever seen, and I was including movies and television shows. Did Bryan take all of his trysts to places as nice as this?

Reception wasn't our destination. The two of us, and our circling cocoon of bodyguards, took the elevator up one floor and spilled out into a hallway. This one also filled with large pots of palms, cane plants, and tall trees.

I flicked between the cameras and the plants positioned by the room doors. *Makes sense now.*

A grand fancy hotel *for* trysts. If anyone checked these cameras, they'd have a hard time making out faces behind the shrubs.

"Beautiful hotel," I murmured.

Bryan squeezed my hand, and a passing thought came and went that Sinjin would likely kill for it. "I knew you would like it."

Did you?

The question almost popped out, but I held it back.

"This way, sir." The guard disappeared behind a tree and a soft chime echoed in the hall. "Room 204."

"Thank you."

Acker and I went in. Alone.

Cash's thinking that this was the best way to get close to him was sound.

Acker placed his phone next to the fruit bowl on the hall table.

I touched the tiny white pills concealed in my bra. *Now to see if part two of the plan goes as smoothly.*

"After you." Acker placed a hand on the small of my back, leading me into a haven as luxurious as the preamble promised. "What do you think?"

Designs had been molded into the walls, displaying dandelion petals through the air. I followed the floating seeds where they rounded the corner, and the king-size bed covered with fluffy white sheets lighter than dandelions became the sight to see.

Turning around, the space laid out before me. The minibar, dining table, and small fridge. Black-out curtains covered the windows. One set was tied back to reveal the balcony at the far end, and in the middle of everything, the floors gave way to a sunken living room—complete with a white leather sectional, big-screen television, and a coffee table where a bottle of wine was chilling in ice.

"It's perfect," I said. "Acker, how about we open a—"

He stepped into my path. "Call me Bry."

"Okay, Bry. Why don't we—"

A soft touch on my elbows stayed my words. He was close. Very close.

Undulating fingers caressed my arms reminiscent of running your hand over piano keys.

"Do you like my shirt?" he whispered.

"Y-yes," I croaked. *He thinks he's here for one thing in particular. Get to the wine and I'll put that dream to bed.*

"You've always liked me in red."

I frowned. Were we role-playing?

"Yes," I finally said. "Red suits you. It... brings out your eyes."

"Your eyes." Acker cupped my face. Reverence made his bronze pools shine. "You truly look just like her."

I cast about for how to get out of his embrace without raising suspicion. "Who?"

"My mother."

My mind ground to a dead halt—all function ceasing as two words tried and failed to be understood.

"I look like your mother?" I repeated slowly.

"Almost." Bryan darted off to the closet, and withdrew a pair of jeans and a plain button-up blouse. "Put this on. Mommy would never dress like that."

Mommy?

He advanced on me. The smile I previously thought charming morphed. "Put it on."

"Fine."

I took the clothes into the bathroom and changed, telling myself this outfit was better than sequin circus seductress. I told myself that and still my skin crawled doing up the final buttons. This man spent a year's salary for a night with his mom's clone. I did not want to find out why.

I came out of the bathroom and discovered Acker changed too. The red shirt remained, but the pants had been abandoned on the bedroom floor. In their place was a pair of tight white shorts that strained to cover an inch of his pale, hairy thighs, and suspenders.

"Mommy." The high-pitched little boy voice that came out of his mouth stood my hair on end. Acker slid off the couch onto his knees. "How was work?"

Flicking to the wine bottle, I moved closer and veered to put the table between us. Acker simply crawled around and planted himself at my feet. "It was good. Fun. Love what I do."

"Aren't you going to ask about my day at school?"

I closed on the bottle. "Ack— Bry, before we get started, why don't we have a glass of wine to relax?" The pills were heavy in my pocket. "White or red?"

Acker frowned. "Mommy, what are you talking about? Little boys can't drink wine."

"You—"

"Ask me about my day at school." The little boy voice dropped for a moment to let a hard edge in.

Frustration and discomfort made me want to scream. The girls were hiding twenty feet from the Kings, waiting for me to come for them. I did not have time for this!

Just play along. I'll be out of here soon.

Taking a deep breath, I plastered on a smile. "How was school, Bry?"

"Good," he said. "I got a hundred on my spelling test and Mrs. Tannen said I was the smartest boy in class." Acker started bouncing on the balls of his feet. "Aren't you proud of me?"

"So proud." An idea came to me. "Mommy is so proud, she's going to make you a special treat."

"Yay!" Acker nuzzled my thigh. "What kind of treat?"

I stumbled getting away from him. "Your favorite. Warm chocolate milk."

"That's not the treat I want."

Revulsion turned my stomach. No grown man should speak in that kind of voice while oozing such lust.

"*Part two is under new management, sweetie. It caters to a very different clientele.*"

"Good b-boys eat and drink what their mommies give them." The words cracked under my fight to not throw up. "If they do, they get more treats."

"Ooh. I want more treats."

I opened the minifridge. On the bottom shelf, mini cartons of white and chocolate milk lay side by side. I poured the chocolate in a glass.

My back to him, I loudly whistled over my spoon crushing the pills. The powder was tipped inside and the drink put in the microwave in the time it took Acker to crawl to my side.

"Almost done," I said brightly.

Acker turned me around, resuming his nuzzling. I glared at the microwave timer and willed it faster.

Beep. Be—

"Here we go." I moved to the couch if only to stop him touching me. He followed on his hands and knees, and then sat up to take the offered glass. "Drink your milk, Bry."

He looked from the glass to me. "Oh, I'll drink my milk." Holding my gaze, he smiled wide, and tipped the drink on the floor.

Acker launched at me. Shooting off his knees, he snatched my collar and ripped. Buttons pinged across the room with the echoes of my scream.

Sequin-covered breasts fell out of the torn blouse. Acker shoved it down and descended open-mouthed.

I dove away and he knocked off-balance, pitching forward. Moving fast, I twisted around and whacked him across the butt. Acker straightened and gaped at me in pure surprise.

"Bad," I barked. "Bad boys spill their milk and rip Mommy's favorite shirt. Do you know what happens to bad boys?"

"I..." Acker stalled like the script had been snatched from him and he didn't know what to do next. "They..."

"They're spanked." I pointed to the couch. "Assume the position right now, mister. Pants down."

"Yes, ma'am."

Acker nearly smacked himself in the face rushing to remove the suspenders and drop his pants. A rock-hard erection poked a hole in the cushion as he bent over the couch, wiggling his ass in excitement.

I thought fast—head whipping from the remains of the pills splattered on the floor to something, anything, that would get me out of here.

My gaze fell on the bottle of wine, and Sinjin's voice roared through my mind.

"I'd be concerned about this country's alcohol consumption if it didn't provide a handy weapon."

"I'm ready for my spanking, Mommy."

I grasped the neck, and the devil in my ear spoke again. *"Use it. Kill him."*

The gross costume was in tatters. My breasts sore from his eagerness leaving scratches. After one of the most horrific nights of my life—the three girls

I couldn't save and the girls I wasn't certain I did—this man forced me into his incest fantasy and assaulted me.

"*Kill him.*"

I jumped on the couch, bottle raised high, and smashed it over his head. Countless shatters burst apart on his skull, showering the floor in glass raindrops.

Acker slumped over the back. Unconscious.

"Sir?" A faint voice came through the door. "Sir, is everything alright?"

I snapped up and tumbled off the seat. I hit the floor hard.

"Sir, I'm coming in."

Time had run out.

Scrambling to my feet, I raced to the hall table and grabbed the phone as the door chimed open. The heels clomped my retreat, stamping on the tile too slow to pace my thudding heart.

"Wha— Hey!"

I fell on the door to the balcony as thunderous footfalls sounded behind me.

"Stop!"

Cold, whipping air blew tears in my eyes. I seized the ledge, vaulted over, and fell to the unforgiving earth below.

Screaming, I dropped past an open window and the shocked couple inside. Brambles caught me. The bushes extracted payment for saving my life, tearing gashes on my arms and cheek. There wasn't a part of me that didn't hurt. I forced the pain down and pushed myself up.

"Don't move," the guards shouted. The clicks of half a dozen safeties going off were heard amid the couple in the window's squawking. "Stay right there, bitch!"

"I don't appreciate being called a bitch by the dickless minions of a pervert!" I took off running, bullets peppering the ground behind me. "Go spank your boss's ass!"

I veered around the building, leaving their threats behind.

Exposed. Bleeding. Chest heaving like I ran for a century. I was a terrifying specter exploding into the dignified, elegant scene.

Those that didn't run away shrieking, demanded to know what happened and if I was okay. I ignored them, kicked off the cursed heels, and ran across the drive, scattering millionaires in my wake.

Where are you? Where are you?!

"Redgrave?" Cash materialized from the shadows under the awning. "What the fuck happened to you? Did Acker do this?" Cash drew his gun so fast, it pulled me up short and I almost dropped on my ass. "Where is he?"

"Cash, no. Forget him. He doesn't matter." I fell into his arms, adrenaline deserting me short of the final stretch. "We have to get to Marco's Pizza now."

MY ARRIVAL DREW ALL eyes to me. Running inside wearing Cash's oversized coat and screaming, "Kaylee," would do that.

"Kaylee?"

"Check the bathroom," said Cash, coming in behind me.

I was moving by the end of the sentence. Throwing open the door, I stopped at the threshold and swept the room. There were three stalls, each one hanging open.

"Kaylee, are you here?" I whispered. "Please, be here."

A small hand gripped the frame, and then a blinking eye followed. "You came."

My knees gave out. I dropped to the floor, arms flying open to catch her. "Of course, I came," I sobbed. "Where are the other girls?"

Kaylee shook her head in the crook of my neck. "They wouldn't come with me. Ilona said she didn't trust you. She can take care of her sister by herself. She told me to go with them, but I didn't go."

I shut my eyes, heart squeezing. "That's okay. I'll find them if I can. Make sure they're safe. Let's get out of here." I stood to leave, holding her hand. The door opened.

Kaylee saw Cash, and ripped free. Crying, she ran in the stall.

"Kaylee, no, it's okay. He won't hurt you."

Honestly, she couldn't be blamed for thinking otherwise. Free of his coat, Cash's well-built physique of rippling muscles and tattoos were on full display. Clinging tighter to him than the white Henley shirt was the leather gun holster. But none of that was what struck true fear.

The sub-zero frost in those harder-than-gold eyes would frighten anyone who had witnessed that coldness in the ruthless gangbangers who beat, terrorized, and sold her.

A ruthless gangbanger like Cash himself.

But as I got on my knees, reaching for her again, I spoke knowing deep down everything I said was true. "Cash would never hurt you. He'll protect us, and take us somewhere safe."

His weight thumped the ground. Cash was on his knees. "That's right, Kaylee. You don't have to be afraid of me, and to prove it"—Cash placed his gun in my hand—"Adeline will hold on to this."

Kaylee poked her head out.

"If I do anything you don't like, she'll kill me."

An extraordinary thing to say to a child, but Kaylee looked at me, eyes seeking, and I nodded.

Kaylee came out of the stall.

She took my hand, and together, the three of us left.

"WHAT IS THIS PLACE?" I asked softly.

Kaylee wasn't sleeping. Her head rested on my lap and the blanket Cash gave us wrapped her up warm, but she was wide awake. Still, I spoke barely above a whisper. The energy needed to do more left me hours ago.

"It's my apartment."

A better description would have been loft, and topping that, would have been luxury downtown art gallery doubling as a living space.

City light streamed in through a wall of windows. For the other three walls, their beauty lay in the portraits, paintings, canvasses, and prints covering the exposed brick. They demanded all the attention, and therefore, the rest of the décor was simple. The couch we sat on. The coffee table, rug, dining table, and the kitchen accompaniments. That was all.

"You have your own apartment? Then, why do you live in the station?"

Cash moved around the kitchen, taking things in and out of the fridge. "My alias is on the lease, but all of us use this as a safe house."

He set a sandwich and glass of milk on the coffee table. Kaylee immediately dug in.

She gave me the okay to return his gun a while ago. She trusted him. Trusted us. And as we waited for the Merchants to arrive, she had told us her story.

Cash returned from the kitchen carrying a first aid kit. "Come here."

I didn't fight him. Getting up, I settled on a dining chair and let him tend to my cuts.

"How did you get these?" he asked, not letting his voice carry.

"Jumped off a second-story balcony into a bush." The toneless voice that came from my mouth didn't belong to me. "How did you get that?"

Cash followed my line of sight to a jagged scar on his arm. "Sinjin. We got into it over something stupid and he stabbed me. He was wild in his teen years."

"Was?"

The dim lights didn't allow me to be sure, but I thought I caught a grin.

"Did Acker hurt you?"

I definitely imagined the grin. No one could follow a smile with the menace leaking from his pores.

"No. I ran from the bodyguards that burst in after I smashed a wine bottle over his head, not from him."

"I will hear the full account of tonight." His gentle touch was at odds with his voice. "Then I'll determine what happens to Bryan Acker and his guards."

I said nothing. What was there to say?

His movements were steady and sure bandaging me up. Exactly as I would've expected from a doctor. The unexpected was the effect he was having on me. The places he touched soaked in his warmth—drawing it deep into myself.

Cash turned over my hand to treat a cut on my palm. I closed over him, lacing my fingers through his.

Twice I'd place his expression as he looked at our hands as curious. But he didn't move. And I didn't speak.

We sat there for a while. Until Kaylee got up.

Cash stood too, sliding out of my grip. "I'll find her some clothes," he said. "She can shower and then get some sleep. The guys are on their way."

I nodded. Tears prickled behind my eyes, and I couldn't say why.

"Thanks, Cash."

"You're a wild card, Redgrave," he replied, walking off. "I would be an idiot if I hadn't assumed something like this would happen."

"WHAT CAN I SAY? I PROMISED life with our bunny would be interesting."

A chin rested on my forehead. Sinjin drew me out of the way, and closed the sliding door on the sleeping eleven-year-old.

"What happened?"

I faced them.

Mercer reclining on the couch. Cash leaning on the window. Brutal a silent figure by the table. And Sinjin—eyes level and serious like I'd rarely seen.

"The auction," I seemed to say. The voice that spoke was still not mine. "That's what happened. Whatever it was, it's not that anymore. Hasn't been for a long time. They cater to *different clientele* now."

Mercer leaned forward, brows drawing together. "What does that mean?"

"It means Corbin tried to sell that little girl to the highest bidder."

"Sell—"

"Yes, sell! Her and two other girls I managed to get out of there, but I don't know where they are." I threw out my hands. "I don't know where they are, or the other three I couldn't help. They're gone, Saint!" I whirled on him. "They could be anywhere in the city with people who are doing fuck knows what to them."

"Adeline—"

"It's not the first time." Tears soaked my cheeks. "The deep shame of everyone behind that stage made it clear they've seen more children than they can live with put on that stage."

He reached for me. I ducked his touch, advancing on Cash.

"I couldn't make out the people in the crowd. I got a glimpse when I came in, but onstage, the lights blinded me. All I know is the bidder numbers for the ones who took the first three girls. Ninety-one. Forty-seven. Twelve," I counted on my fingers. "We have to find out who they are, and get them back."

"Corbin's the one who will have that information," Cash said.

"Then we get him!" I fumbled at my pocket. "I have the phone. This is what you needed to take them down. I got it." I forced it on his palm, closing his fingers on it. "I couldn't go without it, because you're going to stop them."

Saint grasped my shoulders, setting me on the couch. I stopped his retreat.

My nails cut piercing tracks that didn't elicit a flinch.

"Tell me you are."

"We will, Adeline. Their crowns will be wiped clean off the street."

Strike.

"Their businesses smoldering ash."

Strike.

"Their men cemetery fodder."

Strike.

"The Kings are finished in this city."

The final blow landed and Adeline Redgrave fell.

"Then I'm in."

"In?" Cash repeated.

"I'm in the Merchants. I'm in with you," I told Sinjin. "I'll be your bride. I'll perch on your throne. If you're destroying those sick, child-trafficking bastards, I'm going to be a part of it."

"You understand we don't do anonymous police tips," Mercer said. "We don't give warnings and we don't show mercy. If we find the people who took those girls, they will die in a manner violent serial killers would call excessive."

The phantom hand squeezed my breaking wrist.

"Sure you want to be a part of this?" Sinjin swept over the assembled men. "Of us?"

My gaze was steady, and the voice that replied, was mine. "I'm in."

A normal man would've showed disbelief. A moral man shock and outrage. But a blue-haired demon was neither of those things.

A grin curled into Sinjin's cheeks, wide and beaming.

"Welcome aboard. Want a nickname? I'm still partial to Bunny."

Adeline Redgrave fell.

And the person who rose in her place was new, unnamed, and masked.

COLD SEEPED INTO MY thighs. A bitter replacement for the heat the concrete floor was stealing from me. I could've gotten up. Returned to the bed made of pillows and blankets in the living room.

I swiped another finger through my treat and licked it clean.

A figure moved in the darkness.

"When the Brutal's away, the mouse will play." Mercer appeared above the kitchen bar. "Naughty."

"Ever notice how much better food tastes when you eat it with your hands?" I scooped more icing as proof.

"Can't say I have."

"Try it yourself."

To my surprise, Mercer got on the floor next to me. He cupped his hand over mine and tasted the chocolate buttercream. "Mmm. You might be onto something."

"Yeah," I whispered.

It was just the three of us. Mercer slept on the couch and Sinjin tucked me in under him. At some point in the night, I slipped out and found my way here.

"There was nothing you could've done, Adeline. You know that, right?"

My grip tightened on the plastic. "I should've stopped him."

"You did stop him."

"Not before he sold three girls like exactly what they called them. Items. *Objects*."

"He had a gun. You thought fast, came up with a plan, and took him down anyway. You got Kaylee and the others out."

"Two girls, one of them eight years old, are spending a night on the streets because it took me so long to get back to them," I said. "We can do this all night, Mercer. I don't deserve praise."

"I think Kaylee would disagree."

I turned away. Mercer grasped my chin.

The crushingly beautiful face. His hands on my skin. Chocolate and woodsy cologne. All of him became my world.

"We'll find them, Adeline. As of tonight, Corbin's out of business."

"Why?" The question I'd burned to ask sprang forth. "Cash said they bring in millions. They have wealthy patrons and the illusion they're gentlemen gangbangers. Why trade it in for the filth I stepped into tonight?"

"It's possible Angelo doesn't know what Corbin's doing. He handed him the auction, which is the least profitable part of the business. Overall, the escorts make the Kings a lot of money, but not Corbin himself. They set up the auction so the house gets a cut, but it's a seventy-thirty split favoring the talent. Or it was that way," he said. "I suspect the split favors Corbin now. And as for the children..."

"He gets it all."

"Yes."

"Money. It always comes back to that."

"We assumed Candy knew more than she did," he said. "If we'd known, tonight would have gone down very differently."

"Would it?" I gave him a hard look. "Everyone is afraid of the Kings. Even the Merchants or you wouldn't be skulking around, making plans, and using me. If you'd known they were auctioning children off to the highest bidder tonight, would you have busted in, masks on and guns blazing?"

"Yes."

I halted. My rant lost steam before it got started. "You would?"

"Yes. Consent is everything in my business, Adeline. Plus, we've made ourselves clear on how we feel about rape. All four of us would have done the same thing you did tonight. With one exception."

"What's that?" I rasped.

"Felix wouldn't have walked out of that bathroom alive."

"Oh."

"But there's a reason we didn't know," he continued. "Sex trafficking is a nasty racket, and even among the criminal masses, we want nothing to do with those twisted fucks messing with kids. If it got out the Kings are involved in this, they'd still have fear, but they'd lose their respect. That loss comes at a higher cost than you'd believe."

The hand cupping me and the frosting hadn't moved. I didn't want it to. Slowly the poison was leeching out, and I couldn't bear for him to stop.

"You've made the first strike, Adeline, and it's given us the means to ruin them. So if in the back of your mind you're convinced we'll lose this fight and those girls, you can tell that voice to shut the fuck up."

A laugh startled out of me. Part-sob, but still a laugh.

"Hey." Mercer brushed his nose on my cheek, turning me to him on the strength of his touch alone. "You've got the full force of the Merchants behind you on this one. Why wouldn't you? You're one of us."

"Yes, I am." I rested on his shoulder. "Thank you."

Did Mercer know he said everything I needed to hear? Did he say it for that reason? To loosen the knot of pain and trauma I buried years ago.

I burrowed deeper into his side.

Maybe he did spin sweet words to soothe me. What mattered is it worked, and above all, I would make his predictions reality.

Together we scooped another finger of icing. "Hey. What did you mean by consent is everything in your business? What do you do?"

He replied around a mouthful of chocolate. "I'm a whore, love."

I choked. "A what?"

"A whore. Manwhore. Escort. Gigolo if you're feeling old school. Boy toy if you're not." Mercer bent his neck, grinning into my slack jaw and bulging eyes. "Ah. There's the reaction I was looking for."

SAINT

I ran my fingers through her hair. Licked her cheek. Fit her body to mine.

Since the night before when Adeline said she'd perch on my throne, I hadn't been able to keep my hands off her. I'd have fucked her right then and there but she said we couldn't with the kid in the next room.

Speaking of which.

I glanced around Adeline and saw the kid was staring at me again. She was pretty average as kids go. Long brown hair and big moon eyes set in a face plump from adolescence.

"What?"

"Why is your hair blue?"

"Why is your hair brown?"

She giggled. "I'm serious."

"My hair turned blue because I ate too many vegetables. Don't listen to adults. That stuff is bad for you."

Her eyes bugged. "Really?"

"No." Adeline gave me a look. "Don't listen to *him*. Veggies are yummy and they make you strong." Adeline finished chopping the carrots as if to illustrate her point. "You'll love my vegetable stir-fry. I'm famous for it."

I shook my head behind her back, drawing a line across my neck. The kid ducked her head, giggling again, and proved to me at least part of the story she told Adeline the night before was true. Last night was her first time on the auction block. No one had gotten the chance yet to wipe the smile permanently from her face.

The six of us were in the Leighbridge safe house. A bare-bones loft we converted out of an abandoned warehouse. There was one bed and one bathroom, but taking the kid to the fire station was out of the question. There was an entire room filled with dangerous weapons. We weren't entirely irresponsible.

Besides, if half of what Adeline told us of the night before was true, lying low and planning was our next move.

Mercer and Cash were on the couch arguing in low tones. The phone sat on the table between them. Adeline and I were in the kitchen. Brutal was cleaning. And our newest guest kicked her feet under the breakfast bar while she resumed her staring challenge.

"What's your name, kid?" I pulled up the chair next to her. I knew this too but I wanted to hear it from her. Adeline was set on her path. What the kid told me would determine mine.

"Kaylee Trevino. What's yours?"

"St. John Bellisario."

"Like a real saint?"

"I have been called that."

Adeline mumbled something under her breath.

"How old are you?"

"Eleven."

I nodded. *Adeline said the youngest was eight. What the fuck are the Kings into?*

"How old are you?"

Amused, I replied, "Twenty-eight."

Adeline handed her a plate of vegetables to snack on. She nibbled on a carrot despite my warnings.

"Have you met the guys?" I asked.

Kaylee pointed. "That's Cash, but his real name is Killian. Addy will shoot him if he does anything I don't like."

"Good deal. Keep her on standby."

Cash flipped me off without pausing in his speech.

"See?" I snapped my fingers at Bunny. "Take care of him."

"Oh my gosh, guys," she cried. "It is hitting me how unqualified you all are to be around children."

I grinned. Adeline was quickly adopting her old self.

Good. The woman crying and shaking last night had my sympathy, but she wouldn't do. If Adeline's going to be at our side as the city burned, I wanted the fearless, back-talking wolf in bunny's fur. Only she would survive what was coming next, and the ultimate end goal:

Kieran.

"That's Mercer Santos," Kaylee went on. "Mercer bought these for me." Kaylee showed off her new shirt. First on the list was buying her clothes and burning that dress. Literally. I lit a fire in a garbage can that morning and tossed it in.

"He's nice," she said.

Brutal emerged from the bedroom, gloves on and loaded down with cleaner.

"I don't know who he is," she whispered. "Do you know him?"

"Barely."

"What's his name?"

"Ask him."

"Excuse me," she called. "What's your name?"

Adeline broke in. "Kaylee, Brutal doesn't—"

"Baris." Brutal peeled off his gloves and shook her hand. "Baris Alexander."

I slid a look to Adeline, whose hanging jaw made both of us laugh out loud. Brutal winked at her.

"Where are your folks, Kaylee?"

Kaylee dropped her head, fists balling on her lap. "My mom is dead."

I waited for more. None came.

"And your dad?"

She tossed her head, brown hair swinging.

"Is he a good guy?"

"No. He's not." Her voice was getting smaller and smaller. "He sold me."

"Saint." Warning laced Adeline's tone.

I focused on the kid. "Do you want to see your dad again?"

"No." A whisper, but a firm one.

"Would you like new parents?"

That made her lift her chin. "What?"

"New folks," I repeated. "A foster mom and dad. Nice couple. Will keep you fed and never raise a hand to you. They travel around the country. Love playing games. And they've got a ridiculous number of kids for you to play with. You'll never be alone, and like Bunny, they'll take out anyone who tries to mess with you. What do you think? Interested?"

She stared at me.

"If you are, I'll make it happen."

"You can do that?"

"I can." I looked past her. "Cash, when will they get here?"

"Called this morning. They'll be here in a week."

I clapped. "There you have it. New foster parents coming in a week. You can meet them first, of course, then say the word and they're yours."

"Mine? But I don't know them. Who are they?"

"I can vouch for them." I tapped my chest. "They're the people who took me in."

Kaylee looked around at us. She stopped on Adeline.

She held the knife and celery but had ceased chopping long ago.

"Do I have to go? Can't I... stay with you?"

Adeline came around the counter. "We're going to figure out the best situation for you together," she said. "You won't go anywhere that you don't want to go. I promise."

Kaylee's tiny shoulders relaxed. "Okay."

"But this isn't the time to talk about this," Adeline hissed at me. "I don't know these people either."

I tucked Adeline between my legs, securing her around the waist. "It's cool having you with us," I said, "but it can't be forever."

Adeline's glare drilled a hole in my head, but it had to be said. No use getting the kid's hopes up.

"Soon, Adeline, Mercer, Cash, Brutal, and I will be busy hunting down the men your father sold you to, and stopping them from ever doing something so stupid again."

"You are?"

"We are," I said. "It'll be dangerous. We'll be gone all day and most of the night. Some nights we won't come home at all. School, friends, and foster parents kicks sitting in an empty station by yourself for hours."

Kaylee nodded, lips trembling.

"Hey." I tipped her chin. "I'm telling you this because you and Adeline will find the best place for you, and when you make your choice, you'll have the truth. You can handle the truth, right?"

She said nothing for a stretch. "You're going to stop the bad men who took me? The men who hurt Ilona, and sold the others?"

"Yes."

"Then I can handle the truth. Addy has to help the other girls. She can't take care of just me."

Adeline squeezed her hand. "We're not making any decisions today. When *I* know what's true, we'll talk about it."

"Do you know how you'll stop the bad men?" Kaylee asked me.

"We'll find the rats where they hide," I answered, "poison their cheese, and flush them out. Works every time."

"Good."

"You can help us."

She sat up straight. "I can? How?"

"If you told us the names of the other girls and what they looked like, that would help." Cash and Mercer stopped arguing to listen in. "Also, the place the men kept you. What was it like?"

"It was really nice. A hotel," she said. "I didn't know it was a bad place until it was too late."

"A hotel." Mercer, Cash, Brutal, and I shared a look over her head. "That's perfect, Kaylee. You don't know how much this helps."

"Kaylee, want to help me make lunch?" Adeline asked.

The young girl hopped off the stool and skipped after her. I let her go.

My decision was made.

The Kings changed the rules, and now there were none.

Plan A was out. Plan B was in.

I preferred plan B anyway. There was a lot more blood.

Chapter Eleven

A*deline*
"Smile," Sinjin said. "She's watching you."

I glanced up. A band of acrobats jumped, swung, flipped, and soared through the air. An incredible performance that earned gasps, aahs, oohs, and "holy craps" from the audience. But Kaylee wasn't looking at them anymore. She was looking at me.

"If you're unsure about this, she will be too."

"I am unsure," I said under my breath. "We didn't consider child services. What if they can find her a nice family?"

"Cinco's foster care system is shit even when I'm not making a point to a traitorous bastard," Sinjin said. "You can bet Corbin is looking for the girls who got away. If they put the word out there's money in it, her foster parents could get in their heads that she's worth more in the Kings' hands than in theirs. The safest place for her is out of the city."

Sinjin was right. We had this conversation many times, and each time I agreed this was best.

But she is the one I saved. The only one. I have to know she'll be okay.

"What are you worried about? I told you they adopted me after I left the church," said my son of a priest. "And look how I turned out. She's in good hands."

Heaving a sigh, I didn't bother to touch that one. Sinjin maintained that the couple we were going to meet was good to him. He had no reason to lie, but the fact remained Sinjin's ideas of good and bad didn't match normal society.

I said as much.

"Now that I'm here, the picture of you gets clearer. You're the one with the storied past," I said. "It's not every day someone runs away and joins the circus."

He chuckled. "Happens more than you think."

The performance ended on his cryptic note. The six of us tromped down the stands. Kaylee slipped her hand in Sinjin's halfway down. I hid a smile.

A week had passed since that awful night. A week the five of us had holed up in the warehouse loft making new plans and taking care of Kaylee. That they were unqualified to look after children was still true. I walked in on Cash teaching her how to take apart and reassemble a gun. But the guys were good with her in their own way.

Brutal let her help him clean, and when he went back to do it properly, he didn't let her see. Mercer entertained her with books and games. Sinjin's cracks about his people skills came into new light.

Sinjin himself kept up his baffling charm with children. His dry, twisted humor had her giggling for hours. The other night I woke up to Kaylee slipping between us in our makeshift bed. She put her head on Sinjin's chest and fell asleep like she'd done it many times.

Cash remained neither chatty nor warm, but when she asked, he repeated his promise to find the other girls and stop the men who bought her. Permanently.

A promise I'll keep. No matter what it takes.

The sun pierced Cinco's autumn chill, granting us an unseasonably warm day. Perfect timing for Merriman Circus to arrive. Which they did in a big way. Cinco Fairgrounds went from an empty patch of grass to multicolored tents, clowns, acrobats, carnival games, food stands, stilt-walkers, and unicyclers as far as the eye could see.

"Margot and Troy own the circus," Sinjin had told me. "They've taken in more than a few runaways over the years. They're good people, Adeline. Kaylee will like it here."

Cash handed Kaylee a twenty-dollar bill. "See those kids over there?" He gestured to a girl and two boys running around the cotton candy stand. "Challenge them to the balloon toss. Whoever wins feeds Elsie."

The Elsie in question was the eight-thousand-pound elephant grazing on the edge of the fairgrounds. Kaylee was off and running at them in a blink.

We followed behind at a distance, parting the crowd of families and performers. All of us did. Mercer, Brutal, Cash, and Saint fanned around me—silent and blank-faced.

"You sent Kaylee away for a reason," I spoke up. "What is it? Finally ready to tell me our next move?"

"Yes," Cash said. "We couldn't sooner because the kid was attached to your hip, or did you want her to hear the details of how we're breaking into Paradise tonight and having a chat with Corbin?"

I stopped dead in the muddy grass. "Tonight?"

"Can't afford to wait longer," Mercer said. "The others might have covered for you, but taking out Bryan Acker gave you away. After he woke up, I assume he demanded his money back—plus other things. It wasn't a leap that the girl smashing clients over the head, took out one of their guys. By the way," he said, grinning. "Did you really tell his guards to fuck off and spank their boss's ass?"

My cheeks warmed. "Yes. It was a heated situation."

"Priceless." Chuckling, he wandered close and bumped my shoulder. "Speaking of Acker, I should tell you that he remotely wiped the phone. We can't intercept that text for Angelo's location."

"So, I jumped out of a window and was almost killed for nothing." I squeezed my eyes shut. "It's my fault. You said to download the program, not steal it. Of course, he wiped the phone."

"It's not your fault," he said, brushing a flying strand behind my ear. "You had to act quickly. Besides, it wasn't a complete loss. I read his texts before the wipe. There's an unknown number that texts an address every Friday night. Twenty messages from that number and all a different place, but figuring out what they have in common can help us narrow our search."

"That's something at least," I said.

"Something we'll worry about after dealing with Corbin. Who knows, Corbin might answer the question for us."

"How are we dealing with Corbin?"

"Head-on. Right now, the Kings have no reason to think Felix's attack and the girls going missing was more than a crisis of conscience," Cash continued. "But Corbin's not an idiot. He'll take steps to make sure this doesn't happen again."

"What kind of steps?" I asked.

"If it was me," Sinjin said, "I'd move the auction and the girls. If you ever came back, it'd be to an empty hole. Assuming you survived the hit I put out on you."

A fist clenched in my chest. "Corbin's going to move them? Kaylee told us everything she knew about the hotel. It was the only place she was brought to. If he moves them and disappears, we'll have nothing."

"I said that's what I'd do," Saint replied. "As tight as the Kings are, information gets out. This didn't. Corbin's kept a close lid on this. Twice weekly dates with Candy and she didn't know. It's a good bet Angelo doesn't either. Packing up the operation and moving would tip his hand."

"He'd have to explain why or risk the higher-ups taking a closer look into his activities," I finished. "A sociopathic child peddler that's addicted to money wouldn't chance it."

"There's no gain on him putting a hit on you either," Cash added. "Corbin doesn't give a shit about Bryan Acker, and the Kings don't need the world knowing a one-hundred-and-fifteen-pound woman in heels beat their guy with a toilet seat."

"Okay," I said. "Then, what steps is he taking?"

"More guards. More guns. No one in or out that he doesn't know. The back door Kaylee escaped through was jammed by cinderblocks. Our men have staked it out over the past few days. The blocks were replaced with a metal bar and two guys pretending to look casual while they pace in front of it."

My head bobbed slowly as I gazed at Kaylee laughing and playing with the children. "I get it, Cash. The time for costumes, aliases, and slipping in unnoticed is over. The only way to get to Corbin... is to attack."

"Also known as plan B," Saint said. "Full-frontal assault. Open season on the Kings and their businesses. War in the streets, Bunny." He swooped on me, stealing a devastating, ravaging kiss that plumbed the depths of my mouth and pulled a moan from me like I didn't know where I was. "Personally," he said, "I preferred plan B from the start."

"Except the small, but significant issue that I projected one or more of us will die before this is over," Cash said, matter of fact. "Ninety nine point nine percent probability."

"Die?" I recovered from the effects of the kiss quickly. "You can't know—"

"Outgunned, outmanned, and fighting on their turf. It's near enough to a certainty, Redgrave. We can win, but we all won't live to share the spoils."

My jaw clenched. Nostrils flared sucking in short, rapid breaths. I trusted Cash's projections like I did my common sense. Of course, we couldn't enter a war with the toughest gang in Cinco and come out unscathed. My anger and fear wasn't for me.

I narrowed on each man in turn. "What's in this for you? The night you killed Spencer, you said you were 'laying the foundation for big moves that will one day see the Kings whimpering pups at our feet, and the Merchants running Cinco City.' You have your sights set higher than the Kings, but I'm supposed to believe you're willing to die before they're reached?"

Cash spun on me, pulling me up short. "What are you trying to say, Redgrave? Out with it."

"What's the double play? The Merchants plan to rule the city, not die in some underground shithole. I want those girls back. I'll do *anything* to save them," I shouted. "Even if it means I die. Will you? What if we break in there and Corbin hands you plan C wrapped in a pretty bow? You leave him to his business and he helps you bring down Angelo. Would you take it?"

"No."

"No?"

"No," Cash barked.

Mercer's stare was unblinking. The easy grin had vanished. "No."

Sinjin just looked at me, expression saying it all. Then Brutal— Baris gripped Cash's shoulder, moving him to the side.

"No."

That almost inaudible whisper—said to gift my ears only—broke me. My anger leaked out, leaving me the tired, stressed-out mess I was.

"Why is this important to you?" I asked. This time without accusation.

"We told Spencer that night and we'll tell you," Sinjin said. "We will rule this city. The sex." He pointed to Mercer.

"The fight clubs." Brutal.

"The money." Cash.

"And all the rest." Sinjin spread out his hands. "Cinco is mine, and it will exist under our law. The most important being that no one who fucks with kids should expect a long-life expectancy. None of our men will be in that racket. Seeing as every gang in the near future will report to us or be put down, they might as well learn that lesson now."

"I agree." I cupped his cheek. "Under our law, Cinco will change."

"OVER HERE."

Cash motioned to a trailer bordering the fence of the fairground. Saint drew ahead. He climbed the stairs and let himself in.

These are the people who had a hand rearing Sinjin Bellisario. I glanced down at the girl holding my hand. "Are you nervous?"

"A little," she said. "But I like Nova, Dawson, and Jude. They said if I stay, we'll be cousins. I never had cousins."

"They said that?"

Twisting, I fell on the kids Cash told her to play with. They were running and skipping behind us, going along for the ride.

"They're homeschooled," she said. "Every day they get to be here with the animals and shows and games. Nova is already learning to fly like the acrobats."

"Sounds like every kid's dream. Ready to meet Margot and Troy?"

She steeled herself. Chin lifted and shoulders squared. "I'm ready."

Voices floated out of the trailer. "... boys been? Would it kill you to call more?"

"It's been a hectic time at work," I heard Cash say.

"Must be if lost little ones are falling in your lap. Where is she?"

"She's here," I spoke up. Together, we stepped inside the trailer.

The only word I could use to describe it was quaint. Photos in big, clunky frames covered the walls. We walked in on them in the kitchen/dining area. The kitchen space was small, and yet they managed to blanket it with green. Plants hung from the ceiling, sending winding tendrils from their pots. Handmade, knitted chair covers decorated the seats, and sitting on them was an older blond couple.

The man who had to be Troy carried his rugged looks and full head of hair into middle age. His eyes crystal blue and lined with wrinkles. He stroked a beard more silver than blond, nodding at Kaylee.

"Hello."

Margot's long, waist-length hair bled darker than her husband's. She wrapped herself in a shawl matching the color and style of the chair covers, looking like a cozy extension of her home.

First impression not so bad.

"This is Kaylee Trevino," I said.

Kaylee burrowed her face in my side, suddenly shy.

"None of that." Margot bent at the waist, smiling as she drew her away from me. "No need to be afraid of a couple of old carnies." Traces of a European accent laced her speech. "Especially when they have cookies. How about we sit down, have a snack, and get to know each other? That sound all right?"

"Okay."

Margot straightened to guide her to the table and I got a proper look at her.

"Oh my— Mrs. Margot, are you...?" Golden-brown eyes blinked at me. "Killian's mother?"

She laughed. "Last time I checked."

"You raised Sinjin?"

"Caught the little waif under the bleachers pickpocketing the audience," Troy said. "Fourteen years old and scored about eight hundred dollars before we nabbed him."

I goggled at Sinjin and Cash—both standing there eating cookies like it was nothing. "You enjoy this, don't you? First Baris and now a parent trap."

"Excuse me?" Margot looked to *her* boys. "Is something wrong?"

"Nothing's wrong, Mom," Cash said.

"Absolutely nothing," I agreed, following her and Kaylee to the cookies. "I have so much to ask you. What was Killian like as—"

"No." Cash put me over his shoulder. "We'll give you space," he told his parents. "Take a few hours. We'll check in before we go."

"Go on, dear," Margot said. "We'll be just fine."

Cash carried me outside.

"Uncle Killian! Uncle Sinjin!" Dawson, Nova, and Jude ran at us. "I wanna play. Pick me up too."

"Uncle," I said into his back. "You have siblings too?"

"Five. Not including Sinjin."

"Unbelievable. Where are they? I'm meeting them."

"You already did. At the acrobats show, cotton candy stand, the unicyclist, and two of the tightrope walkers. That's all the introduction you need."

The kids, the colors, the carnival, the family reunion I didn't know I walked into, and Kaylee telling us she wished to stay felt like fate's gift before the storm. As the sun set on the empty fairgrounds, I hugged Kaylee tight, whispering promises we'd talk every day and I would visit her wherever she was.

"Will you guys visit too?" she asked.

"Won't have to," said Sinjin. "You'll come to me. Merriman Circus rolls through Cinco four times a year."

Kaylee threw her arms around him. "Bye, Saint. I'll miss you."

The others got the same goodbye.

Kaylee came back to me, pressing her cheek to mine, and said, "Thanks for coming for me."

"I will again if you need me." I placed a new cellphone in her hand. "Remember what I said."

She looked in my eyes. Small. Young. Strong. "They can't take what matters."

"No one can. Goodbye, Kaylee."

I cried on the walk through the grounds. For Kaylee. For me. For the girls out there who thought no one was coming.

The guys walked silently at my side.

"She'll be happy, won't she?"

"Yes," said Cash.

"Were you?"

"Yes." He was a firm, towering presence amid the ghost of his childhood. "The man I became is a reflection on Sinjin, not Troy and Margot Hunt. He's a terrible influence."

A snort escaped me unbidden. I laced my arms around his, dropping my head on his shoulder. Maybe the happy family he left behind still had their effect on him, because he let me. "Hard to disagree considering what I'm about to do."

I met Sinjin's gaze. "Let's take that bastard down."

THAT NIGHT, I KISSED Sinjin on the steps of the fire station.

We had to come back. Change. Reload.

"Know what to do?"

"My role is pretty straightforward."

"Stick to the plan." Sinjin's hand was warm and heavy on my chest. "All of this..."

He moved down. Cupping my breast. Tweaking the nipple through the fabric. Flattening against my stomach. Then gripping my thigh to draw me in.

"... is mine. If you're hurt, I will do something others regret."

I brushed my lips on his chin. Wetness collected in my middle. "Is that your way of saying be careful?"

Sinjin kissed me again. He got into his car, and drove off alone. Another layer of security. The Merchants arrived to jobs separately. They lead different teams of their men. They tried to take Sinjin in once. They wouldn't show up as a group for the bags to be thrown over their heads in one go.

Cash left. Mercer honked his way out. Brutal and I were left.

He stood next to a silver Lexus. Spotless, of course. Brutal opened the door on my approach.

"Are you being a gentleman, or do you not want my fingerprints on your ride, Baris?"

We weren't running late. Our destination was a bar two doors down from Paradise, where we'd wait for our clocks to strike one.

I put my hands over his. "Can I say something?" I asked softly. "Can I say it because you won't ask questions? Because you won't interrupt and you won't tell a soul? Can I say it because I'm selfish? I want you to share this burden in silence, because I can't anymore.

"Can I?" I rasped.

He nodded.

"My name is not Adeline."

His brows twitched. The barest reaction.

"It is, but it wasn't supposed to be. I was meant to be Madeline. After my grandmother. My mom was so high when she filled out the form, she forgot the M." I laughed mirthlessly. "That should give some insight into where this story is going."

Lowering my head, I rested them on our hands. "My parents weren't a couple. A random party, drugs, drinks, and an empty bed upstairs brought me into the world. This suited my mother. Dad had money, influence, and a sense of honor. The latter doesn't always come with the first two. He was a baby daddy who'd set her up in style and pay child support on time.

"We had a nice apartment in Waterford. A car. A checking account. And Mom could afford her habit without choosing between the drugs and feeding me. Everything was perfect for her until Dad lost his job. There was an accident at work, and his coworker and best friend was killed. Afterward, new management took over, fired every boss and supervisor, and hired new people.

"Suddenly, there was no money for the nice apartment, car, and bottomless credit cards." I paused, taking a deep breath, and caught a tear on my tongue. I hadn't realized I was crying. "Dad got a job. He got three jobs. He killed himself trying to support me, and Gianna," I said. "She was his best friend's kid. He couldn't abandon her when he knew Soren would've taken care of me if the roles were reversed.

"But Mom didn't like that," I cried, rocking on my heels. "She'd shout at him that we were his priority, and if she didn't get more money, she'd take away his visitation.

"It wasn't about his priorities, of course. It was about hers. She couldn't hold down a job, and when the money dried up, she carried out her threat. Packed up and moved us in the middle of the night. She refused to let him near me. By that point, it was bad," I whispered. "She had to choose between drugs and feeding me. Most times she chose wrong.

"One day when I was ten, I heard her arguing with her dealer in the living room. I tuned them out. Headphones in and pillow over my head like I always did. Until my mattress dipped."

Brutal's finger lifted. He glided down my wet cheek, spreading my tears.

"From that day on, Mom realized she didn't need money. She needed dealers who liked kids. It went on... for a while. When Dad tracked me down and found out what was happening, he took me away from her on the spot. We didn't return to the apartment to get my things. Ever since, it's been him and me. Looking out for each other."

I leaned on the metal, glass, and plastic separating us, wishing that I was leaning on him.

"I can feel it, Baris." If I couldn't have him, I'd have his name. Strong and unique, caressing my tongue. "Their hands on me. Around my throat. Gripping my wrist. Pulling my hair. I feel what those men are doing to them, every second of every day that they're out there. So, you don't have to worry about me tonight. I won't mess up, flinch, or hesitate. This is one fight I can't lose."

Brutal crooked his finger under my chin. He said nothing—not with words or the special way he communicated.

He kissed my forehead. Soft and light like the voice I longed to hear.

Brutal drew back. I rose on tiptoe and captured his lips.

I imagined their softness. Dreamed they were smooth and warm. My fantasies didn't come close to the reality of kissing Baris Alexander.

Salty tears mixed with his sweet, minty taste. He was stiff, not responding as I moved against him, and I feared I had taken too much.

I stroked his cheek, indulging this opportunity knowing it would be my last. Brutal stopped the thought with a hand curling around the nape of my neck. I was drunk by the first swipe of his tongue demanding entrance. He came around the door and scooped me up. We fell inside the car.

My hands were everywhere. In his hair, running down his back, gripping his ass and bringing him closer still. I was heady with the danger of it. Brutal was to be seen, feared, lusted, and admired. He was not to be touched.

I wrapped my legs around him, trapping him in my embrace. I'd have every inch of him until he made me stop. Though that seemed the last thing on his mind.

He put my hands over my head, and slowly skated over my dips, curves, and bends. The only touch I felt on me then was his. He arrived at my breasts and traced the mounds. Pushing them together, Brutal bent and bit my nipple through the fabric.

"Ahh." My sudden, heated gasp escaped him. The next he tasted on my lips, kissing me and continuing his exploration lower.

I was used to chatter during sex. Breath hot in my ear while a guy—Sinjin—described in graphic details the ways he'd turn my pussy out. Brutal's silence prompted a quiet in me too. He slipped beneath my belt, tugging on my shirt. The bodysuit T-shirt wasn't going anywhere. I could've said if my tongue would let me. I drank from his lips, making soft noises from the friction of his tugging.

My jeans popped open.

Brutal crouched on the ground between my legs. His lips were swollen and glistening. Hair tousled. Collar askew. I was having a stolen moment with Brutal's alter ego. When he came back, we'd be in so much trouble.

My pesky jeans were peeled off me almost sinfully. The obstruction was pushed aside and Brutal descended. His tongue swirled around my clit, teasing and tasting the helpless thing to render me quivering goo.

"Yes, Baris." Entwining in his hair, I held him firm, rocking my hips and bouncing my pussy on his face. An act that lost me a table when I did it to Sinjin in the kitchen. This time, Brutal lost control. He bent my knees up to my head and plunged inside me. Head bobbing, he dipped in and out of my overflowing well hard and wild.

My back cracked in half. Nails broke the leather. Cries fogged the windows. Foot banging on the dash, I snatched the door handle for leverage and popped it open. My head fell out of the car as the orgasm shredded my body. Upside down, I twisted and writhed, my muscles tightening and unwinding at once. The after echo of cries carried out into the busy street beyond the gates.

I lifted up in time to see Brutal rip open the glove box, snatch a pack of tissues, and dive where I couldn't see. His face buried in my thigh as the most delicious sound he could make peeled out of him. I felt pleasure I couldn't convey at being the woman Brutal made a mess for.

"You're the first person I've told that story." I got another tissue and gently cleaned him. "I wouldn't have been so scared to if I'd known I'd get that reaction."

"It's not you who should be scared."

I lowered my eyes, jaw tightening. "Those men are dead, Brutal. Addicts/dealers have a high mortality rate. What matters now is stopping the others."

That statement brought us both back to reality. We fixed ourselves and eventually got on the road. I snuck glances at him throughout the ride. Brutal had reformed into his perfect self, but flashes of the tousled man bobbing between my legs tormented me to distraction.

"Can I say something else?" I ventured. "For a guy who doesn't use it very often, you know what you're doing with that tongue."

His chuckles washed over me.

It helped to joke. I shared a secret from my past that ravaged me to this day. I sensed it at the edge of my soul, attacking the armor for a weakness. Brutal would lock my confession away in the depthless place he kept his secrets, truths, and past. Knowing it was there connected me to him. Made me feel I knew a part of him, if that made any sense.

Why does it have to?

Sobering, I asked, "Is this going to cause problems between you guys? Sinjin mentioned a rather premature agreement to share me if I got involved with all of you. Does it still stand?"

He nodded.

"Good." I traced the shell of his ear. "It turns out you guys are warming on me."

BRUTAL AND I SIPPED our drinks and tried to look casual. The effort for him was pulling off easily. I kept tapping my phone awake to check the time. Brutal caught my hand on the last check and laced our fingers together. It helped to settle me for all of ten minutes.

Our dusky corner of the bar attracted little attention from the few patrons. They watched a game on the television overhead, and made idle conversation with the people nearest them. None of them aware of the events about to rock their street.

The clock ticked twelve fifty-five. Brutal and I rose at the same time.

Outside, the Sunday night partiers raged into the street. The crowd had thinned to a fraction of what it was the week prior. That didn't stop couples dancing and grinding on each other in the line.

I wondered if I was ever that carefree. Growing up with the mother I did meant I was cautious just stepping inside my home. My life with Dad, I was safe from harm but not from struggle. I killed myself working and keeping my grades up. Then it was a crappy apartment and a grueling climb up the kitchen ladder.

Looking back, the only time I ever felt free to do and be what I wanted, was when four men kidnapped me.

I withdrew from my musings, focusing on the guys lounging on the wall. They looked chill to the random passerby—one bobbing his blue-beanie head to the music and the other on his phone. If it wasn't for the bulge under their coats and the fact they didn't walk outside a four-foot radius around that door.

Brutal pulled his gloves on.

"Yo," one of them called. "The entrance is that way."

"I'm walking toward the entrance," I replied. "And you're going to let me in. Tell Corbin Serenity is here to see him."

The reaction was immediate. They whipped their guns out, training them between our eyes uncaring of the witnesses.

"Serenity, huh? You're the whore who beat the shit out of Felix," said Blue Beanie. "Who's this guy?! You've got one hell of a death wish coming back here."

"What I've got are a couple of special somethings I bet Corbin is eager to get his hands on. I'm not here to embarrass another one of you in your own house. I just want to talk." I flapped a hand and the safeties went off. "Call Corbin. Ask him if he's interested. If not, I can always try Angelo."

The guys shared a look.

Anger, confusion, frustration, and a trace of fear flashed on their faces. Ours were blank. I knew the plan backward and forward. This had to work. There was no other option.

Blue Beanie jerked the gun at me. "We're not letting you in. You got something for Corbin, give it up now or get shot."

I blinked lazily. "Either you don't know what the 'special items' are and you're about to make a huge mistake that costs your boss a lot of money. Or you do know what I'm talking about and you're a fucking idiot." I patted my pockets. "I don't have them in here. How am I going to hand them over?"

"Tell us where they are."

"I'll tell Corbin where they are. In addition to outlining our new business arrangement going forward."

"You—"

"Enough of this, Loch," said his friend. "We both know Corbin's gonna want to talk to her." He made no secret of his smirk. "You want in, fine. Give me a minute."

He got on his phone, keeping up his grin as it dialed. "Yeah. It's Sonny. We're outside with a girl named Serenity. She's offering to return what she stole." He laughed. "I'm not kidding. Yep. Yeah. One guy with her. Alright."

Sonny hung up. "Corbin would love to chat with you. Your friend stays here."

I shrugged. "Fine with me."

"Up against the wall."

I did as he said—propping my hands on the wall and enduring the pat down.

"Move," he ordered. One hand held open the door and the other jammed a muzzle between my ribs. "Hands up. Don't try anything. If you even sneeze, I'll put a hole through your lungs."

"I must've done a number on this Felix guy if I've got you this jumpy."

"Your handiwork against Acker while his armed security stood around with their dicks in their hands impressed too. We're not taking chances." Sonny prodded me inside. "Show her friend to his car," he told Loch.

The scant light from outside winked out. I found my way, silently going through the next steps in the—

A shot rang out clear over the music. I whipped around and was hauled back.

"Whoops," Sonny taunted. "I guess your friend will need to be carried to his car."

He shoved me on. I stumbled, righted myself, and was shoved again.

"I up my asking price ten grand for each time you put your hands on me."

Sonny clamped my shoulder. "Shut—"

His hand flew off me.

Brutal got him by the arm and slammed Sonny headfirst into the wall. Brutal shoved his gun arm unnaturally up his back. His scream wasn't heard over the club's music.

I knew from experience how easy it was to sneak up on someone in this loud, pitch-black hallway. I now also knew, two men with guns were no match for Brutal.

He hooked the man around the neck, securing his hold.

"No!" Sonny flailed against Brutal. "No!"

Brutal gave one hard twist, ending Sonny's cries.

He let the body slump to the floor.

Brutal looked to me, eyes seeming to ask, "*Are you okay?*"

"I'm okay," I said. I looked anywhere but the body. "Send them in."

Brutal stuck out the door and signaled to Cash. He returned wearing a mask.

One after the other, my troop of masked men filed into the hallway. Cash identified himself merely with his eyes. They shone with that unsettling intensity as he indicated for me to go ahead.

I stepped into the squalid room, memories tumbling in my head in a dizzying array. The girls walking in their straight, silent line. Felix's bullet shattering the ceramic tile inches from my head. My desperate ramming on the exit. And Corbin down the hall the entire time, tucked away in that room.

He's right in there. I swept over the space. *Not much in my way.*

Eight poker tables and three were full. The men stopped what they were doing at my arrival. The bills fell on their stacks, rising into towers of green that reached chest-high. Three tables. Fifteen men. All counting out stacks of money.

Money they made off the tears of little girls.

Behind my back, I held up three fingers.

"How'd you get in here?" A man with a crown on his shoulder and a scar cutting through his hairline stepped out of the pack. "What do you want?"

"I'm here to talk with Corbin," I said. "Loch also told me to tell you to hurry up and relieve him of door duty, so he can get home and fuck your mom." I made a face. "I said I didn't feel comfortable saying that, but he insisted."

The men howled.

Scowling, my interrogator took his hand off his gun. "Fucking prick," he muttered. "Corbin's in his office."

They turned their attention off me and resumed their counting.

I moved quickly to the side, ducking in the hallway.

The Merchants streamed in. They fanned out along the wall—weapons drawn and aimed.

A shout. Then the first gun went off.

The line surged forward. Bullets rained in a symphony of gunpowder, flashes, and screams. I couldn't carry a weapon being the lure that got the Merchants inside. As such, Cash's explicit orders were that I stay the hell out of the way.

I ran in the opposite direction. I'd keep back, because I had to scour the place. There was a back door. No one was escaping through it.

Sticking my head in the bathroom, I discovered the traces of my fight with Felix. Bullet hole in the wall and a cracked toilet seat. Otherwise, empty.

I went inside the auction room. Rounding the partition, I met half a dozen rows of upholstered seats and no one sitting in them.

Six rows. Ten chairs in each.

That's how much they expected on a given night. Sixty people to buy a child, or sit silently while their seatmate engaged in the bidding war.

Corbin will know who they are. He will tell us.

I turned to leave.

Felix blocked my path.

"Serenity."

The too-big-on-top, needle-legs gangster didn't seem so menacing when he was pushing around little girls. The bandages and black, blue, and purple bruises covering every inch of him changed his profile—as did the gun.

I should've checked backstage.

"I've been looking for you, bitch," he hissed. "And look at that, you came to me. Did you bring the welcoming party outside?"

I fixed on the weapon. "Yes. We've come to ask a few questions about the Kings' setting up stake in the sex-trafficking business. Any thoughts?"

He laughed—a harsh terrible sound. "Corbin kicked the shit out of me for losing those girls. I've been ordered to bring them back and kill you. So my thoughts are: you've got to be the stupidest whore in Cinco. Second, fuck those brats. I'm killing you now."

Felix launched at me, tackling me over the seats.

Bang.

We crashed onto the chairs and bounced off, falling to the floor in a heap. I scrambled off the dead body.

"Don't wander off, Bunny." Mask or no, I knew that Merchant.

He stood from the partition, gun in hand.

"Come on," he said. "Corbin's waiting for you in his office."

The poker room was a nightmare, and nightmares were my specialty. Bodies littered the floor. The stories of their death sprayed the walls and leaked from their wounds in ever-growing pools. Two Merchants were among the carnage. The rest stuffed the money in duffel bags. Another result of keeping the men from interacting. They didn't weep and wail over their fallen comrades.

But I would if it was my guys, and that thought hit me hard. Attachments were being formed in spite of the rules. There was a reason they thought it too dangerous. Reasons that would make themselves clear to me when it was far too late.

Sinjin placed my mask in my hand.

It's already too late.

Corbin was waiting for me as Sinjin promised. Ten guns trained on him, and one gloved figure stood at his back. Surrounded by his impending death, and Corbin didn't bother to look up. The scritching of his pen was unnaturally loud—amplified by mocking.

He copied a line in his notebook, licked a finger, flipped the page, and continued scribbling.

"It's your show," Sinjin said, stepping to the side.

I looked from him to Corbin, then I gave my back to both of them, observing the office. This office was night and day from the pigpen we smashed through to get in.

A complete remodel was done in here. Plush carpeting on the concrete floors. Drywall and cream paint for the cinderblock prison. Photos of him with the VIPs of Cinco society blanketed the space, and his large, ornate desk dwarfed the room. It was too large—as though someone told him *the bigger the desk, the bigger the man*, and he took it to heart.

I studied him, picture beginning to form. His suit was expensive. I'd bet the cost that the price tag would shock me. Light brown hair was swept back in a swirly, bordering-on-boy-band style. If I was honest, he had the classic good looks to make it work.

I bobbed my head. *I know this man.*

"Corbin," I began.

"Just a sec, love." He didn't glance up. "Let me finish this thought."

"You're a dishwasher."

He stopped in the middle of flipping his page. "Excuse me?"

"You're a dishwasher," I repeated. "In the grand kitchen of life, you've always received the scraps. You stood off to the sidelines while others basked in the spotlight. They got the praise."

He slowly raised his head.

"Of course, there is nothing wrong with being a dishwasher. It's an important position in the kitchen, but you didn't see it that way. You thought you deserved better than your station in life, and when the first chance came to move up, you seized it." I gestured around me. "All of this is to remind you and everyone else that you've fought your way to the top. And the disgusting, foul, evil things you've done are to stay there."

Corbin closed the notebook and folded his hands on top. "Serenity, isn't it?"

"Sure."

"I was rude to keep working while you stood there waiting, so you're being rude in return. Let's start over."

This guy was unbelievable lounging like we were about to sit for tea and crumpets while his men lay dead outside.

"Please, sit," he said, motioning to a chair. "I believe you have a proposition for me."

I sat.

"Would it be too much to ask for the mask to come off?"

"Not at all." I peeled it off. "Can't breathe in this thing anyway."

Brows narrowing, he scanned me up and down.

"As I suspected, we've never met," he said, "so what the fuck do you want, bitch?!" He slammed on the table, shooting to his feet. "You steal from me, cost me thousands, drive away a client, break into my club, and kill my men! I better have killed your whole fucking family and butt-fucked their corpses, because if I haven't, I will!"

I whistled. "Wow. There's that insecure dishwasher complex."

"Argh!" He jumped over the desk and was swiftly wrestled into his seat. "What do you want?! Is this about the hit Angelo put out on the Merchants? You're on some mission to take us all out now? Well, I can settle this for you. You can't win.

"The Kings have four times the money. Four times the men. Four times the territory. And twelve times the firepower." He leaned as far forward as Brutal would let him. "And now they know who you are. You'll enjoy my death for a week. Max."

I listened to his speech patiently. "I'm not here to kill you, Corbin. This isn't about the Merchant/King beef. It's between you and me."

He pulled a face, scowling. "I don't know you."

"No, but you do know Shelby, Elle, and Adriana."

His face shuttered closed.

"They were the girls you sold last week. I want to know where they are, who bought them, and where the others are. I'll also take the names and info on all of your bidders."

"You're insane, bitch. Kill me or get the fuck out of here."

I sighed. "I don't appreciate being called a bitch by a— Goodness. You're so beneath contempt, I can't be bothered to waste descriptors on you." I got to my feet. "Bring the dishwasher with us. I have a feeling he'll open up after spending some time in our accommodations."

My march out would've been badass if Sinjin hadn't gotten his hands on me.

He snapped me to him, hooking my leg around his waist and lifting me. I was shoved up against the wall.

Gunmetal grays reflected my parted lips and flushed cheeks. "You have no idea how fucking sexy you are right now." He ground his erection in my middle to prove it.

"You heard her," he barked. "Tie, gag, and put him in the trunk."

For me, "I'm going to fuck you into a wheelchair. We're breaking every damn bed in the house."

My face was flaming and why wouldn't it? Sinjin did not lower his voice.

I cleared my throat. "I would be very interested in discussing the details further *after* we get an evil man to talk and rescue those girls."

"I'm a multitasker, Bunny. I can do both."

With difficulty, I broke free of his spell and followed his—our—men out with our prize.

"Bag," Cash ordered. One of the men tossed him a duffel packed with money. "The rest is yours."

They celebrated in the midst of corpses.

Carrying a grown, bound man past dozens of witnesses was easier than it should have been. We tossed him in Cash's car and left the extra hands behind. It was down to the five of us now to get him to talk. I understood what that meant when I suggested it. I knew what this car was speeding to.

I told them I was in. I said I'd do whatever it takes.

My commitment would be tested like no other.

I sat in silence during the drive to North Quay. Ghostly hands beat and tore at me the whole way.

"YOU THINK THIS SCARES me? Huh? Your toys don't impress me."

Corbin had been yelling and carrying on even before the gag came out. Cash and Brutal hauled him kicking and flailing into the basement. The choice crap he spat as he was suspended off the ceiling was particularly creative.

"I'm not telling you shit!"

Brutal opened a trunk tucked away in a corner and emerged with a sheet of plastic. He laid it out under Corbin's feet.

"You're dead," he said. "Every last Merchant in this city will be hunted down. We'll beat you unrecognizable, you won't need the masks. And as for Queen Cunt over there, I'll sell her pussy to a different bastard every night."

"How quickly you dropped the gentlemen act," I muttered.

"All right, Bunny." Sinjin bowed low, sweeping up his hand. "He's all yours."

"Mine?"

The guys were fanning out. Sinjin hopped on the rack while Cash leaned alongside. Mercer propped against the cage, and Brutal got out another piece of plastic, put it on the trunk, and took a seat.

"You started this," Sinjin said. "You have to be the one to finish it. Not just for you."

A vision of a frightened Kaylee peeking out from a bathroom stall flashed through my mind.

"You're right."

Lifting my chin, I converged on the swinging gangster. "I know you keep payment records and background information on your bidders. You'd be an idiot not to. Tell us where—"

Corbin spat in my face. "Fuck you."

I reeled, revulsion churning my stomach as the gob ran down my cheek. A blur shot past me.

Brutal smashed his jaw. He swung on the hook, head lolling and dazed.

"Let's try this again." Sinjin wiped my cheek.

Keeping hold of my chin, he raised me to meet him. "There's no one right way to this. Everyone has their own style."

"Their style?"

"Take Brutal." Sinjin pressed my back to him, resting his chin on my shoulder. "No tools. No weapons. He extracts pain with his bare—gloved—hands. He feels the breaking of bones beneath his knuckles. Listens to a sweet symphony of screams, grunts, and whimpers."

His words washed over me soft, light, and mesmerizing. Sinjin spoke with a reverence that stilled me.

"In a silent world, Brutal controls the sounds. He elicits your begging and your cries, and he decides when they stop."

We shifted to Cash. "Cash is about guns. Bombs. Firepower and precision. Getting the job done quickly, efficiently, and on his timetable. Mercer—"

"You can bore her with the details about me later," he broke in, grin wide and gorgeous.

Sinjin hummed agreement. "Then there's me."

Again, I moved with him. The marionette on the end of his strings. "Knives."

The wall of blades glinted in the light.

"Blades are thin. Deceptively delicate. They slide through the skin like it was where they were meant to be. A sheath of blood and muscles, and on the end of the hilt, you can feel it. The connection. Their pain is your own. Their blood obeys your command."

Sinjin whispered his love letter to the blades. A private conversation and I the intruder spellbound in his hold.

He selected one off the wall—the knife he put inside me—and closed my hand over the hilt.

"Corbin will tell you anything you want to know with this in your hand."

Corbin laughed at our approach. It made his split lip bleed more, and that didn't stop him. "What do you think you're going to do with that?" he cried. "Look at you. You can't stop shaking."

I was shaking. The knife bobbed harder the closer we got to him.

Sinjin tore his shirt open, ratcheting his howl up louder.

"Oooh. Very scary," he mocked. "A trembling little slut who hid when shit got bloody and scurried in after you handled the situation for her. You think this girl with her nonsense about dishwashers is going to make me talk?" He laughed again. "Come on, guys. Colleague to colleague. Do me the courtesy of questioning me yourself. At least the male model over there throws a good punch."

"Do it." Sinjin guided my hand to his chest, pressing the tip over his heart. "Make him tell you where the girls are," he whispered.

The devil on my shoulder.

"It's a wonder we didn't stamp out the lot of you in a week," Corbin said. "Cockroaches. That's what the Merchants are. You hide in masks and scuttle around in the dark, terrified to take the Kings head-on."

"Do it."

Pinpricks of sweat dotted my face and heaving chest. As cold as the basement was, I burned.

Sinjin's steadying hand didn't push or force. He wanted me to do this myself.

"You'll never find those girls." Red tinged Corbin's grin maniacal. "You killed a fraction of the men who work for me and stole even less of our money. The business will keep running uninterrupted until I get out of here—and I will get out of here."

"This should help," Sinjin said.

Releasing my hand, he dipped inside my jeans. Shock made my gasp louder as he flicked my clit.

"Pain is a gift, Bunny," he said, licking the shell of my ear. "Just as pleasure is. You're freeing our friend from himself."

"Sai— Ah!"

He plunged two fingers inside me and scissored them—rubbing that bundle of nerves as he picked up the pace. Waves of heat radiated up my core, threatening to fog my mind.

Corbin's tirade had come to a blessed end, but Cash, Mercer, and Brutal, they moved in closer. Surrounding me.

"Corbin stole those girls," Sinjin murmured. "He ripped them from their lives, fed them to beasts and killed the people they were. Tonight, he can make it right. He can save them, but only if you help him, Adeline."

Sinjin freed my breasts, exposing their rock-hard secret to watching eyes. He tweaked them mercilessly, tugging hoarse cries from me. I stumbled, knees weak, and my hand slipped. A thin, barely there cut appeared on Corbin's torso.

"Yes," Sinjin said. "Give him this gift. Make him right his wrongs. Confess his sins. Once he does, he'll thank you." Sinjin returned my hand where it was. "Do it, Adeline. It will feel this good."

"N-no," I rasped.

The knife clattered to the floor.

"I can't—"

"You can!"

"—with a knife!" I cried.

I untangled from him, swaying on my feet from the almost orgasm. "I can't do it with a knife," I said. "I create with knives. I make beautiful, delicious food that makes people smile even on their worst day. That's how I do good, Saint. I won't use the same tool on a worthless piece of trash like him."

The walls of weapons gave me more choice than a grocery store. I spotted a club nestled among the antiques. The long handle was smooth and curved, ending in a round head.

"But I can use that."

I claimed my prize, and turned on Corbin. I closed the distance. Hands steady. Eyes clear. Skin cool.

"Tell me where to find the girls."

The wild grin was gone. Replaced by a snarl twitching contempt. "You shouldn't have spent your college money on those fake tits. Maybe then you'd fucking comprehend that I won't tell you a damn—"

I swung, smashing the club between his legs.

"Argh!" Eyes bulging, Corbin's face flushed red to purple.

"Someone who hates children as much as you do has no business having them," I said. "As far as I'm concerned, beating you until your testicles literally burst will ensure another great wrong isn't committed, on top of the pain you've caused."

I hit him again. Corbin's scream rang through the fire station.

"Where are they?!"

"I'll fucking kill you, bitch!" Spittle flew from his mouth. "You're dead!"

I swung the club. Corbin flung his body to the side. He jerked and twisted on the rattling chain, screaming his threats.

"Take him down," I ordered. "Put him on the rack."

"As you command, Bunny."

I didn't need to ask if Sinjin was enjoying this. His erection strained against his zipper. A closer look revealed Brutal and Mercer in the same state. Cash's long coat concealed what may or may not be there.

He and Sinjin moved a thrashing Corbin to the rack and strapped him in.

"We don't even use this," Cash said, voice dry. "You chose your bride well."

"Yes, I did."

I pushed both of them out of my head. All that mattered was finding those girls—Shelby, Elle, and Adriana. A week in hell was a week too long.

"Answer me, Corbin. Who bought the girls? Where do I find them?"

"Half... a million," he forced out, "and your lives. That's what I'll give you. Let me out of here right now and the Kings won't seek retribution."

"We both know that's a lie," Mercer said. "I doubt Angelo knows what your part of the business is getting up to. He won't seek revenge, but you certainly will."

"No." He tossed his head between bound arms. "This can end here if you—"

"If *you* tell me what I need to know," I finished.

I lined the club over his penis. "Last chance."

"Call her off," he shouted. "Take the money!"

I brought the weapon down.

His cry savaged his throat. Corbin's eyes rolled in his head, and he went limp.

"Dammit." I tossed the club next to him. "He passed out."

"Unsurprising," Cash remarked. "Your method is effective, but will result in frequent fainting and vomiting."

"Keyword there is effective. For all we know, they held another auction last night. He has to tell us what he knows now." I marched toward the stairs. "I'm getting water to throw in his face. Or maybe smelling salts for the fainting princess."

Sinjin's voice followed me up. "I fucking swear I'm going to marry that woman."

CASH PROVED TO BE CORRECT about many things. There was a lot of fainting and vomiting involved.

And the method was effective.

"C-Castian Hotel!" Rivers of tears and mucus dripped down Corbin's face. "Stop, please."

"That's where they are?" I asked, raising the hand holding the club to wipe my brow.

I shed my jacket long ago, standing over him in my tight one-piece tee and black skinny jeans. Sinjin said I looked like a warrior priestess preparing a ritual sacrifice for slaughter, and he was going to fuck me so hard I'd transcend realms and meet the goddess herself.

He'd been highly distracting throughout the entire process. Twice he jacked off while urging me to show no mercy. A terrible influence indeed.

"Yes," Corbin rasped. "The children aren't bought... they're rented. Why sell them when we can keep the money going for months, even years? We pimp them out like any other whore. The bidders pay for one night. The rest of the time—"

"They're kept at the Castian Hotel," I finished. "How many children are you keeping there?"

"It's not just children. Some are older. Runaways. Hookers. They'd rather live in a five-star hotel, working a few nights a week than the alternative."

"How many?" I repeated.

"Eighteen girls. Thirteen boys. Fifteen of the rest."

Thirty-one children. My stomach heaved. "Tell us about the hotel."

"I own it." The truth came out slow, but it came. "Everyone from the receptionist to the janitor works for me. To an outsider, it's a regular, high-class hotel. But once you're in, you don't leave. The windows are tinted and can't be opened. The doors lock from the outside. Bathrooms in the rooms. They can even watch television. It's a nice setup.

"You should see what some of those other fucks do," he cried. "Pump them full of so many drugs, they don't know when someone is climbing on top of them. They sleep in crack houses and shit in buckets. I didn't kidnap them! They were sold to me. Some by their own parents. If it wasn't me, they just would've gone to someone else, and their lives would be much worse."

Acid burned in my mouth. "That's your defense? You're the lesser evil?" My grip tightened on the club. "I heard that once. That if my mom wasn't taking me to him, she'd just hand me to someone else, and they wouldn't *love* me." I stuck it in his face, crossing his eyes. "If you try to justify what you've done again, I'll keep hitting till it comes off."

"Alright! Fuck! The bidder list is a notebook hidden in my desk's false bottom. Most bid through the auction, and then drive from the club to the hotel to meet their... item. For the special guests or those willing to pay extra for privacy, they buy a night or more through the website. It appears as a regular site, but will tell anyone who doesn't book with a special coupon code, that we're fully booked. I'm telling you because you'll find out anyway," he spat. "Half a dozen bidders in the book will be marked 'website.'"

"What won't we find out on our own?" Mercer asked. "Security? Guards? Guns? How do we get in and out undetected?"

"You don't. I've got the best security system money can buy. There are cameras on my cameras. The *receptionist* has photos and fingerprints of the bidders, so no one can walk in pretending to be someone else. Also, everyone is fucking armed, and they won't go down easy. If we're busted, it's a life sentence from the state, and a death sentence from Angelo."

"He wouldn't like what you're doing?" I asked.

Corbin laughed. "He wouldn't give a fuck about what I'm doing. But he won't be happy I kept it quiet, didn't cut him in for eighty percent, and then got my ass caught. The Kings don't get hauled out in cuffs on the six o'clock news. And they for fuck sure give Angelo his cut."

"Thank you, Corbin," Sinjin announced. "You've been very helpful. In the morning we'll have another chat just to be sure you've told us everything you know."

"I have! They're at the hotel. All of them. I swear."

"I'm sure they are. Tomorrow, I'll be extra sure."

"Tomorrow? Saint, we can't wait," I said. "We know where they are. We have to go."

"We can't," Cash said. "Sinjin's right. First, we have to get info on the hotel. If it's as guarded as he says, we're looking at a full-on assault. Getting in, taking out the players, and safely moving over thirty children out of there isn't a five-person job."

"We'll get all the guys on this one. Tomorrow, we make a plan to strike," Sinjin said. He lifted the rack and moved Corbin around.

"No, stop! What are you doing?"

"Facing you to the wall for the lady's privacy," he replied. "I'm going to do unspeakable things to her now and would rather you not watch."

He was lifting me over his shoulder in the time it took that comment to register.

"Saint, do I need to remind you there is a perfectly good bed upstairs?"

"Do I need to remind you how long it's been since I fucked you on the floor, on your knees?"

"Two days."

"Exactly. Ages."

The room spun. Next I knew, I was lying on the plastic blinking up at him. Over his head, Cash climbed the stairs out of the basement. Sinjin tugged my jeans off and flung them over his shoulder.

I flipped to crawl away. He snagged my ankle and dragged me right back. He hooked an arm around my thigh and explored my middle. The truth was known in an instant.

"Interesting," he purred. "You're drenched, Bunny. Looks like someone enjoyed their chat with the King more than they let on. Should I be jealous?"

"That was from your earlier fondling."

I'd said it and I'd swear to it. Did I feel a sense of satisfaction deep down over exacting justice against a man who pimped children out to the highest bidder?

Yes.

Alone in my room with the door locked and a pillow over my mouth, I'd confess that I did. But to Sinjin—no. It was the effect he had on me that did it. Admitting this dark prince with his love song to blood and knives was pulling me deeper into his web was not something I could do.

Not before he did.

Cupping his hand, I drove him deeper. "Finish what you started."

"Gladly."

He jumped on the distraction like I knew he would.

I heard a faint click. Sinjin cut my shirt in half.

"Saint, this was my favorite!"

"Don't wear shit that gets between me and your pussy. You're lucky I let you get away with pants."

He punctuated his sentence with one hard thrust, cutting off my unfiltered opinion of what I thought of that.

Sinjin set a demonic pace. Pounded me so hard and fast, he lifted my knees off the plastic and left my toes scrabbling for purchase.

There was nothing like having sex with Sinjin Bellisario. The man lit a spark in your core that set off exploding waves of pleasure for days to come. Seriously, he could just brush past me in the kitchen and I'd be wet and willing for him. No one else could have the effect on me that he did.

At least I believed that until today.

My cheek slid up and down the plastic. He was the wrong way up, but clear as could be. Brutal hadn't left with Cash. Neither did Mercer for that matter.

Mercer leaned on the rack, pants around his ankles and fist stroking his formidable cock.

Brutal, however, did not indulge what achingly demanded his attention. He fixed on me—expression hard to place as his friend and leader turned me inside out.

Peeling my shirt over my head, I tossed it in the direction of my pants.

"Saint," I breathed. "Were you serious about spreading around my employee benefits?"

He chuckled. "I was. Why? What do you have in mind?"

Through my fog, I locked eyes with Brutal. I crooked my finger.

"Come on," I said. "You put the plastic down for a mess. Let's make one."

My silent fighter came to me.

I was weak from Sinjin's relentless pumping. I had to climb up his legs and unzip him. Brutal knelt to give me better access.

Taking him in my hand, I swallowed him whole.

My head bobbed up and down. Faster and faster. Cheeks caving in to suck those intoxicating grunts and groans as an extra treat.

I loved that I could make him utter those noises. I loved that he spoke more words to me in the last month than he did to others he'd known for years. I loved his fingers tangled in my hair, and Sinjin at my back.

I sensed him getting close. Picking up the pace, I relaxed my throat and accepted everything he had to give me.

A sharp hiss sounded over him.

"Damn," said Mercer. "This is not how I saw my night going."

I pulled up with a "pop."

"What? Is this more a Tuesday night deal for you?" I teased.

"Yes," he said, grinning. "But on Tuesday night, I'm not standing on the sidelines."

"No one said you had to."

"Don't tempt me." He pulled up his pants—the remains of his temptation on the floor. "Corbin here just gave me homework and it won't get done if I spend another second feasting on you."

I opened my mouth to reply. Brutal fisted my hair and guided his cock inside. The man didn't need to speak to make his wants known.

Mercer left us to it.

I WOKE EARLY THE NEXT morning. Alone in Sinjin's bed. Ten points for guessing where he was.

Downstairs having a conversation with Corbin.

Naked, I picked his shirt off the floor, shrugged it on, and padded out of the room.

I gave Sinjin the green light to put me on my knees in front of the guys, and spent half the night getting thoroughly fucked in both holes. At this point, I could dispense with the modesty.

Cash parked at our new dining table with his laptop and binder.

"Morning."

He grunted in my direction.

"I feel like cooking something different today," I mused. "What do you think of chocolate crepes with maple ricotta and mixed berries?"

"Steak, eggs, and toast for me."

"You have that almost every day. At least try my crepes. I swear you won't want anything else after."

I got another grunt in response.

I sidled up to him, peering over his shoulder. "What are you doing anyway?"

"What are you doing? Put some fucking clothes on."

"What? Why?"

"You may have Sinjin, Brutal, and even Mercer eating out of your palm, but you're not playing your dangle game with me."

"How can you say that after—?"

"After what?" He shifted from the laptop, giving me a look that blew through the stern and sank my happy ship. "Nothing's changed between me and you. Clothes, steak, eggs, toast. Now."

"Asshole." I stomped upstairs and dressed. "I'm not making two breakfasts," I snapped on my return. "You can eat my damn crepes and like it."

"Stop shouting and listen," Cash said. "The sisters who got away, Ilona and Jazmin Kepes, they're fine. They made it to the Hungarian embassy."

"They did?" My irritation was forgotten. "How do you know?"

"I put Diego on finding them. Checking shelters, hospitals, and clinics. He found a shelter on Lumen Street that took in two girls that night. Thirteen and eight years old. They were taken to the embassy today."

I released a breath I'd been holding for a week. "I'm so glad they're okay. I couldn't sleep thinking of them out there on the streets."

"Now for the Castian Hotel," he said. "I checked out the website."

"What did you find out?"

"He wasn't lying about one thing at least. You can't make a booking. I tried three times with three random dates and got 'fully booked' each time. On the fourth try, the system said there was an error and to try again another time. Any legitimate customer would've given up and booked with another hotel. It's effective for keeping people away."

I tossed my head, eyes rolling skyward. "So there really is a hotel in the middle of our city where Corbin runs his sex-trafficking nightmare under everyone's nose."

"Looks that way."

"What do we do now? Those 'website' customers don't have to wait for an auction to get to those kids. We have to get them out as soon as possible."

"I agree," he said. "Waiting's a bad idea for many reasons. This hotel is four floors and in the heart of Harlow. There's a crew in there keeping up appearances. If one of them swings by the club, finds a room full of bodies, and can't reach the boss, they might panic. Assume Angelo discovered they were cheating him out of thousands and doled out punishment. We can't risk them packing up shop."

"If they move the kids, we may never find them."

"No, Redgrave." It was unsettling the times his eyes held no emotion. It was worse when they did. "They won't run off with thirty life sentences in the back seat. If they're burned, they will kill those kids and run."

His words were a punch in the gut, forcing the air from my lungs. "Cash, we can't wait any longer."

"I know. Tonight. We take down the Castian Hotel."

I TOLD THE GUYS I WANTED in on what they do. Made promises to Sinjin that pleased him to no end.

But the truth is, I had no clue what my part in this was.

Cash's announcement that we must strike wasn't a call to action for me. I stood in my kitchen making crepes and all around staying out of the way as the boys streamed in and out.

Cash barked orders into his phone all morning, relaying to his men who would be going in with us, the weapons to bring, a warning it was a hotel full of children, and why those children were there.

Mercer's homework wasn't clear to me. It seemed his only job was to pace along the upstairs banister and chat with various people while wearing that devil-may-care grin. As for Brutal, he had no orders to give, though I heard him in his bedroom pummeling his freestanding punching bag.

Then there was Sinjin. My Saint. Coming in and out of the basement wearing blood like face paint.

"Cameras on every entrance. A bellhop that stops you at the door and double checks identity," he said on his last stop. "Four bellhops actually. Loitering under the awning, looking natural. All packing."

"In the back?" Cash asked.

"In the back. On the sides. On the roof. On every floor," he said. "Corbin's got them posted on each entrance twenty-four hours a day. No chance of going in quiet."

"We expected that." Cash showed him his laptop. "I've got an aerial view of the hotel. There's cover in this alley. We can get the kids out through there where the vans are waiting on this side street. But we'd need a clear path through the kitchen."

"We'd have to pull them out of this area." He pointed. "Pin them down here. I said we can't go in quiet, but we'll do it anyway. They won't see us coming."

I listened closely as I made the filling. "What do I do?"

Cash frowned at me like he forgot I was there. "Do? You're not doing anything."

"I'm coming, Cash. I said I was in and I meant it. I won't sit at home playing with my whisk while you rescue those kids without me."

"You're a liability," he said, blunt as a truck. "You can't shoot. You can't fight. You won't stab. Someone would have to go in watching your ass instead of their own. You're not coming."

"I can fight," I corrected. "Just because I haven't given you the beating you're begging for doesn't mean I don't know how. My dad taught me to shoot, and refusing to torture a guy with a knife is different from using one to defend myself or kids that need me. I don't need my ass watched. I need you to tell me where I'm going to be and what to do."

"You'll be right the fuck here chilling the case of beer, or three, I'll drink when I get home."

"Saint, tell him—"

"There it is," Cash said. "Dangle's putting that pussy's power to getting what she wants."

I dropped my bowl. "This whisk is going to be dangling out of your—"

"Settle down," Sinjin said. "Both of you. Bunny is coming."

"To get herself killed?" Cash snapped.

"She has to come." Sinjin leveled an unnaturally serious look on me. "What was that you told Corbin about the man your mother handed you over to?"

I dropped my gaze, lips pressed tight.

"This is her fight, Cash," he said. "Besides, I'll be the one watching her ass. No one's touching her."

"I don't need my ass watched," I repeated, but I was just glad he said yes. "Where do I need to be?"

"Behind Sinjin." Cash picked up his phone again, dismissing me.

I looked to Sinjin and got a grin in reply. "Behind me is right." He dropped a kiss on my knuckles. "If you'll excuse me, Corbin and I were in the middle of our conversation about Angelo.

"Call me when we're ready to move out," he said to Cash. With that, he swept out.

I hovered near Cash. Giving up on my crepes, I whipped up a simple meal while impatiently waiting for him to hang up the phone.

"—exact timing. Diego's on this. So is Duke and Remington. They'll have a money stash on the premises in case they have to tear out of there quick. You guys find it, it's yours. That's your pay. Good."

He hung up and I was on him. "Cash, seriously, I want to know the plan. You ordered those guys to bring in a lot of firepower. The place is full of kids. How are you making sure they don't get hurt?"

"Corbin said himself the kids are locked in the rooms all day and night. They won't get caught in the crossfire."

I squinted at his laptop. "I get that they have websites, guards, and guns to keep the nosy out, but too much of that and someone will get suspicious. There are health inspectors, safety checks, and city workers. What do they do when Mr. Blart shows up to check out the kitchen? Tell him fuck off enough times that he reports them? Kill him and risk a murder investigation blowing up their operation? They've got to let him in. The kids are locked in the rooms upstairs, so they can be downstairs putting on the show."

"What's your point?"

"My point is *that's* how we go in quiet. A couple of guys show up as inspectors and they won't need to worry about Billy Bellhop and his gun. They'll walk them right through the front door."

"That's... not a bad idea," he said slowly. "Once they get in the back, they can clear the loading dock. Cut us that path through the kitchen."

"And it's way too dangerous to have bullets flying around kids, even if they are in the rooms. We don't know who's in there with them. One of the *guests* could panic if they hear gunshots."

Cash released a harsh breath, his fists balling. "You're right. But there's no way around it. They have men on every floor. We can't evacuate without getting noticed. Bullets will fly, Redgrave."

"Then, we have to give those men a reason to leave their posts. You said if it starts going wrong, those monsters will cut their losses and save themselves?"

"Yeah," he drew out.

"Then this is what we do…"

WANT TO KNOW WHAT GOES through your head on the ride to certain death?

It's not as sweaty, panicky, and frantic as you might think. No, I felt none of those things.

What you get is an autopilot calm similar to the peace you experience while vacuuming, filing, or taking inventory.

That's what I was doing—taking inventory.

Sorting and weighing the measure of your life does not come easy. Have I done good? Have I committed wrongs? Have I chosen the former enough times to outdo the bad? If this is my last day, have I taken advantage of the thousands of days before?

Eight thousand and four hundred days. That's what I've been given. So very many of those were horrible. There were hundreds of those days that I prayed it'd be the last.

That's why today is good, said that calm, still voice. *To die the day I end that nightmare for other little girls, makes sense in a way nothing else ever did.*

This is why I've suffered. So one day when the time came, I would make it right.

Sinjin cut into my musings. "Remember what to do?"

"I should hope so," I said. "It is my plan."

It took a day to work out the details and who would do what. Then another to get everything in place. That night, we were destined for the Castian.

"It's a good plan," Sinjin said. "You've got a knack for this."

I cut eyes to him, and he was looking back at me—despite the fact he was driving. Gently I faced him at the road.

"That pleases you, doesn't it? That there's a side to me that indulges vengeance. I'm ruling well as your queen."

"Vengeance or justice?"

The quiet question dimmed my smile.

"Is that what you carry out?" I whispered. "Justice?" My hand lingered, stroking his cheek. "What wrongs are you righting, St. John?"

"Too many to name," he said. "Get ready. The hotel's up ahead."

"Why do you do that? Avoid talking to me about anything real. I thought we were past this."

"How's this for real? Put your mask on now."

I bit my tongue, holding back the frustration. Even if this wasn't bad timing, fussing with him would get me nowhere. Sinjin held back infinitely more than he shared. Some days I felt connected to him. Most I wondered if I'd ever truly know him at all.

The end of Lincoln Street loomed ahead. Castian Hotel claimed the corner pocket between a Peruvian restaurant and a bar. You couldn't call this part of the city quiet. People flitted in and out of bars, restaurants, stores, and hotels. A Tuesday night did not compare to a Saturday night in Cinco, but this place was a high-speed video of city night. Life was always on the move.

But no one laughing in these outdoor cafes or strolling with their friends to the bar noticed what was going on right next door.

There was a boldness in Corbin's setup that boiled my blood. He really thought himself a king. Ruling over Harlow, setting the rules, and breaking them as he saw fit. A confidence he held due to forty years of the Kings proving just that. They were above the law.

Until now.

With Sinjin, I was united. There would be a new rule in this city.

"Hello."

Sinjin's voice brought me to reality once again. He pulled to the curb and parked in front of the Peruvian restaurant. He set the phone on the dash as he put on the mask.

"Hello?" A rough, gravelly greeting left the speakers. "Who is this?"

"This is Sinjin, leader of the Merchants. How ya doing, Angelo?"

My eyes bugged. Diving forward, I grabbed for the phone but Sinjin was too quick.

Silence compounded on the other end, risking my death as I stopped breathing—waiting for him to speak.

"How did you get this number?" was the calm reply.

"A new friend gave it to me. I'm calling to let you know I'm about to take care of a problem for you. A few of your associates have gone rogue. They went behind your back and betrayed your authority. We both know something like that cannot stand."

I gestured wildly at Sinjin, mouthing, "*What the hell are you doing?!*"

"Absolutely," Angelo said. "If what you're saying is true, it cannot stand. But don't trouble yourself. I'm quite capable of handling these matters internally."

"It's no trouble at all." I didn't have to see Sinjin's grin to know it was blinding. "Just think of it as you owing me a favor."

Angelo's laugh was as hard and unpleasant as I pictured him to be. "I should think it's you who owes me the favor, Sinjin, leader of the Merchants. I lost a lot of money when you knocked over Jimmy's shop."

"Whoever those handsome devils were, running around in your shop, I assure you it wasn't any of my guys. You don't have to take my word for it. Tonight, you'll see the Merchants in action. Compare that shoddy, half-assed job run by idiots who couldn't take out a single camera, with the mess I make of your strongest and best-defended men. Afterward, ask yourself if you want another demonstration, or to skip to giving me that favor."

Sinjin ended the call.

"Alright, Bunny. Let's do this."

"What the hell was that?" I cried. "Are you insane?"

"That was the beginnings of negotiations. The fight doesn't end tonight." Sinjin settled the mask over my nose and mouth. "Corbin is just one head to chop off the twelve-headed beast. You heard him say Angelo would've looked the other way if he kept it quiet and cut him in. This is the endgame."

Sinjin twisted and grabbed the tool bag. He got out knowing I'd follow. I did at a slower pace.

Gathering my things, I mentally ran through the plan. My stretch of calm was over. This would not be my last night. For me or any of the guys. Ninety-nine point nine percent probability be damned.

Sinjin's knit cap was a beacon bobbing among the carefree pedestrians. I trailed it onto the hotel's drive.

Castian Hotel differed little from the photos I poured over for the last forty-eight hours. Four floors of black-iron balconies, white window awnings, and a portico-covered drive devoid of lights.

Two men in black hotel uniforms came to life at our approach. Their name tags read Terrance and Cory. Just on the other side of the door, two more men watched us.

"Can I help you, sir? Ma'am?"

"We're city inspectors," I said. "Building code regulations have changed for this area. We're checking older buildings to ensure they're in compliance."

City inspectors.

Sinjin and Cash got their hands on two uniforms easier than I could believe. I told myself they got it from a top-quality costume store, instead of off someone's back. Ditto for the tool bag.

As for the paper dust masks, those were a quick trip to the store. They didn't have Ms stitched on the side, but they concealed our identity just fine.

I took a step. "Excuse us."

"Hold on." They both held up their hands.

Cory and Terrance looked like normal guys at a normal day on the job. As long as you took no notice of the loose clothes that made it easy to conceal weapons, long sleeves to hide the crown tattoo, and their general air of "go away" when they're supposed to be the welcome party.

We were definitely in the right place.

"We didn't hear anything about a regulation change," Cory said. "Why weren't we informed beforehand?"

"Everyone in this neighborhood was informed by automated phone calls," Sinjin replied. "Trouble is people usually hang up when robo-Karen starts talking. And that's if they pick up a call from an unknown number."

Cory and Terrance shared a look.

"Want to get on the phone with our supervisor?" I plucked a card from my chest pocket. "He'll tell you everything we did."

"Yes, I would." Cory took the card and drifted off to make the call.

Terrance stayed on us, mean-mugging to make a real city inspector uncomfortable.

"Why are you wearing masks?" he demanded.

"We might have to poke a few holes," I said. "Don't worry, we patch them back up."

"They're legit," Cory announced, hanging up the phone. "Their boss said they're in and out in ten minutes if nothing's wrong."

Terrance didn't budge. "We can't allow you to go around poking holes and disturbing our guests."

"We need to see inside the kitchen, cellar, and the back of the building. You have a lot of guests hanging around there?"

"Ten minutes," Cory said. "That's all you have." He snapped his fingers at the men inside. "First floor only. Do not poke holes."

Finally, we were let inside.

The Castian was all the pomp and arrogance I expected of the club beneath Paradise.

Hell had marble floors. Decorative heat lamps lining our way. Large portraits of serious, unsmiling Victorians on every wall. Their unfriendliness was matched and exceeded by the crew working the lobby.

Two supposed bellhops. A front desk agent in an elegant pantsuit who watched us until we disappeared around a corner. Three people playing cards in the lobby seating area. A man polishing glasses in the bar lounge. He stopped and shut the door in our faces. Lounge closed.

"Kim, stay with them," Cory said. "Help the inspectors to whatever they need, so they can be on their way in ten minutes."

"Sure." Kim got up in the middle of her card game. "Let's go."

"Which way to the kitchen?" I asked.

"That way." She pointed to the silver double doors directly ahead of us.

Kim was a tall woman with short hair and an obvious bulge under her coat. I guessed her official title was security. It allowed her to be obvious.

"Where's the cellar?" Sinjin asked.

"You stay on the first floor."

"Look." Sinjin unfurled a map and held it up in front of their faces. "The new codes say cellars have to meet these minimum measurements."

Carefully, I backed toward the kitchen.

"I don't care what you've got going on down there," he went on. "I just need those measurements."

My pulse raced a mile a minute. All the guards had to do was look up from their poker game. Kim could chance a peek around the map. If they did, it was over.

Digging in my tool belt, I rescued the canister. I edged the door open and tossed it inside.

"You can do the measuring, and I'll wait here."

"What is this for?"

Another object went flying into the kitchen.

I straightened and went to Sinjin's side. "Building code regulations," I repeated my mantra. "We're checking older buildings to ensure they're in compliance. Won't take long—"

"Holy shi— Fire!" The card player leaped to his feet. "There's a fire!"

"What the—?" Kim ran to the door. She flung it open and billowing smoke poured out. "Get a fire extinguisher!"

"Can you see the fire?" I asked.

"It's over there! I can get to it!"

"It's too late. There's too much smoke." The Kings rushed to see. "Where's the fire alarm?"

"It doesn't work," the desk agent blurted.

"What do you mean it doesn't work?" I cried. "Just get out of here. Everybody, out!"

Kim didn't need to be told twice. She nearly knocked me down racing for the exit on the heels of her card buddies.

"Fire," Sinjin sang. He popped another smoke bomb and tossed it at the couch. "Run. Run for your lives."

"Stop laughing. They're not out yet." I peered around a pillar.

The guards, bellhops, and desk agent bottlenecked at the topiaries.

"Got a Samaritan," Sinjin remarked.

The lounge bartender went for the stairs, shouting "fire" all the way up.

"Sometimes it pays to do the right thing," I said.

"Doesn't pay for long."

The Kings escaped, spilling onto the drive. Through the glass doors, I watched their bodies jerk and writhe in a hail of bullets.

The Merchants streamed inside, leaving them where they lay. They were a terrible sight to behold in those ski masks and silk shirts. A sight the children did not need to see.

"Head up the west stairwell," Sinjin said. "The children go down the east."

"Be careful," I said. "A kid might run the wrong way. Don't shoot anyone who isn't shooting at you."

"Move!" shouted a ski-masked Cash. He, and two figures I knew well, broke off from the pack making for the west stairwell. "Take this."

Cash held out a gun.

"I don't need it."

"Then you won't have to use it." He shoved it into my hand. "At least you'll have it."

He and Brutal were off before I could make him take it back.

I spun on Sinjin. "Saint, take it."

"We don't have time for this, Bunny," he said, hooking through my belt loop. "There's a pile of bodies on the doorstep. We need to leave this party before it's crashed."

I swiftly shed the uniform for the black, long-sleeved romper underneath. Sinjin caught me trying to leave the gun in the pile and stuffed it in my pocket.

"I'll take the fourth floor," Mercer said. Mercer got a spare mask out of my tool bag and made a trade. Less a frightening monster and more the helpful man directing you out of the fire. He didn't wait for us to tag along.

Uniform on the floor, Sinjin pulled me after him, and then I ran out in front, tearing up the steps. Sinjin set off another bomb under the staircase.

Together we burst onto the second floor. The guard patrolling the hallway spun with his gun at the ready.

"Fire," I cried, waving at the smoke already seeping under the door.

"Who are you?"

"Does it matter?! That way is blocked. We have to use the other staircase."

He spun on his heels, breaking out with no regard to the people locked in the rooms. Our footsteps thundered behind him.

"Hey!" He skidded to a stop on the landing, scrambling for his gun. The door swung shut as he dropped. After a beat, Cash tossed his key ring inside.

"I say again, great plan."

"Fire!" I shouted. "Get out! There's a fire."

Sinjin and I waited.

He scanned the doors, eyes hard. "This floor must be clear."

A door banged open at the end of his sentence. A man tumbled out wearing one shoe and rushing to do up his pants. "Where's the fire?!"

"Let me help you, sir," Sinjin said, jogging up. "If you go right this—"

Sinjin slammed his skull into the wall. He stopped his shrieking with a knife to the throat. "I have a feeling I'm going to enjoy this more than usual."

Four keys hung on the ring. I tried them on the door he came out of. The lock gave in to the second key.

"Hello?" I called. "Don't be scared. I'm not here to hurt you. You're safe now. I'm getting you out of here."

I entered the hotel room, treading softly on the carpet. A messy bed met my eyes. Then that other shoe. Stepping around the dresser, a tiny face peered at me from the corner.

The phantom hands took hold of me. Grabbing, twisting, ripping, tearing until my eyes held the despair reflected in his. As I gazed at the state of the room and the helpless child cowering within, a hard pit of hatred lodged in a corner of my soul where it couldn't be removed.

Clarity dawned on me bright and steadying, revealing the way forward, and at the end of my path was a creature of heaven and hell more terrifying than Sinjin Bellisario could ever be.

"Hi, sweetie," I said gently. "I'm going to take you someplace safe, okay?"

Louder, I called, "There's a little boy in here, Saint."

I crouched down. "Ready to go?"

He let me fold him up in my arms.

I helped him dress and carried him out. I draped my hair over his eyes to shield him from the last look at his abuser. I faced him at the wall.

Sinjin hauled the whimpering scum over the threshold.

His knife flashed, cutting a graceful arc through the air. A red line appeared on his neck. Blossoming into rivulets of painted waves.

I watched him die, and the creature unfurled her wings—waking to bestow judgment.

He stumbled over his feet and dropped out of frame. Sinjin let the door swing shut on his body.

She named it just.

"There's no fire," I said. "We'll go down in the elevator."

Door to door, Sinjin and I coaxed the kids out of the rooms and into the elevators where Brutal and an assembly line of Merchants were waiting to lead them to the vans.

Mercer's homework was arranging the transport. He was also in charge of arranging a safe place on the other end. These children, teens, and runaways who did not live here as willingly as Corbin claimed, trusted that place was for them.

"Take this blanket. It'll be okay." I draped it around the girl's shoulders.

"Where are we going?" asked the small voice.

I led her out, murmuring about the warm bed, food, and safety waiting for her far from this gilded prison.

The elevator dinged open. Saint blocked the door, waving the kids through. I sent her to him and made for the final room in the hallway.

Opposite me, the exit to the east hallway creaked.

Time slowed.

A bald head covered with ink stuck itself inside.

The bartender.

As if in delayed motion, I watched his face crumple in a frown, then blow apart in outrage as the city inspector led his charges into an elevator.

I saw this, but Sinjin didn't.

Sinjin stood equal to us both. Too far for even my scream to reach him in time. To warn him of the threat, push him to cover, or for him to respond with the swift lethalness that made my angel invincible.

Face twisting, the lone King yanked out his gun, and I fired.

A scream ripped from my throat—ringing above the shrieking children.

My first bullet struck true. It clipped his shoulder, spinning him to the threat he hadn't noticed. He fired and a splintered hole materialized in the doorframe inches from my head.

I emptied the clip. Seeing him jerk and twist was an act I couldn't connect to myself and my finger squeezing the trigger.

Tipping into the hall, he crashed to the floor.

Dead.

"Bunny."

The creature released her hold, abandoning me to the ringing in my ears, cold grip in my palm, and Sinjin's shining reverence to the warrior priestess.

I flung the gun away from me.

"Saint—"

He shoved me against the wall, ripped off my mask, and stuck his tongue down my throat. The kids were safely down the elevator. It was just him, me, and the man I killed.

I broke away gasping. "No, Saint! I can't— I can't believe I—"

"You're fucking incredible." He pushed me back, cupping my whole face in his hands. "And you're mine."

There was a finality in his words that silenced me. It muffled the small part of Adeline Redgrave that still existed—for both she and I knew with absolute certainty that with this act my fate was sealed.

I was his.

SINJIN, MERCER, AND I evacuated the final floor.

I lifted the last child into the van and buckled him in. Mercer drove off with a parting honk, leaving me and Sinjin behind.

We moved quickly. Cleaning up the discarded uniforms, tool bags, gloves, and then walking out the door.

We were a couple striding arm in arm down the street as the wailing sirens and cops blew past.

I BRUSHED THE CLOTH over his chin and caught on his stubble. Sinjin bent his head back, allowing me to continue the journey down his throat.

Wringing out the washcloth, pink water dripped into our sudsy bath. I continued my task—cleaning the blood off him.

"You haven't asked," I murmured.

Sinjin thrust his hips, driving deep inside me. My cry bounced off the porcelain.

"Asked what?"

"If I'm okay."

He flicked his tongue over my nipple. "You're riding me, Bunny. If you're not okay, hop off."

I was riding him, and I couldn't seem to stop. Sinjin filling me whole was the only thing anchoring me as we bathed in the blood we spilled.

"I killed a man, Saint. You haven't asked if I'm okay."

"Am I supposed to?" Moving to the other nipple, he met my dips to his thrusts.

"Saint," I breathed—part remonstration, part moan.

His hair was silken webs between my fingers. Hot, flushed, and hazy, I held him close.

"What was the alternative? The guy would've blown my brains out. Could you have lived with that?"

I tightened on him, and drew a groan through his teeth.

I could not have lived with that. In the core of my being, I knew I'd have killed every King in that building rather than let them have Saint.

"No."

"There is no moral crisis. You did what you had to do, and what you would do again. Don't probe further. Do not ask yourself if you're okay. You are."

"Say it," I whispered.

He didn't ask me what.

Sinjin licked my lips, snaring them in his trap. I'd make no more requests of him that night.

Together, we sank below the water.

"—POLICE DON'T KNOW WHAT to make of the scene they uncovered last night at the Castian Hotel," stated Marcia Stupple. "Seventeen bodies were found on the premises. Of the deceased, Congresswoman Veronica

Kenzie, tech mogul Case Leonard, and Alvin Brown, founder of Brown Manufacturers were identified among them."

Mercer, Brutal, Cash, Sinjin and I watched the news in rapt silence.

"In the meantime, across the city, almost fifty people—the majority of them minors—were taken to St. Lucie's hospital where the hospital administrator was prepped and ready to receive them. All claim they were prisoners inside the Castian. Held against their will and subjected to horrors at the hands of their captors, and the hotel's guests alike. They say they don't know the men and woman who rescued and delivered them to the hospital, but they thank them for saving their lives."

Sinjin picked up his phone. I didn't try to stop him this time.

Angelo skipped the preamble. "I expected your call much sooner."

"Sorry for the wait," Sinjin said. "I was tying your last gift up in a bow."

"You killed my people." It wasn't a question. "Exposed Corbin's extracurricular activities. And you made it look like it was done by the Kings."

The last part was true. Corbin's cameras had cameras, and though they couldn't see our faces, they had no trouble picking out the strategically placed golden crowns on our necks, shoulders, hands, and biceps.

What police would make of the kidnappers and child traffickers slaughtered by their own people, who then turned around and saved the captives was their business. Either way, someone would answer for this news story breaking on every channel, and the cops had the Kings going backward and forward.

Most importantly, the children were safe. The phantoms had gone.

I could breathe.

"You're welcome."

"Forgive me if I suspend my thanks," Angelo said. "Leonard, Brown, and Congresswoman Kenzie were valued customers of mine. To my other valued customers, it appears as though I cleaned house with no thought to who was caught in the crossfire. Or worse, I don't have control over my people and they're running around slaughtering each other. I've lost ten important clients today alone.

"I will say this, Sinjin, leader of the Merchants, the job done on James & Co. Jewelers and the one you pulled last night is a child's scribbles compared to the Mona Lisa. I've paid for the insult of believing you responsible for that shoddy work, and now you have my full attention."

"Then, listen close." Sinjin leaned forward, bumping me off his lap. "The war on your customers, clients, and businesses stop when I get a few things from you."

"What would that be?"

"Your gang, money, and territory—"

Laughter poured out of the speaker.

"—and Kieran."

The sound ended so abruptly, I thought the call dropped.

"We'll discuss the mercies I'll grant you in person." Angelo's hiss slithered up my spine. "One day very soon."

Click.

"Kieran?" I spoke up. "Who is that?"

"Hold on." Sinjin dialed another number. "Diego. Tonight. You're on."

With that, he hung up.

"On for what? What's going on?" I swung my gaze from guy to guy. "Seriously? Are we still keeping the maid in the dark?"

"No," Sinjin said clearly. "We're not. Angelo's not ready to break. Diego will get him there."

"He was never going to give up his gang for the death of those Kings and some bad publicity," I said.

"Course not," Mercer said. He draped a leg over the arm of the chair, reclining with his glass of wine. "We're not taking over the Kings unless we kill him. That was always the result. But one thing we can't get if he's dead is what he knows about Kieran."

"Who's Kieran?"

Sinjin stood up, standing before the television. "We said we'd be the law in this city. There's someone who already is."

"Someone who is the law?" I repeated. "Who? This Kieran guy?"

"Yes."

"I've never heard of him."

"No, but you've seen his work."

I made a face. "What? Stop talking in riddles, Saint. Who's Kieran?"

"You've heard of a fixer, haven't you?" Mercer snagged my attention. "A kingmaker. Someone who sets all the pieces on the board in your favor."

"Yeah."

"Around twenty years ago, whispers started rising about a guy named Kieran. That's it. Just Kieran. It was said you could bring any problem to him, and he'd make it go away. Mistress threatening to expose your affair and destroy your political career? Gone.

"News of your embezzling about to break out? The police evidence disappears. Want to collect the insurance money on a building you own? Take a vacation and when you come back, it'll be a pile of ash.

"Kieran didn't stop there," Mercer said. "He made as many careers as he saved. Mayor Katz didn't have a chance of winning until he was shot in a drive-by while playing in the park with his daughter. Sympathy catapulted him up the polls, and the rest was history. There was never proof, but some credit Kieran for him, and the power acquired by many others in our little slice of heaven."

"Wow," I breathed. "So, you want to find this guy to hire him? Have him hand you control of the city?"

Cash made a harsh noise. "No, Redgrave. Let him finish the story."

"Kieran was formidable. Ruthless. Effective," Mercer continued. "Everyone went to him, Adeline. Rich and poor. It's unknown how many clients he worked with, and the number of secrets he's created or kept hidden. What we do know is he kept meticulous records, receipts, and proof in his ledger, and once he had enough, he turned on all of them."

"He's used that ledger to control the city ever since," Cash finished. "Crowning himself the king."

"Oh my gosh. Again, how have I never heard of him?"

"Where would you overhear talk about underground kingpins? While you're shelling shrimp in Salvatore's kitchen?"

My glare was withering. "I've lived in rough neighborhoods. Been around more unsavory types than you have, Cash. The only Kieran I know was a kid in elementary school who put his boogers in his lunchbox."

"He prefers it that way," Sinjin said. "He doesn't want to be known. Doesn't need to be. Kieran stays in the shadows, pulling strings as it suits him. That ledger gives him total power, Adeline, and while he has it, the rest of us are just peasants squabbling over the leftovers."

"Whoever owns the ledger," I said, "owns Cinco."

"That's about the size of it," Mercer confirmed.

I shook my head. "But hold on. You said this was twenty years ago? How is he controlling anybody with scandals that are decades old?"

"Just 'cause he closed up shop, doesn't mean he's out of the business. No one knows who he is or what he looks like. You could be spilling your life story to him in a bar and have no idea. He's an expert at finding what he needs to know. He's only added more to the ledger over the years."

"Don't his old clients know who he is?" I asked.

"They never dealt with him directly."

Sinjin retook his seat next to me. "We know one thing for certain. He was, or is, in the life. Mafia or gang—doesn't matter. He got his start on the wrong side of the law."

"Where does Angelo fit in?"

"The Kings are the oldest gang in the city," said Cash. "They've survived for years. Virtually untouchable. More than one person has assumed Kieran and a certain ledger have contributed to their long lifespan."

"You think Kieran is a King?"

"No," Sinjin admitted. "I think he *was* a King until he struck out on his own. Now the bastard's middle-aged and basking in the penthouse-life with that ledger close by. Whipping it out when necessary to protect his former brothers."

"To find him, we have to tap old gangsters like Angelo for what they know," Mercer said. "He has to know something. *Someone* has to know something. We'll find them."

"The ledger is that important?"

"The ledger is everything." Something in Sinjin's voice struck me. "There's no point to any of this without it. A puppet king is no king at all."

"A puppet king?" Ripples hummed under my skin as I peered in Sinjin's eyes, and the boys in turn. "Kieran doesn't have something on you guys... does he?"

Silence pressed in on me.

That's an answer in and of itself.

THE CONVERSATION WAS over after that. I couldn't get more out of the guys on what Kieran held over him, or just how far they were willing to go to get that ledger. It turned out they didn't answer because they planned to show, not tell.

Kaylee and I texted while I prepped the artichoke-stuffed beef tenderloin. I told her the girls were rescued and authorities were working to find them safe homes. She asked me if their rescue had anything to do with the Castian Hotel, and the bodies piled in and outside.

I was thinking of a response to that when Sinjin called me.

"Bunny, get in here. My lap's waiting for you."

Rolling my eyes, I said, "Your lap has to keep waiting. I'm buttering beef."

He stood—no doubt to pick me up himself—and the reporter floated to my ear.

"—in Harlow. Multiple buildings on fire."

I snapped my head up. Sinjin was there, hoisting me around the waist to carry me where my attention had gone.

The boys were seated in the living room. Mercer and Brutal watching. Cash switching from the screen to his computer.

"As you can see, firefighters are working tirelessly to put out these blazes. Between the timings and concentrated locations of these fires, early reports are pointing to arson."

"Saint, did you do this?"

He plopped us both down on the armchair. "Yes, indeed."

I was too stunned to speak.

"Fires," he said. "I got the idea from you."

"You didn't get any part of that from me," I snapped. "I created fake fires to chase away child traffickers. Those are real!" The screen mocked me, displaying the burning warehouse in stark, HD clarity. "How many?"

"Twelve," Mercer replied like it was nothing. He was reclining on the couch again, sans the wine. "The phone you nabbed off Acker wasn't a waste. He had the locations of the last twenty spots that hosted Angelo's casino."

"Our friend in the basement gave us twenty-one," Sinjin said. "The location it was supposed to be held this week. We burned it down too."

"Were there people in those buildings?!"

He bobbed his head. "Yep. We burned little Tracy and her entire family alive." He scoffed at my gasp. "Of course there weren't people inside. Angelo chooses buildings with little foot traffic."

"Diego checked them in case," Mercer assured me. "That's why it was thirteen buildings and not twenty-one. The others were beneath clubs or restaurants."

"I just... This is too far."

Sinjin's eyes hardened. "Have you changed your mind, Bunny? Are you out?"

"I didn't say that."

"Good. Because this isn't far enough. Cash," he said, though he looked at me. "Adeline's going to help you with the rest. I'll be downstairs."

Sinjin stormed out of the room.

"Uh," Mercer sighed. "I hate it when they fight."

Steaming, I spun on Cash. "What are you doing?"

"See for yourself."

Cash held up a book. I recognized it immediately.

"That's the list of bidders."

"Names, numbers, addresses, and *preferences*," he said as I joined him. "Angelo lost ten customers due to the Castian. He'll lose a lot more when the people on this list get texts from Angelo, demanding they pay him half a million dollars, or he'll reveal those preferences to all of Cinco City."

"Won't they call to bitch him out? He'll just tell them he had nothing to do with it."

Cash smirked. "And admit someone outside the Kings got their hands on this and is using it to fuck with them? Think that'll sit better with them?"

My smile matched his. "No, I do not."

"Angelo hasn't made the call yet. He will after this."

I flipped the notebook open, finding where Cash left off on the list. "Saint missed the mark if he thought this would punish me. I'm more than happy to cosign tormenting child molesters." I grabbed his hand as he reached for the computer. "As long as we carry out the threat. All of Cinco finds out what they are."

"Mercer's got a journalist friend dying to break the story. This was only going to end one way."

"Tell me what to do."

That night and early into the morning, Cash and I drafted individual texts to those on the list who slipped the net at Castian. The names that came up were sobering.

Politicians. Business people. Musicians. A former actor. One woman was on the board of a children's charity.

The texts were written, number spoofed, signed with the name Angelo, and sent at four on the dot.

Task done, I rolled into bed for a few hours of sleep. I was up again to make, and burn, breakfast when Saint decided our tiff was over and he carried me upstairs to bed.

The call didn't come on Thursday.

Friday came and went without a ring.

By Saturday, I was pacing the kitchen

"Why hasn't he called?"

"Should I pop over and ask him?"

"I'm serious, Saint."

He was relaxed on the kitchen stool and lazily trying to catch me as I went by.

"What if they all handed over the money and he's sitting pretty counting his bills? He's probably laughing at us right now."

Saint finally snagged the hem of my peplum top. He towed me in and tucked me between his legs.

"First rule of dealing with blackmailers," he said. "Never pay them. Everyone knows it doesn't stop after the first payment, and Angelo could drain them dry with what he knows. No, Bunny, I'm sure they're not paying him. What they're doing is hiring a hitman for a fourth of the cost to take him out permanently."

I blinked. "What? But then— What about Kieran? I thought you wanted that talk with Angelo?"

"I'll get it." Sinjin swept my hair over my shoulder and followed it down my back. "If a hit is put on him, Angelo will find out an hour after it's done. Once he looks into what the hell is going on, he'll make the call."

Resting my chin on his chest, I asked, "What happens after? After you take down Angelo? After you find Kieran?"

"Cinco is mine, Bunny. You know that."

"I mean what happens to us?" I whispered.

His response was to carry me upstairs. I was naked and curled up at his side with my head tucked under his chin when his phone rang.

Picking it up, he showed me the screen.

Angelo.

"Angelo," Sinjin answered. "What can I do for you?"

"The day has come."

The room temperature dropped ten degrees. Corbin thought his shouts and threats were intimidating. He must not have truly pissed Angelo off. If he had, he'd know this was real menace.

"You and I will meet to discuss this attack on my business, and how it will come to an end."

"Gladly. Mind if I pick the place?"

"I insist on it," Angelo replied. "I want to know where you feel safe, Sinjin. Where you lay your head. Where you eat, drink, and piss. I want to know what brings you joy, and then I want you to watch while I return the favor, and burn it to the ground."

"We bring one," Sinjin continued like he hadn't spoken. "One man, or woman, with you. Show up with fifty guys and I disappear."

"Where?"

"Twenty-Five Cinco Casino. VIP room. Ten o'clock."

"Leave your mask at home."

Click.

I shuddered. "He's not a guy you want to meet in a dark alley. You don't want to meet him in a brightly lit alley either. Who are you taking with you tonight?"

"You."

"Me? Why?"

"Cash, Brutal, and Mercer will be outside stopping whatever plan he's got to kill us the minute we step out the door."

"Oh. Makes sense."

Chapter Twelve

Saint

"I'm just saying it doesn't make sense," Adeline went on. "The place is called Twenty-Five *Five* Casino. Why not call it Twenty Cinco? How did no one catch this?"

Adeline had hold of my chin, keeping it pointed at the road. "Are you blabbering because you're nervous?"

"I don't blabber, jerk. I'm easing you into the conversation. When you smell a real one coming, you snap up like a clam," she said. "You had this place ready to go. Why? What am I walking into?"

"You'll find out in two minutes."

Stupidly named though it was, Twenty-Five Cinco Casino stood out. Theaters, restaurants, shops, and another casino surrounded it, but your eyes were drawn to the neon lights shining brighter than the rest.

I turned into the parking lot knowing somewhere nearby, Cash and the guys were staked out waiting for Angelo to make his move. I helped Adeline out of the car and escorted her inside certain he already made it.

Twenty-Five Cinco was alive on a Saturday night. Bells, chimes, and clacking chips sounded on a looping soundtrack. It was the only music I liked listening to.

We went through security. Both of us patted down, sent through the motion detectors, and her bag checked.

On our release, I led Adeline to the bar by the hand. She wasn't wearing pants for me to hook my finger through the belt loop. I reached to do it automatically and her hand was there, ready and weaving her fingers through mine.

I glanced at the linked hands as we went. I noticed others looking at us too. The attractive couple.

Couple?

The loving boyfriend and girlfriend.

Love?

Minds made up, their glances and quick smiles decided the answers to the questions. What was my answer?

That they could not tell me.

"Two bottles of Armand de Brignac," I told the bartender, "and whatever the lady wants. Send it to the VIP room."

"Right away, my man."

We continued on to the back, skirting the tables and servers carrying drinks. I dropped out of her grasp. She took it back.

"Angelo and his man might be watching. Don't want them reading into the hand-holding," I explained. "He's looking for a weakness."

A smile played at her lips. "Am I your weakness?"

"I can't go more than an hour without dousing up on that pussy, so the evidence is sound."

She laughed. "I hope your weakness extends beyond your dick?"

She'd been doing that a lot lately. Trying to steer me into making a definite statement on what I felt about her and our being together. Was this a girlfriend thing?

I stopped it with those in high school when I figured out how easily I could get the sex without the commitment. Why bother with anything else?

Of course, nothing was that simple with Adeline.

"You also make a mean prime rib."

She fell silent—eyes drilling a hole in my head and pouring that fire inside. That was why it couldn't be simple. She was like no one else.

Always fighting. Always pushing back.

Gold and red velvet doors peeked through the crowd. A guard stood watch. He threw out his hands when he saw me.

"Sinjin," he crowed. "Been a long time."

"Hey, Jalen." We shook. "Work's kept me busy. This is Bunny."

"Addy," she corrected. "Let me guess, you're a long-lost foster brother? Sinjin's uncle? Maybe his fraternal twin? I've walked into so many surprise family reunions this month."

"Nah. I'm just the guy opening and closing the door." He cut to me. "Which I did for two gentlemen an hour ago. They're inside."

I nodded. I expected this.

"Send him in within the next twenty minutes."

"Will do," said Jalen.

He did his job, letting us inside.

The VIP room made its name for privacy and luxury. There were no windows in here. Squares where windows should be, were made of silver grating and a dark red backlighting. Different tables were set up around the room—for poker, blackjack, and the private meal two men were enjoying in front of a big screen playing yesterday's soccer game.

I picked Angelo out of the two without trouble. I knew what he looked like. Knew he favored silver wingtip shoes and his face tattoos covered a scar with a hidden story.

"Ah," Angelo said. "You must be Sinjin."

"I must be."

"Full name." He wasn't asking.

I wasn't holding back. "Bellisario. Both parents dead and I have no siblings. If you were planning to kill my family, I'm afraid you'll have to jump back in time."

He tsked. "Shame. Orphans add a layer of difficulty to our business. I'm sure you'd agree."

"I do. They're a bitch."

Angelo waved that away. "We can discuss that later. We haven't finished introductions. This is Tony."

Tony was two hundred pounds of lethal muscle awaiting the signal to kill me. We shook like new friends.

"And"—Angelo fixed on Adeline—"who is this?"

"Your men know me as Serenity," Adeline replied.

"Your real name?"

"I don't know you at all."

"Angelo Castillo, leader of the Kings," he said. "Your real name?"

She hesitated for another second. "Adeline."

"Beautiful." He lingered on her—longer than I liked.

"We're busy men," I said. "Let's not waste any more of each other's time."

He finally flicked off her. "I agree."

Adeline and I took our seats in the armchairs against the opposite wall from Angelo and Tony. First rule of negotiations: Never be within strangling distance.

"The attacks on my business stop today."

"What? Still no thank you? The Castian Hotel was a gift."

"As I said, I handle my matters internally. Corbin Dumont will be taken care of for the wrong turns he took, and for telling you where to find my casino. Is he still alive?"

"For now."

"Then, his return is another condition."

I leaned back in the seat, drumming my fingers on the arms. I couldn't conceal my grin. "What are the rest?"

"The Merchants are over. You've claimed no specific territory, but I will settle for your money, weapons, and you."

I cocked a brow. "Me?"

"You have a talent better used toward working for me. You and the men who lead alongside you. Your gang will become Kings. Not all of you, of course," he relayed calmly. "Most will die. But you won't and you can't ask for fairer than that."

"My life in exchange for becoming a King. Why do I sense coming into the fold won't be quite that easy?"

Angelo was looking at Adeline again. "Easy is not the word I used," he said. "You'll be beaten severely. Fingers, ribs, and many bones broken. When you recover, you won't earn a paycheck until you pay off the money you've cost me in the last five days. You should know that number has hit seven figures."

"All right," I replied, tone light. "Now for my terms. I want Kieran."

I now had his full attention. Expressionless, he said, "That request did not make sense on the phone, and it doesn't make sense now. How can I deliver you Kieran? I don't know who or where he is."

I smiled. "Don't sell yourself short. You've been in the game for as long as he has. You've heard the whispers. You stood in awe of the legend. You know about the ledger. I don't buy that you haven't searched for it. Everyone who knows of its existence is after it, and you have the resources to get closer than most. You'll tell me what you've discovered about Kieran and the ledger, then the attacks stop."

"What about my gang, money, and territory? Have you given up on your other demands so soon?"

"Nope," I said. "I'll get those after I've killed you and every King who remains loyal to you."

Adeline shot me big eyes, silently screaming at me to pull back.

"I prefer that ending, to be honest," I said. "It's no fun if you just hand it to me."

"You are a disrespectful little pup," Angelo hissed. "You believe this makes you appear strong. It simply makes you stupid."

"If we're skipping to the insults, you're a geriatric, paranoid shit who thinks we're back in the days the Cosa Nostra ran the streets. Times have changed, Angelo. You don't rule by respect or even by fear. You rule by blood.

"You want my gang? Kill me and take it. I will never kneel before you."

Angelo was silent through my speech. His expression wasn't. He cycled through each stage of rage.

"You will, Sinjin Bellisario. I can promise you one thing. You will."

A man in black pants and a red vest walked inside. Two bottles of wine were tucked under his arm. His name tag flashed the name of the casino and Nikolai.

"There we have it," I said. "We've laid out our terms. Time to find out who leaves satisfied?"

"How do you propose we do that?"

"Blackjack."

If I expected surprise, I didn't get it.

"Putting your fate in a card game," he said. "Against a man who's been stacking chips since before you were thought of. I'm forced to amend my opinion on your intelligence."

"Putting my fate in card games is what I do. You won't give up Kieran and I won't give in to you. Seems to me our only choices are to kill each other right here, or let the matter be settled out of our hands."

Angelo studied me for a long stretch. In the background, Nikolai shuffled cards.

"All right," he said. "I will play your game and, most importantly, honor the results."

"Let's get—"

"But I'm changing the terms." Angelo closed the distance. "If you win, I'll tell you what I know about Kieran and the ledger. If I win, I take her."

"What?"

"Excuse me?" Adeline cried.

"I take her. You can keep your gang, and your lives. The girl comes with me and I'll accept a truce between us."

"No."

He cocked a brow. "No?"

"No!" Adeline echoed. "I'm not going anywhere with you."

"She's not a part of this," I said.

"She's here. She's a part of this."

"No."

"Good bye, Bellisario." Angelo headed out. "Hopefully, your fruitless search for Kieran turns something up in the days you have left. When your blood soaks the streets, I'll have the girl then."

Tony threw open the door to watch my last chance stroll out of it.

"Wait."

Angelo paused all too easily. "Yes?"

"Saint?" Adeline whispered, sliding her hand into mine again. "What are you doing?"

"You'll honor the result," I pressed. "If I win, you give me Kieran and a truce that lasts until nature takes its course?"

"I will."

"Then, it's agreed."

"Saint?"

Angelo backed into the room, the triumph curling his lips. "And if I win...?"

The words scorched my tongue coming out. "The girl goes with you."

"Saint!" My hand was flung away. I couldn't look at her though she jumped in front of me, grabbing my jaw to turn me where she willed. The betrayal in those brown pools poured in and scorched the rest of me. "What are you doing? You can't t-trade me."

Her voice broke, and my resolve along with it.

I opened my mouth to tell her to trust me, and glanced at a watching Angelo. I told her with my eyes instead.

Trust me, Adeline. I always have a plan.

"Let's not waste another minute." Angelo swept out a chair, getting comfortable at the blackjack table. "I'll have a glass of that."

Tears collected on her lids. She wasn't hearing my message. She couldn't see it.

I reached for her.

"Don't!" she screamed. "Just don't."

I withdrew, jaw grinding. She couldn't see what I was doing then, but she would.

"Let's play."

I took my seat. The chair two down scraped over the carpet.

"I'm playing too." Face soaked with tears, and her chin was raised. Shoulders steady. "You can give me a glass while you're at it. Actually, I'll have the whole bottle."

"What are your terms?" Angelo asked. Amusement laced his tone. "That you stay by your boyfriend's side?"

"Sinjin knows my terms."

Sinjin.

"We're continuing a previous game."

I tried again to catch her eye. *She always knows what the fuck I'm thinking. Why not now?*

"Ready, lady and gentlemen?" Nikolai asked.

Angelo signaled for him to get on with it.

"Ladies first." He placed the deck before Adeline.

Adeline laid her card facedown. She dropped a ten for me, and a three for Angelo. A nine fell on her facedown card.

The game began.

"Hit."

"Stay."

"Stay."

"Hit."

Angelo and I went back and forth.

Adeline dealt my final card.

Twenty-one.

We switched. I took over dealing and both lost against me.

Angelo's grin was gone. He snatched the deck, roughly shuffling and dealing out the cards.

"Hit."

"Stay," Adeline said.

"Stay."

"Hit." A queen of spades landed on her pile, putting her over.

"Stay," I said.

Angelo flipped his facedown card.

Sixteen.

I stayed.

He hit.

I won.

"Argh!" Angelo swept the cards off the table, showering the floor red, black, and white. "You cheated!"

"How? You handled the same deck I did. Was it marked?"

He swung to Nikolai who stood impassively off to the side. "You work together. That's why you suggested this place."

"This is sad, Angelo. I won. Honor the terms," I said, "Tell me what you know about Kieran."

Adeline sat silently through the exchange.

Planting his hands on the felt, he leaned over the table, and said, "I will make good on my promise."

Something hard pressed into my skull.

"I promised you'd watch while I destroy everything you touch."

I held still. "How'd you get a gun in here, Tony?"

Angelo laughed. "Security's only as good as the price of their bribe."

"I've always said that," I replied.

"This is good. Play cool." Angelo rounded the table. "To have a worthy opponent whimpering and mewling at the first hit reflects badly on me for being taken by someone so pathetic." He put his hand on a still Adeline's shoulder.

"You're going to watch me walk out of here with your girl. After, Tony will escort you outside to an idling van and the men waiting inside for you. As I mentioned, you will be severely beaten. While you recover in the deep, dark hole that is your new home, I'll visit regularly to update you on my progress wiping out every Merchant in Cinco."

"Last chance," I said, voice calm. "Tell me about Kieran."

"Shall we, Miss Adeline? I—"

A faint click sounded behind him. Nikolai, aka Memphis, leveled the gun on Angelo's neck.

"Look at that. We're at a good old-fashioned impasse."

I felt the second he twitched.

Tony swung the gun on Nikolai. I pushed up his hand, sending his shot wide, and grabbed the bottle in front of Adeline. A quick smash and the jagged pieces were in his neck.

Tony grabbed me on the way down. We collapsed on the floor amid Angelo's shout.

Adeline pushed her seat back and stood. She walked away.

Angelo lunged at her.

Bang!

He dropped clutching his arm—cursing and shouting fit to bring the place down around us.

Adeline stepped over him and kept going.

"Adeline? Adeline!"

She walked out the door.

Shoving the dying man off me, I raced across the casino floor. "Stop!"

"No."

I held her arm, making her stop. "You can't go out there. Angelo's guys are waiting for us."

"I don't care," she said, pulling free.

"At least wait until Cash and the guys clear them out."

"Goodbye, Sinjin."

"He was never going to win!" Everyone in my vicinity stopped what they were doing—gaping at us. "You know that. I don't lose."

"Yes, you do." There was no heat. No fire. No pushing back. This cool, toneless woman, I didn't know. "We're done."

She turned her back on me, continuing on.

"Adeline!"

I ran after her.

"Hey." Hands seized me, hauling me back. "Walk it off, man. Cool down."

"Leave the lady alone."

I fought free of my captors—punching one across the face. Skidding outside, I swept the street for her, but that bobbing head of auburn-gold was gone.

Cursing, I returned to the VIP room.

Memphis groaned on the floor by Tony, blinking awake. The remains of the final wine bottle covered him.

They were the only two in the room.

Angelo disappeared.

CASH, MERCER, BRUTAL, and I spent the night searching the streets for her.

Angelo's waiting party was taken out. Then we dispatched the second one that came for me as I ran to my car. The delay gave Bunny a significant head start.

Three in the morning, I walked inside the fire station. The others were still out looking for her.

That friend of hers and her father's retirement home. I'll wash off the blood and then break inside both.

I trod past her door.

Thump.

I stopped.

Clang.

"Adeline?"

The shuffling on the other side stopped. Then another thump.

"Adeline." I fell on the wood, pounding and ramming it. "Adeline, let me in!"

The frame splintered but didn't budge. The obstructions were back in front of her door. Her sign she wanted me out.

"Fuck that."

I shot down the hall and yanked down the stairs to the attic. When the builders remodeled this place, they stashed the floor-to-ceiling fireman's pole behind four walls rather than rip it out. It was why we bought it. The secret door in Adeline's closet gave us an escape route if we were attacked. It also let me spend nearly every night with her.

Sliding down the pole, I dropped off on the small platform outside her door. My busting in made her shriek ring through the station.

"What the fuck?!" Her huge eyes trailed me staggering over the carpet. "Where did you come from? Is that— A secret door? How long has that been there?!"

I didn't reply, taking in the scene. Adeline's bags were open on her bed.

"What are you doing?"

"What does it look like?" She snatched up the discarded dress she wore that night. She was in her jeans and T-shirt. Shoes on and laced. "I'm leaving, Sinjin."

"No."

She kept packing, stuffing her clothes in a suitcase. I grabbed it and flung it across the room. It dented the plaster crashing into the wall.

"Feel better?" Arms folded and eyes darkening, she was my snapping she-wolf once again. "Because it changes nothing. I'm leaving."

"Why?"

"Why? Because you threw me on the table like I was a five-dollar poker chip!" Now she was screaming. "That's why."

Then I was shouting too. "I wasn't going to lose! Blackjack is my game. The advantage is always mine."

"That's not the point." She tore out her hair. "Why don't you see that?"

"What don't I see? Even if by some fucking miracle he beat me, I'd have killed him before letting him walk out the door with you. You're overreacting."

She tossed her head. "Overreacting? Damn hell, Sinjin, it's so obvious you don't have a clue what to do with a girlfriend. Here's your first tip: don't bet her in your war against a merciless gangbanger."

"Our war," I said. "I thought you understood what it takes to get to Kieran."

"I don't give a fuck about Kieran. I don't know who the hell he is and neither do you," she flung. "I'd never risk myself for that guy or his mythical ledger, but you made it clear you'd risk me. Power is that important to you. *Kieran* is that important to you. And I'm a means to both ends. Admit it!"

"He killed my father!"

Her shout died on her throat. Adeline stared at me, jaw working. "He what?" she breathed.

"My father was killed. Murdered on the steps of his altar because of Kieran. I know who he is."

She took a step back as if to distance from the truth. "Why would Kieran kill a priest?"

"He didn't." The words spilled out unbidden. The dam was broken. They couldn't be put back in. "When I was eleven, a man started visiting the church. He'd hid his face. Stuck to the shadows on his way to the confessional.

"It became a regular thing. This faceless man arriving weekly to spill his sins to my father. One night, men broke into the church. They dragged him out of his office. Beat him to a pulp. All the while demanding he tell them what *Kieran* told him. He refused."

The scene unfolded with sharp clarity, sending me seventeen years in the past.

My father broken and bleeding on his knees. The cross he gave me cutting my palm as I clutched it, praying for help.

The man in the black hood and blue sneakers slipping past me through the pews.

"My father refused to break the seal of confessional... until they found me."

"Sinjin..." Adeline trailed off.

"They held a knife to my throat," I said. "Pressed till they drew blood. Tell them about Kieran or they'd gut me like an animal.

"He told them," I rasped, "and they killed him anyway."

Adeline dropped her eyes—too slow for me to miss they were shining. "So, that's why you're doing this. It's always been about Kieran."

"My father betrayed everything he believed in for the walking, talking incarnation of his sin. His one moment of weakness lost him the respect of his community and peers, and then it cost him his life. Someone will answer for that, Adeline, and that someone is in Kieran's ledger. The name of every man and woman in this city so desperate, they'd hire two thugs to murder a priest. I took care of those bastards years ago. There is only one person left, and one person who knows who they are."

She wiped the tears from her eyes. "Sinjin, what happened to you and your father was horrible. I can't imagine the pain you've lived with all these years. Or the hatred. But you asked me that night if what we were doing was vengeance or justice? I thought it was justice.

"I was willing to do what I had to do to end the Kings because we were doing good. We were proving that someone comes. When the helpless are cheated, or a child is trapped in hell. The Merchants will come."

A snarl leaked through my teeth. I was hot—sweating. A torrent was rising in me and I didn't know where to direct it. A first for me. "That's a real sweet sentiment, Bunny, but that's not who we are. It never has been, and you don't get to play shocked and naïve now. You knew what I was when we started this."

"What I knew is you wanted me for me. You protected me. You kept me close. You loved me." She laughed harshly. "I knew that until tonight. Shocked and naïve is damn right. I asked you that day if I was the woman on your arm, or a card in your deck. Tonight you finally gave me my answer."

"He was never going to take you! What part of that don't you understand? You're mine. That's not going to change."

"It is, Sinjin."

"Saint!"

"Sinjin!"

She bent over her bag and shoved in the clothes that had fallen out. "I'm leaving. The kids are safe. Angelo's running scared. I've done what I needed to do, Sinjin. I won't be your pawn in a war between you and Kieran. If my place isn't by your, Brutal's, Mercer's, and Cash's side as your equal, then it isn't here."

"You're not leaving." I threw the bag again.

A hard force tackled me. Adeline and I tumbled into her armchair, tipping it backward. My head cracked the wall. Adeline smacking and shaking me kept me pinned.

"What are you going to do, Saint? Put me back in the cage? Threaten to kill my family? Are we back to this now? Because that's what it will take!"

"Why?!" That was all I could shout. All I could think. "Why are you doing this?"

"Because you don't love me!"

The confession was a death knell that stopped us both. We tangled there, chest heaving, battle raging on in our eyes.

"You don't love me, Sinjin," she whispered. "You don't let me in or show me how you feel. Mercer won't lift his veil of mystery for a second to reveal something real. Brutal still holds back with me. And Cash doesn't want me here. I'm falling in love with men who don't love me."

"Stop."

"You don't love me, Saint."

The torrent was building. Swelling. Battering the shields. "Stop saying that."

"Then, you say it." Her tear dripped down my cheek. "Tell me you love me, and I'll stay. Tell me I'll never be a choice between you and Kieran again."

"Adeline—"

"Say it."

"Adeline." I took her face in my hands, and she was gone.

She climbed off and walked away.

The torrent exploded.

I picked her up, shoved her against the wall, and crashed my mouth on hers. Adeline shoved me off, screaming. I flew at her again.

We stripped each other violently. Ripping and tearing the clothes off our bodies. We fell on the bed—mouths and hips connected.

I didn't know if I loved. I shut myself off to that emotion and all others when the last person left who loved me died as the price.

Adeline kept digging. She tore and searched and demanded something inside of me I wasn't sure was there.

That night, she lay beneath me. Her breaths were soft and slow in sleep, barely disturbing the pillow. You wouldn't believe this woman was the unrelenting force of destruction against everything I thought I knew.

This I do know. She's not leaving.

Adeline Redgrave is mine.

ADELINE

I woke alone the next morning.

I didn't have to seek Sinjin. I felt him in my body's kinks and the soreness in my middle. I smelled him on my skin. I sensed him somewhere in the house, waiting for our final showdown.

I rescued my suitcase off the floor and set it on my bed. I continued my silent, solitary packing.

I finally heard the story of St. John.

The full truth of how he became this man. The knowledge of his father's terrible end, and the hatred that changed his course.

I had all of him, and now I knew it could never be me. In the end, Sinjin will choose Kieran.

It was proof there was a shred of mercy within him that he refused to placate me with false I love yous.

But half of him was not enough.

It was too cruel to ask me to live in a house of men who didn't want me. Who'd use me for sex, food, or as their protégé in their rise to the criminal top, but no more.

I couldn't do it. Not like this.

It was no use if they didn't love me too.

"Adeline."

Sinjin stood in my doorway, carrying two mugs.

"Is that for me?" I asked softly.

"Yes."

The barest smile tugged at my lips. "You fetched."

"For you." Sinjin held out the tea. The very act looked like it hurt him. Knocked him off balance. "I'll do more things for you. I'll bend. I'll open. I'll break. If you stay."

"It's simple, Saint." I cupped his outstretched hand, feeling the warmth spread through him to me. "I'll stay for as long as you want me, if you love me."

"I... want to," he got out. "Show me how."

"I can't." My last shred of hope crumbled to dust, taking my tears with it. "If you have to want, it means you don't."

"Adeline—"

"Go, Saint. Please."

He went.

His footfalls thundered on the stairs. The front door slammed shut. I was alone.

I finished packing and began taking my things to the car. My car. I'd have to return it, but I could ask Gianna to do that in a few days when I stopped bawling long enough to speak.

I ran my hands over the hood of the white Chevrolet Camaro, thinking of the boys.

Mercer will crack some joke and disappear into his room when he finds out I'm gone. Cash will show no reaction to what he feels either way.

Brutal was hard to guess. Part of me thought he'd track me down and put me where I belonged like he'd done so many times. Another part of me hoped he would.

Why does it feel like I'm going through four breakups instead of one?

I closed my eyes, summoning the power to get in the car and leave.

Because I fell harder than they did, or possibly ever will. You can't stay, Adeline. Get in the car.

I reached for the door handle.

A creak sounded, turning me toward the gate, and the man pushing it open.

"Hello?" I called. "This isn't a fire station. People live here."

He didn't stop what he was doing.

"Hey," I said louder. "This is private property."

He finally turned to me, and pulled out his gun.

Screaming, I dove on the gravel. Shattered glass showered me from the blown-out window.

I ran.

I bolted for the station and threw myself inside as cars squealed into our lot.

They found us. The Kings had found us, and I was alone.

Fumbling for my phone, I dialed the first number I could think of.

Bang! Bang!

"Hello?"

"They're here!" I knocked over the knife block ripping one out. "The Kings are breaking into the station!"

Bang! Bang!

"Come—"

The phone was torn from my hand. I spun—knife out, and Corbin brought the club down on my arm. I cried out as it skittered across the floor.

The ruined man was more terrifying than the weapon he readied for another strike. Bloodstains soaked his shredded clothes. Cuts and bruises covered his body. Blackened his eye. Swelled his lip.

"I told you to take the deal," he said. "Now it's our turn, bitch."

He swung, hitting me across the temple. Pain exploded in my head.

Then everything went black.

"...DID WELL."

"Thank you..."

My eyes fluttered open. Blurred, spinning figures surrounded me.

"...end this pup."

I tried to focus and a burst of pain scattered my thoughts. My skull pounded.

What happened? I went to put my things in the car and...

"Ah. Finally. Hello, Adeline." One figure in particular stopped spinning. My world cleared on Angelo Castillo. "Nice to have you with us."

"What... did you do?" I rasped.

"Nothing yet."

Blinking, I took in the men in my living room.

One.

Five.

Eight.

Thirteen Kings standing at attention behind Angelo and Corbin. A bandage encircled Angelo's left arm—the single evidence of our ill-fated game of blackjack the night before. He crossed his hands in front of him, finger tapping on his gun barrel.

I lifted my arm, and found I couldn't. My hands were bound to the stool.

"We can't get started until your boyfriends arrive," Angelo said. "Don't worry, I already called. They'll be here soon."

I asked one question. "How?"

"This is how." Corbin got in my face, holding his hand up between us. A foul stench washed over me, wrinkling my nose. Days locked in a basement had not been kind to him.

But it was nothing compared to weeks locked in a room while your rapists were trotted through the door.

"Broke my thumb." The swollen, purple appendage backed him up. "It was simple from there to get out. Which I did last night. While you were having your lover's spat, I figured out where I was and called Angelo. Those medieval torture devices make nice décor, but there's a reason we've moved on."

I scoffed. "Well done. You slipped the trap and found a way back to Daddy. I wonder if that'll earn you enough forgiveness for creating this mess in the first place."

He slapped me across the face.

"I didn't start this! You did," he hissed. "You came into my club. Stole from me. Killed my men. Attacked our business. You wanted a war, you got one." Corbin twisted to Angelo. "Boss, please."

Angelo relaxed in Mercer's favorite chair. "Go on," he said, waving a hand.

That was all the warning I got. The punch knocked me to the side. The chair tipped and I crashed to the floor. The unbroken fall jarred my bones. I crumpled there dazed and shaking as the third blow landed.

Corbin tore my hair. He bloodied my nose, and split my lip. One working hand did not slow him down.

"Wait till your boyfriends get here." Corbin hauled me up only to push me over again. My head struck in the same place he hit me, breaking my resolve not to cry.

"They'll watch me hold you down and fuck your worthless cunt," he poured in my ear. "I will get untold pleasure from carving that blue-haired son of a bitch to pieces in front of you. I'll start with the fingers and end with his dick."

Corbin lifted me, setting me upright. "I will enjoy this so much, I'll have to fuck you again." He squeezed my face till my lips puckered. My muffled scream leaked out as he kissed me. "How about a taste?"

"No!"

Corbin made to rip my shirt. I snapped forward and head-butted his nose.

"Argh!" He stumbled, but came roaring back. My shirt fell in pieces around my wrists. "I might sell you to Bryan Acker permanently." Corbin cupped my breasts, squeezing and tweaking my nipples painfully. The men hooted and laughed. "Make back the money you cost me in full."

"Get off!" I thrashed, rocking the chair. I'd risk cracking my head to get away from him.

Saint! Cash! Mercer! Brutal! Where are you?!

"After me and the boys have had our fun with you, of course." Corbin sucked my nipple into his mouth. He moaned loudly as he tossed his head, tongue wagging and lapping me up.

Revulsion lived under my skin. I ached to flay it off and burn it at the feet of Corbin's stake.

"You will regret this," I hissed. "I will kill you, you filthy, low-life beast. Make you feel every bit of pain you caused."

"That's enough," Angelo spoke up.

"I'd like to see that," Corbin said, swinging my breasts by the nipples. "But I wonder how that's going to happen without your gang backing you up."

"I said that's enough."

"The Merchants are dead, *Serenity*. And we'll start by shooting their leaders as they rush through—"

Angelo put his gun to Corbin's temple and fired. The man dropped dead at my feet.

I stared at his body in disbelief.

"You were right," Angelo said calmly. "Bringing us here wasn't enough to earn my forgiveness. I let him have his revenge. Reclaim his dignity. But the greedy fuck has caused me trouble for the last time."

"What do you want?" I asked, fixed on the gun.

"You know what I want. You knew it last night."

Shouts sounded from outside. The front door banging into the wall reverberated up the high ceilings.

"No matter how this ends, Adeline," he said. "You're coming with me."

"Angelo!" Saint roared.

"Uh-uh! Guns down!" Angelo spun me around. He hooked me around the neck, and dug the barrel into my aching temple. "Now. Or I blow her brains out."

My Merchants blew in like the avenging angels Saint swore they weren't. Breaths ragged, hatred etched in their face, and guns steady. They approached Angelo without fear.

"What did you do to her?" Saint demanded even as Angelo's men circled them.

"This was Corbin's doing." Angelo gestured to my nakedness. "I stopped him before he could do worse. But I won't stop them"—I flew into waiting arms—"if you don't get on your knees!"

Angelo's men tore at me. Three of them ripped me free of my bindings and pinned me to the floor. My pants were shoved down my ankles.

"No!"

"Stop!" all four of them bellowed.

"On your knees!"

Sinjin found my eyes through the crush of chaos. He looked at me, only at me, as he sank to the floor.

Mercer, Brutal, and Cash followed one by one.

"Drop the guns."

They clattered to the floor.

"Well, well, well," Angelo began. "What are we going to do about this, boys?"

You could hear the kitchen clock tick its seconds; it was so quiet in the room.

"I'm experiencing a dilemma. I desperately want to kill you. You disrupted my business and cost me millions in lost clients. If you were anybody else, you'd be skipping to hell alongside Corbin right now. But there's my problem," he said. "You're not just anybody else."

Angelo strolled the length of the kitchen, relaxed and shooting the shit. "None of you older than twenty-nine, and you four built a network of crime I can't untangle. I had people searching for weeks and couldn't find you or your men. I couldn't find your money. Your territory. Your enemies. You're ghosts," he said.

"Ghosts who struck the first damaging blow to the Kings in forty years, and I can't help but think the Kings will last another forty with you as a part of our ranks." He pointed the gun at Sinjin. "I made the same offer to your leader last night, but now I'm asking again... with sweet Adeline's virtue on the line. Accept my generous offer, or watch her be violated in the worst possible way."

Groping fingers probed my middle.

"Stop!"

"Get your fucking hands off her," Sinjin shouted. "We'll do it! I accept. I'll join the Kings."

Sinjin. He swam in my vision. *What are you saying?*

"Will you?" Angelo asked. "What happened to the pretty speech you gave last night about ruling in blood. You'd give up your gang when I stepped over your corpse and took it. Wasn't there also something about never kneeling before me?"

I watched Sinjin's jaw tic from across the room. His rage was living electricity charging the air. But he didn't fight back.

He didn't get up.

"I shouldn't have said that," Sinjin said. "I apologize. Let her go, and I'll do whatever you ask."

"So will I," said my perfect Brutal.

"Me too," said Mercer.

"We'll be Kings," Cash said. "I've got twenty suggestions off the bat for tightening up your weak-ass security and dealing with your traitorous men. Let her go."

"Hmm. I'm not convinced," Angelo said. "I'll need to hear that apology again. Add a 'boss' this time."

"I'm sorry, boss," Sinjin said.

Angelo waved his hands. "One more time. All together."

"I'm sorry, boss," they chorused.

Hatred licked at my soul. The vile scum was loving this—holding my violent rape over the heads of my men. And my Sinjin—who swore he'd never kneel, beg, or bow—did all three for the woman he didn't know how to love.

Stupid, fucking fool.

I wasn't sure if I meant him or me. It fit us both.

He told me he loved me in all the ways he knew how, and now that I finally heard it, it's too late.

And Brutal who I said wouldn't let me in. It wasn't into his world that I needed entrance. He wasn't opening the door because he was coming out of it. Talking to me. Comforting me. Laughing with me.

Mercer holding me on the kitchen floor as I cried. Cash promising to avenge the wrongs done to me.

It was I who needed to learn what love was.

"Thank you, gentlemen. I believe you're sincere," Angelo said. "But on further reflection, I don't see how I can trust a bunch of sneaking bandits who scuttle around my city like rats. You'd turn on me at the first opportunity, and I'd expect nothing less."

Angelo leveled the gun between Sinjin's eyes.

"Kill them."

"No!" I screamed.

Crash!

The window blew out. Glass rained down in glittering slow motion, drawing every eye but mine, pinned as I was.

I saw Angelo fall. Witnessed his knees crumple. Face contort with pain. And his gun go flying.

The Kings spun on the ruined window, shooting out into the sky, and the Merchants seized their chance.

Mercer, Brutal, Cash, and Sinjin riddled the men on top of me with bullets. They collapsed over my body.

"Adeline, take cover!"

I didn't need to be told twice. A shootout erupted in the converted fire station of North Quay.

I wriggled out from under the bodies, yanking my clothes up.

Cash flipped the kitchen table over. The boys ducked for cover as I dove behind the couch.

A blanket draped over the side, tickling my hair. I pulled it tight over my exposed breasts.

Seven of Angelo's men remained. They backed into the mantle, behind the coffee table, onto the staircase, and up to the second floor. Holding a line that couldn't be crossed for the person shooting from outside hadn't stopped. A spot of fortune that made us no less outnumbered, and my boys still trapped behind that table.

The air was choked with gun powder. I couldn't hear my heart pound in my ears for the shots going off in an endless chorus.

"How do we get out of this?"

I stuck my head around the couch.

Angelo crawled across the floor, pulling himself forward with his good arm. He reached the stairs and tumbled down, disappearing out of sight.

"I don't fucking think so."

Keeping low, I army crawled in quick pursuit.

"Redgrave," Cash shouted. "What are you doing?"

"Taking cover!"

A bullet struck the floor in front of me. Picking up speed, I reached the stairs and pitched down, sliding none-too-gently to a frantic Angelo yanking at the knob.

"Ah!" I pounced on him, securing him in a choke hold. He had no chance to escape me. I kicked open the basement door and threw him inside. His shouts echoed up the stairs as he hit each one on the way down.

Straightening, I dusted myself off and fixed the blanket properly around me. I skipped downstairs, kicking the door shut behind me.

"Oh, Angelo," I called. "Where did you run off to?"

I hit the bottom step in time to see him snatch a gun off the wall. He twisted and pulled the trigger.

Click.

Click. Click.

"Those aren't loaded, dumbass."

He kept frantically clicking the trigger. I put this lapse in common sense down to the bullet wound seeping blood from his shoulder.

"I'm glad we finally have this chance to talk." I took the gun away and flung it across the room. Hopping on the rack, I smiled at the hapless banger struggling to keep himself upright against the cage.

"Where to start?" I sang. "Oh, yes. What is it you think you know about me, Angelo?"

Sweat dotted his forehead and upper lip. His face was bleached of color, which I put down to the bullet and me—thank you very much.

"I know exactly who you are, Adeline Redgrave." He spat on the floor. "How could I not? But I'm guessing your boyfriends up there don't have a clue?"

I couldn't hold it in anymore. I laughed—full-blown belly laughs that made me tear up. "Not a one," I said. "Absolutely no idea. I mean, I didn't plan to be in the bathroom when they killed Raiden Spencer, but there I am taking care of a drunk chick, and they just walk right through the door. It was like Christmas."

I climbed off the rack. Each step closer drove him back into the cage. "I was interested in the Merchants from the start. I needed a gang to infiltrate, and they were new and untested. I thought I'd hang around some unsavory types like Raiden Spencer and Hazel O'Hare, and let them point me in the right direction. That worked out *so* much better than I thought."

"Stay back," Angelo cried as I crouched next to him. "Back!"

"Let me tell you something—I don't know if you know this—but you men are scarily easy to manipulate. Those chiseled hunks of men up there didn't think for a second that I haven't been exactly where I wanted to be all this time. I made sure of that, putting up a hell of a fight at the beginning."

I pulled a face. "Okay, I did almost lose my nerve when the cage got involved." I flapped a hand at it. "Tried to kill Sinjin. But once we got over that little tiff, it's been smooth sailing."

"Why are you doing this?" he cried.

"Isn't that obvious?" I laughed. "I'm after Kieran, you stupid old fool. *I* am going to find that ledger, and this city will live under my manicured thumb. It's the way it should be. I am my father's daughter after all."

I bopped his nose. "Speaking of Kieran, this would be a good time to tell me everything you know about him."

"I don't know anything," he said quickly.

I tsked. "Now, don't lie to me, Angelo. I don't like being lied to. One more time, tell me who he is."

"I don't know!"

Getting to my feet, I grabbed the bars of the cage and dug my boot into his hurt shoulder. His screams bounced off the soundproof walls.

"Who is he?!"

"I d-don't know! I swear, I don't know!"

I stomped him again. Then again. Then twice more for the insult of attempting to win me in a game, and allowing that Corbin trash and his men to assault me. I dug in deeper for that last one.

Then I did it again.

Angelo whimpered on the floor, tears soaking his cheeks.

"It doesn't stop here, Angelo." I moved off, circling the room. "To borrow a phrase from my love, I will be the law in this town. For your crimes against children, the Kings will be rubbed out like smudges from the earth."

Back to the wall, I slipped a knife off the hook.

"Once I have the ledger, every other gang from the Blood Brothers to the Rolling Ninety-Nines will fall in line. The mayor will jump at my beck and call. The elite of Cinco society will bend their head for me to wipe my muddy shoes on their backs. Or they'll die."

I crouched before him again. "I suspect my boys, the Merchants, will have something to say about that. I didn't give a shit at the start, but damn, if they haven't grown on me. Sinjin and Brutal got me so twisted up, I couldn't hold my sweet-little-cook routine when their pants came down. Sinjin was right that I haven't been with men like them."

"Men who understand me."

I sighed. "I'm truly falling for them. Turns out love isn't total bullshit and it's turning me inside out—which is unfortunate because it doesn't change my plans one iota. It scared me last night when Sinjin offered to trade me. I need to be exactly where I am, by their side, so when they find the ledger, I'm the one who claims it. That's going to be one nuclear fight, but future me will deal with it."

"Listen," he rasped. "You don't have to kill me. The Kings have more money and men than the Merchants ever will. We'll find Kieran. That child sex business was Corbin, not me. The Kings are out of that racket for good. You and I can work together."

"Is that what you were hoping we'd do when you tried to win me off Saint? I don't appreciate being treated like an object, any more than I appreciate being called a bitch."

"That wasn't what you think. I was trying to help you. For all his bluster, Bellisario stood next to you and didn't see what he had. You should be standing at my side. Running the Kings as partners. It's not too—"

"Shh," I crooned. "It's okay. Enough of that begging. It's making me see you as even more pathetic than I already do."

His expression shifted so quickly, I blinked and the snarl twisted his features. "It's not me who's pathetic. Look at where you've fallen. Spreading your legs for any blue-haired thug if it gets you on top. You're pitiful!" he spat "And your time is done. You'll never find Kieran."

I waited for him to end his silly speech. "A while ago, Saint told me about styles of killing. What your choice says about you. How it tells your story with brushes dipped in pain. Stabbing, shooting, beating. Who was I? It wasn't until then that I really thought about it," I mused. "I don't have a style per se. I think what I really prefer is—"

My hand flashed out behind my back, sinking the knife in his neck. Angelo's eyes bugged. He slapped helplessly at my hand, blood gurgling from his mouth.

"—when they never see it coming."

I wiped the knife on the dying man's pants, and sat back to wait.

And wait.

And wait as the battle raged upstairs.

"Adeline?!"

"Finally," I muttered. "You better not have any diseases," I snapped at Angelo's body.

I pressed the knife above my hip, and sliced. Ichor gushed from the wound.

"Ah!" That scream was not fake.

"Adeline." Sinjin ran into the room, trailed by Brutal, Mercer, and Cash.

I curled up next to Angelo's body—clutching my side with the knife between us. It told the tale.

I burst into tears. "I tried to hide down here, but Angelo was waiting. He a-attacked me. I had to kill him, Saint."

"It's okay," he soothed. Sinjin gathered me in his arms. "Everything's going to be okay. I love you, Adeline. I'm sorry I wasn't here."

"It's okay." I turned my sobs up to maximum, hiding my smile in his collar. "You're here now."

"This will never happen again," Mercer said. "We'll protect you."

I bit my lip in case a sob came out as a laugh.

Oh, boys. I know you will.

If you'd like to read the next book in the series, Cash, click here.[1]

---

1. http://mybook.to/CashBookTwo

Cash

They ripped me from my safe, perfect world and bound me in chains.
Now it's Cash's turn. The cold, hard, analytical leader has a problem he needs me to solve, and he's not asking.

I'm driven deep into the world of cons and corruption. I can't tell if anything around me is real. Least of all the smiling, pleasant people.

Someone is playing us for a fool, and it might be me.

The time will come when I have to make a choice: Right or wrong?

Love or money?

Me or Cash?

All I know is, one way or another, the war between us will end.

Keep In Touch

Join Ruby's mailing list for news, teasers, and more: https://www.sub-scribepage.com/rubyvincentpage
Join Ruby's Facebook Reader Group:
https://bit.ly/3bNuCOq

ABOUT THE AUTHOR

Ruby Vincent is a published author with many novels under her belt but now she's taking a fun foray into contemporary romance. She loves saucy heroines, bold alpha males, and weaving a tale where both get their happy ever after.

www.ingramcontent.com/pod-product-compliance
Lightning Source LLC
Chambersburg PA
CBHW022114310726

48972CB00007B/2030